WELCOME
— TO —
GODDESSOMA

TERRY WHITE

ISBN: 978-1-956373-56-1 (sc)
ISBN: 978-1-956373-57-8 (hc)
ISBN: 978-1-956373-58-5 (e)

Welcome to Goddessoma
is dedicated to John Milius.

I have never met him, yet the seed
of so many stories that unfold in my mind
is his image in *The Wind and the Lion*
of the Raisuli with sword held high
charging across the beach man-to-man
horse-against-horse to rescue Mrs. Pedecaris.

CHARACTERS AND PLACES

In Satamabode
Sugorai, the palace city
    Qurmadi, Seed Bearer
    Varanos, Heir to the Seed
    Deserena, Daughter of the Seed
    Murosaya, Assessor Martial of the Abode
    Panjael, son of Murosaya and Captain in the Protectors
    Ghoru, Captain in the Protectors
    Nacros, son of Murosaya and Cadet in the Protectors
Alambarat, a fortress city near Ryadabode and Prayadevale
    Calivara, Dowager and mother of Qurmadi

In Ryadabode
Virnipal, the palace city
    Pavim, Queen and Regent
    Khoroas, Heir to the Seed
    Sevrese, Daughter of the Seed
    Bhalkavar, General of the Protectors

In Hanarabode
    Pharmos, Seed Bearer
    Ruryo, Assessor Concordant of the Abode

In Prayadevale
The monastery of the Sulatin Order
    Athayam, the Intercessor
    Luzarain, the Conductor
    Daiyenso, a monk
    Saina, son of Murosaya and student monk

In the Garland Forest
    Shib, leader of the ferines
    The Preceptor, a hermit and immortal

EPISODE 1

Outside his window Saina saw bodies drifting in a vaporous glow. One open eye could not explain it, so he rose from his bed and shook the sleep away. He cautiously leaned out the window and watched the trails of light—serpentines threading the forest outside the monastery walls and ascending beyond the rooftops up the mountainside.

He knew at once this event was not truly taking place within the air in front of him. It was in the aether, which lay behind the sensory perception. It was an extraordinary materialization of souls returning to the Goddess—something dreadful must have happened in the mortal world to cause so many deaths.

No other students were at their windows. No monks were about.

Why am I always shown this and no one else?

It was not the first time he asked that question. On the rooftop of an adjacent wing of the building were the two aetheric figures he would expect to see. They were perched as always at the spot on the roof where they fell to their deaths so long ago. But tonight they did not stare across at him. Their attention was as fixed as his on the parade of death.

It was one thing to be able to witness it, but to interact inside the aether was a higher skill. He could do it. He backed up slowly and sat upright on the end of his cot. His eyes closed. His breath and heartbeat settled to nothing.

His mind was more resistant to peace, for questions and impressions spun through his head. Even so, the odd but familiar vibration spread throughout his body, leaving him light and still. He felt his spine slipping slowly backward to the cot, while the tether of the aether pulled his spirit out of his body to float into nothingness.

He tumbled in the formless silence, feeling his awareness expand into the Body of the Goddess—into Her endless firmament and pervious ground where everything was contained and everything could be known.

He came to rest perched as always on the tiled roof with the two boys—just as they were ten years before when he had carelessly brought their deaths. His fault. His dare. His rebellion. And forever the stamp on his character by which all the other students and monks in the Prayadevale monastery judged him.

They sat slightly apart from him, two free children dangling their legs over the roof's edge far above the courtyard. He remained behind them, aware that, while his own consciousness was a decade removed from theirs, they must replay the game and reenact the fall he goaded them into without him.

He paid them no attention, instead watching the parade of souls gliding into what must be the peace the Goddess offered them at their deaths.

In Goddessoma all time was contained in one moment—any moment one wished to examine. All action in the aether was clouded and slow, as if in water rather than air and easier to examine. All senses mingled so that sight could take the form of hearing or touch.

The glow he perceived in the stream of bodies was as much a hum passing through him as a light—made up of the celestial entities that controlled everything in mortal life from this realm of Goddessoma. Her legion of gods and devils, Her votaries constantly engaged in sustaining Her creation and effecting Her destruction of life at every moment.

His teachers lectured with such words as an explanation of Goddessoma, yet they could not give students the experience. None of his fellow students spoke of this experience, and he doubted his teachers shared it. Nor did he feel obliged to inform them of what he knew.

One of the boys suddenly spoke—a vaporous message that entered Saina's mind directly.

Saina's father is dead. He just came through—and on his son's birthday.

The other boy added, *I saw him, too. Everyone here is from Satamabode. Saina's home.*

Saina now focused on the truth of this last statement. He had not returned to Satamabode since he was sent to the monastery ten years ago, since before these two companions died, but somehow he knew all these deaths were connected to him. Some were bloodied with cuts. Some were killed by fear. But what was not true in their assertion was that his father was among them. And for that matter Saina's birthday had already passed.

He does not know, they repeated.

He ignored them, becoming more mindful of the faces drifting by. They rose in his mind and turned away like fish in a sunlit pool. He still saw no form he could call his father. They were wrong.

Yet he wondered if he would even recognize his father. Murosaya was Assessor Martial of Satamabode, commander of the Protectors. The most important man after the Seed Bearer. In these ten years he never once came to the Prayadevale monastery and never once asked that Saina be released for a visit to his home. That was not necessarily cruelty, since admission to the Sulatin Order brought an end to all ties to family and to the Ten Abodes. But to a child it felt like punishment, and now to a young man of twenty it was no less than cold-blooded.

Suddenly one figure drifted closer to him, wearing the emblem of the Seed Bearer of Satamabode. It was Qurmadi. If he was dead, then Murosaya as Assessor Martial must have died first—as a matter of honor. As Qurmadi drifted away there was a flash of emotion on the aethereal face. Saina could not interpret it—fear, pain, contrition? He felt a shiver through his porous body—the Seed Bearer and all these Protectors and, if the boys were right, his own father were all dead? This was warfare between Abodes? Not in a thousand years.

His mind wrought to find a rational explanation. Anger rose in him. But this landscape was made of much finer elements. Such conjecture and emotions from the mortal world were enough to suddenly shut the door to the aetheric counterpart. The tether pulled him back into his material body once more. He was aware of the bed against his back and did not even open his eyes. In moments the visions vanished in his sleep.

In the streets and alleys of Sugorai, the palace city of Satamabode, cries of terror and exhaustion echoed and vanished in turns as block by block the city was conquered. Murosaya, Assessor Martial to Satamabode, felt the flaming midday sun burn his brow but his failure burned deeper.

Seed Bearer Qurmadi had died in the night. The old sovran's regret and resignation were nothing to his cowardice. Murosaya tried to get him to safety through the old tunnels beneath the palace, but the thought of their haunted darkness so terrified the Seed Bearer that he convulsed in a whimpering frenzy. Murosaya had nearly dragged him through the palace corridors, but at the dungeon door he screamed one time too many, and clutching his chest he fell in a spasm and died.

Now the city of Sugorai was about to follow him, and Murosaya was left to a rat's escape with his the Seed Bearer's successor. At this moment the Heir of the Seed Varanos crouched with his father's fear a few steps behind him. Murosaya despaired at the semblance between son and father—the only difference was how the son exaggerated the father's worst traits.

It was the Assessor Martial's burden to serve unquestioningly and yet brace their frailties. But today the Heir would be allowed no opinion, let alone giving orders. Murosaya would get the young man to safety—he would not allow the Abode to collapse under his stewardship. If this Heir died, then the Seed died. A thousand years of lineage gone in two days.

If only one of them could convince me I am doing the right thing—that saving the Seed is worthwhile.

Hanarabode's army and their foreign mercenaries had swept to victory in Sugorai like a flame put to oil, violating forty generations of tradition, in which the armies of the Ten Abodes fought only outlying invaders. And that was an uncommon challenge. The borders were manned by more administrators than soldiers. Now Hanarabode invaders rode through the western hills and ringed the city before anyone believed their intent.

But even so, they would have failed before Murosaya's Protectors, the largest and best trained among the Ten Abodes. It was this mind-poison weapon that brought Satamabode defeat. Demons released from harness, panicking the defenders into giving up the gates, breaking down all resistance step by step into the Seed Bearer's durbar.

How could Seed Bearer Pharmos of Hanarabode have conceived of this attack? Not possible in any world. It all must pin to the chest of the Assessor Concordant—Ruryo.

And now, when Murosaya should be retaking every footstep that had been given up, he had to send his army out of the city where the weapon could not reach them. His one remaining responsibility was to keep this spiritless Heir alive. It was the only way to extract support from the other eight Abodes. A city conquered and its riches stripped away, the land stolen, the people subjugated—these the other eight Seed Bearers would condemn loudly but act on slowly. Yet to lose the Seed of an Abode was an act they surely could not allow.

He rose when his scouts came back. He had only a small force— twenty handpicked Protectors, plus the twenty of Varanos' personal Protector guard sworn to him ahead of the Assessor. Any more would have drawn attention from the Hanarabode Protectors who were already perched in the highest towers of the palace and on rooftops across the city. By now they knew the Seed Bearer was dead, and only one target remained to complete their victory—Varanos.

The Assessor listened and then decided a way out of the city. There was one obscure square in a poorer district near the eastern outer walls— nothing to attract looters. It had a water channel that drained into the great river that surrounded the city. If they could reach it and then avoid drowning the Heir in the ducts beneath the walls, he could unite with his remnant force led by his son Panjael out among the eastern hills.

He pulled the Heir up and pushed him toward his destiny. Varanos ran erratically, wild-eyed and breathless, but the soldiers knew their business and corner by corner they eluded would-be captors. They stopped in the shadows of a narrow alley behind the shops of the square he chose. The canal ran on the other side of the square. There was only a small distance to cross unprotected.

Varanos suddenly grew more timid than even Murosaya could credit. His head shook and he backed up. He was not going into the square to expose himself. Murosaya thought he would panic and scream as if one of the terror weapons had hit him.

"Gather yourself! You are Seed Bearer now. I can get you out of this city, but you must follow my commands. Do you understand?"

The Heir was nearly as old as Murosaya's son Panjael, but he cowered like a child. The Assessor nodded to two of Varanos' Protectors to carry him. They looked awkwardly at each other.

Murosaya felt fury. "You do not serve the Heir any longer. This is the Seed Bearer. He is my responsibility now. And you all answer to me!"

Suddenly a cry broke out from one of the shops lining the alley. A woman's voice, and then a man shouting in a foreign tongue. It was easy to guess what was going to happen.

Murosaya felt a different fury rise in him. He moved quickly out into the square and found the door to the shop the sounds had come from. Three of his own men followed him, scanning overhead to count the mercenaries that must be watching.

The Assessor stormed into the shop. He may have had utterly failed his Seed Bearer, but this woman stood for the thousands of citizens in the city he had forsaken as well. He had to do something about it. One symbolic act for his honor.

He passed through the shattered goods on the shop floor and into the family quarters beyond. He saw the woman's legs pushed back and her naked calves kicking and straining under the man's grasp. One mercenary—easy to identify for the crust of hardened skin that grew on the backs of their race.

The poor woman's thin arms were pounding against her forehead so her mind would not feel the man's violence inside her. Her clothes were ripped away, her exposed breasts shook with the convulsions of his movements.

Murosaya's hand closed tightly on his sword. *This,* he thought to himself, *is my daughter—a daughter of my Abode. It is my fault he can take her.*

He grasped his blade with both hands, doubting that at his age he retained the strength to pierce the man's crusted back. He crossed the room in three steps brought his sword across his chest for a strike into the man's ribs from the side. The blade twisted and opened the chest. Blood burst from his heart and sprayed the air. The woman was drenched. She screamed louder. Her eyes sought Murosaya's but there was no recognition. This was not a woman who was ever likely to have seen him close up. She was not grateful that he coated her with her attacker's blood. The man's dead weight was upon her. His hardness still pushing into her. The spasm of death only made the rape more ferocious and repulsive.

Murosaya shoved the body off her. She scuttled to a corner, crawling into a ball of pain and wretchedness. He made a feeble movement to comfort her, but her hysteria was too acute. He backed away and turned to go. What more could he do for her? His rescue came too late for her to care. So it was for the entire city.

Varanos, you'd better be worthy of these people!

He emerged into blinding glare of the square. His men had moved ahead to secure it. The dead mercenary apparently was a straggler without companions.

Murosaya saw the Heir's curious expression. He was not fearful of the canal, he was trying to get his guards to take charge. A dark impression flew through the Assessor's mind—he could not give it meaning. *What has Varanos done?*

He pushed the Heir to the edge of the canal. Varanos squirmed. Murosaya felt a rush of unbelievable energy and pain in his ribs. He saw an arrow sticking out through his cloak. Everything stopped still for a long, long moment. The shouts around him could not penetrate the silence.

He sighed roughly. "Ohh, damn this miserable day!" Then he collapsed into the arms of his men.

Murosaya found the face of the Heir looking at him, frantic and speechless, alarmed and relieved at the same time. But his mind was drifting into the distance, unaware of the fight going on around him.

"Murosaya, I didn't know this would happen to you."

The sun darkened Varanos' eyes but enlightened Murosaya. He could see lies and guilt in the blinking.

He had saved the traitor to Satamabode, not the future of its Seed. The suspicious events of the months past now made sense—he realized the treachery had been going on for years. It was the dead queen's doing. Her legacy to this young man was to invite the invaders on his behalf. Now he was impatient to welcome his new allies.

Murosaya felt violent disgust, but only a whisper could emerge from his lips, garbled by the blood bubbling in his throat.

"Varanos, what did they promise you? It cannot happen. Ruryo does not need you. When you fail him in any way—and fail him you will—you will be dead like me within a day." He paused and laughed and coughed blood. Perfect clarity came to him. "Too bad your mother did not live to see this," he croaked. "She bred you for it—her plan…"

He wanted the Heir to feel a bite of poison from his words—his only weapon to avenge Qurmadi's death. But he lost his thought and it came to nothing. Varanos was gone. The fighting was over. He was being carried to the canal in the sunlight. It was only then that he noticed how light his body was, carried along not by his men but by a current of celestial beings. Not the canal, not the burring sunlight of the Satamabode summer. It was their light.

But as wondrous as it was, Murosaya fought it back. He called his men to him. There were a few left. Varanos and his traitors were gone. His mind was flooded with impressions, and his thoughts tumbled among them. What was the one last order to give—if he could just pull the thought out of his drifting consciousness?

"Panjael leads you now—he is the new Assessor Martial. Go to him. No counterattack. He must go to Alambarat. Get the Daughter of the Seed. Sanctuary in Ryadabode. General Bhalkavar of Ryadabode knows—he will help Panjael."

He coughed roughly and felt another surge of blood warm his lips. Lips that were cold, as was his body, even in the sunlight. With what little energy he had left in his arm, he grabbed the hand of one of his men.

"Remember these things. It is all I have. Panjael. Alambarat. Deserena. Regent Pavim. Bhalkavar." He felt sentience wavering. What was he forgetting? Something more critical than anything else.

"I remember." *Of course! There is a way to correct all this. This is what I kept secret so long. Where is it now? So much to remember and sort out.*

The thought was racing away into the distance. He had to stop it. He had to stop dying and speak this one last message.

"Tell Panjael the Sulatins at Prayadevale … the boy … Saina is there. The scroll. Where is the scroll? One of you has it. The package I gave you."

His men looked around and shook their heads. They assumed he was delirious.

"Tell Panjael … make certain Saina gets the package…. It explains everything." He put every last impulse of strength into his hand and gripped the officer's arm. "Do you have it all? Saina. The scroll. All these years … the Sulatins furious at me. Remember…."

He felt all strength depart. He struggled once more to make sure his commands would outlast him. *Saina must keep the scroll … study every word. Ahh—I forgot. Yesterday … Saina's birthday.*

But he could not tell if they heard him, for they were far into the distance. Then through the emptiness he sensed spectral eyes watching him and countless forms—some were ghosts, some gods, some devils—a host of swirling movement and brilliant light that was somehow alive around him and within him.

He shuddered, but it seemed to make sense after all. This was the world the Sulatins talked about. Goddessoma. The divinity encompassing and permeating everything. This was what the original sages of the Ten Abodes could see. These are the beings that gave them their power.

Well, what a surprise.

He heard his own laughter. A deep satisfaction came over him—yet a longing equally deep at the same time. His last link to the world was a thought of Saina—regret for what he had done to the boy. And to the boy's mother. He remembered love there and seemed closer to it now than ever. And closer to the love of his first wife—the mother of Panjael. Her eyes were among those regarding him. He was thrilled but a little frightened to see her again.

Are you here for me?

I am. Welcome to Goddessoma, Murosaya.

Murosaya's men watched the last breath escape him with a rasp. The most senior spoke.

"Put him into the canal. Let him drift into the river. It is a dirty kind of funeral, but at least he will be carried away from the place of his defeat."

As the body departed the man whispered, "Sorry, no one knows what package you described. Somehow I don't see Assessor Martial Panjael worrying over it. Not while he chews on the idea his father was killed by his own men."

∘∘∘❧❦❧∘∘∘

Varanos and his remaining escort of Protectors waited in the main courtyard of the Sugorai palace. The day was won, the fighting had stopped, cries of fear and confusion receded. With a golden sunset a sense of quietude covered the city, almost denying the outrage of the past days.

For Varanos there was no serenity. It was his palace, but he was left waiting to be received by Assessor Ruryo of Hanarabode. It was too strange and irritating. Nearly as bad, the courtyard held scattered groups of the grotesque tribals wandering about, sometimes staring at him and casting aspersions no doubt in their clumsy tongue. Were they even informed of his status?

For that matter did the Hanarabode Protectors know what was going on? It felt altogether dangerous. What good were these few Satamabode men around him? Not just his guard, but also cowering Satamabode administrators in the shadows, wondering what they were to do with the Assessors they served all dead. He did not want them approaching him for orders and explanations.

He paced uncontrollably through the grove of trees that shaded the vast courtyard pond. At last a figure swept through the palace doors into the open air with dozens of soldiers in his wake pushing along servants who had not fled the palace. It was Ruryo.

Heir Varanos' chest pounded with expectation. He wanted to believe Ruryo was his security. But the man did not look protective, nor even like an Assessor. His dress was as plain as could be seen on an innkeeper. His eyes were perfectly still, yet they took in everything at once as he glided down the steps. The sun shone on his forehead and on the thinning dark hair bound at the back. Not a powerful figure like Murosaya, but far more dangerous.

Once in front of Varanos, Ruryo raised his brows and lit up his eyes with appreciation and praise—a different man entirely from the one a few paces before.

"It is victory, then—victory for the Heir of the Seed!" he enthused. His arms spread to include Varanos' traitorous saviors. "And here are your loyal retainers—all well deserving of great favors from you and from your allies in Hanarabode. Soldiers, I have prepared a celebration in appreciation of your contribution to this day. Come. Follow my men into the palace. The Heir and I will join you shortly."

Varanos watched his men depart and with them his momentary sense of security. The sun was lower than the city walls now, and lights were being lit, multiplied by reflections in the pool. They walked in a large circle around the water as they talked.

Ruryo continued the same warmth, pressing Varanos about his experience in the streets, commiserating with him about the presumption of the late Assessor Martial Murosaya in dragging Varanos all over the city. Meanwhile, the bureaucrats watched in shock from the distance where they were now under guard. Varanos wondered about their loyalty as they watched Ruryo's manner with him, but suddenly he did not care—they had no choice. He was Seed Bearer.

Ruryo saw where his attention had wandered and said quietly, "Have no concern. They have been told that they would be tortured by these barbarians from the plains. After we have a conversation, I will see that they understand you stopped me from doing so and that you welcome them to join you in the new Satamabode."

Varanos huffed softly. Every decision was stolen from him.

They arrived at the entrance steps. Ruryo went ahead just fast enough to make Varanos catch up the whole way. Varanos did not fail to notice the presumption. Anger was gaining on fear in his mind.

Later, inside the palace he did not join the men for some time, as Ruryo stopped in corridors to ask leisurely questions about the rooms and halls. Varanos could see his answers were of no interest, that Ruryo was merely counting time. He reached for Ruryo's elbow and turned him. Ruryo smiled and ignored the touch.

"You have explaining to do. What of those weapons? What was all that? Everyone was terrified. Why did you not warn me?"

Ruryo looked smugly into the Heir's eyes and nodded slowly. "That was my secret. If you tell someone a secret it cannot remain so. But this becomes the way of warfare henceforth. Which, of course, means the assurance of victory." He laughed with an air of contempt. "What will the Abodes and the Sulatin Order make of it—don't you wonder? The arrows have a band of clay that breaks open when the point hits. Out comes a cloud of poison for the mind. When the eight remaining Abodes hear of it, do you think they will come to your rescue?"

Varanos opened his mouth but had no answer. He shook his head. The rescue phrase startled him—as if it was not hypothetical.

"Of course, from your perspective Satamabode has not fallen. The Seed is not in peril. That will steady them."

"Who made the arrows?"

"An ally I did not mention to you." Ruryo enjoyed the confusion he caused. "An alchemist. When I was negotiating among the tribal nomads, he was searching the land for a mineral they have out there on the plains. He would not say which, nor would he say where he was from, but he was on good terms with these tribals." Ruryo shrugged and smiled ironically. "They have no discretion. I discovered they had informed him of our goals. Normally, that would have called for his death, but he came to me claiming a weapon he had invented that could briefly render a warrior incapacitated and awestruck. Well, he claims its manufacture calls upon the power from demonic forces within the Body of the Goddess. Ridiculous, obviously, but that is how an alchemist talks. In the end it is simply a powder and some liquid separated inside the hollowed shaft. On impact they fuse violently and a gas emerges that penetrates and disturbs the senses. Nothing so mysterious."

"But it wasn't temporary—men died. Horribly."

Ruryo smiled. "Yes, there is the real mystery, but it had nothing to do with the alchemist. His concept was to render your enemies incapable of fighting, overcome by fear." He let out a low laugh. "I added something of my own. I soaked some of the points in poison. I gave these to the mercenaries and told them which uniforms and insignias to aim for. The panic of your soldiers was entertaining, but you cannot expect an alchemist to understand what creates victory. It's not simply fear. It's death—only death."

"Why give such a weapon to foreigners? It's dangerous—isn't it?"

"A calculation, yes. But I cannot be responsible if the mercenaries have something they haven't disclosed." Before Varanos could question all this Ruryo opened the door to a small meeting room from which came laughter and shouting.

"Now we will join your Protectors, if you please," said Ruryo.

Inside the Heir saw his trusted men drinking and lounging with women. Ruryo quickly explained that these women belonged to the tribals, but stolen from some other nomad people. This explained their very dark color and the absence of the porcine skin.

Varanos found the women quite beautiful and elegantly dressed. Not so different from his own sister Deserena if their skin was a tone lighter. Then realization dawned. "Why—these are my sister's clothes," he whispered.

Ruryo gave a thin judgmental smile. "Your sister chose to escape to Alambarat."

Varanos objected. "What are you going to do to her?"

"Retrieve her. She will be safe here with you. I am sending a force to secure Alambarat tomorrow." It was only as much information as he would grant the new Seed Bearer. He pointed to a heavy jar on a table near them. "It would be a grand gesture if you were to pour your men drinks for the toast of gratitude."

Varanos chewed his lip hesitantly. "Is that really necessary? I mean, these men—"

"These men," Ruryo cut him off without any sign of anger, "put everything at risk for your cause. Killed their Assessor Martial for you. Their choice has made them dependent upon you forever. How do you measure the value of that?"

The men looked at him expectantly. Varanos was appalled. Their expressions seemed to invite him to join them. One of the women with a flowing green silk skirt raised it to her hips and mounted her soldier's lap. The two of them held cups out, and she smiled at Varanos as she began undulating on top of the soldier. This inspired another to tear open the ties that once bound Deserena's bodice. Her breasts rolled softly out into the hands of her partner.

Varanos shot a look to Ruryo.

Ruryo smiled. "Well, my Heir, they *are* soldiers, not members of the first families of the Abode. This is how a soldier celebrates victories in his dreams." He spread his hand. "Riches." Beside each man was a chest of precious objects. "Sensual relief." The mounting woman moaned as if she could understand the words. Ruryo shrugged and picked up the jar from a table. "Here, fill their glasses. Talk to them. Bestow your respect for their ways, not your censure."

Grudgingly Varanos took the jar and lifted the ladle to fill the cups. Drink spilled onto the carpet. He stiffened himself. "Men," he tried to say with authority, "come for another celebratory draught."

"No—no. Take the jar round," Ruryo corrected.

Varanos looked mortified. As he approached each one, the women teased him. One reached out and ran her hand along his thigh, gripping lustfully at his crotch. The drink sloshed from his hand. Her partner laughed at his own sovran.

Varanos' eyes widened. The woman continued her stroking. He backed away quickly and found that he bulged beneath the fine cloth of his pants—in front of common soldiers.

The women laughed. The men laughed. Varanos could hardly breathe and nearly let the jar drop to the floor.

Ruryo stepped in, handing Varanos a cup he himself had poured, and said, "Your toast?"

"Well, I—I hadn't anything prepared. I mean, well, thank you. Thank you all." It was done so awkwardly the men grew a little tense, even in their pleasures. They looked round at each other and held up their cups at the same time.

Ruryo laughed. "This is the ending you have earned, all of you. Drink up."

There was laughter and release. Heir Varanos brightened to see them raise their cups to him and pour the draughts down their throats with vehemence.

Ruryo put his hand on Varanos' elbow and drew him aside again. Varanos was both indignant and calmed by the touch, and wondered how differently things would now be done in Satamabode.

Ruryo's penetrating eyes settled upon Varanos' own. "Tell me what happened with Murosaya. I suppose the shock of watching the man fall was terrible for you?"

Varanos swelled slightly. "Not at all. Murosaya was arrogant and sanctimonious. I hated him. All my life. His sons, too."

"Well, no reason to continue to hate him now. His loyalty to you served you very well in the end. You must learn that every obstacle is an opportunity. Welcome every impediment and you will find something you would have missed had you not stopped for it. When enemies oppose you, they show you the way to defeat them."

"What are you possibly talking about?" The sounds of sensual pleasure around him were irreconcilable to this discussion.

"I will try to make it easier for you. Murosaya is the man I am most glad is dead, for he alone was worthy of our respect. Unknowingly, he was your best ally during his life. Whatever quarrel your mother had with him for all the years of your life, it created her desire for revenge, driving her eventually to me by the good fortune of how the Seed Bearers intermarry among themselves. I gave her the strategy, but it was she alone who calculated perfectly how to suborn your personal Protectors—all driven entirely by hatred for the Assessor Martial. You do not see reason for gratitude? But even in his opposition to your mother, he was trapped by his loyalty to your father and then naturally to you. What was the right thing for Murosaya to do? Save the Seed he could not respect—lose the Abode he served with love. I hope before he died he realized how he was fooled."

Varanos turned away at the memory of his last look at the Assessor Martial. "He knew. Too bad my mother did not live to see it."

"Yes. I regret I was never able to learn why she so mistrusted and despised Murosaya herself. But that is all over."

The celebration suddenly exploded with the shrieks of women and rage of men. The soldiers of Satamabode went down to the floor in fits, clutching themselves. Naked women were thrown aside to die on their own. One of the men stretched his arms out to Varanos with a curse gurgling incomprehensibly in his throat. He crawled closer. Ruryo remained in his place but the Heir shrank back. The last man fell to the ground with bloody foam about his lips. His empty cup rolled to Varanos' feet.

The Heir looked terrified toward Ruryo, as if for help. "What is this?"

Ruryo cocked his head, "I had some poison left over."

Varanos looked as if he might throw up.

"Ohh, no-no," Ruryo laughed. "You had none of it."

"But—but, why did you do this? You just made me say I owed everything to them."

"Mmm. That is the truth. But this is not a day for loyalty, as you so ably demonstrated to Murosaya and to your father. Today, the principle is discretion. How could I trust men such as these to understand either principle?" He gave smile colder than the last. "Discretion—today. Tomorrow—well, we must see."

Varanos watched the life pour out of the figures on the floor. Suddenly he wondered about how his mother had died. And when the same might happen to him. He hated Ruryo, but instead of bringing blood to his eyes the feeling brought tears of anxiety.

Ruryo would not put the Heir at ease in any way. "Now—of Qurmadi's and Murosaya's last orders. Tell me everything that went between them."

Varanos shook his head weakly. "Their orders? I don't know." Suddenly he remembered a fevered conversation the previous night. "One thing. I heard him tell my father that he had the Abode scroll. He told my father it would go to Saina in Prayadevale."

"Who?"

"Saina. Murosaya's second son. He had three. Saina and I were close in age. He was supposed to be a companion for me when I was a child, but we disliked each other. I don't remember him beyond that. He was sent to the Sulatins."

"But what is the importance of this?" demanded Ruryo.

"What do you mean?"

"Satamabode is about to fall after a thousand years, and the Seed Bearer and Assessor Martial dither about the Abode scroll?"

"I don't know." Varanos grimaced at a last moan from the floor— the woman who had handled him.

Ruryo laughed at length. He walked slowly about the bodies and looked at the new work of his poison as he spoke. "Now you can understand why I have brought this transformation about? It is your own fault—all you royals. You are the guardians of all the rights and gifts of the people of the Ten Abodes. If someone fawns before you, he becomes rich with control over the land or the rivers or the sea and heralded as the first families of the Abode. Had they backbones they could have taken those things for themselves. They gain all the produce of the fields and forests and the metals in the ground, if they will agree pay for your luxuries. And you still have greed enough to tax your people, who actually work for you. Why? Because you possess the Seed—because your birth is recorded in a scroll that is so precious it must reside only in the hands of the Sulatin Order in Prayadevale." He laughed again. "And yet for all that apparent grandeur and potency, I can arrange the defeat of one Abode so easily." He paused and added under his breath, "And the rest as well."

Varanos drew himself up for a moment's attempt at nobility. "*You* arranged? What of my mother's part and my own? You just said—"

Ruryo gave him contempt enough to wither him. "I have watched you for years from the distance of Hanarabode. I have studied this Abode and every other for a decade. I know every weakness. Your mother did not find me—I lured her. You are all figurines I have moved about now and again. To Seed Bearer Pharmos of Hanarabode, I offer my deference. That is because he is needed in a particular way at present. You, however, I have little need of now that your function is completed. Know the difference."

Finally defiance surged in Varanos. "Did you kill my mother?"

"She doomed herself as the enemy of her own husband. Qurmadi killed her. You killed her by being weak and presumptuous. Now you will confine your thoughts and actions to what I order them to be. As my own Seed Bearer does."

"Damn your heart—if you have one! I could tell Pharmos what you just said. It would be your last day on earth as well."

"Ahh, such a child still. And would that not be just the thing he would expect you to say in order to place yourself between the two of us? That Varanos really believes he is destined to rule Satamabode. Do not trifle, Varanos. Stay in your place. Or join your father."

"I am the new Seed Bearer of Satamabode. That is a function you cannot ignore. Without my Seed, there is no line, no Abode. You just admitted as much."

"Ahh. Yes, and you may just be the one who exposes the myth of the Seed once and for all." He smiled with a power that terrified Varanos.

Soldiers of Hanarabode entered and the bodies were dragged away. Ruryo ignored them and ignored Varanos as well, going deep within.

Varanos rubbed the sweat from his brow, wondering when this would end and what would become of him. To his surprise, he saw the very scroll of such interest to his father and Assessor Martial in its oilskin bag on the floor behind a divan. It simply rolled away as one of the bodies was removed. Murosaya had given it to the care of the

Protectors for the escape. It had fallen into the hands of one of Varanos' own instead.

He said nothing to Ruryo. If Ruryo thought it was on its way to Prayadevale—so what? If Ruryo had such contempt for the Abodes, the Seed Bearers, and the Sulatins, then let him find it himself. He wandered toward it and let his heel guide it under a divan.

"Is that all? Can I go?" asked Varanos. Then it dawned on him that he had just begged leave of an Assessor—and one from another Abode!

Ruryo let his mind come back to the Heir. "Yes, if you like. But I think I would like you to issue your first directive as Seed Bearer."

"And what directive is that?"

Ruryo nodded. "Exactly. You should always ask first before you give a directive. That is our relationship now. What I want is your order to instruct my men to kill Saina, second son of Murosaya, in Prayadevale."

"Why waste your time over a student monk?"

He received a withering look for his impertinence.

"You will have him killed so that I won't waste any time over him."

There was one other witness to the murders of the traitorous soldiers of Satamabode in this room—and before that the death of Assessor Murosaya and before that the death of Seed Bearer Qurmadi. His name was Daiyenso, a monk of the Sulatin Order.

No one among the revelers or deceivers in the room had seen him. Nor could they have, for among his Sulatin abilities was the teaching called *Withholding the Light*, a skill derived from knowledge of Goddessoma, as described in one of the Abode scrolls. With he could stop the release of any light that struck the body and leave a shadow within the shadows for anyone to see.

Daiyenso was both of the Order and apart from it. Since his youth he had been used as an observer of the actions of the Ten Abodes— even places beyond the boundaries of the Ten Abodes. He remained unknown wherever he went, even within the halls of the Prayadevale monastery itself—but for the highest members of the Order.

What Daiyenso observed over the past few days could shake the ancient foundations of life and lineage in the Ten Abodes. Yet, he had no intention of reporting events to his masters in Prayadevale first. Before them, higher than the Sulatins, he had another loyalty—one he found on his own or more likely found him.

Alone now in the deadly room he released the light from his body, picked up the scroll of Satamabode and calmly left the palace. With his unusual limp he headed toward one of the less attractive gardens of the city where an aged and remarkable fig tree stood, its branches spreading far from the main trunk and held up by a small jungle of downward growing shoots that were now covered by a ruthless vine from below.

In that refuge he sat and performed another of the Goddessoma powers, known as the *Compression of Distance*. His mind pictured an unknown cave lost in the Garland Forest, a region forgotten by travelers, hunters, woodcutters, or humans of any kind. There his master waited, ten days walk from Sugorai for someone with his injured feet, but only a moment away in the aetheric darkness.

He spoke the ancient syllables in his mind and felt space stretch out from his body in every direction. The garden gave way to the universe of Goddessoma, and delicately he let his attention drift toward the cave. He was carried past the thousands of eyes of the ghosts and spirits and gods and devils who inhabited the realm. He tumbled into this crowded void with the sensation of turning inside out. Then nothing—not movement, not time, not boundaries.

When awareness of his temporal body came back, he could feel the rough surface of the cave instead of the leaves where he had been seated. He opened his eyes to the blue-white self-effulgence just beyond his arm's length. Inside it was the figure of the man. The light was of his being and his making. He gave a barely noticeable bow of his head.

"You are agitated, Daiyenso. These days bring burdens, shocking and disgraceful acts—which now I ask you to relive for me. But you understand why? The alternative is suffering that would afflict many more and for many more years. I reiterate, that is why the Goddess allows us to intervene—we simply condense the sum of suffering and distribute to ones who are strong enough or tainted enough to learn from it."

"I accept that," Daiyenso replied. "All my life I have watched the Ten Abodes slowly dying—along with the Sulatin Order. The sacred duties of both remain unfulfilled. But even as I have observed this, maybe hundreds of years of disintegration lie ahead. By your presence and guidance renewal will come more quickly. The cost will be borne by only a few. The rest may never notice. It is an honor to be of service for that end."

"Even for those you just saw killed?"

Daiyenso paused, recalling the effect of the poison with revulsion. "Within the Body of the Goddess everything is either being born or dying."

"Yes, the ironic truth that all birth is preceded by dying and all dying is followed by birth. To renew the Ten Abodes is the same process. There will be compensation for all—for some in this life, for others in another one. I remind you of this so you will take care to clean your mind of any impressions these events leave with you."

Daiyenso nodded. "To witness a poisoning is to be poisoned. I have not achieved the equanimity you possess."

"Yet enough to speak of the events now without injury."

Daiyenso nodded and related the invasion, the attack on Sugorai, the deaths of the Seed Bearer and Assessor Martial, the venal deceptions and misguided intentions. He knew this man could see it all without him, but Daiyenso refused to ponder what he was asked to do.

The master nodded intermittently but made no comment and asked no questions until the end was reached.

"Now tell me about the young man in Prayadevale."

Daiyenso drew breath. "Saina. His father's last order to be passed on to the first son Panjael was to recall Saina from the Sulatins and give him the scroll. The scroll was waylaid but I retook it and will deliver it to Panjael with your permission." He paused. "Ruryo orders Saina to be killed but does not yet comprehend why or how that would help his cause. It is just his instinct and his habit of mind. It would be pointless."

Daiyenso saw the master smile, and his hand wave slightly without leaving his lap. He sensed that his teacher perceived a weakness in his thoughts.

"No need for you to intervene after you deliver the scroll. Nothing is ever pointless. From Ruryo's attempt on his life Saina will learn the risks he faces and the importance of his attention. That is valuable. In time you will offer him lessons when he needs them or suggest directions. But always first, see what he learns on his own. The best knowledge is that which is most economically gained."

"Then it would not help if I could study the scroll? It will be foreign to him."

"Mmm. Initiative is important for this one. He has been taught and learned too well to wait passively. He must rise by himself—or not at all. The possibilities and combinations in the field of action are always innumerable. Why not? Goddessoma, which animates it, is infinite. The boy begins with nothing special about him beyond his circumstance. He must gain an understanding that his actions matter. Then he must perceive and pass his tests for his confidence. If you know more than this you will inevitably be drawn into his action—and that harms him in the beginning. He will learn more from his obstacles, and eventually others will be drawn to help him because of what he has achieved. By that time your guidance will be welcomed."

Daiyenso saw in the light of the man's presence a smile hidden behind the long strands of hair and beard and somehow at odds with the nakedness of the body.

"You see," the laugh bubbled over again, "not long, everyone will be drawn into his action. The wind blows in the green grove and tosses every leaf. Some fall, but most are left. Let him blow softly in the heat of this season, softly again in the time of the rains. When spring comes and new growth is vibrant—that will be the time for him to come forward. My time as well." The laugh came like the wind he just spoke of.

"Go now to Panjael and make your delivery. Then to your superiors in Prayadevale. They will have many concerns that you can allay. Between those two stop in Alambarat and you will find a Daughter of the Seed—not the one from Satamabode but from Ryadabode. She has inadvertently come into peril. It is an unforeseen circumstance. A leaf that should not fall. That is the risk of intervention—causing the need for correction. Your help assures my vigilance."

Daiyenso bowed slightly in assent from his seated place. But he felt the barest hesitation to rise.

The master added, "Unless there is more you want to tell me."

It was said softly as a question. The truth was, it was an order. Daiyenso understood he could not hide any thought within this cave or anytime in this man's presence.

"It is only the weapon you warned me about. The alchemist. I heard the story Ruryo told, and it sounds so unlikely. Of course Ruryo has little respect for truth."

"Mmm. An alchemist. We will examine this later. Everything in the right sequence. Now is the time for the scroll to find its owner. So go." Yet he held up his hand. "Understand that Ruryo seeks a higher truth. He is not evil, but to reach that higher truth every act he undertakes drains him of compassion or even empathy."

"From what I have witnessed, I am surprised. A higher truth."

"Mmm. But not the highest truth. And everything below that mark must appear contaminated and malefic by comparison."

A summer night mist was rising off this insignificant tributary to the great river that sustained Satamabode. Panjael, son of Murosaya, stood in the midst of hundreds of his fellow Protectors, who had escaped from Sugorai. They had regrouped under the broadleaf trees in the eastern hill country, exhausted in the darkness, avoiding cook fires or any other risks of detection, stunned by the new sensations of defeat.

The pale luster of two of the three lunar sisters sinking toward the horizon gave just enough light to expose the bitter smile on Panjael's lips. He slowly shook his head. He had revealed to them his father's death and the more shattering implications of the Heir's apparent betrayal. He accepted the mantle of Assessor Martial in front of them and quietly outlined the plan to rescue Deserena in Alambarat.

In hardly more than a day he had risen from the rank of captain to commander by attrition. And now Assessor Martial—but with the irony that each advancement left him with fewer resources to command.

When he ended with his promise to command them eventually to victory, he heard few fervent sounds of assent. The physical strength and emotion had drained out of their bodies. Most sat in silence, alone, nervous and dejected—exactly as he felt. He advised them to take a short sleep before their march and wandered slowly through them toward the river.

There he removed his boots with difficulty and rested his feet in the waters, stirring the moonlight on the surface. He forced his thoughts away from the day and on to tomorrow. But that only led him to contemplate his father's past prescience. To have sent the Seed Bearer's daughter to Alambarat proved fortuitous. But if he had suspected this attack beforehand, his knowledge brought very little advantage.

And now Murosaya's last orders to Panjael seemed paltry—not what he would have expected as dying wishes. Get Deserena sanctuary with Regent Pavim in Ryadabode. Deliver a scroll that had now disappeared to Saina in Prayadevale. Not a thought for retaking of Satamabode, let alone vengeance upon the traitor who sold it out. Panjael saw nothing but exile and a plea to the other Abodes to make it all right. It was not his father's way. And not his.

He heard a soft footfall behind him. As he turned and drew his blade, his surprise nearly sent him into the water. It was a Sulatin monk.

"How did you come here? What do you want?"

The man crouched by the water's edge. "I have come with something from your father. My name is Daiyenso."

Panjael instinctively braced. "My father sending his orders through a Sulatin? Try again."

Daiyenso remained impassive. "I was in Sugorai. I know he wanted you to give your brother Saina an article of much value. I have it."

"Yes? And I know how it was lost, so account for how you have it now."

"I witnessed the Assessor Martial's death. Your father's men lost track of the scroll. I was able to follow it and retrieve it for you to carry out his desire. Your suspicion is unnecessary."

Panjael felt anger rising up—that a Sulatin should have seen Murosaya die and he did not. Behind the resentment was sudden suspicion that the Sulatins played some part in his Abode's defeat. He took a long breath.

"Can I take it that you followed the Heir as well? You can confirm his guilt?"

"Yes. They took Varanos back to the palace along with the package. There he joined his ally Ruryo, the Assessor Concordant of Hanarabode."

"Varanos with an ally? Arranged by his mother, no doubt."

"Long ago. Ruryo has been master of both of them. Their weaknesses have matched his strengths."

"Oh? This is known by the Sulatins? So you are allies as well."

Daiyenso shook his head. "No. I give you a simple conjecture based on character. My Order knows nothing yet of these events. Nothing of how they came to be. And nothing of what will come. I will report to them presently, but I have come to you first, only to see that your father's orders can be carried out. He alone saw signs of treachery—he was too generous to believe it sooner and had too little time to thwart it. You have the time now."

Panjael stared at the unmoving and unmoved face in the dim light of the moons and mist. His conviction that the ancient Sulatin powers were all delusion was not lessened, but he had no rational explanation for this man's story or his being here.

Daiyenso extracted an oilskin bag from under his cloak. "Here is the scroll of Satamabode. It contains the teachings of the Founding Seer and the history of the Seed of your Abode."

Panjael shook his head. "I've heard of it. Do you expect me to believe that with it I will take back Satamabode?"

Daiyenso ignored the question. "These Abode scrolls are kept in Prayadevale. To the Sulatins they are a valuable source of knowledge. When the Heir Varanos was born the scroll was brought to Sugorai to record the birth. In spite of the Sulatins' demands all these years, it was never returned. Murosaya took responsibility so that Seed Bearer Qurmadi would not be blamed. Now no one left alive knows their motives, but the Sulatins want the scroll. You now you have the scroll. Your father's instruction was to give it to your half-brother Saina."

"I know my father's instruction. Why are you acting for him and not your Order?"

"You have to trust me. I will tell you this. Your father knew that the scroll and your brother will become important to your cause. I do not know why, but it must be prudent to respect his plan."

Panjael gave a dark smile. "Well, I trust myself now. I don't need a scroll or my brother. I need to know how to defeat the weapon that won them their victory today. Do the Sulatins know that? Obviously my father did not."

"Doubtful. Your father wanted"—

"Stop telling me what my father wanted. Who are you? A Sulatin spy! I owe your Order nothing. I owe my father the payment I will extract from the traitor Varanos when I defeat the Hanarabode Protectors and their pigskin crusted mercenaries."

Daiyenso hesitated. "You know that is not possible yet. And if you take revenge on Varanos, you will end the Seed of Satamabode. You then have nothing to gain support from the Order or the other Abodes."

Panjael leaped to his feet. "Fuck the Seed. If the Seed had any power, this conversation would never have to happen."

Daiyenso nodded and a smile spread across his lips briefly. "That is what Ruryo believes."

Panjael's hand tightened on the sword handle. But the man was right, and he had put Murosaya's dying wish before his duty as a Sulatin. The act deserved Panjael's respect.

Daiyenso released the scroll to Panjael's hand. "I am not one to give martial advice. Only to remind you that your father was a masterful strategist. There is something to discover in his thoughts. To that end, I will disclose one more statement I overheard from Ruryo. He is sending a force to secure Alambarat tomorrow. And a coda to his order is the demand from Varanos for the murder of Saina. It is sensible to conclude Saina does have importance to you, and there is urgency behind your father's wish."

After a long stare into the Sulatin's moonlit eyes, Panjael turned away and called, "Captain Ghoru!"

In a moment the officer was in front of him. Ghoru was much older than Panjael but seemed the more potent of the two.

"I want you to help me carry out my father's last wish."

"Mmm. Murosaya's last wish. That is an honor."

"Yes. Apparently, according to my new counsellor…" Panjael turned to acknowledge Daiyenso, but the Sulatin was gone.

Ghoru twisted to see who the new Assessor was looking for.

Panjael swore softly. "I mean to say I want you to go to Alambarat tonight with horses enough for full speed all the way. You must reach it by dawn. Then up the mountain to Prayadevale. My half-brother Saina is there—a student or maybe a monk by now, I forget. Tell him I need him with me. Ignore whatever objections the Sulatins put up. You will have to give them a report, so share what I told everyone and add that behind the acts of Varanos is a greater villain named Ruryo who devised the attack. Give them something to think about the next time they talk about preserving the Seed. Bring Saina down the mountain. I told the men, we are going to Alambarat. I will change that order. I will take a small force to get the Daughter of the Seed out of there."

"Not to defend the city?"

"Can you imagine that weapon let loose in such a confined place? I cannot put our people at such risk."

"Then this war is as good as over." Ghoru kicked at heavy grass at the river's edge.

Panjael shook his head slowly. "We will all reassemble at the ruins at the head of the old road through the Garland Forest. There we will decide how use what strengths we have."

Ghoru nodded. "We cannot hide in the hills forever."

"No. We need the other Abodes."

"And quickly." He saw his commander's glance at a bag on the ground. "Is there something else?"

Panjael balked. "No. Just that. Just tell Saina our father called him to service. I will take care of the rest of my father's wishes myself."

As Panjael watched Ghoru leave he began to pull himself free of the leathers of his armor and clothing and then stepped naked into the river. He lay down in its waist-deep water and let his head fall slowly back beneath the surface. It was there, submerged in the darkness, that suddenly the meaning of the package became apparent. It was nothing but coin—the currency of the Sulatin Order.

His body rose out of the water. *I will give the Sulatins a choice. They can recognize Varanos as Seed Bearer, in which case they lose the scroll—and I devote my life to Varanos' death and the end of the Seed. Or they change their stupid rules and let Varanos' sister carry on the heritage with me as consort ruler of Satamabode.* He paused and added to himself. *In the latter case I will devote only a moment to Varanos' death.*

He smiled to himself until doubt came. It did not sound like a strategy Murosaya would have devised. Yet everything in Murosaya's thousand-year-old world was irrevocably shredded and crushed. Panjael claimed the right to break free and start the next thousand years.

Satisfied for the first time this day, he dressed and walked among his men with a new story.

EPISODE 2

Saina was the only student in Prayadevale from Satamabode. The few who preceded him were already confirmed monks and therefore removed from all ties to any one Abode. Why the other Abodes sent many more students was a mystery he did not want solved. The obvious answer—to him and to the younger students—was his guilt and therefore Satamabode's punishment for the death of the two boys. True or not, today he had another dark spot placed upon his character.

A rider had come from the valley below with the story of the Hanarabode attack. Conductor Luzarain had assembled all the monks and students to relate the facts. As they exited the assembly hall with dread and confusion, everyone stared at Saina, offended—he assumed—by his lack of reaction. No one would have guessed that he had already learned of the event from his visit to Goddessoma two nights before.

For his own part he could not understand why the victim should be accountable for Hanarabode's crime. There were students from Hanarabode, but they were only children and somehow earned forgiveness. He wanted to shout back that he had not even set foot upon the soil of Satamabode for ten years. He wanted them to understand that his father Murosaya was the righteous player in the drama. Instead, he withdrew to his room. He went out the window—earthly body this time—and perched on the rooftop where he was used to facing failure and burying pain.

It was also where he practiced pursuits no one else cared for—the lineage studies, or more accurately the animals he tended in the lineage studies and those he had learned to befriend around the monastery.

Right now he focused on the screech of a circling hawk in the late afternoon wind. He watched the bird with envy and gave an echoing cry. The hawk descended with broad flapping wings and landed on the crown tiles above him. The bird appeared to ignore him, keeping his eyes fixed on the distance, but Saina understood such manners and did the same.

"You are so fortunate, my friend," Saina whispered. "Today is just another day to you. Hunting is good?" He spoke aloud, but it was the picture of his words in his mind that he knew animals understood. That he could talk to them and hear their replies in his mind was apparently a Sulatin power recorded in the scrolls, but one so obscure he felt it would add to his dark reputation, so he never asked.

The prey is in hiding. Your kind crowd the trees and the roofs down the mountain. Hunger today.

Saina swallowed. *More fighting?* That meant Alambarat and the foothills. *Would they come to Prayadevale as well?*

The hawk turned his eye to the ground below. He heard it before Saina did—a call from one of the teachers. He leaped into the air and swooped down into the courtyard to gain power before streaking high up the mountainside.

Saina felt the force of wings beating the air and envied it. He swung back into his window and ran down the stairs to meet the teacher on the ground.

"Now the messenger from Satamabode wants to see you."

Saina felt suspicion. "Why me?"

"That is certainly not for me to guess. You will see him privately with Conductor Luzarain." But in truth he did know, because he added at the Conductor's door, critically and perhaps with a measure of satisfaction, "It appears he wants to take you back to your Abode."

A tremor ran down Saina's spine.

Inside, silhouetted in front of the window, was the corvine form of one of the two leaders of the Order—an earthbound match for the hawk in the air overhead. Conductor Luzarain was the exemplary Sulatin, admired by all the young monks and students—astute, eloquent, radiant, and fearsome. Everyone said he must have mastered the powers, though such things were never to be talked about let alone seen by students. If his demeanor was any clue, it was not hard to imagine he possessed them all. He was a living statue, perfectly balanced and quiescent, filled with presence like the mountain against which the monastery was built.

A personal audience with the Conductor was more than uncommon, so Saina took a long calming breath as he crossed through the doorway. But suddenly an impression more extraordinary came to him from the other man leaning against the wall. Upon his figure was something Saina had never seen—the tunic of a warrior stained with blood from an enemy's death.

He watched in awe as the man shifted off the wall and walked in front of the Sulatin Conductor, circling to the other side of Saina with an appraising sweep, igniting the air in the room with power that was nothing like a Sulatin's—more compelling and much more dreadful. Yet, of the two figures, Saina decisively felt this was the one he wanted to follow.

The soldier had no time to acknowledge Saina's regard. He spoke roughly—not an attitude heard among the walls of Prayadevale.

"Saina, son of Murosaya, Assessor Martial of Satamabode."

Saina managed a quick nod.

"Yesterday, moments before his death defending Sugorai as well as the treacherous Heir of the Seed of your Abode"—he paused as if picturing it in the air in front of him—"your father ordered your return. I wish I could take you to him alive, but this was his last command. He was killed by traitors serving the Heir of the Seed. You will have to rely on your memories of him now. I have the pride of my own service to him as an honor above all others." He took a deep breath and crossed his arms on his large chest—as if there was nothing more to say. Then for the sake of formality he added, "Captain Ghoru," and let his head bow with a slight tilt that held a measure of respect along with a caution.

The Conductor watched Saina's hand, prescient about what was about to happen. He saw the beads slip down from Saina's wrist to his fingers as the mental counting began. The names of one hundred and eight gods who governed the hundred and eight energies of Goddessoma. Under stress, what else would a Sulatin student do? And he knew from that alone that Saina would stay with the Order today.

He cut in to explain Ghoru's mission, not for Saina's benefit, but to regain control against this explosion from the outside world. "The captain wants to take you to your half-brother Panjael, who is now Assessor Martial of Satamabode."

The officer scowled. He was not interested in having an interpreter. Saina saw for the first time a soldier's instinctive dislike of Sulatins and wondered how widely such resentment existed. He studied the earring Ghoru wore—he was aware that everyone wore an earring in the world outside to signify their craft or profession. But among Sulatins no outward signs of distinction were allowed. Ghoru's emblem was an officer's sword no longer than a fingernail, but when he was not pleased it shook under his ear like the threat of a real one.

Ghoru gave Saina a wry smile. "I was expecting a boy. This is a man. Are you ready to depart?"

The Conductor raised his brows. "Saina is a man, it is true, but he is not yet a Sulatin adept and looks forward to years more of our training. I think you should give him the choice of whether he wishes to reenter the world of the Ten Abodes or continue his commitment to our Order."

"If he has not yet reached the adept level"—there was a measure of sarcasm in his voice at the pretension of the word *adept*—"then he has no more commitment to this place than to his father. Is that not right?"

With the merest tilt of his head Luzarain conceded the point.

"Well, Saina, of course, you are free to follow this path or not. Which is it to—"

"I will go."

Luzarain gave him a piercing glance. Saina lifted his arm imperceptibly behind his back and the beads returned to his wrist. Luzarain was not fooled and gave a wan smile.

Ghoru was ready to move on. "So it is. Do you have a horse for him? I have one sound mount left. The others galloped past exhaustion and I set them all free along the way."

Luzarain spread his arm to indicate the mountain valley that held the monastery—"There are farms here that have horses—not familiar with battle, however."

"Could you arrange a trade with one of the farmers? We must leave just before dark in case we find the battle has moved to Alambarat. These are unpredictable times."

Luzarain turned with a look that said he had enough of warriors. "There is another trail that bypasses Alambarat and ends in Ryadabode. It can be travel on foot."

"So there is. But a horse is my request."

Luzarain gave an elusive smile. "I must preside over many meetings because of your news. Surely you can imagine. I will inform someone of the task."

"I can easily imagine your talking about it. I need to do something about it. And I will be ready to leave very quickly, Conductor."

Before he was swept up in the captain's wake, Saina stood fast. "May I ask? When did my father die—precisely?"

"Midday. Yesterday." Ghoru counted fingers quickly and gave the date.

"Not the previous night?" His brow wrinkled with confusion.

Ghoru shook his head.

Luzarain gave him a sharp look. "A prescience?"

Saina blinked at the Conductor's perceptiveness. But realizing suddenly that he had no obligation from this moment on to share his mind with Luzarain, he lied. "No. A mistake."

He felt light and fluid as he raced through the corridors to empty his room of his scant possessions. Currents washed through his mind and every vein and nerve rose on the tide.

He was no longer a student Sulatin, for whom every act was meted out. Material life in Prayadevale was reduced to a routine of choicelessness. Everything was simple. And in that simplicity the mind could devote itself to what was truly complicated, with the hope that someday all that complication would become simple as well. Now he was at the edge a world where all this was reversed—where one not only wished for a particular outcome but even fought for it.

Still, when they later rode out he looked back at the last sight of the monastery walls and felt his throat tighten. Surprisingly he felt gratitude, not judgment. These years had forged something within him in spite of his attempts to disown it. It was the presence of Ghoru that made him realize he could no longer be passive. He must understand what he was taking with him. He looked again at the captain, expecting out of habit that his thoughts were being judged, but the soldier's eyes were fixed on the top of the mountain that buttressed the monastery walls.

Saina followed the look. A wisp of smoke drifted over the peak above them. He had never seen such a thing before.

"It may be a blessing you are leaving this place." Ghoru laughed darkly. "Or not. From a fire in the mountain to a fire in the basin below. You can't escape."

Ghoru turned his horse into a canter. Saina's farm horse objected, his fears instantly apparent. He was used to the security of a shelter at night. He had never been out of sight of his farm or the valley. He could only repeat the same thought in different words. *I am not leaving. I won't go. Won't you listen? I hate this other horse. He hates me. I'm going back.* He wheeled around, strained against the reins, and stomped his foot three times.

Saina could not hold him by force, but he stroked the neck just below the mane and thought, *I'll see that you are safe. Everyone is confused now—me too. But things will settle soon. You will be able to trust me.*

Ghoru had stopped his horse ahead and was watching. Saina felt obliged to whisper the words aloud as well. The horse gave in enough to allow Saina to turn him and pick up a canter, which Ghoru's horse joined.

"You may not have much time in a saddle—or even a saddle, come to think of it—but you know more than most riders about what is carrying you. Be care, though, whatever you promised this horse, you probably won't live up to it. Not when you see what awaits you below. He is smart to panic. He's no farmer now. And you—not a monk."

Sometime later they reached a bridge across a crevasse where the trail to Alambarat ran more steeply. Saina' horse put up a long mental fight with Saina before crossing it. When Saina finally reached the other side he felt a flood of relief surge through him—not over the horse's struggle but because his Sulatin life and all its order and quietude was behind him. Everything the horse regretted, he rejoiced.

Like the monastery of Prayadevale, the much older city of Alambarat down the mountain grew out of rock generations before—before the artistry of cities and palaces like Sugorai when threats from wandering tribes required impregnable walls. The huge boulders of the foothills at the base of the mountain range dividing the northern and southern Abodes were crushed and molded into a fortress city. That left only one direction for growth—upward—creating a city of hives cascading over narrow winding alleys and connected by culverts bringing water to neighborhood pools from the snows above.

One large square survived in which citizens could assemble, and this afternoon the Hanarabode Protectors and their mercenaries were gathered there after testing for resistance and finding none. Before they arrived Panjael had rescued the Daughter of the Seed and warned the city to acquiesce and wait to fight another time.

It prevented the use of the demonic weapon, but nothing would have dissuaded the mercenaries from looting. As the shadows grew long everyone feared the dark this night.

In one of the neighborhood pockets sat a blind beggar of undetermined age. Thin and long and dusty, he looked more like a heap of firewood under a blanket than a man, except that he mumbled without interruption. It was not a profitable spot for begging—at the back of a minor theater far from the public entrance. Actors were usually as poor as he or if flourishing they were headed to pleasure not charity. But the blind man would have to be deaf to think there would be a performance this evening or anytime soon. Now that the invaders owned the city, actors, beggars, and first families alike were marked.

Across the alley another person was watching the blind man intently from a shabby doorway—a young woman in ill-fitting clothing with a face scarred about the eyes as if she had suffered by fire. She held in her hand a black kerchief like the one the beggar wore—the traditional mask of the blind and misshapen.

Her eyes were not damaged, in fact they were trained on him studying and mimicking his demeanor—the carriage of his head and the manner of his mouth as his unintelligible words flowed forth. She was disappointed with the results. Then she looked both ways down the street and up to the windows above. No one regarded her, and she felt safe to cross over to him. She placed a coin in his hand, and crouched to examine him as he offered his meager form of a blessing.

Hooves and armor clattered beyond around a corner. Then came shouted orders and muffled shrieks of confusion—no telling if they were coming nearer or leaving.

She attempted to leap away, but the beggar held fast to her arm. In her panic she slid to the ground beside him, wrestling free and edging backwards. He pushed her behind the blanket that covered him before the soldiers scuttled by. They did not descend far enough to see them, the alley looking so unprofitable. Silence came again.

The young woman panted and shook off the blanket, backing away from him. She could not look at his face for the blanket was now over his head. It was the sight of his feet that drew her eye. He sat cross-legged with the soles turned up. They were marked in the same way as her face, burnt as if he had stood upon a stove. Except—her scars were false, his were not.

She was uncertain he was fully aware of her—whether he had saved her with intention or merely panic. Should she speak to him? Tell him what was happening? But the same martial sounds were rising from unknown locations. As a stranger to the city she could not know where soldiers might come from next. She had to get back inside, for discovery would bring disaster.

Running back to her door she met a sight that made her gasp. Another arm took her in—this one thick and strong and quickly recognized.

"Where have you been?" came a gruff whisper. A huge-chested figure with no hair upon his head or face loomed above her.

"Oh, Bhalkavar, you scared me witless!"

"Hush! Not by name." Then he laughed and whispered again, "General Bhalkavar is known widely for his manly looks—even at his age. Just because he loses a handful of hair, you should not have reason to doubt this fact, eh?"

"No, you look terrible. Not a handful of hair—you have been sheared. Why could you not allow him to use his make-up, like this?" She fingered the drying scars upon her face.

"If you please," his whisper continued, "it is not appropriate for a Daughter of the Seed to comment on the appearance of one who serves her Abode so well." He stretched his neck as if to let her consider his new appearance more carefully. "It was necessary, for I may have fought beside some of the troops of Hanarabode in the border campaigns. This hair and beard have been rather memorable in times past—making quite a general's presence, I believe. Theater makeup could never have hidden Bhalkavar." Then he drew his hand across his chin. "He promised me it would not swell up. Was he right?"

"No, you look like a bladder full of fresh cheese."

"Ahh. You look rather bad yourself, thank you. And that was the point, after all. Come back in. This annoying fellow says he has to put one more layer on you to preserve the effects. What have you been doing, anyway?"

"Mmm, there is a blind man just there across the street. I was learning how to hold my head and such."

"He is not there now." He took her shoulder in his hand. "Don't be imprudent. Trust me and assume everyone else is not your friend."

In the next room they were greeted again by the artist who had been working on them for some time. He was gray and thin with age. And every word he spoke had the cadence of the stage and a gesture to embellish it.

"Let me add just a few more touches—please. You two may be the last who will ever know my skill. I do not expect these scabby mercenaries to appreciate theatrical arts." He finished with a long sigh as his flourish.

His frail hands stirred at pot after pot, mixing rapidly until he obtained the color he wanted. Then he held the mess over a handful of glowing coals in a tray and worked the softness back and forth.

"We were in the middle of a great season. The actors were so full of themselves when I brought them my new supply of clays and paints just before summer began. It was a large purchase—I should add, on credit. And I will never see it paid for. I will never see them again. Well, you know—they may play kings and warriors and virgins all evening, fighting each other for center stage, but when the real enemy descends upon them, these actors fall to the ground and pray the scenery covers them."

"That's hardly fair," Sevrese complained, "Every craft must have its true heroes and villains."

"Yes, of course. You are wise for your age. Apparently, that applies to Heirs of the Seed, too. Ahh, here we are. Not too warm? Blink now. Again. Again. Yes. A moment to cool, then the scarf.

"You know, I was an actor in my early days," he chattered on, "but never first in the company. My lines were meager. Seldom even a change of costume. I had so much free time I began to experiment with all this." He gestured round the room filled with dusty pots and vials. "I have invented much of what you see in our theaters nowadays. No doubt you came because you heard of me?"

Bhalkavar saw something disingenuous in the man's look that even an actor's pretense did not cover. The general knew they had been recognized. A Daughter of the Seed was beneath the makeup.

"No," replied Sevrese, surprised at the artist's notion. "It was pure coincidence that we came across this little passage to avoid the crush of people earlier. The theater gave me the idea to look for some costume that would disguise us were we to run into the mercenaries. We must be away to our Abode without any more delay."

Without being noticed, Bhalkavar shook his head at her candor.

"Well, of course," the artist went on, "I knew you were not from here. Your timing for a visit was unfortunate. And it would be prudent for people of means to not be visible for a few days. May I ask, which Abode is yours?" He met Bhalkavar's glance and retreated nimbly. "Of course, it is none of my business. Why I ask is that I have traveled widely in my trade over the years. Most of the famous acting companies know of me or use some of my mixtures today. For example, some years ago my services were purchased by a theater in Ryadabode."

"Make your point," said General Bhalkavar impatiently from across the room. It had been likely that this man knew them—he was one of many risks to calculate while getting out of this city. But at least he had the courage to admit it and try to make an offer of loyalty.

Or—more likely he is afraid I will kill him when he done.

"Ahh. I was just thinking—your need for disguise must of course be followed by a need for secrecy. And I thought that you might fear—"

"Yes?"

"Well, I wanted you to know you need have no fear of my speaking or—"

"No, friend, far from that, you have just increased the need profoundly," the general replied without emotion, as if to push this man into a corner and judge the response. "When people go to such pains to be candid, it is certain they are not."

"What is the meaning of all this?" cut in Sevrese.

The men were both silent. Neither moved.

"Bhalkavar?"

He rolled his eyes. "This fellow is trying to tell you that he knows our potential value as captives, and the knowledge does not inspire his greed."

"I am supposed to be blind, not deaf. It is your distrust that does not inspire me. What choice do we have but to take him at his word?"

The general took a moment to run his tongue over his lips and hold his voice down. "We have choices."

"Surely, you had not intended"—she cut herself off, realizing their predicament was too deep for her general to make any allowances. He was entirely right. Only he could be trusted, for his honor would force him to any length to protect her. "But we are in debt to him now," she added without conviction.

The general stared at her as if from another world—one in which a necessary death or two would raise no protest. Then he looked at the artist, blinking slowly once. "All right, if I believe your pledge not to betray us, prove to me you were at least a good enough actor not to blunder, should someone trace our path to your door."

The man shook his head. "If I could guarantee that, then you should wonder if I were acting now."

Bhalkavar smiled ruefully.

The man went on, bolstered by their small expressions of faith. "No, sir, I would rather you have confidence in my art. It is good enough that, while *I* might have discovered you, henceforth, no one else will. In fact, I would claim that if this beautiful work was uncovered, believe me, it is I who would be recognized for it. No one else here in Alambarat could have created this. Not in the Ten Abodes, if you want the truth. So you need not kill me, for if your escape fails your captors will surely see to that deed."

The general looked exasperated.

Sevrese laughed quietly. "It seems the modesty of theater people is close to that of generals, so it follows their sense of honor could be equivalent."

This was met with a raised brow and a grunt. Hearing noises from the street again, the general walked out to investigate. As he left he added, "All right, then show me more of your art. You two write us a play quickly. We need more than disguise, for we need to be able to answer every challenge credibly. No one will leave this city unchallenged."

Outside, the general could smell fear in the air. The leaders of Hanarabode obviously had very limited control of their mercenaries once these tribals found themselves within grabbing distance of treasure or pleasure.

He was glad it all was over so quickly. Glad that Hanarabode found a weapon that decided the outcome by its sheer power—though he had not seen it. Panjael was probably right to use it as the excuse for abandoning the city. But it convinced the general not to join their flight.

Unfortunately he mistakenly believed he had more time. Ruryo was more formidable than expected—Murosaya paid a price for patience, but Bhalkavar was not going to pay again.

If two of the best generals in the Ten Abodes are too slow for Ruryo, it is certain the remaining eight Abodes will dither forever—when striking immediately with several times his forces would stamp out his impudence. Instead they will cry for a way to patch it all up somehow with the Sulatins' blessing. Not my Abode. Not Regent Pavim. But now I have tied her hands by putting her daughter in jeopardy. Murosaya's premonitions were flawless—if only he could have seen through the Heir of the Seed.

He went back inside, wondering again what became of the blind beggar Sevrese had seen. He found her triumphant, and for a moment felt relieved.

"All right, we have names, you and I, and a past, a present, and a future that will throw the soldiers off course but not so complicated that it trips us up. I have adapted an adventure tale I remember from my childhood. You probably have no idea who the sprite Cheki is, do you? She lives in Goddessoma and comes into the world to watch over horses and protect them against the demons of Goddessoma. Her warnings are what make then shy at things we cannot see." She gave a quick bow. "My name will be Cheki."

"A horse tale," said the general wearily. "I explain to the soldiers from Hanarabode who stop us that you are a sprite—so no worries?"

She ignored him. "You are Mohidram, who was a horse-coper in this tale. Cheki rescued him, which tracks with our current predicament."

He gave a wan look.

"Most recently, you brought fifty mounts down from Ryadabode, and you had sold half. You were on your way to Sugorai with the rest, but they were stripped away from you by the retreating forces of Satamabode. You made your way back to Alambarat, looking for compensation for your loss. Now that Hanarabode has taken over, you want an introduction to their procurement officer. You want someone responsible to make amends. And, as they will consider you a nuisance, they will pass you through the gates gladly."

"Ahh, good," agreed the artist. "That is good—the part about your restitution. You did not tell me that before. It will be very convincing if you make demands—as if you have no reason to escape, on the contrary. But you did not tell him about Cheki. You see, Mohidram, she is your blind relation. You are the last of her family. She lost her sight in an accident at a cooking stove."

Bhalkavar studied it. "What would I be doing with someone like you in tow?"

"Why, Mohidram, Cheki's very name is luck to your trade. I am like a magnet stone for your horses. They listen to me. You would have cursed your own success to send me away." She narrowed her look. "Or you regret not having sent me off in someone's service once your success was ruined, but who would take a blind girl? Is that more to your liking?"

The artist beamed. "Either way, this makes a wonderful story. Many more details are coming to me even now. One day I will complete this play, if you would permit me. But I know you must be away and I need to show you all about the carriage of a blind person so you will not be caught out."

"No, I have studied your beggar in the alley."

"What beggar?"

"I saw him while you worked on Gen—on Mohidram."

"He does not work this alley. I know all the beggars that depend on this theater. They work the front. And no blind ones. Are you sure you were not followed."

She did not answer directly. "He had old burns on the bottom of his feet."

The artist shook his head, unwilling to accept it.

Bhalkavar took no chances. "We will go now. Here, fellow, for your artistry. It is not sufficient for your help." He tossed a small pouch of coins.

The man caught them and held out his hand to give them back. "Keep them. Money is as dangerous as the lack of it now. If you will permit me, I have one more thing for you. He held out his hand on which a silver jewel rested.

Bhalkavar gave a look of surprise. "I would not have thought of it. An earring for a trader. Where did you get this?"

"Well, we have to be prepared in the theater—for any role."

The general acknowledged the gift with a nod. He reached for his sword lying on a bench.

"Oh, sir, no-no—you cannot take that. What trader would have such a sword?"

Bhalkavar was adjusting his it under a cloak. "This may not be in your play, but out there I will feel better with it."

Sevrese stood by, appraising him. "He is right, though. This disguise must be our only weapon or it is nothing. A sword like that will bring a hundred questions. It has your name sign right on the hilt!"

"All right." Bhalkavar put the blade down reluctantly. "Take it. But if it is found here your throat will no longer be good for swallowing. And careful—that sword has been my soul for many years."

Sevrese touched the general arm. With her scarf covering her eyes it was too dark in the room to see his face. "I do not ask you to make this sacrifice. To give up your soul."

There was stillness for a long moment.

"It is just an expression. The sword is a piece of steel."

"No, it's not. You mean it exactly as you said it, and my safety does not demand such a cost."

The general rubbed his head. *She has a temperament as great and as strange as her mother's. Why can't she just leave this one thing alone?* But he knew she would not. Once she or her mother took a stand, however ridiculous, their feet fused with the stone below them.

The artist stepped between them. "I have a poorer sword—part of a soldier's costume. It would serve your disguise, and I will bury yours safely beneath the floor for you to reclaim. Surely in a time of disorder as great as what we are witnessing today, souls can be exchanged between blades."

Bhalkavar took the prop and added, "It's an honor to accept it and your help."

∽∘∘❧❦∘∘∽

Saina awoke with a hand over his mouth—Ghoru's. There were voices in the distance and hoofbeats on the road beyond the trees.

A groggy first thought came to him. *Ghoru need not fear—I am used to being silent for months at a time.*

Seeing him calm, Ghoru let loose his grip and stood up. The real danger was his horse, who might call to new companions or appeal for rescue. Both mounts looked tense—ears erect, eyes stretched, nostrils searching, tails high. Any moment one of them would sound a call, and all would answer.

Saina tried to think his way into their minds, but they were closed to him. He moved to comfort his with a hand, but a wave from the captain held him back, warning that any change in a horse that tense might release a long nervous neigh. He explained in a whisper that once they have become alarmed in their own horse way, better to let them be horses for the moment. They stood tall, listening long after the sounds had died to their human companions. Finally, they relaxed and returned to the grass at their feet.

"Was it a Hanarabode sortie?" Saina asked.

Ghoru nodded. "Satamabode Protectors have withdrawn to the plains. If these riders find nothing on this road up to the bridge, they will turn back."

"Captain, why would they search this road? No one comes to Prayadevale, and the monks do not pose a threat to anyone."

"True. Unless you are."

"I?"

"It is possible someone else knows Murosaya sent for you."

"I still don't understand. My father paid me no visits and never called me to him in ten years. Why is it so important that he does so now? Especially to his enemy?"

He studied Saina and then shrugged. "I confess I don't see it. No offense meant. I would say the same about everyone I met up the mountain there. But it was an order before your father died and an order your brother Panjael obeys. Captains don't ask why."

"The Sulatins say there is always a reason for everything."

"You believe that?"

"It is fact. Belief does not enter into it. Most of a student's life in Prayadevale is devoted to finding answers why. And there are many such questions where the answers are never satisfying. Even the very old monks are still searching for better ones."

Ghoru laughed. "It is a good thing you are all celibates."

"What difference does that make?"

"I have loved women throughout my life and never understood why they feel as they do?"

"I've never thought about that. It's not part of the training."

"Mmm. That's because even the Goddess doesn't know. When we get down from this mountain, I think you will need some training. You're a good looking young man, and my guess is you will soon discover there is nothing to get from that monastery better than a woman's arms wrapped around your neck."

Ghoru's words were a foreign language. "I would rather discover the art of war—in case that is the reason I am called."

"Let's ride and I will tell you all about fighting enemies and loving women."

Saina took a deep breath. "I know you're making light of me. I'm curious about one thing. What do soldiers—or anyone else have against the Sulatin Order?"

The captain frowned. "I suppose because the few Sulatins I have encountered seem so pious and judgmental. That fellow I met up there with you, for example. True, I am trained to bring death, but what has he ever done?"

"The Goddess is both creator and destroyer. The Sulatins accept that warriors must represent Her destroyer aspect. Maybe it is you who is judgmental."

"Maybe." Ghoru gave a low grumble and finished placing his saddle. Then he said, "There's something else I am judgmental about. Why for ten years you have never been back to Satamabode. I am not a father, but that seems a little cruel of Murosaya."

Saina mounted. "For that I have no reason and now I will never get one. I suppose the Sulatins are wrong about reasons after all."

"A dying wish. Perhaps he thought to make peace with you. Then there is our departed Seed Bearer, who kept his son close, and see what happened to him?"

"I knew Varanos when I was a child. I remember he liked to trick me—and my brother Panjael—with lies. Panjael taught me many ways to anger him so his parents would refuse me as his companion. It worked, but later I was sent away to Prayadevale, so it didn't work the way Panjael thought it would."

"Well, the Heir got his revenge against your brother. Now Panjael gets his turn again."

Ghoru noticed the horses' ears and turned them deeper into the trees. The riders returned and passed.

"Lazy. They didn't even reach the bridge. Maybe they've given you a pass. Wait a bit longer and then we will descend. But not to Alambarat. The city is now captive. We have to find another trail."

They first caught sight of the light of Alambarat through the trees after a long slow ride down the switchbacks. Ghoru halted and turned his horse in front of Saina.

"We can't go much further, but it's still too steep. We have to continue, but if we are attacked on the road, leave the horse and dive into the forest cover. I don't know where you will come out, but make your way south. Find the ruins at the old Garland Forest trailhead. Panjael will leave someone there to meet you."

Without thinking, Saina asked, "Do you have arms for me?"

It sounded absurd—hanging in the air while the captain appraised him. Then he reached into the pouch behind his saddle. "Since you asked, take this." He bumped Saina's arm in the dark.

When it came into his hand, Saina realized it was a short sword—good only for close fighting, but he was stunned to be holding it. He pushed the weapon into his waistband. "You probably have low expectations of me as a warrior."

"I think you have learned more than they taught you. Sometimes you can measure a man in a moment. Other times it is a complicated business—that's more your case. But if we are forced to fight, with that blade you need to act fast and shock your opponent before his reach makes it useless. No worry, it is my duty to keep you alive, and you will notice that I have never been killed myself. We can do this."

Further on, as the thick forest spread out to make room for the boulders of the foothills, Saina saw movement in the moonlight. He turned to warn Ghoru but intuitively he looked up. The two boys who haunted the monastery roof had followed him through the aether. He looked around and saw light gathering in the trees as if expecting new souls for Goddessoma.

He doesn't know he has the power. He doesn't understand his gifts. He needs to know. He must accept. This is the time!

These whispered words stopped him dead in the middle of the road. Suddenly Ghoru pushed the farm horse ahead, and Saina turned toward a cleft among the boulders just off the road. The sound of riders from below seem to shake the trees.

"Keep going further in. Get off the road!"

The two boys leaped from their post into a cleft between boulders and led Saina deeper where the horses could be turned.

The approaching riders broke into a canter to give their mounts more surge on the upward turn. Saina could make out the voices—some foreign, others not. There were two lanterns swaying—one in the lead and the other trailing—but the light was flashing so wildly they missed the cleft and passed by. Saina started to move, but Ghoru hissed him to a stop. Another group of riders was following. Slower so their sound was just under the clamor of the first party. And no voices, no lights.

After they passed a short time went by in silence—nothing but the occasional breaths from horses' tension and the flicking tails and shifting legs in a tight and uneven spot. Suddenly, above them on a switchback up the road it was clear a fight broke out. Saina heard for the first time in his life the clash of swords and cries of pain.

Quickly it was over and hoofbeats came back down, this time at a gallop.

Ghoru's horse stamped and the captain eased him out. "It's either our enemies or our comrades fleeing. Either way, I must meet them. You will be safe here."

He was gone only moments when the beat of the horses and yelling and cursing were echoing through the darkness. One rider very near the cleft went down with a cry and the lantern he carried rolled toward Saina. The man scrambled into the cleft frantically to avoid his pursuers. Saina's face met his in the streaks of light and shadow. The man's sword hand went up instinctively, and Saina just as instinctively raised his to fend it off. He forgot Ghoru's instruction, and scrambled to pull the short sword out of his belt.

In the suspension of that moment Saina gaped into the face of an officer of the Hanarabode Protectors, once his Abode's neighbor, now his mortal enemy, straining to bring a blow down upon him. His blade slid from Saina's shoulder to his rib without penetrating past the thickness of the robe, but then Saina felt a second thrust enter his side at the lower ribs.

His pushed his own blade deep into the chest of his enemy, who let go of his sword before it could cut Saina any deeper. They both fell away, one dying and the other growing lightheaded.

The two boys watched as an aethereal light came out of them and into his wound. He felt a surge of energy rising upward through his spine to meet it. The gods within the Body of the Goddess were challenging Her devils. He would be saved or killed by their choice. His heart was pounding wildly, yet there was some stillness behind it, from which his own energy emerged. He felt an ocean of Her power, as if his will could dismiss the killing forces of Goddessoma and let the healing beings work. Yet he remained calm and uninvolved in their work.

The same conflict was raging inside his attacker as well without the man seeing it or knowing it. His life was draining away against all his desires, as the devils shut down his organs one by one. He was staring at Saina with a mind far off in memories.

Ghoru crashed into the cleft and stopped—stunned by what he saw in the weak light of the officer's lamp. He knelt to feel the man for signs of life or death.

"Who kills me?" the Hanarabode officer gurgled. He was looking upward to Ghoru.

"I am Ghoru, Captain in the Protectors of Assessor Martial Panjael, who is son of Murosaya. But if you are so interested in how you die, the kill goes to this one. He is Saina, also son of Murosaya. He and his brother will chase all of you snakes back into your den and throw in the rest of your demonic weapon. You should die now to avoid that."

The man had only a few words left. "No. Not yet." He held a finger weakly pointed at Saina. "You are Saina? Varanos ordered you dead. Ruryo, I should say." His eyes glazed as he saw the blood-filled cloth of Saina's shirt, and he smiled. "He sent me to find you. I did." He took a rasping breath and rose slightly with pride. "You took my blade in your side. Your blood is on my hand. You will die before me. I am sure of that. So I think I have served well enough. Served Ruryo. And your own Seed Bearer as well. I have the honor. Not you. Not Panjael. Not you, Ghoru" Then his mind went deep inside for the end.

Ghoru frowned. "What did he mean? Did he cut you?"

Saina gathered enough breath to speak and swallowed. "I felt—something."

Ghoru's hand went to Saina's side. "Is this your blood? Your robe is cut open. That's not a good place to be cut, son. Your hand, please."

He pulled Saina's hand from the wound and felt the slick blood all over it. But there was no open wound. Only a long scab that appeared to have closed days before. He picked up the sword and saw blood on both sides still wet. "What is this—Sulatin magic?"

"Who is Ruryo?" Saina asked hoarsely,

Ghoru was still looking for signs of the wound. "The Assessor Concordant of Hanarabode. The only one among your enemies with a mind to design all this. Without him, you would still be at peace up the mountain."

"I ... should ... thank him."

"Wait until you know he hasn't killed you. Come on. Panjael sent a patrol to get us out. That's who last rode by and defeated the riders above."

The fire from the lamp oil suddenly died to nothing. Riders were circling at the entrance to the cleft.

One of them shouted. "Ghoru—is he there?"

A rush of sounds swept through the cleft—groaning leather and rasping metal and heavy breath—and all evidence of Goddessoma was covered up by this mundane but dangerous world.

Ghoru pulled Saina and the horse out and was greeted with laughing relief from the riders.

"There is one more in there. A captain of Hanarabode. Not a very brave one. He deserted his men up above—but he could not escape my friend's blade here. Saina, son of Murosaya, half-brother of Panjael. And a hero in the only victory for Satamabode in these few days."

Saina was suddenly surrounded by excited soldiers, and their officer drew Ghoru aside.

"We found a way up through the forest, so we can guide you down. Panjael waits at the old ruins with the Daughter Deserena." He added in a low tone, "What is it about this young man?"

"Not our place," Ghoru whispered.

"I know, I know, but—well, I mean, a Sulatin?"

Ghoru put his hand to the officer's shoulder. "Do not dismiss so quickly what we don't know. He has their powers. I saw that. So Murosaya's order must mean something important. That is enough for me. And for you."

The man nodded in agreement. But then Ghoru felt something in his comrade's manner change. "What are you thinking?"

"That I want you to take the boy and my men and meet Panjael. I want to go to my family down there in Alambarat. The mercenaries are probably running free in the city. Is it desertion?"

Ghoru spat. "It's commonsense. Do it. I will take care of what others think—including Panjael. Take his robe. Your family will be surprised to know you are a monk now."

Moments later they took off again. Saina was now dressed in a Protector uniform and carried a full sword against his leg. He passed for a soldier—a thought that took command of his mind for the rest of the journey.

"Unbelievable!" Bhalkavar was furious.

Sevrese's own impatience was fueled by his. But she knew her words had to be swallowed to not alert the line of people they were caught in. And so did his.

She whispered forcefully, "Mohidram, you should please calm yourself. You sound like some old general used to ordering everyone."

He took hold of himself and merely grunted. "I should have known they would close the gates last night. I spent too long with that artist."

"No. We will get through this. We have gotten through the others. Describe to me what you see." She fiddled with the black kerchief over her eyes.

"What is going on, my dear blind niece and eternal burden, is another damned checkpoint and another line a hundred long. No one is in control of this army! It's not for security. They are just harassing refugees and stealing whatever these people managed to get through the last checkpoint. I have told my Mohidram's story five times now since dawn, and I will not go through it again."

"You were only good at it once." She swore under her breath. "There is nothing left to steal. Not even your actor's sword, sharpened for nothing."

As they moved with the line the morning sun finally cleared the mountains and spread across the city. Ahead there was a bridge over the riverbed that took the runoff from the city and hills to the great river where Sugorai stood. The summer water level was down by half but still a strong enough flow to make the bridge desirable.

Along the river on both sides were troops scattered without order, most peacefully asleep for the first time since they crossed the Satamabode border. This last checkpoint served the unofficial greed of the nomad mercenaries, not the Hanarabode Protectors.

A disguise was not enough now. Every citizen, despite the rank they held a day before, hid all distinction and made up their own implausible stories in their effort to escape. But the mercenaries could not have cared less since they did not understand the stories, and looked upon trifles as riches.

Bhalkavar scanned the area very carefully and spoke low to her. "I see two Hanarabode officers lounging nearby, while twenty tribals control this line. Their officers find the command of mercenaries distasteful. No discipline here. You must listen to me very well." His voice remained low, but he put an edge to it.

She felt it and her body tightened. "Yes?"

"It was I who chose this particular disguise of yours, not the artist. We could have concealed your identity with less effort. It was to hide your attraction that he scarred you this much—so that you would be the last person a soldier would look at with longing. Do you understand me?"

"Of course."

"Good. Unfortunately, these tribals are no so discerning. Do not carry yourself as a weakling. But not with any of your usual pride either. Just disappear behind me. Ahh." He swore. "Too late. They've started."

A woman's cry rose from the refugees in line ahead, as three of the mercenaries pulled her out. Bhalkavar's eyes went to the officers. Would their Hanarabode masters put a stop to it? No, they were wandering toward some bushes by the river, uninvolved.

Good, he thought with disgust—*have a piss. Make it a long one.*

"All right, Cheki. Do you think you can ride one of these nomad ponies tied there near the bridge?"

"I cannot see them very well. But, of course—I can ride anything."

He knew that was true. "You will get them after I play with these soldiers a little. We will cross the bridge at a gallop. You must keep going even if I make a brief stop or two. If we are separated, just get up into the Garland Forest. I will find you. Now, it will take a moment for me to organize this. Stay in line until I call for you."

"Will you help that woman?"

He huffed. "The world is full of problems. You can't make all of them ours."

She withdrew the cloth from her eyes as he moved off. Her heart was pounding. She watched as he stole up to the officers first, who were now in the middle of relieving themselves.

"Here is a model of leadership for us all, eh?" He spat on the ground behind them.

They turned their heads to him, but before they could fully turn around without making a mess on themselves, he moved in behind and drew one of their swords from its belt. The man stood ludicrously exposed, but instead of attacking him, Bhalkavar cut the other one with a furious slash from neck to waist, drawing an explosion of blood. The remaining partner stumbled away, but without a weapon he froze in terror. The blade came across his stomach and returned to cut his throat. It was over before anyone else around them even noticed.

Bhalkavar pulled the other sword free from the first corpse, turned and rushed the mercenaries who were attacking the woman from the line. They slowly understood this was an enemy coming.

The three pulled the struggling woman roughly off the ground and put her out as a shield to the wild man approaching them. Bhalkavar slashed the arm of one, and the woman rolled free with a severed hand still gripping her. The second and third fell to two rapid cuts opening their necks.

Four other mercenaries who had been surveying everyone in line with similar intent called out an alarm and rushed toward the general.

He met their charge like a bull and scattered them. One by one they attacked, but he blocked each movement in turn. His own blows fell so quickly it was difficult to say which sword hit which man.

A few of the remaining mercenaries simply ran back toward the city walls. But there were still enough left to attempt to surround Bhalkavar.

He gave the call to Sevrese, and she ran past him toward the horses. The men followed with no order. He rushed them as they gained speed. They tried to halt but tumbled over one another. He killed three more as if they were flies. The others withdrew in panic. He raged at them.

"How did you ever get this far! Rats fight better than you."

Sevrese reached the horses, leapt upon one and took the lead of another. They were nearly out of control, but her legs were used to guiding horses without the help of reins and these small strangers gave in to her immediately.

The general threw one of the swords aside and gathered the reins of two more ponies who followed her, wheeling them around to mount one. They all drummed across the bridge, and the general pulled up to see who would follow. Two riders were coming toward the bridge from the distance. Both were Hanarabode Protectors on tall fighting horses. They could easily run down the ponies.

He dismounted and pushed the ponies ahead, raising his remaining blade to await the first mounted Protector.

Sevrese glanced back and realized what he was going to do. She screamed to stop him.

The first of the Protectors galloped ahead with spirit and Bhalkavar awaited him like a statue. He raised himself in the saddle to cut the general down, but the statue suddenly leaped into the horse's path. The horse swerved, the rider lurched and Bhalkavar's blade split him before he could rise.

The horse backed away from the falling body, and Bhalkavar jumped the dead man's horse. It staggered and recovered as other rider came across the bridge at a gallop—standing in his stirrups with sword in both hands raised above his head.

Just before the officer delivered his blow the general caught him under his arm and sent him into the exposed rocks in the riverbed where his head was cracked.

Bhalkavar grabbed the other mount's reins as his own horse whirled on the bridge. He galloped toward Sevrese, who at the right moment stood up on the pony's back and leaped to the saddle next to her without breaking stride.

They disappeared into the hills further before any others could follow, save four of the ponies.

From the distance Saina could not see into the glade where Panjael's Protectors were concealed, but instinctively the beads dropped into his hand. The mental chant began on its own, as it always had. Approaching his brother after all this time in any circumstances would have rattled whatever peace he carried down from Prayadevale. But this background of events made him feel as foreign as the tribal mercenaries.

His farm horse seemed to sense the resistance and was overcome with dread, spinning once and nearly tripping—dangerously close to unseating his rider.

Saina recovered from the lurch and actually thanked the horse for distracting him, offering him serene mental pictures of the valley farms surrounding Prayadevale. He realized quickly that only gave more pain.

Listen, we are both alike in this adventure. You a farmer, I a monk. Neither of us knows the next thing to do. But we can trust these men—and their mounts from now on.

The riders picked up a faster pace and swept into the trees to a mass of soldiers greeting them.

Saina dismounted to the sound of his name.

The voice was hardly familiar, but the sight of Panjael was even more unexpected. It was a jolt to any pretentions of family reunion. *This*, he comprehended, *is what a warrior looks like.*

He was a lion. Stunning black eyes flashed a greeting to every man there. His close black beard was muddied with dirt and effort. He was twenty-nine and faced the cruelest test of leadership—complete defeat.

"Not a proud day on which to meet again, eh?"

Saina bowed slightly, "Panjael, I am here to serve you."

Panjael's returning smile was inviting and indifferent in turns. "Come on. Let us sit in the shade and talk." His solid sword arm went around Saina until they sat. "No longer the lifelong student. Now you have a messy little war to round out your knowledge."

Saina guessed that anyone from the outside took the Sulatin life to be a lazy one, and he could not help resenting it. But he knew he would be hard pressed to compare bodily austerities and agonizing mental exercise to what he saw around him at that moment.

"I am sorry about our father. I—I did not know him as you did. To hear of his death ...." He stopped, having no real feeling to offer.

"He cared about you. He always got reports of your progress. I even heard our Seed Bearer Qurmadi ask him about you once. He must have proud of that consideration."

Saina was surprised and showed it, remembering the face of the Seed Bearer entering Goddessoma.

"I know it seems peculiar since he always kept you so distant. I asked him once why this was so."

"What did he say?"

Panjael shrugged and shook his head. "He would not explain and only said it was best for you. He was not an easy man. He served an Abode that was always the strongest and the richest of the Ten, but in his generation the cracks in that strength began to open. So, somehow it ends like this. In his lifetime, Satamabode fell. Imagine him contemplating his place in our history as its last Assessor Martial." He gave another shrug and looked into the distance. "Next to last, I suppose. Perhaps his name will be mercifully spared at that, and the true degradation may be mine to earn." He laughed.

Saina knew well how it felt to endure shame and dishonor for actions he could not control. At least, he believed he could not control them, but everyone else in Prayadevale blamed him, no matter how they labored to explain the accident otherwise. Panjael did not seem to want empathy, nor did Saina want to compare his guilt to his brother's.

Quickly he tried to remember something from their shared past. Murosaya had married Saina's mother the year of his birth—after the event. Panjael's own mother had died the year previous. Saina's mother in turn died when he was eight. Other than these facts, there was little to look back on.

He shook off these impressions and brought himself back to the demands around him. "Can you tell me why was I summoned, Panjael? Captain Ghoru said it was our father's specific request. Do you know the message he had for me?"

Panjael took his breath slowly. "He sent a package for you. I will show you later. We were forced apart by the battle. He saw the city was lost and decided the preservation of the Protectors came ahead of it. He sent me away with all those who had not been cut off and captured. By then Qurmadi was dead, so the Heir had to be saved. That was Murosaya's duty and his last mistake. You have heard it from Ghoru— Varanos betrayed his Abode, likely poisoned his father, and had ours murdered as well. I don't know the reason he wanted you back, but I know what I need you to do. I need you to go back to Prayadevale."

Saina gave a look of incredulity.

"No—I don't mean as a student. I have a mission for you there—for the Abode."

Saina's mind descended from confusion to disappointment. It should have been more than this. It should have been something that changed his life. A mission to Prayadevale—what was that?

"I thought ... well, surely there was something from him ... something about me ... after all this time." Saina felt his teeth clench together, then loosen. A single hollow laugh escaped him and he looked into the trees to hide any bitterness in his face.

Panjael took this in. "Saina, we all have our places. And our gifts. Maybe there was more. Maybe Murosaya had something else for you. Perhaps it is in the package he wanted you to have. I am sorry you have been robbed of his word, but now I need you for myself."

Saina gave half a shake of his head. "I will do whatever you want. Of course I pledge that."

"Good enough." Panjael took another deep breath and glanced round his shoulders once. "What do you think your Sulatin Order makes of the attack at Sugorai?"

"Captain Ghoru gave his report to the Conductor and the Intercessor in Prayadevale, and they in turn told all the students and monks. But I left before they revealed any interpretations or plans. It is hardly possible they would share that with students. I really don't know how they take it. There has never been such an event for a thousand years. How can anyone fathom it?"

Panjael looked disappointed for a moment. "Yes, it is unique, but all of the people involved are rather typical. Though Ruryo stands out. Speculate. What will they think of Varanos' role in it and what their precious Seed is worth these days?"

"In the lineage studies I learned that the Seed is not considered a factor in character. The Sulatins say the Seed of the Founding Seers is the only way to assure their cognitions are permanent. While anyone can cognize Goddessoma, that cognition dies with the person. Only the Seed of the Founding Seers is passed generation to generation. They cannot sanction what Varanos has done, yet the fact remains that the Seed has not been lost. Perhaps, if there was an alternate Heir, they would exert pressure, but there is none."

"Mmm. That depends on how you define Heir."

"But only one thing defines the Heir. Does he carry the Seed of the Founding Seer of the Abode? That is why the births are all recorded in the Abode Scrolls."

"There is a Daughter of the Seed."

Saina shook his head. "The cognitions of the Founding Seers are carried by the Seed. No female has this."

"Ahh, Saina, it is a feeble story. It is more likely that Varanos' offspring will be murderers than seers. It is time for the Sulatins to have one practical idea. And you are going to tell them what it is for me, as you agreed the moment we met."

Saina nodded cautiously. "You want me to tell them Deserena should rule Satamabode."

"Mmm, no. Not tell them. Convince them. She carries the Seed. I will rule as her consort. Very practical."

Saina felt his mouth open, but he had no words—none that would come out. *The Seed is absolute. Practical or not. There is no convincing against a principle that is absolute.*

"You seem hesitant. I understand your dilemma. But our father foresaw a way to convince the Sulatins—a last resort for our Abode. I told you he left you a package. It contains the scroll of Satamabode."

Saina blinked. "The scrolls are in Prayadevale. Completely protected. Even the students have never seen one."

"One of them is not in Prayadevale and has not been for many years. It is in my tent. Murosaya kept it when the Sulatins came to record Varanos' birth, making them very upset with Satamabode. He ordered me to use it to make peace with them."

"But with Varanos alive there is no threat to the Seed."

A low laugh rumbled in Panjael's chest. "I am going to remove Varanos from the discussion. He will pay for the murder of our father with his life. The Sulatins have only the time it takes me to complete that pledge. If they want to line up women for Varanos to impregnate, they should hurry. Once I complete that task, I will rule Satamabode as consort of Deserena, Daughter of the Seed."

"I understand."

"If they refuse not only will I end the Seed, but you will burn the scroll. How will this sound to them—the *Nine* Abodes? Not the same power to it."

Saina's eyes went to the ground.

"You don't think you can make that threat. Look around. How can I take back Sugorai and Alambarat without the backing of the other Abodes? How can I obtain their Protectors without the sanction of the Sulatin Order? My offer is less polluted than sanctioning a murderer for the sake of what squirts into his pants—that would shame the Sulatins forever."

Panjael let a wry smile cross his lips. "Saina, what the Sulatins fail to understand is that Seed Bearers do not rule the Abodes. Men like your father do it for him. One of those men proved it very dramatically days ago at your father's expense. His name is Ruryo, Assessor Concordant of Hanarabode. I don't know what he is planning, but he has a weapon no one can best, so the Seed Bearers and the Sulatins should be worried. I am offering them a bandage that will close this wound. I am willing to face Ruryo and his weapon with their support. This is what you must convince them of. My price is the death of Varanos."

"My mission is to make them pay that price for the return of the Scroll, but with the loss of the Seed." Suddenly Saina realized that Ruryo could make the same threat on a larger scale. He will kill Varanos, rule Satamabode—and repeat his work nine times. He said nothing to Panjael

"You think about how you do it. In the meantime, here are my instructions to you Saina. Take the old road from here to Ryadabode to avoid Ruryo's men. Meet with the Regent Pavim in Virnipal. She is influential with the Sulatins, and I believe her General Bhalkavar tried to help our father discover Ruryo's plot. I know Murosaya tried to send Varanos and Deserena to Alambarat to visit the Dowager. Ryadabode Daughter of the Seed was supposed to meet her, but it did not take place. Regent Pavim will grant Deserena sanctuary."

"Is the Dowager safe?"

"She is not our problem. Next return to Prayadevale as soon as possible—make certain you secure the scroll somewhere you can retrieve it when an agreement is reached. Do you understand all I have told you?"

Saina nodded, thinking, *You want me to prevent the downfall of all the Abodes by accelerating it.* "I will do my best."

"Right." Panjael spread his hands toward the mountains behind him. "Here we sit near the ruins of the city that began Satamabode. Your Founding Seer may have relieved himself on this very spot. Now it reveals the next phase of your life. Auspicious enough for you?"

Saina tried to look enthusiastic. "The Garland Forest is where the ferines were hunted—is it true they still exist?"

Panjael laughed. "If there are any left I am sending one warrior with you for protection. Your brother Nacros."

A ten-year-old shudder went through Saina.

It appeared to delight Panjael. "He's almost grown and not quite as annoying as you remember him. A good fighter—brave, skilled, and reckless but effective against a ferine attack."

As if he was called, Nacros was walking toward them. "Do we leave now? Saina! Good to have you back—in time for three brothers to die together making the traitors pay."

Panjael waved him forward. "Don't let him decide when you die. I rely on you to follow my instruction. There is no chance Nacros will."

Nacros gave Saina a clumsy embrace. He then gave an earnest grip to Panjael's arm. "No harm will come to Deserena. I assure that completely."

"What I want from you is get deep into the Garland Forest as soon as possible. Ruryo is smart enough to learn of this escape, but I doubt he would invest the men to track you so far."

Saina coughed lightly. "Ruryo is searching for me as well."

Nacros looked amused. Panjael said nothing.

"Captain Ghoru knows. We were attacked by Hanarabode Protectors above Alambarat. One of them said Varanos ordered me killed. But then he said it was actually Ruryo."

Nacros raised his brows. "How did he fail?"

Saina felt his pride welling up. "I killed him first."

Panjael gave him a clap on the cheek. "Good. Exactly. Nacros, watch them tying the packhorses—make sure it is to your liking. I have one more thing to show Saina."

They hurried into the Assessor Martial's makeshift tent of leafy branches—the escape from Sugorai having left them with no supplies. Next to it was another of slightly higher craftsmanship. Saina guessed it housed Deserena.

Panjael tossed Saina an oilskin package. "There is the precious scroll. I want to have a last word with the Daughter of the Seed." He exited quickly.

Saina's eyes bulged at the bag. Once alone he carefully unpacked it and rolled it open slightly. A scent came up from the depths of the past. He closed it immediately, fearing its fragility. Then he heard whispered voices. It was Panjael in Deserena's tent. Saina could see them barely through the branches. They were arm in arm. It was a potent sight, the two of them. She, sleek and flawless—he, perfectly tooled and shining. Silk against leather.

She seemed to be pleading with Panjael. Saina heard only parts of sentences. "Unendurable … how can I survive … the security of your arms … the pleasure you give me … what will I do?"

They melted into each other and their lips pressed together interminably. Saina could not look away, though he knew he must. They broke their kiss only to caress each other and gaze into eyes. Then again a compulsive embrace. She spoke his name so many times, it seemed the only word she knew. Her tears came and went between their kisses.

At last, it seemed Panjael would part from her. But then he let her hand trail from his shoulder, down his stomach, and around his hips, until it found the desire between his thighs. There she put her energy, eyes closed, sensations rolling through her body as she played with him, until at last she took his hand and pulled him closer as she bent to the ground. He was on top of her, pressing his whole body to hers. Her legs wrapped around him.

Saina forced himself to back out of the tent in silence. It was not until he was at some distance that he could fathom his feelings at the sight of their passion. He had sweat tears rolling down from his temples.

The Intercessor Athayam sat with legs folded on an unembellished couch. A low table was placed in front of him with one meager oil lamp and a tea setting upon it. Luzarain and Daiyenso were each seated on a mat atop the stone floor on opposite ends of the table. It was nearly sunset, and narrow shafts of sunlight strayed in through the carvings on the shutters.

While Conductor Luzarain's authority concentrated within the Order, the Intercessor's spread out from Prayadevale to the Ten Abodes. As a friend and advisor to the Seed Bearers, he was regarded as confidant and conscience—inspiring them to align their duties and their actions with the principles of the Founding Seers.

His body reflected a past of great strength that had slowly given way to a long and dignified decline. His head remained erect as always, his hair hanging down over the front of his shoulders, long and white, folded behind his beard. His calm hands were crossed in his lap. To break the silence he stretched effortlessly for a small carved bowl and raised its contents to his lips. He took the liquid slowly, holding each sip in his mouth a moment before swallowing. Then he returned the bowl to the table and took up the cloth beside it to wipe any droplets from his beard.

"I am very relieved," he began at last, "that the Daughter of Ryadabode has encountered no harm—so far. And Satamabode's Daughter Deserena. Both escaping through the Garland Forest. I should like to send word to Regent Pavim, to ease her distress." He paused, reflecting. "But, perhaps not, since we have no certainty of their safe arrival in Virnipal. Even if the war does not follow them, there may still be a danger from the ferines."

He drew a deep breath. "You have given us an excellent report, Daiyenso. Hanarabode's success is deeply shocking, but better than protracted fighting, I suppose. While we think of this news as all of single story, there are two crimes to consider. I see reasons to separate them. One is the murder of a Seed Bearer by the Heir of the Seed, the other an attack by one Abode on another."

Luzarain tapped his finger lightly on the table. "We have no proof of the first. Daiyenso overheard Varanos attempt to accuse Ruryo, who denied it—or at least sidestepped it. Did you see it happen, Daiyenso?"

"I observed his dying. It could have been fright. But the way Ruryo is distributing poison, I feel safe to say he arranged the death."

"But where was Varanos at that time?"

Athayam shook his head. "You are cutting the blame too thin, Conductor. Is it not fair to say Varanos brought death to Assessor Murosaya? He did not draw the arrow or let it go, but he created all the circumstances required to complete it. His intention in all the communion with Ruryo was to reach the status of Seed Bearer. He might have expressed displeasure with the notion that Ruryo had somehow poisoned Qurmadi, but even if the Seed Bearer died of fright, Varanos initiated the fright. There was never any chance for Qurmadi—or for that matter Murosaya—to live beyond the attack."

Luzarain waved his hand gently and nodded.

"Now," continued the Intercessor, "it seems to be our time to react."

"But, Athayam, we should not react to the crime—the two crimes, if you like. We must react to Assessor Ruryo's success."

Daiyenso nodded. "That is the point, Athayam. This never was a Seed Bearer's action or an Heir of the Seed's action. Even more accurately we can trace the origin to the mind of Varanos' deceased mother. None of it would have gone beyond speculation, were it not crafted by Ruryo. And to our discredit—my own chiefly—we failed to see it."

"Which is why," added Luzarain, "we cannot expect the Seed Bearers to muster the will to act against it."

Athayam scratched his beard lightly. "Mmm. A family quarrel that Ruryo managed to turn into a catastrophe for the Ten Abodes. His craft, as you put it, has exposed two Abodes and the Seed Bearer families who rule them as fools and murderers."

"Worse than that, Athayam," began Luzarain. "If we let Ruryo's intentions be paramount, it must be concluded he intends the end of the Ten Abodes and the Sulatins. His next action must be the execution of Varanos."

Athayam again swallowed tea and turned his cup several times in his hand, contemplating. "Why would he want to destroy our connection to the Founding Seers?"

Daiyenso shifted slightly and drew the others' looks. "What Ruryo wants to prove is that a connection with the Founding Seers does not exist—never has. His plan is exactly as Luzarain described. At the moment of his choosing, he will kill the new Seed Bearer to prove that the people of Satamabode are better off without one."

And with that act he will expose ten Abodes and their Seed Bearer families as well as the Sulatin Order as fools and liars.

"That statement may be the key to inspiring the other eight Abodes to concerted action. What do you think, Daiyenso?"

"We cannot forget the weapon he conceived. I saw the effect many times. Warriors were terrified and rendered powerless. Inspiring the Abodes to warfare will be difficult when he aims that weapon at them. They may abdicate in order to save their lives. After all, if Assessor Murosaya could not contend with the weapon, what Abode can?"

Athayam's brows rose. "If the weapon is the difference whether Varanos lives or dies, what if we can counteract it? There is surely enough alchemical knowledge in our library to undo its power. It appears to harness the destructive forces of Goddessoma. We can harness the creative powers of Goddessoma. Luzarain, you should assemble the best within these walls to work on that goal."

"Of course."

Athayam took a long breath and released it. "What puzzles me, but not the two of you, is how to comprehend Ruryo. If I accept what you say is his plan, it still does not explain his motivation. Is this all a conceit? Audacity? Insolence? Luzarain, what do you believe?"

"As unused to this as you might be, just as Daiyenso agrees with me, I agree with him. Ruryo holds a glass to the faces of the Seed Bearers and Sulatins alike. To the Seed itself. Even to the Founding Seers. He provokes the question—is this truly the only way to rule? He is a villain in his means, but he is an idealist in his goal. His question places him— and anyone else—in the center of existence. He sweeps away Founding

Seers, cognitions, Seed Bearers, and Goddessoma itself. In its place he offers rationality and expedience. What if that works just as well?"

"But why?" Athayam looked incredulous. "That is madness. Besides, life in the Ten Abodes is fruitful and propitious. What warrants violent change?"

Luzarain gave a hollow laugh. "If one queen's bitterness can spark a plan to bring down the Ten Abodes, how is this propitious and fruitful? Ruryo has attacked our one weakness, Athayam. We cannot prove the value of Founding Seers, cognitions, Seed Bearers, or Goddessoma."

"Daiyenso, do you still agree?"

Daiyenso stared into his cup. "We do not have to take the perspective of Ruryo to explain these events. I have a very different view. I think you can guess it."

Athayam took this in for a long moment. "The return of the Preceptor."

Luzarain instinctively shifted his weight on the cushion, evincing his displeasure. Daiyenso set down his cup and drew himself up on his.

Athayam understood each reaction spoke more than words. These two were the great rivals of the Sulatin Order, and no one but he knew this truth. Both had mastered advanced Sulatin powers, yet neither was free from envy of the other. One was the Order's leader, the other a shadow in the shadows.

"Daiyenso, do you believe the Preceptor will resolve this?"

"I believe he caused it—acting on behalf of the Goddess. I believe he will resolve it—acting on behalf of the Goddess."

"Yet," Luzarain broke in, "he chooses not to satisfy the Seed Bearers or us by his presence. We have only your conjectures as to whether the fall of the Ten Abodes and perhaps even the Sulatin Order could be the inevitable prelude to a revival of the knowledge of Goddessoma."

Daiyenso gave a slight wag of his head. "Only the precedent he gave us when he founded our order five hundred years ago."

Athayam gave a soft murmur. "If either of you is right, this entire discussion avails nothing. We can take action or not with the same result. But I cannot ignore the need for action."

"Except," added Luzarain, "we have one curiosity that has not come up in this discussion. An action started with so little apparent significance that we pay no attention. That is a mistake, I believe."

"What action is that?"

"The summons for Murosaya's son Saina, our pupil until a few days ago—and the union of Saina with the Satamabode scroll."

Athayam nodded. "Yes—and it goes back even further. The mystery of Murosaya's withholding of the scroll after Varanos' birth." He nodded. "At least Daiyenso can verify that the scroll is safe for now and there are signs of a revelation of what Murosaya intended. But with all these dangers developing all that may be old news already. So for us it remains a curiosity and little more."

"Because of that," added Daiyenso, "it gathers power by remaining out of everyone's reach."

"I see that point." Athayam looked at Daiyenso, but the face was blank and the lips sealed. "Then we must wait until Saina emerges from the Garland Forest. If all goes well Saina and the scroll will be in Ryadabode in a few days. Not very long after that if I am not mistaken falls Regent Pavim's birthday. Let us all three go to Virnipal and give the Sulatins' blessing on the celebration. There we can gently force the issue of the scroll with this young man who has left us."

Luzarain nodded. "Perhaps Daiyenso would be willing to extend an invitation to his ally in the forest as well. I think forcing *him* on the issue of the scroll will be more enlightening than anything Saina can offer."

The two rivals stared into each other's eyes in the dim light. Neither gave the smallest measure of ground away.

Assessor Ruryo moved through the immense corridors of the Sugorai palace like a fractious young stallion. His pace under the lattice carvings high above threw flickering shadows and brilliant flashes on the herd of soldiers, messengers, and servants in his wake.

He gave agitated but exhaustive lists of tasks required for the arrival of Seed Bearer Pharmos to the servants. For nearly every item there was at least one obstacle to confront, and each one he sorted out for them—resigned to knowing that he himself could have finished all of their work in a portion of the time.

The soldiers gave their reports in turn, always slightly behind his shoulder as he moved along. None of their words ruffled him. He seemed to see their descriptions in some changing landscape in the air before him. It was as if the whole of the lands of Satamabode was subdued within his arm's length.

At last came the messengers' reports, for he had already established a thorough communication service in every direction from Sugorai. Most were only confirmation of his expectations. It was only one which truly intrigued him. And this one brought the train to a stop before the door to the great durbar of the Seed Bearer of Satamabode.

"So you are telling me you know the whereabouts of the son of Murosaya. The second son, you mean—I don't care about the other two for now."

"Yes, Assessor, he is—"

Ruryo instantly held up a hand to stop him. "Tell me the source."

"A member of the Protectors of Satamabode, wounded and captured outside Alambarat. He was trying to get into the city dressed as a Sulatin, which was suspicious. We worked on him but he only confessed to be one of the Protectors that fled Sugorai after our victory. Later he admitted coming to Alambarat for his family. Then realizing his family was at risk he gave in and told us his mission had been to save the son of Murosaya."

"So he told you this to avoid death to his family?"

"At first."

"What next?"

"The tribals were given a chance with him. They made him tell us Saina had escaped into the Garland Forest. There is an old road"—

"Yes, yes. And this he offered to prevent his own death?"

"No, sir. To obtain it. The tribals are reportedly very thorough with torture."

"Mmm. What did he know about this Saina?"

"He killed the officer in charge of a party you assigned to find him."

"Did he? Some Sulatin magic I suppose."

"No, sir. Blade against blade. But he was badly wounded and used Sulatin magic to heal himself."

"Don't be ridiculous. It was probably a scratch."

"I believe it is the truth. He exchanged his uniform for Saina's Sulatin robe for the escape. The whole side was stained with blood."

Ruryo shook his head angrily. "This all means nothing. The Garland Forest story may be a ruse." He let the thought loose in his mind until it formed fully into action. "No point trying to find them there. I have confirmed that the old road does not enter Ryadabode. They will first have to join the current road coming over the mountain from Alambarat. Have a force waiting for them there."

You will be met as you climb that last run to the border, young man. And no Sulatin magic will help.

"Is there no word about the Daughter of the Seed?"

"Which one, Assessor?"

"Ahh, yes. First Satamabode. Since she escaped Alambarat, she must be with Saina. The Ryadabode Daughter and that general? No doubt they too are in the Garland Forest."

You will all meet me at the border—it is too convenient!

Not the first time Ruryo answered every question himself. Only one remained. What did Panjael, a man he had never encountered in person, have in mind? This question only Ruryo could answer. He watched the fingers unroll from his palm as he counted off the facts.

First, faced with the ruin of the leadership of Satamabode and all its defenses, Panjael is left with a small army of Protectors—too small to retaliate and too large to hide. He retrieves Deserena, Daughter of the Seed of Satamabode, and sends her to Ryadabode, obviously for sanctuary—adding the general and Pavim's daughter to help purchase an alliance with her. But a paltry Abode like Pavim's is worth nothing.

Second, the machinations of Murosaya, Saina, and this stupid scroll remain obscure. I have ignored this factor—worse, made light of it, as with the Sulatin powers. Panjael can use that scroll to negotiate with the Sulatins. I must find that scroll and destroy it—remove it from the field of action.

His third finger unrolled.

Panjael needs to avenge his father's death. Varanos hates him, so it follows that he hates Varanos. He will have no scruples about killing his Seed Bearer.

His little finger straightened.

He cannot defeat me. His anger toward the Seed Bearers and the Sulatins will grow as they fail to lend him their support.

He looked at his hand with the fingers extend. Then he laughed clapped both hands together as if he was squeezing a fruit to juice. He saw Panjael with no army to speak of and a few dubious allies and a burning revenge in his heart.

I know you, Panjael. You are coming to me. Good, for I have a job for you.

Hidden deep within the luxuriant greens of the Garland Forest in the noon sun, a band of ferines lounged in the heavy branches midway up the trees. They took their rest high enough to view the distance down the slope, watchful of any movements.

The young ones could not rest even in the summer heat. They were more nimble than the adults. Yet to develop the powerful bulk around their shoulders and shanks, they rose easily to the higher branches where they could stand upright and sway.

The older ones opened an eyelid once in a while to watch them, but they preferred to doze on the beds they fashioned in the stronger branches below. But for all of them sleep was fitful today. The disturbances in the basin below over the past days left them uncertain and anxious. They felt the fighting in the air and in the tension of the hunter birds that had left the open sky of the basin to perch here in the mountain forest for now.

Silence was never easy for ferines. Their deep chests, supple jaws, and spreading noses combined uniquely to give them voices more melodic than any singing birds. And of all animals their connection to the Goddess was deepest—their sense of Her presence in every object more inspired. Songs of praise sprung from one, and all the others knew instinctively how to join in.

They made songs that exalted the forests—noble trees, timeless rocks, ever-changing clouds rolling over the slopes, the celestial shafts of light, the gusting currents of air that fan the leaves. The songs extolled the rains and the gathering of the droplets into the ruts, which grew into streams and then washed into the ravines, passing far off into the great river basin and then renewed with the wet darkening of the sky. They honored their fellow creatures—food-givers, food-takers, food-sharers, allies, enemies, helpers, pests. And the multitude of plants—the sustainers, the shelterers, the healers and poisoners alike.

There were story songs—the histories of ferine masters and matriarchs and the songs of play and of work. But there were also songs of the conflicts—when long ago they fought a great fight against demons beside the humans. And in a more recent time when the humans hunted and tried to imprison them for their own pleasures—and the great fight for the ferines' own freedom that followed. Those last songs were on their minds now that conflict had broken out in the basin. They sang them quietly, just enough to ease the tension until the Goddess sent them some sign of Her desires.

In the meantime they waited, hoping for the one they called the Being Surrounded by Light to appear. Shib, their leader—very old and still powerful—had talked of the Being Surrounded by Light since his youth. He was one of the ferines who had been captured and caged. But unlike the rest, Shib did not escape. In fact he did not even try. He was kept down in the basin in a garden in the big city in a large pen that could never have held a ferine who wanted to break out. One look at the power of their muscled frames should have told the humans that. But the Being Surrounded by Light asked Shib to stay there. The Being Surrounded by Light promised him he would not be mistreated, and he asked Shib to watch and listen to everything in that garden until he could understand the humans when they spoke and even when they thought.

Shib sacrificed his freedom for years until the Being Surrounded by Light gave him permission to go. And when he returned to the forest all the ferines were in awe of what he was capable of. But more in awe when he brought to them the Being Surrounded by Light, who lived in a cave in the Garland Forest ever since.

It had been many seasons since the Being Surrounded by Light had emerged. Only the oldest like Shib could recall it. The rest only wondered, would he come? Shib thought so, and he would not let them give in to their fears about what they heard from down in the basin and what it might mean. He knew that Being Surrounded by Light would give them the thoughts to prepare for whatever was coming. Maybe those thoughts would be of peace and contentment. But privately he believed Being Surrounded by Light would ask them to go to war.

They had urged Shib to go to the cave, but this was never done. Shib told them that Being Surrounded by Light was by his own nature alone and silent. And that must be respected always. So Shib now waited with them, letting a foot dangle from his makeshift berth, occasionally rolling his head toward the sounds in the distance.

When there came chattering in a distant tree, he knew someone had seen something. Now there would be answers. A growl followed a shrill call and then more chattering, until at last everyone was up and involved. This was it. Everyone knew it had to come. Unable to keep their fighting in their own world, humans had entered the forest again.

Shib came down to the forest floor with the rest of them. Word had come with song from a down-mountain troop. Shib listened along with the others, but he did not react with their anxiety and urgency.

This is no source of fear, he told them in his way, offering a wave of his hand before walking away with a ferine's limping gait. *Are they many? No. Two riders first. Then another three more.*

He gave the ferine's snorting laugh. *Such a threat! Do all of us attack at once?* They could not meet his silent stare, but he knew they needed to fend off anything that could possibly menace them.

So, we can alarm them in the night—if they come this far. No harm to that. A fair warning.

Many growled and cheered this idea.

Then I will ask Being Surrounded by Light what more to do. He patted his head to say he would send the question.

Now they jumped and shouted and sang. They trusted Shib.

EPISODE 3

Late in the morning, Bhalkavar and Sevrese saw the party following them far below. They studied them at length from the security of trees and rocks above.

"Three riders. Two wear Satamabode Protector uniforms. These old eyes cannot make out the other." Bhalkavar rubbed and blinked, but nothing became clearer.

"You may remember I am the blind one," Sevrese grumbled and considered them longer in silence. "The horses are confusing. In front is a cavalry mount, alright. But in the middle is a true beauty—delicate conformation and gait. Not a trail horse at all. And then there is the last rider who looks to be on a plough horse without a saddle. Yet the packhorse is a soldier's mount again. Ahh. The middle rider is a woman—explains the horse. She is dressed very cautiously. Maybe an officer escaping with his wife with and an orderly. There were bound to be refugees coming this way. They are not a danger. Let them pass us, as we hide."

She stretched back against a rock, wishing the elevation would at least afford relief from the heat. She had never been pushed this hard. From the intensity of the fight itself—not the least the bloody memory of a Bhalkavar she had never conceived so vividly—to the crossing over this uncompromising terrain without supplies, this was not an adventure she felt born to.

She rolled onto one elbow to take another look at the riders and to survey the expanse in the distance—the far-reaching basin of Satamabode. It was magnificent. And empty. One pasture or ploughed field or orchard after another on which nothing moved. So austere compared to the verdant mountain valley and sparkling lake of her Ryadabode.

Beneath the make-up she continued to wear at the general's insistence, her eyes widened painfully. She propped herself higher. Then she glanced at the general, who was deep within his own mind, waiting with the infinite patience of a perfect warrior.

"I have a surprise for you, Bhalkavar." She smiled. "No, for this surprise I must address you as Mohidram."

One eye squinted to regard her. He could feel the irony in her words. Then he shot a look at the riders. "What?"

"It looks like Deserena is coming to visit me instead."

"Are you certain?"

"Yes. Quite certain. I would not forget the face of a Daughter of her beauty—even at a distance. Even veiled. Will she be followed?"

He strained to judge the figures below a moment. "Mmm. At this pace they should have been caught by now. It is too late to get ahead of them unseen, but we will have to delay considerably to stay out of sight behind them."

Sevrese sighed. "They have a pack horse. Provisions. Real food. Your berry fast is wearing thin, and there will be even less to eat as we finish the climb."

He nodded. "And—they may need us. They are obviously seeking sanctuary with your mother. Not much of an escort, but good for not being noticed." He reflected a few moments. "Does she know you well enough to recognize you like this?"

"I doubt it. As you know, I rarely seek the company of the other Daughters of the Seed, nor have I given any effort to finding potential husbands. We last saw each other at a Seed Bearer gathering, where we found nothing in common. She knew she comes from the gem of the Ten Abodes, and she expects companions to seek her, not the other way round." Sevrese paused. "What about the Protectors knowing you?"

He gave a huff. "You made it clear I am more disfigured than you are. We will keep our little play alive."

She realized what he intended. They would offer help, yes, but if they were captured in Deserena's company, a poor blind girl would draw little attention. It was not what she would call honorable, but she could not bring herself to raise that question. She adjusted her disguise.

He rose and hailed the three below. As he stood over her he gave a low whistle, "The one in front has drawn his blade and comes ahead. Oh, young fool—let us not have trouble with you."

From below, Saina heard the shout with a shudder of anxiety. He would have held back and returned the call, but Nacros sent his horse leaping up the slope, cutting through the brush to shorten the switchbacks. Saina moved his own horse next to Deserena's, and both of them took up a faster pace. The bouncing trot made every joint and every muscle ache to his limits.

The pain took his mind back to Prayadevale—how on the fourth day of a fast, of which he had much experience, one's capacity for irritation and resentment usually became eruptive. Sulatin students would sit together in groups in the afternoon discussions, vehemently rejecting each other's arguments over some point of study or glowering in silence with lethal plans against each other circling in their thoughts. It was part of purification, and when it was over, after the black moods and headaches, at least came some uplift. He doubted that the stabbing weariness of all this riding would end with any relief.

Suddenly Nacros shouted from above, waving his blade in front of his head.

"Stand—both of you!"

Saina called for his brother to wait, and pressed for a gallop, nearly falling for want of stirrups. Deserena's horse left his behind.

Sevrese and her general were already standing. He called back, "You ask for what you already have, sir. You see all of us—only two and with no ill intent. The girl here is blind and no threat to you. We only wish to greet you so you will not judge us a threat." He lifted his arms and with an elaborate smile asked, "Are we your prisoners?"

"First you will tell me who you are!" demanded Nacros.

"A horse-coper with the simple name of Mohidram. Here is an unfortunate niece I care for named Cheki. We can hardly warrant your sword."

"Oh, really? Well, trader, where are your horses?"

"In the trees, hidden just above. You can see them if you slow down."

Nacros strained. "I see only two. But I see blood upon your shirt and a Hanarabode Protector's sword in your belt. What kind of a horse-coper are you?"

"One who knows how to fight his way through the checkpoints in Alambarat. We had a few ponies that joined us by choice, but they found fulfilling lives in the grassy hills before our climb. And how did you come to be here?"

"That is not your concern."

Deserena and Saina caught up and dust stirred all around them. Deserena looked down to hide her face even with a veil. Saina waved to clear the air and get a look at the man standing atop a boulder. He was as calm as Nacros was agitated—with the same silent power Saina had seen on faces of rare Sulatin monks. Luzarain's face for one.

Mohidram suddenly laughed. "Greetings. As I was telling this young man. I brought a small herd to the outskirts of Alambarat only a few days ago. News of the invasion had not reached me. Those barbarians stole almost everything, but I had revenge upon at least one of them"—he gestured to the red marks on his shirt—"and stole two of their Hanarabode horses as well. So you see? We struck a blow for Satamabode. Since we got away we have been wandering in these mountains trying to locate the old road. I know the forest only from the other side—to tell the truth, I once came to this forest in search of one of the Garland trees for a gift to a woman I admired. But I never got so far as this western slope."

"How is it you were not followed? Have you seen any sign of anyone since your escape?" Saina asked.

He shook his barren and sunburnt head. "There is safety in these mountains. But unfortunately the Ryadabode side is too dangerous to descend. We need the advantages of the pass. A long journey back from where we came. Then a short ride on the Alambarat road to the Ryadabode border crossing. I expect it will be heavily manned now. If we are all trying to reach that Abode, then perhaps we are better off together at least through the Garland Forest. Even if we are not followed by your enemy, we will be watched by the ferines."

Nacros looked at Deserena and Saina. "An old hawker and a cripple. They are a burden to us. Let's ride on."

"Nacros—" Saina tried to cut him off.

At the same moment, Sevrese leaped to her feet as if she would attack, but the general pushed her behind him quickly.

Saina intervened. "Nacros, can you try to weigh things just once? I say we let these two join us." Then he turned to Deserena. "If you do not mind, perhaps they will be agreeable company for you as we travel."

From the look he saw cross her eyes behind the delicate veil, he guessed he had given her the first cause for amusement she had experienced in many days. Saina concluded he was lucky she did not take offense.

Nacros returned his blade with an unreserved snort.

"How many days will we be in this forest?" Saina asked the trader.

The general looked at Deserena before answering. "Mmm. Well, as I recall, if we can crest this slope today, then a night and another day. The high valley is considerably easier—a flat basin for most of the way."

"That would place us for a night run from where we emerge to the border. That is an advantage, isn't it?"

"It could be. But no guarantees." He spread his arms. "I am a horse-coper after all. My talent is fabrication, as this young man observes." He shot a glance at Nacros. "I'm sorry, I notice you hold a cadet rank. I am not sure how I should address you."

Nacros scowled and spurred his horse further up the trail.

Saina dismounted and gestured with a nod to Bhalkavar to separate with him. The general took the meaning and walked off a few steps from his blind companion.

"I apologize for my—my fellow Protector."

He received a shrug in return. Saina liked the man's eyes even more now that he could see them closer. They held compassion and knowledge, not deserving the reputation of his trade.

Saina ventured, "You must recognize that we are a rare type of refugee."

"Ahh. Yes. Please do not misunderstand me, but one of you is obviously of great consequence." He gave a faint wink. "And, I have a guess who this might be."

"Good. I think it would be foolish—even shameful—to try to disguise ourselves."

"Ahh. Not at all. Prudent, I call it."

"Well, I may be alone in this, but better to be forthright when we must depend on each other."

Bhalkavar shrugged again. "You are probably right, but I would have respected you just the same had you done otherwise. Sometimes a lie is necessary and does more good than harm."

"Let me also confess that I have borrowed this uniform. I have spent a decade of my life as a Sulatin student. Only now have I left Prayadevale."

"Ahh. You borrowed the horse on the way."

"He has done me great service." Saina let go a long breath. "Service is what I wanted to discuss with you. A cadet and a monk can hardly provide a woman of stature what she needs. "Is it possible—might I ask"—

"My girl can help, of course." He laughed once and glanced over at Sevrese.

"Ahh, thank you. I do not want to cause her great difficulty." He had in mind that Deserena would. "Is she without sight altogether?"

"A little remains in a good light. Her intuition makes up for it, I suppose. It was an oil fire—the stove exploded."

Saina swallowed hard. "I am sorry."

"Yes. Pity, she lost her mother in the accident. The rest of her family was lost in other tragedies so that now I am all she has. But I see that she earns her way. And I might say, she is excellent upon a horse. As a child before she lost her sight and even now. Horses listen to her, more than to you and me. You will find it amazing that, even blind, she will find her way through their eyes. She will not hold you up."

Sevrese slowly made her way toward Mohidram's voice. Saina regarded her at length, imagining what lay behind the black scarf. "Welcome then, to both of you." He offered his own name and his brother's but referred to Deserena only as their lady in flight.

"Mohidram has consented that you would provide some assistance to the lady in our company. Whatever is possible would be greatly valued. But is that satisfactory to you, Cheki?"

"My uncle is a very thoughtful man, though all horse-copers look to their own advantage. I understand what she needs." She softened her voice. "Anything you feel to pay, please give it to Mohidram. He will be very poor since he made the mistake of going to Alambarat with such precious merchandise in the middle of a war."

Saina shot a look at the horse-coper, who gave a weak smile. "No need for that. Besides, they say a monk has no pockets." He turned away to avoid Sevrese's arch wit.

"It must have been very frightening there for you."

"Because I cannot see? I imagine it was worse for your lady since she saw everything. But she had two able guardians."

"Ahh, no, thankfully she got away before the fighting. And my warrior skills are very limited. As I told your uncle—"

"Yes I overheard. You have Sulatin training. Can you not offer divination or astrological calculation as a skill? Then we would not need anything else."

"Ahh, in these areas half knowledge is worse than none, but I have some skill with healing—and animals."

"We share the latter."

"I expect so. You are named for a sprite with those skills."

"Yes, not many would appreciate that connection. Horses, especially, have great sensitivities."

"Even a farm horse, as I have learned. I am afraid there is some of that in the lady I asked you to serve?"

"She's a farmer?"

"No-no. I mean, that is, the sensitivity you spoke of?

Sevrese gave a wide smile. "Will you lead me to her?"

Saina saw Nacros had helped Deserena to the ground and now led her to shade. He was kneeling before her very like a protective dog. "Ahh, let me consult with her first. She did not know I would request this of you."

Nacros' posture jolted Saina—he realized for the first time that both his brothers were in love with this woman. To his relief he saw nothing on her face but obliged indifference to Nacros. While Saina knew he was ignorant of all these matters, commonsense told him Panjael was beyond any advantage Nacros could claim.

He went to them hesitantly and was met with two stares as he spoke—one resentful, the other bewildered. "If you agree to it, the girl Cheki is willing to give you service."

"You are serious? Saina, she is blind. What am I to ask of her? A bad servant is worse than none at all. I will end up doing everything twice myself."

He shrugged, embarrassed. "I am told she has a little sight left."

Deserena look weary. "Alright. I will try. But consult me first in the future."

"I apologize."

Nacros rose to upbraid him, but Deserena intervened.

"It was generous of you. And thoughtful. It's just that I feel very"—she could not speak. Tears came down her cheeks and she turn away from them.

Nacros pushed Saina ahead of him and then admonished him anyway.

"While you are at it, consult me first in the future. How does a monk imagine he can make these decisions?"

"I am no longer a monk. I am on a mission from our father. His dying wish. What are you doing here?"

Nacros opened his mouth but had no words to answer with.

Saina watched his brother walk away with deep embarrassment at his attack. He wondered if his ten years in Prayadevale could be trusted to have taught him anything.

Maybe Murosaya was right to abandon me to the Sulatin life. A few days back in the Ten Abodes, I am no better than the querulous child he sent away.

——⋅∘∘❈∘∘⋅——

They found the road and toward sunset the fugitive party came upon a garland tree. The pine forest that held Prayadevale was much higher elevation than this mountain chain, and here the leaf trees mingles with the tall cone-bearers. Even so, only here did the garland tree survive to live up to the forest's name. Only Bhalkavar, who was past fifty years, had ever seen one before.

All five stopped their horses as the tree came into sight. It was an ancient one, huge and spreading both branches and roots as far as the massive trunk could support them. Some bent to the ground and made new trunks in support of the main one. As if in respect, the pines left a clearing around it so that no shadow was cast upon its blossoms.

By rights it was past the season for such display, but late rains and hot days had prolonged it. The flowers poured out of the foliage like a lady's fur wrap, circling the branches in layers. In the slanting light of the end of the day, the tree could have been mistaken for a thundercloud in the deep sky beyond. As the sun dropped to the horizon the flowers glowed yellow, orange, red, then violet as if each was its natural color.

Deserena expressed the awe the sight deserved—with unintended irony, "I have seen nothing so wonderful even in Sugorai."

Saina was quiet but filled with a sense of the celestial. In Prayadevale, divinity was always abstract, unadorned—like the halls of the monastery. But this was the work of a divine artist at play.

They all dismounted and walked their horses closer.

Bhalkavar smiled. "We are very fortunate to have been led here by our respective trials."

Nacros growled, "Good fortune at a high cost."

Saina intervened to prevent Nacros' insolence. "Mohidram, you said you once travelled this road for such a prize."

"As a young man." He seemed to enjoy the reverie. "It took me quite a while, but I found a garland tree. You see, before those times it was something done among the first families of the Ten Abodes—a very romantic notion to send someone deep into this forest to gather these flowers and present them to a lover. A great effort, of course, but, as it happened, at the time I was infatuated with someone, so it occurred to me to do the same. I was in Virnipal, and at the right time of year—late spring—so how could I not try? I found such a tree even bigger than this one, though she is majestic, too. They all are. The young ones do not even blossom, so it is these older giants that produce the splendor in this forest."

It finally occurred to Saina that Cheki could appreciate none of this. He asked if she would like to feel the flowers and offered to climb for some."

Bhalkavar cautioned with and outstretched hand. "No, my friend. The bark contains a poison. It travels from your hands into the body and you will be delirious for a week. That is what makes the effort so impressive. Not only does one have to journey here and then find such a tree, but he has to fashion a device to reach the flowers without injury."

Sevrese shifted toward Saina. "Thank you for your offer, but the perfume is as rich as the sight must be. No one has remarked on it, but there is no flower quite its equal in scent."

Deserena took a deep breath and said, "She is right. Here we must camp for the night. This spot exactly. We can enjoy this perfection through the night and the dawn. Just like our predecessors must have. This is perfect."

Bhalkavar scanned the area, thinking of defense, water, fire—never aesthetics ahead of security. He quietly asked Nacros his opinion.

With a scowl inappropriate to the moment he replied, "Well, easy enough to defend, I suppose. The surrounding peaks will block firelight."

Bhalkavar added, "The stream we have been tracking probably pools here in this meadow, so bathing is available, if that is desired."

Deserena gave a slightly haughty look to imagine that her personal habits could be under consideration by a horse-coper—no matter what his past romantic notions. "Yes, later your girl can assist me there, if she pleases." Suddenly tears were again flowing from Deserena's eyes. She shook her head with eyes clenched. "I'm sorry"—

Saina attempted to go to her, but he froze, not conceiving any way to help. He looked to Mohidram, but the horse-coper was just as confused. Then Sevrese took unsure steps toward her, put both hands on Deserena's shoulders, and pulled her close. The tears gushed and her body shook. Saina and Bhalkavar avoided watching and avoided looking at each other.

Deserena finally composed herself and drew in a breath that straightened her spine. Sevrese lowered her head and backed away just enough to prevent Deserena from having to speak to her directly.

Instead she whispered to no one, "Excuse me. I must sit down. When I find some of my things in the baggage... and it grows a little darker... I would like to find a pool to wash. I will come get you." Then she left them.

Sevrese knew the two men were looking at her. "Everything pressed on her at once. I could feel that. I think the notion of bathing in the open made her realize how much she has lost. Is it true?"

"Everything," said Saina quietly. "It may never come back. I admire that you knew. And that you did that for her."

Saina watch Mohidram lead her away before the talk trapped her. He whispered something Saina could not hear, but he saw Cheki's shoulders rise slightly.

He realized beyond his admiration he had no idea what to think of her. The only women he had known were idealized—the goddesses he had studied as symbols and principles. Taking all of them in sum as the Goddess, he could claim he knew that She created and destroyed and created again. Everything vibrated with a rhythm that was Hers. He knew these two women were not goddesses, but they were reflections of Her. Her power was the power within them. But it was a mystery to him how that power might feel within and why it should be hidden in what looked like fragility. And finally why it should come out of nowhere with such strength? He felt as though it was too late for him to ever understand after Prayadevale. Ghoru had warned him.

Later, when the two women left for the privacy of the stream, he felt relieved to join his male companions. They built a fire and started a meal and talked quietly about the security of the camp.

Saina asked Mohidram if he had experience with ferines.

"I have seen them, but not close. When I was very young it was just after the time they were hunted, and they were of a mind to retaliate. I was told they can tear their way out of any cage. They can open any lock you could fashion. They are only as big as a small human but their shoulders and legs are powerful. And frighteningly fast. Sometimes they walk like a dog, other times they run like a human. Their eyes are wide apart, more like a horse and I believe they can see much more than we can. I have no idea what their minds are like, but back then they were considered closer to people than to any beings they lived among in the forest."

When the young women returned, they all ate quietly until the moons began to show in the sky, and the snow-white blossoms became resplendent in silver. Deserena seemed happy but tightly controlled. She took to her bed on the ground and turned away from the fire without any acknowledgement. The others followed.

It was much later, when the horses took notice of movement in the trees. But before they had expressed more than a few quick snorts Nacros was up and armed. He dashed in different directions, finding nothing but awakening the rest by his efforts. Otherwise they might have slept on peacefully, missing, or even lulled by, the voice that floated above the trees in the distance, an eerie tone somewhere between a songbird and a wolf. It was beautiful until Bhalkavar gave it a name.

"Ferines," he growled.

The fear of the name lent menace to the sublime mystery of the song. The notes rolled through the night in a serpentine, extending through every nerve of the body, wrapping tightly like a snare that cannot be escaped.

Then in unnoticeable degrees it transformed itself into a chest-pounding shriek. Instantly a score of hairy forms flailed and leaped among the five travelers. They hit at the human's legs, pulled their clothing, threw their bedding, and threatened with bared teeth face to face. It went on for a few eternal moments before they were gone into darkened silence.

Neither the general, Nacros, nor Saina had dealt a blow in return. They now stood incredulous. Then they shook themselves and spread the smoldering fire into half a dozen more to surround their small camp, increasing its protections. It looked like a miniature battlefield.

"Let them wail all they want. They never cross fire, I'm sure," taunted Nacros.

But fire did not stop them. It only gave the three men and the two women the fright of a clearer look at the attackers in the second wave.

Sand-colored, stringing hair fell across the ferines' shoulders from their heads—more like human hair than fur. Gray skin showed on their front but their coats were heavy over their muscled backs. They stayed out of range of weapons, rushing in with sporadic bursts, letting the fire light them with hideous rage. Their crying howl was intimidating enough, but it was their eyes that made Saina freeze. He had never seen eyes that deep in a wild beast—framed by bony brows and a wrinkled and flattened nose and the paint-like shadows cast by the firelight. The effect made them terrifying but not wild at all. To strike back against them—something with that much understanding—was impossible for him.

Deserena was convulsed by shaking and cries. Sevrese was kneeling over her, but had her own fright to deal with, feigning blindness with such a need to see.

Only Nacros' wild swinging connected, and one body fell limp before the fires. But before Saina could call out in its defense, he followed it down. Something very heavy connected with the back of his head.

It was the horse-coper he saw over him when he awoke. Saina could not speak his question, but Bhalkavar knew what it would be. "A few of them had clubs, it seems. They make their own weapons—can you imagine that? And I have seen soldiers attack with much less discipline. What fighters they would make." He realized the truth of his military life was about to show itself, so he corrected the direction of his words. "You were the only one hit. Everyone else is alright, don't worry. Your lady was shaken, but Cheki has her calmed again."

"But how is Cheki?" Saina struggled to whisper. "Imagine all that and not being able to see." He did not wait for an answer. "Perhaps it would be a benefit." He sat and rubbed his neck.

Nacros came up and, without even inquiring of Saina's condition, added in an offhand way, "They carried off the dead one."

"What?" came the general's disbelief.

"Just like soldiers. I had kicked it outside the fires. Just now I looked and it was gone without a sound. I barely saw them in the bushes before they disappeared."

Bhalkavar walked away to survey things. Nacros waited for the next attack. Saina listened to the Daughter of the Seed quietly crying.

"That is not all they took," Bhalkavar announced from the edge of the light. "The horses are fine, but your packs are in shambles."

Saina stumbled over to see along with Nacros. Deserena came after them, since nearly everything was hers. Her face was wet and distressed, and she scanned the wrecked bundles with resignation.

Then Saina noticed Sevrese slowly making her way toward them. It did not occur to any of them at that moment—including Sevrese herself—that this should not be possible. They saw only what was different about her. The cloth was gone from her face, and the frightful scarring across her forehead and eyes and trailing down over her cheeks was finally fully exposed. In the firelight it was shocking—as much as the faces of the attackers.

Deserena recoiled. It repulsed her, but then to his surprise Saina saw a wave of compassion come up in her face. She rapidly sorted the scattered clothing around her and pulled out a brilliant scarf laced with fine threads of gold. Without realizing her error she held it out to Sevrese, as if she would reach for it. Without realizing the same thing, Sevrese reached for it instinctively.

Bhalkavar interceded quickly. "Your scarf was torn away by one of the ferines, Cheki. This noble lady offers to replace it."

He started to wrap it round, but Deserena could not stand to see his artless attempt and came forward to finish. Sevrese thanked her simply, and it was over simply. But for Saina something about the encounter struck deep.

His knowledge of rank was very narrow. In Prayadevale he had seen only the occasional struggle of individual natures to push themselves forward—foreign in a world where every student in simple cloth is like another. He knew nothing of the subtleties of condescension from above or the inevitable resentment and envy from those who watch privilege from below.

He realized how limited was his view of the Daughter of the Seed as someone indulged and self-pitying—a judgment so obvious to one who has nothing, even as he admitted that her loss was incalculable. Tonight she put aside her pain for someone else.

No one does that only once—she has another side I cannot see.

Nacros and Bhalkavar drifted into the darkness following the trail of the baggage. Deserena returned to her own survey nearby. Saina was watching Sevrese, who stood absently because she could not knowingly stare back.

But as she could actually see more through the cloth Deserena had chosen, she became very uncomfortable in his gaze, without any power to avoid it. She sat in a heap, calculating that if she really was blind there was nothing more to do. She felt a warm wet trickle on the back of her hand. She fought the impulse to look at it, trying to smell it to see what it was. She wanted only to be free of his searching eyes.

"You're cut," Saina managed from his reverie.

"I fell down back there," she whispered. "I think I hit a broken branch. It is nothing."

For years he had been studying the medicinal science of the Sulatins, yet he could only vaguely recall the combination of herbs to clot blood quickly—and where could he find such things in the night?

And why is my heart pounding at the thought of helping her?

He was paralyzed, realizing he was proof of Panjael's prejudice against the Sulatins. They watch. They never do anything. What good is knowledge if no action comes of it? But then he felt a stirring of that source of energy within—the same force that had surprised him on the road with Ghoru. It seemed to lift his hand as if to seek out her wound by itself. He took her arm and felt the slick smear of blood as his hand slid up to find the gash. He felt torn skin, only the width of a finger, but deep enough to bring forth a flow of blood. A simple bandage would stop it, but instead of finding cloth among the wreckage, his fingertips pressed the tear back together. Heat came but not from his hand—instead through her body toward the wound. His hand had only unveiled the aether so that he could see the action. Minute impulses silver-gold in aetheric color brought a tingling vibration of Goddessoma that would bind together anything rent.

Sevrese felt it as well and forced her eyes to stare evenly ahead—but for one hasty glance at his face. She saw that his own attention was centered within himself—maybe in his hand, even in her body. The notion overwhelmed her.

Then he gave out a breath as if something was released and he had to let go of her arm.

He wondered suddenly if her blind eyes could draw the power as well. He raised his hand toward her, but he felt nothing like the other wound. Neither his hand, nor the flow of Goddessoma within her would act on her blindness—as if it was not there. He reasoned, because it was long since healed in the only way that it could be.

Her own hand came up and moved his away.

"Sorry. I didn't mean to intrude."

"How did you stop the blood?" she whispered.

"It's nothing. A Sulatin trick. But I wondered if I might try it on your eyes. It didn't work. Sorry."

"My sight is not a wound. Destiny brought this to me."

He wanted to question what she meant, but Nacros broke in. "The food packets are intact. And this." He held a case belonging to Deserena—the last wealth of Satamabode—and then put it under a cloth, away from a horse-coper's view.

A sudden fear sliced into Saina. "Nacros, did you see the oilskin bag? It was the only thing of mine in the baggage."

Nacros answered with a younger brother's annoyance. "Look at all this mess? I don't know." Then he reached down and held up the very package—empty. "Is it this?"

The scroll was gone. The original record of cognition of the Founding Seer of Satamabode was being dragged through the woods completely exposed. A thousand years of treasured confinement was wiped out in a moment. Saina's fear turned into sickness descending upon him. He could have dropped to the ground, his knees seemed so weak. All that held him up was his concern that no one must know what had been in the package.

"So what was it?" asked Nacros.

Saina's mouth opened but hesitated. "A memory. Our father gave it to me."

Nacros snorted. "Remembering will not bring back the past, Saina."

The scroll gone—his emptiness was greater than the night the two boys died.

For a long moment they all remained silent with their own thoughts. Even the garland tree could provide no more peace tonight.

Pavim, Regent of Ryadabode on behalf of Heir of the Seed Khoroas, stood in the soft shadows as the early mountain sun warmed her palace in Virnipal. She was just inside the balcony doorway of the small chamber used for private meetings with her Assessors. Below she could see the reflecting ripples across the long crescent lake that shaped the valley of her Abode.

The door closed in the room behind her, as her Assessors departed. They had no counsel to offer her. She knew the same discussions were being conducted in each of the eight Abodes not caught directly in this conflict. She could not imagine any one of them had answers to the most basic question. *What now must we do?*

Absently she took a step forward onto the balcony until the sunlight warmed her hair and brought up the streaks of white that showed her five decades. Over the years her form had remained thin and intense, her face chiseled with aquiline pride.

Her eyes filled with tears again, as they did incessantly in private ever since the first word of the attack came up the road from Alambarat. Her anxiety was unbearable. She wanted to believe, as shocking as it was that one Abode could violently wage war on another, even the lowest soldiers were incapable of harming a royal member of another Abode.

No officer could order it. Not against her Sevrese. But the rumors of the mercenaries brought shudders—and a helpless feeling that her daughter and her general were lost to her.

Another figure at the edge of the balcony saw the breakdown coming. He came to her, put his arms about her, and let her forehead rest against his chest. Khoroas, her younger child, nearly twenty years, delicately handsome, dark hair waving off his shoulders in the wind, whose life was lived without the presence of his Seed Bearer father.

He carefully guided her further out toward the west facing corner of the balcony where she could gaze at the thick Garland Forest covering the western line of mountains that defined her realm.

"He has her up there. I know he does. Bhalkavar will protect her like the lion that inhabits his soul."

She took a long breath. It shook her as it escaped. "I know, Khoroas. I know. But even as I know, any doubt cuts through my conviction like the sharpest blade. I cannot help it. I fall apart." Her nose drew in a watery breath, as she wiped her cheeks of tears.

"Well, she is strong, too. I would never say as much to her face, because she thinks she is even stronger than she is. But you cannot imagine she will have any trouble following Bhalkavar wherever he is forced to take her."

"No. But weighing on top of their danger are all the meanings and consequences of this tragedy for the Abodes. I harden myself to one distress, and I fall into the depths of desolation about the other. What will come to our way of life and our future? Will Sevrese survive it?" She bit at her lip. "Damn Pharmos. What a hateful, duplicitous devil!"

"And what would you have for his punishment?"

She stepped away from him and then turned round. "You think everything you just heard here was futile, don't you? I can tell from your voice. Resignation."

He rubbed his eyes nonchalantly. "Well, the combined military of eight Abodes would certainly make Pharmos' delusions disappear— except for the weapon we heard of. Yet even without it, every chance at concerted action is mired in precedents and traditions that undermine it. The Abodes have been equals so long, they have lost any possibility of leadership or consensus. Yes, Mother, that seems futile to me."

"We need the Sulatin Order to force concerted action."

Khoroas laughed and shook his head. "The Sulatins are more paralyzed than we are when it comes to the consensus of the Ten Abodes. The action you want falls to us. Let us initiate it and let the other Abodes follow as they will. Someone must lead by example."

"I see," she countered. "And you would take our small force of fighters under Bhalkavar's leadership right down the mountain and teach these mercenaries a lesson. Would you ride at their head?"

"Do you think me a coward?"

She softened. "Khoroas, I know your qualities. You do not lack courage by any measure. But neither can you take risks that you do not see the consequences of."

"And this explains why you are Regent, though I am of age? I am still a child to you because I have no prudence? Well, Satamabode knows the value of prudence today. Prudence is what trapped my sister in the middle of this fight. Meanwhile Hanarabode knows the advantages of risk. I want the same outcome you want. And your way will not bring about."

He went to a table just inside the open doorway where refreshments remained from the long meeting. He poured a sapphire-colored drink of fermented berries grown on the nearby slopes. Pavim looked away.

"I am sorry, Mother, but you have to see that your world has never been as secure as you thought it was. Now change has blown through the Ten Abodes to prove to you just how incapable anyone is of stopping it. Your generation can wring its hands, but the change was inevitable."

She kept her gaze to the granite peaks and the trees and the sky in the distance. "My generation? What will yours do? I take it your proposed movement against Seed Bearer Pharmos is not to restore my world, then?"

He smiled into his cup as he took the last of its contents. "I would not sweep it away. Simply, I see no reason to let Pharmos—or whoever is doing his thinking for him—have control of what the world will be."

Now she looked at him, up and down. "So you welcome upheaval as long as you retain power over it. But *my* world, as you characterize it, is *not* my own, but the world given to us by the Seers of the Ten Abodes and by the Preceptor who came after. And changing that world is to slap at the Goddess. There is no good to come of it."

He came to her again and put his arm around her shoulders. "Mother, you love that world. I merely live in it. Or play in it—like I am molding clay." He kissed her cheek. "I think as a child I was rather clever with clay, wasn't I? No, I forget—that would be Sevrese. But you should give me a chance. Otherwise you are stuck with what Pharmos wants. Your fellow Seed Bearers are looking to their own security—or their own gain—while you shed tears for the past."

She mused a moment. "You and clay. I seem to remember you were talented, if fashioning lascivious figures of your nurses is art."

"Ahh. Well, I haven't noticed any shortage of lasciviousness in the world that you hold so holy, so don't make that out as my innovation. The Sulatins teach me that this Seed of mine is precious, and like all the Seed Bearers that have come before me, I take that as a duty to be generous with it."

She gave him a wry and weary smile. Whatever mysteries were held in the Seed of her late husband, the ones of that sort had passed to the son more noticeably than anything the Founding Seers imparted.

Khoroas assumed he had lightened her burden with lewd absurdity, and he took his leave. Pavim, however, was not so easily cheered. And certainly not by a young man's carnality. She paced slowly on the wide balcony, wondering about the one thing he said—*or whoever is doing his thinking for him.*

True enough, she concluded, *Seed Bearer Pharmos is the least plausible maker of this new world. This takes a mind that is at once ambitious and patient—exceedingly so.*

She had not been to Hanarabode in many years. And while Pharmos had been Seed Bearer a few years longer than she had been Regent, his Heir was still a youth. She had heard nothing of the Hanarabode Assessors from her general to think them extraordinary.

The one face that came to her mind was a young assistant to the old Assessor Concordant the only time she saw him. By now he must be in his thirties. Still young enough to reject the past, as Khoroas so quickly did. Yet mature enough to do something to change it. The name that came to her memory was Ruryo. She could not recall the face clearly, but cloudy memory and intuitive speculation combined to create a man who could control a Seed Bearer. She sent for her Assessors to return—they knew their counterparts in the other Abodes. She wanted confirmation that this was her enemy.

As she waited she looked one more time to the mountains and mouthed a prayer for Sevrese and Bhalkavar. Then she turned and crossed the threshold back into the room, realizing her fears were inflating ominously.

Unlike the others, Saina dreaded the end of the road through the Garland Forest. He would have to act on his own for the first time in his life. At stake was the security of Deserena, for the future of Satamabode, perhaps even for the extinction of the Seed Bearer tradition—and he had no idea what to do. Stripped of his Sulatin robe, parading in a warrior's costume, who would possibly listen to him, had he anything to say?

Certainly not the Sulatin leaders. Likely not the Regent Pavim. For that matter, not Deserena or even Nacros. As the old weathered road allowed it, he found himself attached to the blind girl with a sense of relief that he had nothing to prove to her.

They were at a high elevation now with little undergrowth. The road was apparent because trees had never sprouted on its rock hard surface. They followed it at a walk up gentle slopes and down easy ravines, stopping in the meadows to graze and water the horses. They saw nothing of the ferines. They said little to each other.

In one long valley where the road was wide, Saina and Sevrese fell in step together. Sevrese broke the silence, as Saina struggled to think of something to say.

"Ryadabode is such a beautiful place. So my uncle tells me. I like the feel of the air—that much I know. And the lake—I know it is just water, but I am convinced it has a perfumed scent."

"You have spent a lot of time there?"

"Mohidram makes a circle through the Ten Abodes selling in one, buying in the next."

Saina's voice had a mark of frustration. "I wish he could tell me about Regent Pavim."

"Ahh. Mohidram knows her well. He supplies her with the finest horses. He is a great favorite of hers. Or so he tells me—he tells me everything about the family. What would you care to know?"

Saina hesitated. The horse-coper was just ahead of them and surely would hear anything she said. He did not want to get her in trouble with her uncle.

Before Saina was about to speak out to him, Mohidram turned. "It's good, Saina. Ask what you wish. Cheki, better that you tell him about the Daughter of the Seed. I find her a little irritating, but you seem to think differently."

"Yes, the Daughter—Sevrese is her name, am I right, Uncle? He says that because she is the best rider and the most discerning of all his customers. Horse-copers have been known to embellish the truth, but he admits she always sees through him."

Mohidram waved dismissively without turning then trotted ahead to distance himself.

"Much better than the Heir of the Seed. His name is Khoroas, if I am not mistaken. I think he is a libertine. But you want to know about the Regent. Ask me your questions."

"I—I don't really know where to begin, but"—he laughed once—"I must have a thousand questions—yet not one."

"While you think," Sevrese intruded, "if I may first suggest, your horse is getting sore on the left front. Do you not hear the step?"

"No I didn't." Saina went silent a moment, picturing in his mind the sore leg and questioning the horse's mind in turn.

Oh yes. Sore. But I have had worse. Don't stop here where I am scared.

Sevrese was puzzled by his silence but could not think how a blind woman could question him. She simply blurted out, "What is the matter?"

"Ahh, sorry. I was just asking him—I mean"—

"Asking him? Do you talk to animals?" she laughed. "You seem to have abilities I had no idea about."

He colored. "I feel impressions from them—from animals. And they turn into thoughts in my mind. Animals have voices for warning, yet I find they have much more to say in their thoughts. I seem to be able to hear those thoughts. He tells me he is sore, but more than that he wants to get out of these mountains and back to his own. So how can you know the condition of his leg from the sound of his step? I find that more a mystery. I don't hear it at all."

"I learned from him." She dipped her head toward Bhalkavar. "Horses have a very rhythmic walk. With one under you, you can feel the rhythm in your seat and your legs. When the beat of the hooves is not right, you know your horse is sore—especially where the ground is hard like this. But you have no saddle, I am told. That makes it even easier. Not as easy as just asking the horse, of course."

"Yes, either way is good. More important, now that I know, what should I do?"

"If you can see ahead that we are on the flat for a time, then you should dismount and lead him. Or, you could trade for the pack horse now that there is less of a load. It is a better mount for you. I am surprised you ride this fellow."

"Oh—he and I both lived our lives in Prayadevale. And he was frightened to leave. I had my own misgivings, and I imagine that we see each other as comrades in our escape into the unknown." He dismounted and walked beside her, his head even with the bend of her hip and leg.

"Why did you leave?"

He hesitated, deciding what he could say. "I was summoned by my father, Assessor Martial Murosaya. But he died in Sugorai before I could reach him."

"That is sad. Assessor Martial—I had no idea."

"Well, I hardly remember him. I was sent to the Sulatins ten years ago, and this is the first time I have been out of Prayadevale. But what I realized in these few days—unlike my horse—is that I wanted to leave the Order. Leaving is so rare an option, I never gave it a thought before."

"Why do you feel it?"

Everything he thought to say suddenly sounded pretentious in his mind. He shrugged but realized it went unseen. "Just an intuition."

She felt his awkwardness. "But you wanted me to tell you about the Regent."

He tried to bring his attention back. "Is she a good rider?" He looked up and saw her smile.

"Yes, she is. She is a woman of accomplishment and principle, respected and loved by her citizens. You know the Bearer of the Seed died many years ago. She has reigned as Regent more than a decade. Because of her it is held that among all the Ten Abodes Ryadabode is the one that has most devotedly preserved the traditions of the Founding Seers. Although that also leads some to say Ryadabode is a little backward. It is all because of the Regent's own respect for custom. Knowing that may be of help to you. After all, the Sulatins are the custodians of that tradition. You understand, I am not in a position to know much more, but that is what I know from my many visits. She is generous—I would add that. So, whatever your intentions, I am sure she will regard them with discernment and grace."

"I believe you put Ryadabode above all the others. You must have had happy times there. And this is very helpful. You have given me much to think about. I think you see more than anyone would ever credit you."

She was instantly embarrassed—justification for this deceit suddenly felt unacceptable. "Thank you," she murmured. Then to change the mood she asked, "Can I ask you something?"

"Anything. Although my experience is very limited."

"But that is the experience I want to hear. What is it like to be a Sulatin? I would like to hear everything."

"You would? That makes you very rare." He took a deep breath. "Where should I start? The Founding Seers cognized the great truths of Goddessoma. What is the nature of creation and destruction? What is our purpose in it? How we must live? What is beyond our lives?" He paused. "You are probably aware of all this—it is just that I don't know what is obvious outside of Prayadevale."

"In some ways, you are the blind one." She laughed.

"I think you are right. As the knowledge faded over time, the Preceptor appeared and formed the Sulatin Order. He trained them to sustain the Founding Seers' cognitions. Five hundred years have passed again. The Sulatins were given custody of this knowledge but it is the Seed Bearers who actually have the ability to continue it."

"What is the difference?"

"Everyone can experience Goddessoma. But only the descendants of the Founding Seers have the gift of cognition. That means they can revive the knowledge and the experience through cognition."

She was about to ask if he had met any Seed Bearers, because what he said seemed preposterous. Instead she asked, "How is that so? How is the ability passed on?

"Through the Seed. Something in the male holds it and passes it on." He felt embarrassed to talk of the Seed with a woman, after years of discussing it in the lineage studies.

"You mean the sticky fluid that a man implants in a woman contains the key to Goddessoma?" She paused and then with a voice full of irony added, "That makes a good story for an Heir to the Seed to tell a girl."

Saina coughed.

"And a woman has nothing to do with Goddessoma? How could that be true when a mother giving birth is the very symbol of the Goddess's creation? Is that why the Sulatin Order admits no women? And the other thing—if a woman gives birth to a girl, why is the Seed not in her as well?"

He flushed, thankful she was blind. "The Sulatins spend a lot of time studying the nature of lineage. I don't know the answer."

"They have been studying for five hundred years? Have they studied any females? Any Daughters of the Seed?"

"No." He winced. "Plants and animals." He took a deep breath to prepare for the onslaught he knew would come. "You are certainly removing any doubts I had about leaving Prayadevale. No student there is a match for you. Maybe no monk either."

She laughed. "You give me too much credit, but I think I would love that life."

"You studied horse trading. That inspires you to question what other people say. That should be a subject in Prayadevale." He paused and then said seriously, "I have watched what you have done for our lady, and I am grateful. But I want to add ... that I admire you. The Sulatins make much out of the power of attention—you give her your attention. It is not a simple thing like seeing. Attention is from the heart. I hope she will express gratitude as well."

Her hand waved slightly to say it was nothing. "It is no matter. These things are best left unsaid. She was not brought up to endure tragedy and emptiness."

"True, but I am helpless. I know nothing of women. Aside from the farmers around the monastery I have not even seen a woman since I left Sugorai that wasn't carved from rock."

"Now, that I have to question. You have been close to the Goddess. Think of the rest of us just like that. Treat us as goddesses, and you will have no problems." She laughed again.

He was without a response—not knowing if she was being playful or her advice was perfect.

The road narrowed, so he mounted and they fell back in a line.

They stopped in the last direct rays of the sun before the mountains hid it for the night. Bhalkavar announced he would scout ahead to see whether they could attempt the run to the border at night.

Nacros was furious, imagining how many ways the horse-coper would betray them, but he was unwilling to leave Deserena to Saina. When the general returned they learned another night in the forest was required. The road to the summit was lit with torches. Dawn was the only chance—and depended on sleeping Hanarabode Protectors.

Another night in the forest gave more anxiety than the prospect of outrunning cavalry. Deserena rolled into ball under blankets. Nacros sat rigid a few steps away with his blade drawn.

Far into the night, Bhalkavar and Saina each awoke while the others finally slumbered in peace. They rose silently, not knowing what had roused them. They both saw the cause at the same time. There was a light in the distance among the trees—not fire, not anything they could think of.

They set off to a distance from the camp where they could speak and observe it. Neither had an explanation.

Then it began moving, and they rushed to follow over the uneven dark ground. They stopped short with hearts heaved in their chests when a ferine face rose up in front of them.

His large eyes were sparkling with moonlight, and he searched them for any sign of hostility. They stood perfectly still. He raised a hairy hand at last and scratched his chin. *Shib*, he announced and patted his chest. *Sorr-eeeyy. Aaattack.*

The two of them were speechless.

He pointed toward the glow in the distance and said, *Beeen-srrounddiidd-bi-liit.*

"What's that?" whispered the general.

"Being Surrounded by Light?" answered Saina. Without the picture in Shib's mind Saina would not have heard the words correctly.

A kind of smile stretched the snout on the hairy face of the ferine. *Eee azz yur scrrrooolll. Nowwwee help youuu.*

Saina put his hand out. "You are Shib. I am Saina. We need your help."

Shib laid his long arm alongside Saina's. "Siii-nnahh." Then he turned, leaped up a nearby trunk and disappeared.

The general turned to Saina. "Did I just hear an offer to help us?"

"That's what I heard."

He rubbed his shaved head. "The ferines and some being of light. This is going to be a little hard to explain in the morning."

Saina scanned the forest. "Look. Where the light was, a fog is moving into the trees. What does it mean?"

"It means we should wake the others and try to get to the road at dawn. The fog will hide us if there are troops there waiting. It is a short and steep ride from there to the Ryadabode checkpoint. We couldn't ask for better help than that."

In the chill of the mountain darkness Luzarain sat alone at the end of a long table in the library of Prayadevale. He was surrounded by five hundred years of Sulatin interpretation of the scrolls left by the ten Founding Seers. Despite the late hour his eyes shone bright in the lamplight as they scanned the words unwrapped in front of him.

He stopped and leaned back upon his chair, contemplating what he read for a long period of silence. Then he meticulously rolled up his sources, replaced them in their protective boxes, and resorted them accurately on the shelves. No one would ever know what documents he selected and what subject he studied.

Finished with the library, he extinguished his lamp and walked barefoot and soundlessly across the stone floor toward his room where an attendant monk waited for him. He lowered his head so that his eyes glared under his thin brows.

"I have discovered something I wish to explore on my own. I will not be available tomorrow for any administrative matters or for any queries or for any other business. This will take my full attention. Perhaps even beyond tomorrow. You will admit no one. You will tell no one."

The man nodded.

"So who can be allowed to see me?"

"No one?" He did not want it to sound like a question and hastily repeated, "No one."

"Athayam?"

"No."

"And who can you tell anything about this?"

"No one."

"Not even Athayam?"

"No. No one."

"And if someone asks me what I was researching, who will I know spoke of it against my instructions?"

"Not I."

Luzarain put his hand on the man's shoulder. "Good. Much concentration is required. I rely on you to allow me that freedom. This experiment is important for the Order. You can see that. Sleep here with your chair in front of the door if you must."

Luzarain entered his room and stretched slowly. Then silently he went through a series of movements to temper both mind and body and sat down upon his bed with his legs crossed beneath him. He smiled.

Tonight, Ruryo, I will know your mind.

His long search for the instructions to the power known as *Witness to Another Awareness* was now fulfilled. This was another of the necessary Sulatin powers he ordered himself to master. The hardest was the pursuit of alchemical expertise with the *Command of Elemental Power.* It had taken him a decade. The relatively minor *Compression of Distance* and the more difficult *Compression of Time* allowed him to watch events that had already unfolded or would, but it did not give him a way to affect the events. With this one he could enter the mind, learn its character, witness its thoughts—and with that knowledge his reach into Ruryo's plans would lengthen.

With eyes closed, with the formulas repeating soundlessly, his consciousness spread through the aetheric atmosphere, bouncing and tumbling through celestial forms and disembodied souls, seeking the one he had named in the formula.

He had no notion of passing time, of night or day, of earth or firmament. That world was insubstantial once inside the Body of the Goddess, and he had no use for it tonight. He wanted only Ruryo's logic and the intense creative energy he applied to it.

His attention was so focused on that goal he never sensed the entrance to it. When he felt the enormous pride and the driving anger and saw the very devils who informed the man's character like worms in a wound, only then did he know where he was.

He listened to drum-like echoes of Ruryo's deepest desires. To gain hold over his Seed Bearer. To suborn the Heir of Satamabode. To shape the ideal order to replace the Abodes. To undermine the Sulatins. To dispense with the Seed and thereby eradicate the Ten Abodes in favor of the One.

Luzarain drew no small satisfaction from the discovery, since the thoughts were his own from years ago. He had not given them to Ruryo. They had both taken them from the forces within Goddessoma—with a vast difference. Luzarain had understanding of Goddessoma that Ruryo would never gain. Ruryo believed the ideas were his, missing entirely that they were nothing more or less than the instructions of the Goddess Herself as She destroys and creates the mortal universe in every moment. These thoughts were eternal and inevitable. They were the function and play of the gods, goddesses, and demons of Goddessoma.

Luzarain was not fooled by the illusion of continuity. In Goddessoma there was no beginning and no end—creation and destruction were simultaneous and perpetual. Every thought, any desire was everpresent. Ruryo's mistake was a belief in originality.

But tonight he wanted more than this—not the foundation of Ruryo's mind but the edifice he was building on top of it. He wanted to see the man's actions in advance. And when he asked with the formula to enter that realm, he understood the depth of destruction Ruryo had reached.

He saw—and felt—death everywhere in Ruryo's mind. Death of Seed Bearers, Death of Assessors and first families. Death of mercenaries by the thousands. Bloody and excruciating and completely unwarranted deaths. True these were natural commands of the Goddess in her destructive aspect, but because Ruryo had no recognition of Her, they became his own commands. He wanted to kill all of them for his own merit.

It made Luzarain sick to be in this mind. Not one death meant anything to the man.

Why does he make things so violently complicated? I give him a weapon to spread fear and weakness, and he must add poison on top of it. I give him the loyalty of these poor nomads and he will destroy them when they would be pleased with their paltry greed. Now he wants to take down all the Abodes and the Sulatins to follow. It can be done. It should be done. But he believes he is the creator of his acts. He is as incapable of seeing what is just and fitting as Daiyenso's boy Saina! Why does the Preceptor put our destiny in the hands of miscreants and fledglings?

But then he could see no more. He tumbled back into waves and tides of the vast aetheric ocean of space and time and desire until Ruryo was a world away. His disappointment was hard, but his self-censure was greater.

He realized his mistake. He could not experience the thoughts of another and at the same time judge them. The Goddess did not judge him. He was Her creation and Her destruction in proportions. But Luzarain had not her omnipotence.

His only conclusion was that the command over Ruryo that he sought was not to be his. He had given Ruryo tools with which to construct the future, but he could not control the hands that put them to use.

Then a larger realization followed, and one that shook him to his depths.

The destructive power of Goddessoma was far beyond mortal imagination. It was not reasonable or sympathetic or temperate. No one could restrain it. And that Ruryo should take more from it than Luzarain envisioned could be no surprise. Ruryo was not reasonable or sympathetic or temperate. Those were Luzarain's restraints on himself. A rare sensation came over him. Doubt.

What have I done?

"This is where we run." Bhalkavar spoke in a heavy whisper. "I found no one guarding this road on the ground before it joins the Alambarat pass. If they are watching, they are on the ridge above and behind the rocks and brush along the road. They invite us in to pick us off as we walk the grade to the border crossing. But instead we gallop through the fog to foil their trap. We do not have far to gallop. Our horses are fresh. We have surprise. Just hang on—the horses will run as one and need no guidance. Still the gallop on this grade will tire them before the crossing and make us easy targets if the fog fades. But let's trust our luck and meet together in Ryadabode short time from now."

Nacros gave a haughty breath. "We don't take orders from a horse-coper. Let's ride."

The general took the point, Saina stayed behind Deserena while Sevrese moved in line behind him. Nacros trailed. As they picked up a trot, Saina sensed the limp just as he had been warned. The horse's head bobbed to compensate for each sore step.

I have no relief to offer, Saina told him with his mind. *Once you take me over that crest I will see you to the lushest farm I can find and you will have pasture for a lifetime.* The horse did not answer him. He was attuned now to his own comrades.

The fog was thick and everyone was a blur in front and behind. Only the hoofbeats as all the horses changed in unison to a cantor told where they were. Next the rising grade forced the horses into a surging gallop.

Saina found Sevrese passing him. He pushed harder as the incline increased but his horse was not capable of keeping a cavalry pace. His breath was labored and loud.

Shouts rose on both sides of the road and on the slope above the pass. Arrows hissed above them. Saina urged his farm horse. He felt exultant. They were moving so fast, he was certain nothing could stop them.

But as they ascended, the fog suddenly thinned to nothing. Saina could see the border outpost ahead—and every enemy eye could see the five of them. Arrows now rained from all sides. He felt he was moving very slowly, and it seemed they could never make it.

Bhalkavar yelled for the outpost ahead and urged his horse even faster. Saina heard the shafts clatter on the road just ahead and felt the wind of one of them stream by his head within a hand's breadth.

His farm horse screamed. There were two arrows in his rump and two more pierced his neck. He gasped for breath with a gagging snort and faltered.

Saina lurched forward and slipped over the horse's head to the ground. The horse skidded forward and his head came to rest in Saina's lap. The beast's eyes stared into his own.

I brought you to this! was Saina's guilty thought.

But in return he heard, *I am saved—She is coming!*

Saina watched the eyes roll back with shock. Blood was flowing rapidly, soaking the horse's rugged mountain coat. *You see the Goddess, don't you? She will know what you should do. And thank you!*

For an instant, Saina saw the aetheric world—the sprite Cheki pulled the spirit of the horse from the ground, swung onto his back, and road upon clouds with mane and tail flowing behind. He looked sleek, head high, ears perked, tail erect, legs curled in the highest step he had ever taken.

The arrows still came. Saina rose and ran.

But next he heard Deserena scream ahead of him. He could see a shaft in her shoulder, and her body slumped forward. He strained to reach her but there was no hope on foot.

Sevrese drew her horse abreast of Deserena and slid onto Deserena's horse to take charge. With only her legs to control him, she held the wounded Daughter and urged the horse faster up the slope.

To Saina watching, it was as fluid and bold a move as any that the spectral Cheki could manage. He was in awe to have witnessed it.

But he was also in awe to see Mohidram so far ahead, seemingly, leaving them to fate. He turned to check Nacros in the rear, and to his dismay his brother had reversed to face the pursuit alone.

Sevrese's riderless horse was slowing. Saina caught him and mounted with difficulty. As the horse spun he watched below as Nacros rode into a volley of arrows and emerged unharmed, waving his sword at a dozen riders, one of whom brought him down.

On the neck of his charger he disappeared into the fog.

It was a hopeless act—dispiriting, not inspiring. It angered Saina to see his brother possessed by such a futile form of bravery. The image of sharp blades slicing into his brother's body made his stomach heave.

Yet it slowed the enemy and saved the rest of them.

He turned and galloped on and saw the horse-coper Mohidram unaccountably leading a column of the Protectors from the border outpost of Ryadabode. In a moment they thundered past him and sent the soldiers of Hanarabode into a rout.

Saina rode on and saw Deserena reach the border in Cheki's protective arms. His own horse, sensing the end, gave a leap and a kick and Saina pitched off, losing consciousness when his head hit the road.

EPISODE 4

Captain Ghoru sat in the corner of a nearly empty tavern in the poorer section of Alambarat. It was late in the night, and he had been drinking carefully since evening. For the first time in decades he wore no signs of his profession, and instead when required to name it he claimed to be a cutler. It was the only trade he possessed enough knowledge of to make it his disguise.

He leaned his head against the wall with his eyes closed, listening to the three musicians as they neared the finish of what would obviously be their last song on this day. They held back nothing and let a surge of energy loose, each of them in turns glancing at the others with a private smile over some small surprise in the playing only they would recognize. By the end their tempo charged the notes like a captain's warhorse reviewing the line.

Ghoru felt the vibration of the strings and skins beat inside of him until his solid body began to sway, rubbing the wall behind him. When their fingers stopped the vibration continued. He felt out of control— the sensation everyone in Satamabode lived with since the mercenaries were unbridled. He left his eyes closed and took another drink.

The drum player stretched out his legs from his mat on the dais. A set of hand drums rested between his legs, and scattered about were other percussion pieces he used to punctuate his rhythms. The lead musician slowly tested the strings and then rubbed the long neck of his dombura several times with an oily cloth. The drone player and vocalist was a woman of some attraction to Ghoru, but when he opened his eyes at last he found her too withdrawn from their play to return any interest he might show her.

He rubbed his eyes and his face and scratched his bearded neck, taking another long pull at the tall metal cup that held his final intoxication choice for the night. The cup was rough at the edge and some of the foam from the drink spilled onto his beard, running down in drips to his pant leg. He looked down to see a bluish stain on his crotch and groaned. He had only this pair of trousers—hard to obtain after the city had been stripped by the mercenaries.

Now, do I stand a chance with this dark pretty one if she sees me as a drooling old man?

He was not without money. When Panjael disbanded the Protectors, he split equally the treasury money Murosaya had sent with him out of the city. It was a generous portion, as over half of the Protectors were prisoners—thought to be moved to some camp west of Sugorai. He was not inclined to spend it as long as it was their share as well. So in secret he had taken some private revenge upon more than one mercenary in the past few nights, recovering a measure of the loot they had taken. Of course, this belonged to citizens of Alambarat, but there was no way to return it without notice—and in fact he was not so concerned about the citizens as he was about his comrades in the Protectors.

He even thought about how he might invest it. While goods were scarce and expensive, an establishment like this one could be bought for almost nothing. Everyone wanted out of the city and out of Satamabode and out of continuous anxiety. When the victory of Hanarabode was all figured out, perhaps some returning Satamabode protectors would like to run a tavern.

He looked again at the singer, who was lowering her instrument into a carrier bent over in a way that motivated him to speak. "No more?" he called softly from his table against the wall. "Such a voice. Beautiful voice."

She looked up and saw his gaze on her breasts. She rocked back and gave him a knowing but challenging look.

Unfortunately it was the string-player who answered. "You are a wonderful audience, sir"—his hand went to his heart—"but these are not the days that inspire songs and cheer. And no one shares your enthusiasm, I am afraid. Not out there, nor in here." He gave a wave to mean the dreary handful of lone drinkers and the beaten people of the city.

Ghoru raised his cup to the man but kept his eyes on the woman. She was giving him heavy-lidded consideration with her large brown eyes. Her lips made the smallest of smiles—weary and wistful. He held her gaze with all the quiet, seasoned manliness he could manage. He wanted her to think about mature vigor, as he felt this was his only asset, and to imagine a night of tranquil carnality to slowly soothe her melancholic thoughts.

He was just about to get up, to test her curiosity about him. It was there—he could see it—but he had so much langour to overcome. He wanted to place his fingertips lightly on her lips, open them, kiss her, and then let his hand caress its way into her blouse where her warm, scented softness lured him. As if she felt that impulse from across the room, she raised her chin very slightly. Her fingertips laced up the strings of her bag as if they were unlacing his vest. She was in the bed of his mind—he considered the real thing a certainty.

He fervently hoped she had a place of her own in this city. The rooms here would probably be stripped and depressing.

Suddenly the door was pushed open loudly and slammed against the wall.

Everyone's heart jumped, except for Ghoru's. His was trained to transform shock into defense, and the impulse drove hand to the dagger inside his vest. It waited there with forced patience.

He caught the odor of tribal nomads turned conquerors—brought all the way from their homeland and their herds. They stumbled in from the night with a will to partake of civilized life—albeit the lower level of Alambarat society. One of them tripped badly at the door and crashed into a table. He laughed deliriously while his next two comrades kicked at him with unstable blows and fell to the ground with him.

Ghoru withdrew his hand from the blade's hilt. There was still a very good chance he would be using it tonight, but he did not want them to notice he was thinking so.

The sleepy patrons were now as alert as they had been in days, and they looked frantically for other ways of escape. One went cautiously for the stairs to the rooms. Two others were edging along the wall in the shadows, waiting to make a break for the door. Another was cowering behind the barrels that made up innkeeper's counter.

The musicians were all frozen, knowing that these newcomers would inevitably demand something of them. They knew they would indulge them, if only to save their instruments from being commandeered.

The intruders were drunk to lightheadedness and gratification but not so much that their complete collapse would come any time soon. They were quite willing to bluster, having learned well that aggression never goes unrewarded once victory was theirs. One left standing at the doorway surveyed the room and strutted into it. The first to fall was now on his hands and knees and began stalking toward the dais. His eyes were on the ankles of the singer. She backed up a step. He grinned as he reached for her legs.

He called out to his comrades to fall in behind him, but they were already up and searching the room for something to steal. The innkeeper made his play, holding clay jars of drink in his arms to entice them to a seat before they took or broke anything. It got their attention, but when he happily shouted out a reduced price, they ignored him. They did not understand the language of their conquered subjects and had no intention of transacting with him anyway. They stood and pulled the liquor from his grasp and sat atop tables facing the musicians, pounding out rhythms from their own lands and shouting for songs no one knew. Their words were no clearer than a dog's barking.

Except to Ghoru. He had fought nomads in every one of the border campaigns. He had captured their predecessors years before, used them to ransom some of his own soldiers—and if it had not worked out he would have killed them without hesitation. It was that kind of warfare out there. People of the Ten Abodes dismissed these actions as mere skirmishes, but not those who did the work. These fighters came in the night to slit throats and steal horses and women and anything else of value. And they were very good at it. Even drunk. He knew enough of the languages out on the plains to follow the meaning of their outbursts. And he was willing to wait in silence for as long as it took. He had debts to collect from those distant days, and many more from the past few, including the torture and death of the friend who rescued him and Saina.

The entertainers knew when refusal was unavailing, and quickly took out their instruments and took up a song. There was no voice to it, for the woman did not want to call attention to herself in any way. Playing the drone defined her perfectly. The mercenary who had menaced her sprawled back on the floor and watched intently.

The mercenaries did the singing. And the yelling. And the jesting. And the guffawing. And finally one of them noticed Ghoru against the wall behind them in the lowest light of the room. He eyed the captain with a vicious scowl, made more grotesque by their hardened blotched skin coming out of his collar. He nudged his partners. They looked round and studied him. They knew he was a soldier. They understood hard eyes.

But instead of acting on their impulse, they grabbed the innkeeper and told him to basket up the jars that stood behind his counter for their comrades. They were leaving. And among themselves they decided that on the way out they would kill one more of the enemy they had been paid to defeat.

The innkeeper could not understand their words, but he knew their intent, and his attempts to act ignorant bought him nothing but trouble. The strongest of the four pushed him roughly. He tripped backwards and hit his head against one of the barrels, leaving him either unconscious or with the ability to play it so.

Two of the mercenaries went for the liquor and began looting. The clumsy one, who had put his claim first upon the woman, now moved toward her, for he was taking her out along with the drink. She kept her seat upon the cushion, as if he could not intimidate her. But that inspired him to do so. He sat down beside her and leaned forward to sniff her dark hair. Her teeth and eyes flashed a warning. He never noticed and reached forward to hold her chin with two fingers and enjoy her defiance before crushing her.

At that moment Ghoru chose to rise. But he did not defend her. Instead he stretched his arms toward the ceiling, yawned loudly, rubbed his head, and started for the door.

None of them was willing to let him go with such casualness. The seducer stayed by the woman with his eyes on this new danger, but the others rose and took steps toward Ghoru, the ones with their arms full of heavy jars of drink cut him off from the door.

"Say—you have any money left? Give it to us," challenged the front one. They laughed at one more defeated defender of Satamabode.

Ghoru shrugged in agreement and felt his pockets with some confusion. Then he looked around on the floor. "I had gold here," he said in a broken-phrase version of their tongue. "I had gold here somewhere, but I dropped it. Quite a lot. Don't go. If you help me find it I will stand you drinks all night." He looked down at the fallen innkeeper. "Ohh—no, I gave it to him for safekeeping. There in his vest, I'll bet. Come, let's get it and I will buy you each a drink. More drink. Gold."

They listened as if Ghoru was the stupidest of any of the stupid inhabitants of the Ten Abodes. How could he buy them drinks when they had all the jars in their hands? The front one grunted and bent over the innkeeper to take the gold. The others stared with interest. Ghoru leaned down as well, but his dagger had slipped into his hand and as he reached under the searcher he jabbed the artery in his throat.

The man gave an empty scream and pitched forward, spilling blood across the floor. Ghoru's other hand gripped a fallen stool, brought it up across the nose of one of the other two, crashing a sidelong blow into the shoulder of the second. The jars went everywhere. Ghoru's knife went deep into the throat of the second man and blood poured out of his nose. He pulled the man's sword and slashed the two he had stunned with his blow.

Now Ghoru turned on the seducer and smiled. The man did not come forward. His fear was great, but he realized he had a weapon Ghoru could not combat. He grabbed the singer roughly by the hair and used her as his shield while he drew his own blade, taunting Ghoru to come at him. Ghoru responded with one step. The man had nowhere to go, so he pushed his sword under the full breasts of the woman he held. Her shoulders stiffened as she raised herself higher away from its edge, but in her eyes there was a look of trust for Ghoru. He let his brows rise slightly to agree with her.

He smiled and shrugged and dropped the sword to the floor. When he saw his opponents eyes follow the sword falling, Ghoru's hand flew forward and the knife sailed into the arm that held the sword. Had the aim been off, it would have entered the woman's chest. The mercenary screamed and the singer forced herself free. Ghoru raced to him with a knuckle blow that crushed his throat and a backhand to the man's temple that knocked him cold.

The woman was shaking. He grabbed the man's sword and put it to his ribs. He motioned her to put her hands to it. She crouched beside him and together they split his beating heart.

There was a frozen moment of silence and stillness in the room. Then the drummer and the string-player scrambled to their instruments and repacked them rapidly. They grabbed for the woman to flee with them but she stepped aside. The innkeeper rose, feigning confusion, but he had seen it all. The remaining customers had already fled.

Ghoru looked from one to the other. "Wait a moment," he said.

He went to each of the dead bodies and pulled from the all manner of pocketsize loot—money, jewelry, icons. He dropped them into a pile and then knelt over it. The others came close.

To the male musicians he tossed some coins and rings. He looked up at the singer and spoke to her companions as he held her gaze.

"She is not singing anymore."

Her companions looked at her, confused, but she did not let Ghoru's eyes release hers.

"He's right. Go on."

They did not wait a moment more. Dead mercenaries were likely to end an entertainer's career.

Then Ghoru turned to the innkeeper, who was experiencing uncontrollable panic with each thought about what had happened.

"I am lost!"

Ghoru reached out and slapped the man's knee playfully. "It's all my fault. You want out?"

"What do you mean?"

"Here, take the pile." He gathered up all the remaining loot and pulled out a pouch of gold. "Oh, Here I had it all the time. It's yours. I now own this place."

The innkeeper nodded wildly, scooped up everything and ran out the door.

Now he met the woman's eyes again. "I might need a partner."

"Good." She reached for one of the fallen jars that was still intact and put it to her lips. When she swallowed some of the liquid rushed down her cheeks and hit her dress at her crotch. She looked down and then looked at his pants and laughed. He drew her against him and gave her a slow smile. "What's your name?"

"What's yours?"

"Ghoru, innkeeper—once a warrior.

"I am Nymia, once a singer—now wife of the world's preeminent innkeeper Ghoru."

"That was quick."

She wrapped her arms around his neck and took his lips with hers. Then she added, "Do you want to consummate these transactions or not? First, we get rid of these bodies and the blood they spilled. Then we will try out the beds upstairs."

"You are a romantic girl."

"No, I just have high standards. You are the first to meet them."

At dawn she woke him by rolling on top of his chest. He savored the softness of her breasts against his skin as if they were filled with honey. He kissed her very long and pulled softly at her lips with his. At length she rested her face under his bearded neck and caressed from his ribs to his hip.

She whispered, "My Ghoru, will you stay with me and always protect me like this?"

"Do you have many enemies?"

"I thought I did. Every mercenary in Alambarat terrified me." She pressed close to him. "But not now."

He stared at her face looking up at him. "Everyone in Satamabode fears them and hates them. With good reason. Or is your reason stronger?"

She turned her head. He felt tears on his chest.

"You don't need to say it. I can imagine. Are you alone because of them?"

She nodded. "I had only my sister, and they"—words would not come. "You knew, didn't you? That's why you wanted my hand on the sword when you killed him."

"I suppose I guessed your thoughts."

She took in and let out a long breath. "I hope you always do."

They lay against each other until she drew herself up.

"Let me guess your thoughts."

His eyes invited her. "I think you will leave. You are loyal and trustworthy and you made promises before you met me that cannot be ignored."

"Like what?"

"You are a Protector, not an innkeeper. Someday you will go off to fight and drive these invaders out of Satamabode. You Assessor Martial will call for you and you must take your place. You already promised. If not him, then you promised yourself."

He took a long time before responding. "Panjael, son of Murosaya, disbanded the Protectors. He told us it would not be forever. He told us that we would hear things about him that would shake our trust to the ground. But we should not judge, only wait. He would call us."

"So I am right."

"No."

"Why not?"

"Because I don't think he can do it. As much as I love him because I loved his father and because he is as good as his father, I am certain this hole he is in is too deep. His father could not climb out of it, nor can he. He will never be in a position to make that call."

She propped herself up and stared at him darkly. "Then Satamabode is lost forever?"

He was still for a long moment, stroking her back with his fingertips. "No. There is another—maybe. I met him and rode with him and briefly fought beside him. I don't know why, but I am more inclined to serve him. He has something that Panjael does not. I don't know what it is, nor does he yet. If he finds it and his chance comes, I will join him. For my comrades. For your sister. For you."

She kissed him passionately and pushed her body against his with all the force she had. "Then I will not resent it. But you must stay alive."

"That is one of your high standards. No worry—I can meet them all."

Saina had no memory of the border outpost since his head hit the ground. Most of the journey from there to Virnipal was passed in fitful sleep and dizzy wakefulness. The Regent's physicians were convinced quiet rest would heal him quickly, so he was left alone in his new quarters in her palace. He had a sleeping and bathing room and an outer room for guests and meals. Ten times the space of his quarters in the monastery and exactly the same amount of company—none. Yet the softest bed he had ever rested on made up for the anything missed.

Before dawn, as he was used to, he rose and washed from a cold basin to the surprise of the servant who came each morning to fill the small bathing pool with hot water. He fretted about the expense of the fine clothes the man brought him and tray of what he assumed were royal foods he distrusted.

When the servant opened the balcony curtains he apologized that the view faced the mountains behind the palace. Most visitors preferred the other side looking upon the city and the crescent lake, because nothing ever happened in this direction.

Saina smiled and thanked the man, then stood on the balcony to gaze toward the place where half his life had passed. Where nothing ever happened—and that was its virtue.

His thoughts drifted back to the road through the Garland Forest and all that had been lost. Nacros. The scroll. And, as he had been told, Cheki and Mohidram, who passed on to the next horse trades in the northern abodes.

The image of Cheki's rescue of Deserena haunted him more than any other memory, but each one compounded. He ached to acknowledge her gifts to him. And more—just to talk to her, as they had talked on the trail. He wanted to understand someone so capable of daring and yet so unlikely to succeed at it. Even without the blindness, hers was a remarkable act—one that parted a curtain for him. Through it he glimpsed power of the Goddess. It was an act of grace.

But now this woman was no longer part of his life. The emptiness had no end.

Eventually the door opened, and the reverie moved on. The servant spoke to him but he could not listen. He heard people filling the outer room. He let the man take him by the hand and lead him through the door, where he faced the Regent herself, standing apart in front of the others, apparently surprised to find the room so small.

She eyed him carefully though not disapprovingly before speaking.

"I am Pavim. Here are my Assessors and a few others from our first families whom you will be introduced to formally later. Here also"— she gestured regally over her shoulder—"my son, Khoroas, Heir of the Seed and the Daughter of the Seed Sevrese. I know you should be left to rest, but I did not want you to feel apart. We are pleased to offer you our hospitality."

Saina lowered his head appropriately. He thought the Heir seemed sensual and bored, though he had to admit his opinion had been primed. Sevrese wore a veil, so he noted nothing except her absorbing gray eyes.

One mystery was resolved now. He was relieved to see that the Daughter of the Seed Sevrese's misadventures with General Bhalkavar in Alambarat had evidently ended with acceptable results. He was glad not to have to negotiate with her mother in the face of the alternative.

The Regent preempted any questions. "We believe your Daughter of the Seed Deserena is recovering well, but she will need time. I have given her sanctuary here for as long as she needs it."

"Satamabode thanks you," he replied.

And so much for the needs of my diplomacy.

She waved it off. "No less an obligation could be contemplated. There is this condition to it. She will remain here as my ward. We will formalize this later when the precedents are sorted out and the Sulatins have been consulted. We are plunged into events without precedents, I am afraid. As her guardian, I will help direct her efforts for Satamabode."

Saina did not know what to say. The implications, her motives—he saw none of it. *What has Deserena to say of such a relationship? What does Pavim's control mean to Panjael?* Saina felt so far off his path, he did not understand which direction was ahead.

She paced a little, as the room allowed, and began talking not so much to Saina but as if to Satamabode itself. "You should have some confidence that the future of Satamabode remains tenable, but there are many difficulties. This Assessor Ruryo is someone very foreign to my mind. I have gathered as much information as I can in so short a time. What I see is a man with a philosophy of *expedience*—if such a thought can be dignified as philosophy."

Her gaze leaped toward the mountains beyond the window—to Prayadevale. "Forget his Seed Bearer Pharmos, for surely he has ceded his authority to his Assessor. Surely your Seed Bearer Varanos is forced to do the same. Ruryo rules two Abodes now. But even Ruryo is not our enemy. You know what is at risk here? I will tell you. What if his expedience proves of value? What if the people of Satamabode find they are really better off for it? Set aside for a moment the destruction of one Abode—the battle is over the worth of all our traditions. The war will continue until we all resolve our doubts about what is sacred and what is simply old. That question shows this attack singularly aimed at the Sulatins. This is your war."

Then she looked at him sharply. Her eyes nearly pushed him back a step. Her words went far deeper, pressing within where all his questions of the worth of Prayadevale and the Ten Abodes were stored. He did not have time to dwell there and forced himself to meet her gaze without looking confused and foolish, as he in fact felt. She relented.

He spoke. "I agree with you."

It surprised her, but it did not stop her.

"We will have a meeting soon, when Deserena is further recovered. Until then, you have the freedom of the palace and the gardens and beyond, as you like. But I would ask you not to leave Ryadabode until things are much clearer."

Her manner made him realize that this freedom arose not from consideration of any sort owed to him, but from his insignificance. She expected his departure, but prevented it only from prudence. He had no part to play in her plans. Her claim that this was his war lay flat on the floor to be trampled.

He caught the eyes of Sevrese, which in an instant turned away from his. They inspired him, for no reason apparent to him, to at least pose one question as the Regent turned to go. It was inappropriate but he could not hold back.

"Can you tell me one more thing?"

She did not turn to him completely. "And what is that?"

"We had two companions on our escape. A horse-coper and a young woman. I lost them and have no way to find them. Can you help me?"

"They are gone."

"But the horse-coper—I understand you deal with him regularly. The young woman said so, and she expressed much admiration for you."

"Did she say that?"

"She did, and if that is true, is it possible you could call them back?"

Suddenly—and for reasons obvious to everyone but himself—his subject charged the room with energy. Every face was looking away. Khoroas was laughing silently. Sevrese had backed into the furthest corner.

Pavim now faced him again and narrowed her eyes. "What is so important to you about them?"

"The girl saved Deserena. That was my task—and my brother's. She completed it for me, and I must tell her—I'm not sure what— that she was remarkable in her courage and her skill and her selflessness. I see it again and again in my memory. I must at least tell her of my gratitude. And for the inspiration. Forgive the comparison but it is all

I know—she showed more mastery in that moment than any Sulatin adept I have known."

"Indeed." Pavim took a breath and looked around the room quickly. "I was not told of this."

"It happened in a moment. I was the only one to witness it."

Her whole manner changed toward Saina. The overbearing tone left her. The condescension disappeared. "Tell me what you saw in detail."

As Saina narrated the blind girl's self-possession and her physical strength and her skill in riding, the room went silent and motionless. All eyes stared ahead, unable to meet anyone else's.

"The truth is," he finished, "as Deserena's shield she could have taken a dozen arrows, but that did not cause her any hesitation. When I thought about it this morning I realized I had seen the grace of the Goddess." He felt a shiver run through him as he spoke the words.

Pavim looked at the floor then around the room. She whispered, "That is a beautiful expression, Saina. But when one acts selflessly, she gives the result to the Goddess. I am certain She hears your gratitude. That will have to suffice—it should suffice."

He saw Khoroas with a look of respect, and for the moment Saina withdrew the judgment that had marked him as smug and unlikable. From her corner Sevrese was looking awkwardly toward the balcony, distracted and fidgeting.

The Regent regarded both of them before speaking and bringing her gaze back to Saina. "But it is not possible to speak to this young woman now. You must leave your next meeting with her to fate."

Saina gave a small bow. "I accept that—reluctantly."

She gave him a hesitant smile then looked away. The Regent's eyes were moist with tears.

Panjael sat on the edge of a divan in the same apartment of the Sugorai palace where his father resided for the past twenty years. He had taken it after Saina's mother died, abandoning all his holdings to serve only his Seed Bearer for his remaining years.

Panjael's elbows pressed hard on his knees and his shoulders hunched forward. His head was bowed and his eyes stared at the patterns in the carpet. It was not a pose Murosaya had ever adopted.

Ruryo stood in front of the window opposite him. The same corner window Murosaya used to look out of many times a day to see anything going on in the Protector barracks across the river to the west and the large maidan where they trained north of them. A shaft of afternoon light was cutting through the air, leaving Ruryo's face in dark in shadow and drifting dust. He waited for Panjael to speak.

Words would follow only after Panjael had thought through this staggering pact Ruryo proposed. But it was difficult to find a starting point to evaluate it. Panjael was now looking at every one of the promises he made to himself—on behalf of his father, the Protectors, the citizens of Satamabode—seemingly fulfilled by Ruryo.

He swallowed and asked the first question that came into his head. "How—how would you have me lure the mercenaries away?"

Ruryo shrugged. "We pay them. We give them half now and the rest when they reach the border to their lands. That will probably assure the death of many of them as they fight among themselves to increase the size of each share. But, as you must have calculated, all your Protectors captured in our attack are detained in a compound near the border. You can rearm your men, and have a measure of revenge ... if you pledge them to me."

"Not to your Seed Bearer?"

A thin smile spread across Ruryo's lips, and his eyes lit up the shadow for a moment. "Would you pledge them to your current Seed Bearer?"

Panjael did not answer. Ruryo gave a single nod.

"Why did you even bother buying your mercenaries? Your weapon made up for the lack of numbers in Hanarabode's army."

"So the great Satamabode would experience its deepest fears and suffering. It was not a military decision. I am Assessor Concordant. My role is to sustain justice, harmony, and rectitude. The mercenaries allowed your citizens to measure the value of all three. My Abode's Protectors could not inspire that—even with the weapon. Now the mercenaries must be removed so I can restore Satamabode to its previous glory and even surpass it."

"You are not here as a conqueror." Panjael did not make it a question.

"No." Ruryo straightened his leaning body and began to slowly pace the room. "The first families of all the other nine Abodes have always resented the shadow Satamabode cast on them. You simply have too much of the bounty of the Ten Abodes. You should see my Seed Bearer parading the palace in Qurmadi's gold-threaded robe waving that horn scepter with the inlaid stones."

"That is why Qurmadi had to be killed—to appease the envy of Pharmos and the other Seed Bearers? Then why my father?"

"Well, that was the desire of Qurmadi's late queen. I cannot say what Murosaya's offense was, but she apparently held her anger for a very long time. I learned of her rage just as a matter of Seed Bearer gossip some years ago. That was the first element of my plan. I contrived to meet her at a Seed Bearer assembly one year. It was not hard to encourage her to think beyond emotion to action. And of course Varanos was her weapon. She as much as sold him to me, and through coded letters and clandestine meetings we gave the boy hope of accelerating his ascent to Seed Bearer. All he had to do in return was provide information he gained by playing up to his father."

"She died too soon to enjoy her victory."

"Well, her plans were rather limited in scope. I don't think she would have been all that satisfied with my own. Her death was well-timed, and her son sustained her passion. It was Varanos who let us know about Murosaya's every suspicion and gave us the right day to attack before he could prepare a defense."

Panjael realized Ruryo had arranged the queen's death—and Ruryo saw the realization emerge along with seething anger against the entire Seed Bearer family.

"Don't judge them so harshly. It is always interesting to witness the motivations of one person to kill another. You, for example, are here to kill Varanos."

Panjael could not prevent his eyes growing wide.

"It was good plan. Obvious only to me. But were you to succeed everyone would see you simply as a traitor. No matter what a Seed Bearer's crimes, an Assessor cannot pass judgment and penalty. You know that, and I know your character—so both of us know it is impossible. You kill only because you are attacked—the code of your profession. That is why I give you a mercenary army to put to the sword."

"Heir of the Seed Varanos attacked his own Abode. My killing him defends it. I have justification for my act. The Sulatins have not come to verify his claim."

Ruryo shook his head. "I care nothing for justification and less than nothing for Sulatin oversight. I want the people of Satamabode to realize that their success and peace have nothing to do with the Seed. Varanos invited the mercenaries. You banished them. Imagine how they will think of you versus the would-be Seed Bearer."

"So I kill as a matter of service and honor. And what do you kill for?"

"I kill people who get in my way. I am going to reform the Ten Abodes. I want you to take part in the victory. I accepted your return and the reason behind it, because I wanted you to pledge to something greater than either revenge or righteousness."

"Do I sacrifice my original objective by pledging to the new one?"

"I have kept Varanos alive because it gives the other Seed Bearers and the Sulatins fodder to chew. You can hear them condoning his father's questionable death because at least the Seed remains. Imagine their confusion when they learn he is dead—as if they shit their pants during a procession.

Panjael blinked. The man had the heart of a statue. He used the queen, used her son, used the mercenaries—all of them must die once their usefulness ends. *I am letting him use me, but I at least have his warning.*

"Are you ready? Collect your Protectors and sweep the mercenaries out of Satamabode."

Why does he trust me? I could perform this act and return to fight Hanarabode again.

"I am not afraid of you, Panjael. You will not turn against me as long as I respect your service and your honor. Your men will follow you for the same reason."

Now Panjael rose and Ruryo gave him the place at the window.

Then Ruryo turned. There will come a time to end the Seed of Satamabode. I will respect your revenge as well, but that is not why you will take that action. The wider view than the one this window affords."

Without looking at his new master behind him Panjael asked, "What is the wider view?"

"That none of the Abodes requires a Seed Bearer. Prosperity buys the loyalty of the people. That for a thousand years they should believe their prosperity depends on some spiritual fantasies transmitted across generations by the sexual fantasies of Seed Bearers is beyond understanding. They will realize that. They will get used to the absence of men like Varanos and Pharmos with little effort. A death or two—perhaps the Regent Pavim for good measure as well—and the rest of the Seed Bearers will abdicate. It is all planned very carefully."

"Without the Sulatins, I suppose."

"Mmm. No one will notice that."

"And your plan places you atop what remains?"

"There is a place for anyone who can absorb the vision. Can you?"

Panjael turned at last to face him, thinking of his own designs to convince the Sulatins he could rule Satamabode as consort of Deserena. It was a paltry, even farcical stratagem. It evaporated with every word Ruryo offered.

He nodded.

In return Ruryo offered, "We have a pact."

Neither congratulated the other. Neither so much as smiled.

Saina no longer awoke before dawn. Nor did he take the meditation position on the floor as he had done thousands of mornings before this one. When his eyes opened this morning he saw the walls washed with red and gold of sunrise. He gave a look out the window to see the mountains and the clouds above them glow in the sun's first rays. It was all beautiful, but it did not dissolve his thoughts about his utter failure to serve Panjael as he had promised. This new beginning he envisioned for himself since leaving Prayadevale was in need of a kick.

His servant entered with a summons by the Regent.

"This early?"

"Regent Pavim always rises before dawn," he answered. "She is always at work at sunrise. Her discipline never wanes."

And there is my kick.

Saina allowed himself to be pushed toward the warm bath and then quickly dressed and hurried to her private hall.

When he arrived in her presence she broke off her discussion with the assessor who was in the room. The man gave up his seat to Saina and backed away. Pavim was dressed in white, adorned only by strands of light coral. She sat on the edge of a wide couch with one bare foot under a knee and the other one grounding her to the tile floor.

Just as Saina settled, Deserena was led in as well, her shoulder still immobilized in a sling. He rose at once to offer her support, but there were three servants and two physicians to seat her at the other end of the Regent's couch. She seemed no longer in pain. She had dressed with care and looked brilliant in contrast to the simplicity of the Regent.

"What is the progress report?" the Regent inquired. The physician started to speak, but she cut him off. "From you I hear every day. Let the patient speak for herself."

Deserena smiled and breathed deeply. "Your physicians, your attendants, your many gifts of comfort—all these are far more than I could have asked for. I am happier than I ever expected possible."

Pavim gave a subtle wave to deflect such gratitude. "They would have been given even under better circumstances. Considering the outrages you have undergone, nothing we do for you even approaches compensation."

Deserena's sincerity was deep. "But you have made me feel that many of my losses have been replaced."

The Regent returned a smile of measured warmth. "That is a generous thought. I have only to place my own son and daughter in your position and ask what I would want for them. I can offer no less to you."

"They have both been very generous as well."

Saina grasped how much he had been excluded from. And why. *To Pavim I am at best the lowest of the Sulatins. I cannot be trusted as Deserena's friend. Why am I here today?*

Abruptly Pavim spoke to him. "Now, Saina, as you are here on behalf of the Daughter of the Seed, and as she is under my protection, I want to share with you and Deserena the news coming from Satamabode."

He took a breath, slipping his tongue once over his lips. He tried to read her face. No sign of good news appeared. But she masked how bad it might be.

"I have been informed by Prayadevale that only a few days ago, the tribal mercenaries were forced out of Satamabode."

"But that is very good news," Saina offered. "By Panjael and his Protectors?"

Her gaze dropped. Saina took it that he had spoken presumptuously.

"Yes, that is true—but things are not as they seem. In fact, there are rumors that the mercenaries were massacred between Sugorai and the border. The number of deaths, if this is true, is appalling. While I am satisfied to know the people of your Abode have relief from the treatment of these invaders, I am at a loss to explain what sort of person treats allies this way."

She looked at Deserena, who was now on edge.

"You must be prepared for what follows. Both of you. It is not a victory for Satamabode, though your enemies would like it regarded so. Your half-brother Panjael has apparently committed his Protectors to Seed Bearer Varanos—thus allowing the Seed of Satamabode to continue. However, we know that Varanos is under the control of Assessor Concordant Ruryo of Hanarabode. Therefore, in truth, Panjael serves Ruryo. Your Abode is no better off that when you escaped. I cannot in good conscience allow you to return."

"But why would Panjael do this?" She cringed with sobs.

Pavim let her cry and then calmly explained, "Here is what I have been able to learn from the Intercessor. I have to trust it is true, even if I do not know how the Sulatins have this knowledge. You have already been made aware that your brother allowed the invasion as part of a plot launched long ago by your mother against each of your fathers—Qurmadi and Murosaya. You have also told me privately—and I assume that Saina knows as well—that Panjael intended to reclaim the Abode with you, Deserena, as ruler while he became your consort. Is this what you were to propose to the Sulatins?" She glanced at Saina.

"Yes, in part."

"So in addition to the betrayal by members of your family, Deserena, you have been betrayed by someone who pledged himself to you. And he has done the same to you, Saina. None of this is rumor any longer, dear Deserena. The Intercessor Athayam has written me that all these stories are corroborated. I certainly give you all my sympathy for the devastation your family wrought on Satamabode. You are the one innocent victim to survive their misguided or else evil designs."

She turned to Saina and drew a long breath. "You are a victim as well. And, whatever plans you made with him on behalf of Satamabode or Deserena are now meaningless. If you agree, then you are welcome here as long as you wish to stay. I appreciate that it will be difficult for you to return to the Sulatins, but I have some influence with your superiors and will use it on your behalf if you choose. There is the option to return to your homeland, but I would be relieved if you did not take it."

Then to Deserena she added, "For your sake, and as a duty higher than any other I know, I will press the other Seed Bearers and the Sulatins to reverse this catastrophic direction that events have taken. To have any hope of success I must ask you to reach for all your strength and take your role as the symbol of defiance against all that has been lost now. Please think about that."

Deserena's face was still streaked with tears, but she regained composure. She nodded and spoke slowly. "Yes. I see your meaning perfectly. I will find the strength you ask for. You are the symbol of that to me."

Her words drove a thought through Saina's mind. He had to speak it. "So, one can say that Satamabode is not altered in principle by any of this upheaval. It still has a Seed Bearer. The mercenaries have been removed. No doubt it can be worked out that the Hanarabode

Protectors can withdraw. Does this mean the Sulatins will not condemn what has happened? That they will sanction Seed Bearer Varanos?"

The question clearly troubled Pavim, who shifted in her seat. "That is undetermined."

"Forgive me but how could it be otherwise? There was an attack but now there appears to be peace. A Seed Bearer died but his Heir survives. The Abode is intact. The Seed is intact. According to the Seed Bearers and the Sulatins, everything has happened as it should."

Pavim regarded him thoughtfully. "Unfortunately, your facts are correct. However, I am not satisfied that facts explain anything. We cannot ignore how these events occurred, who carried them out, and why. By your tone it seems you are not satisfied either."

"Because how and why will reveal that a grave danger remains." He looked at Deserena and could not go on. Pavim saw his look and quietly nodded. She understood him and shared his concern, but would not allow Deserena to hear it.

What if the new Seed Bearer is killed?

The beads dropped into his hand again, and he started to pass them through his fingers. He saw Pavim eyeing his hand with curiosity, but she said nothing. Instead she moved herself so that she bent before Deserena and stroked her hair.

"Poor child. One wound after another. But you are safe with us. I want you to feel your home is here. Though I know you will probably not feel to do so, I want you to attend a celebration planned for me. I am told the lunar sisters on this appointed night will spread across the heavens at even intervals, each in her own phase. I never have been capable of understanding our lunar cycles, I admit, but in addition to the play of the moons, it is my birthday. And we always take the long barge out on the lake for the evening when such events conspire. In easier times I know you would agree to accompany me. But now I wish even more fervently that you will be with me. It is not a time for celebration, but it is also not the time to forego celebration. And do not worry—I will keep you secluded from any festivities or attentions you do not want. You may keep your privacy as much as you wish. There is only one person I would ask you to speak with. The Intercessor will be arriving for the event. He will bring us a higher interpretation of events than I have given you. Let us hope that will provide some comfort." She twisted her head to Saina. "My invitation extends equally to you, Saina. Will you both accept?"

Deserena managed a faint smile. Pavim took Saina's assent for granted. That was fortunate for all he could think of was the wonder that Pavim commanded the attention of the Intercessor on her birthday. In all his years at Prayadevale he had seen the Intercessor a handful of times—only in gatherings that required the largest audience hall, where Saina sat far back with the other undistinguished students. Yet it appeared he sends Pavim confidential reports and for her birthday crosses mountains. So, who could claim the better connection to the Sulatins? She bested him at everything.

"Thank you," whispered Deserena. "I will be honored to be part of your celebration. I only wish I could offer"—

"Those are thoughts you should put out of your head. I accept your generous intention as present enough. You cannot be a burden here, my dear. I do nothing for you with any intent to compensation of any kind. If you decide to offer me a gift, then give me your continued determination."

The audience ended—at least for Saina—when the Regent surrounded Deserena with all the attendants. He withdrew and found a servant who could lead him back, for he had little concept of the palace geography beyond his own room.

On the way the servant was hailed down a hallway by a booming voice that shook Saina.

The servant turned to him and asked, "Can you wait one moment please. General Bhalkavar calls me. I think he has mistaken you for a servant as well. Please forgive the manner of his call." The man seemed very embarrassed by the general's mistake.

Yet it did not register with Saina. He heard the title *general*, but the voice that called was unmistakably the voice of the horse-coper Mohidram.

When the figure at the end of the hall came into the light, he saw the same massive chest and arms. The same face—but a growth of beard and hair had begun. All at once it was completely obvious.

How ignorant can I be?

The general now realized his own mistake. And he also realized what was completely obvious—this was no time for hesitation.

"Saina." He spread his arms. "So, I could not avoid you forever. I can't even apologize for the way I called just now, when the far greater apology should be for my lies."

Saina looked him up and down a dozen times trying to make it otherwise.

Bhalkavar rubbed his hand over the short hairs on his head. "Saina, come. Not here. Come." He sent the servant away.

He pulled Saina along until they came to an alcove where they could sit. Saina crumpled on the bench.

But before Bhalkavar could speak Saina found myself saying, "There is no need to explain. It is all clear now. I am only surprised that no such idea ever occurred to me."

"Stop. Listen to me. Our disguise got us out of a trap at Alambarat. We had to decide whether we could discard it or not before we reached safety and—well, for many reasons I chose not to let you in on it. I hold lying next to cowardice. I was wrong. I am sorry."

"No, I quite understand. You were right. You had the security of your Daughter of the Seed to guard. I had mine. I would have kept her identity secret as well, but it was too thin a veil." Then he remembered Sevrese's veil at the first meeting with Pavim. And all he had said about the horse-coper and his blind girl. He groaned.

"You don't understand yet. You don't understand why we left you abruptly at the border."

"Well, that I admit. I thought—"

"Sevrese was thinking only of Deserena, so we left as soon as we could. How awkward would their relationship be now, if the truth were known? Deserena has no idea about her. They can be friends because of it. And you must know by now that Deserena needs every friend she can find. My disguise was not as complete as Sevrese's so I have kept myself away from the palace. Of course, someday it will all be revealed, but it is impossible when so many blows have suddenly hit her. It is just as well that you and I should run into each other, because you had a right to know now. I am sorry that we resorted to such a trick. Maybe it is one we will laugh about together someday, but now you have every reason to resent me."

Saina wanted the freedom to laugh, but only a faint one emerged. After a long breath, he said, "No, it is not that." Their eyes finally met. "It is not you. She was so magnificent—your Cheki. I—I—saw in her something—something great. It is hard to see that memory evaporate."

"I heard about what you told the Regent. I can tell you it went deep in her. And it earned you her respect. But why despair? Sevrese's actions were real—only not so supernatural as they would be for a blind girl. Whatever her name, handicapped or not, she has character, Saina. In time, even great character. Like her mother."

He nodded. "But for all this time she has been in my mind. I have longed for her—I mean, longed to know her." He suddenly did not know what he meant. He certainly did not mean to say that. Not to Bhalkavar—Sevrese's protector. He swallowed uncomfortably. "It is such a shock."

The shock, however, was now becoming clear to him. That until now she had been an ideal, but attainable—at least in his imagination. Conceivably he could find her someday, and then—well, one could imagine. Now she was a Daughter of the Seed—right here in the palace with him, yet farther beyond his reach than the horse-coper's niece could ever wander.

He saw that his accidental confession made the general embarrassed. He could only think of one thing to say. "General—I can get used to calling you General—your timing is a little troubling. I just learned from the Queen that my brother has sold out Satamabode for all time. Now this. There is no Sulatin training for it."

There was a long silence between them. Bhalkavar broke it with a low whisper.

"Saina, go easy on yourself. News like this would make even a Being Surrounded by Light crap."

Saina spit with laughter and the general joined him.

When they settled at last, Bhalkavar put his hand on Saina's shoulder. "You must be upside-down with confusion. Agree to something with me, will you? If you need anything, you come to me and I will see that it happens. Anything. You agree?"

Saina nodded, and immediately an idea struck him. "Can I ask for one thing right now?"

"Whatever you want."

"Don't tell Sevrese we have talked."

The general frowned, thinking it through. Then his brows rose. "The boatride? Yes, that could be amusing. It is some days away, and I imagine she is fretting how to avoid you. I like it."

When the Intercessor Athayam first caught sight of the city of Virnipal from the crest of the trail, the entire valley and the lake were already in shadow. Even so, the highest tower of the Regent's palace still held onto the last ray of the slanting sun. The eastern mountain wall was deep purple with cerulean sky above and one golden spire alone and straight.

He took it as a moment of natural harmony and at the same time the perfect symbol of the Regent's adamant orthodoxy.

"Captivating, isn't it?" Athayam murmured to Luzarain. "I would like to sit and look."

The Conductor nodded. He was not one to admire beauty aloud, but he knew about Athayam's habits, cultured by so many visits among the rulers and first families of the Ten Abodes. In their company the breathless appreciation of form—particularly the refinements in the land and palaces they reigned over—was always considered to be the highest taste.

Luzarain left Prayadevale only as an aetheric traveler. He let the gods decide beauty. They created it, destroyed it, and there was beauty in each act. He did not need the sun's rays striking lofty bit of plaster to remind him of that. But he remained quiet and still for as long as Athayam needed it.

"You have said nothing about Daiyenso for the whole of our journey, Luzarain. He will come, don't you think?"

"Mmm. You mean Daiyenso or the mysterious Preceptor?"

The older man stretched his legs slowly. "That is giving Daiyenso a great deal of credit. If the Preceptor were to come, it would not be because Daiyenso convinced him or even requested it. I am resigned to the notion that he is who Daiyenso claims him to be. You will not accept it because it steals away what little control we have over events."

Luzarain nodded. "I am practical. Ruryo is a usurper, to be sure, but given the state of the Seed Bearer families, not a usurper without cause. I must respond—to his acts and to the thinking that spawned them."

"You believe it is all manageable. That we can contrive solutions to please all." Athayam sighed. "That gives you the appearance of Ruryo's ally. Do you really want to abandon all our tradition with compromise?"

Luzarain gave a light laugh. "You think the Preceptor will *not* throw tradition out?"

Athayam was silent. There was a sound below them on the trail. It was Daiyenso.

"Ahh, greetings." Athayam remained seated. "You arrived early and came to meet us?"

Daiyenso bowed slightly to both of them unwilling to say when he arrived.

"You come alone." Luzarain smiled.

"The Preceptor remains engaged. But perhaps we can speak about his existence tonight with Regent Pavim."

"To what end," Luzarain asked. "A birthday present?"

"Well, yes, it would serve that purpose. She must realize that the Seed Bearers are content to turn their eyes from Satamabode. Instead of a sense of futility, we can offer a more inspiring interpretation of all that has happened and all that will happen."

"With reservations about the nature of your friend in the forest?" challenged Luzarain.

"With uncertainty, not reservation. There is always uncertainty."

Luzarain shrugged. "Which inspires faith. She has more faith than the rest of the Seed Bearers combined. You are probably right."

"The tower is no longer golden," remarked Athayam, gazing toward the city. "I have conviction that Daiyenso is right. Hope should not be in shadow. I will speak of the Preceptor as a possibility. If you assure me you two will not turn it into a debate."

The other two caught each other's look and each let the corner of his mouth twist with a measure of amusement.

Athayam stood up and put his hand on Daiyenso's arm. "What did you mean? The Preceptor is engaged. Engaged with whom?"

Daiyenso met his eyes. Then Luzarain's. "He seems fond of ferines in the Garland Forest."

Athayam's brow furrowed. "Does he? Perhaps I will not stress that point to Pavim. Ahh, look. She sends a party with lamps to escort us as the sun falls. We will not be late."

Shib's band of ferines slid from their roosts in the forest canopy down to the ground. One songmaker let his voice flow into the night, while his companions began a pulsing rhythm hitting sticks against logs, hands against bodies, tongues against cheeks. Together the sounds rose like a wind in the night and into songs some would find soothing and others haunting.

As the drumming became compulsive to more and more of them, the pressure to move together multiplied, until several lines began snaking through the growing darkness, twisting round trees and each other and sometimes breaking through, merging at last into one closing circle.

Everything in the forest was awake—the ferines, the trees, the birds and the branch crawlers and creepers, the humming insects, the ground scratchers, the underground diggers, the spirits of the dead creatures, the gods, the devils. The Goddess was pulsating in Her aetheric world, and both worlds twisted together, spiraling, merging until there were no boundaries between bodies and minds and souls.

When the center of the dance closed together, the leader of the line cried out and voices broke everywhere and the song collapsed.

And at that moment Shib came into the gathering. Everyone parted around him or took up into the lower branches of the trees. Silence and several hundred pairs of glowing, amber eyes greeted him.

His chest expanded and he tapped it with his finger. It was the sign of a promise.

He will come, he told them.

This was greeted with a chattering flurry, ending finally in another orderly cadence that might have come from the threshing of drying reeds.

Being Surrounded by Light will come. We will gather more bands together. He has shown me a human who will live with us in our forest.

There was a sudden murmur of alarm.

Shib shook his head vigorously. He held up the scroll of Satamabode in both hands above his head, as if it contained the man. *In here long ago we served him. Now, again, is for us to join. Being Surrounded by Light. He says it is so.* And again he tapped his chest for certainty.

There were low howls of excitement, mixed with shrill calls to quicken the day of his coming.

Shib's lips spread to show his own exaltation. He shouted. *We serve the human wellx.. and Being Surrounded by Light will take us to live in the light ... forever.*

There was no containing the noise that followed. But in time it found a rhythm that transformed it into melody and made the bodies move in time once again. This corner of the Garland Forest shook through the night.

EPISODE 5

Saina walked along the shoreline in the fading light surrounded by a crowd. No one knew who he was, but no one paid him any mind. Ryadabode's citizens were all finishing preparations for the parts they would play when twilight came. Dozens of decorated boats bobbed up and down at the water's edge on both sides of the wide pier that anchored the Regent's barge. Others had been launched from coves around the lake and were spread across the water in the distance. Everywhere there was laughter and shouting, musicians rehearsing, cook fires billowing, and incense wafting.

He was used to somber rituals, and chaotic celebrations by thousands of people were a mystery. For these citizens the upheaval of an Abode over the western mountains cast no shadow, unlike for their queen. And in turn their good wishes would relieve her aching mind.

Saina's own birthday was only days away and for the past ten years all he received was a review of his horoscope and the past year's forecast inaccuracies. His astrology was seriously flawed, as it was yearly explained to him, which was why events such as the deaths of his friends would plague him all his life. He was glad this year to miss these acknowledgements.

In that mood, when he heard his name called, he naturally winced. He looked ahead and saw the Heir Khoroas parting the way through the people to reach him.

"Are you lost? The man sent for you in the palace could not find you. Come. I will take you aboard now. I have a few things to attend to early. Come on."

Saina saw Khoroas' eyes size him up momentarily with a distant smile on his lips. He slid around to Saina's side and took him by the arm like a benign jailer, guiding him back through the crowd and onto the grand boat he was commanded to board.

"Many of these people will take to the water with us. Every boat will have lanterns that will light the lake. And then from the shore they will float toy boats toward the barge with lamps inside and offering wishes. Everywhere lights and reflections of lights all over this part of the lake. It's very beautiful." He gave a cordial laugh. "It's a wonder the barge does not catch fire and sink. Maybe by the time I become Seed Bearer, Ruryo will arrange such an offering wish." He shrugged. "My mother, as you will see, is thoroughly loved."

Saina had no idea how to carry on a conversation of this type. He found himself only nodding and making assenting sounds as Khoroas continued to introduce him to all the features of the royal barge with flourish after flourish. Saina did not understand the intention. Or if there was none, he could not see why so much breath was spent on things one could discover oneself.

"Saina, if I may ask your permission, I would like to serve as Deserena's companion tonight. I know you are sensitive to your obligations to her, but allow me to set you free of them, if I have earned your trust."

Saina's mouth opened, but he did not want to share all the troubling thoughts that these words generated in his mind. He nodded, "Certainly."

Then Khoroas gave him a reassuring grip on his arm and left him as quickly as he had caught him up.

Saina leaned on the rail and watched the ripples flash silver and blue in the fading light. Khoroas was now the third suitor for Deserena, and Saina, as always, was expected to keep out of the way. By now Deserena's romances held little interest for him. He had his own intentions to deal with, and they filled his mind with doubt. He wished he had the impertinence to suggest Khoroas keep out of his way with his sister for the evening. But he knew the gap between lover and a monk—between a Daughter of the Seed and man without purpose, without prospect, without even an Abode.

Guests began to arrive onboard—the first families of Ryadabode. Soon the numbers were large enough that he edged aft as far as he could. When that was not enough he took the stairs to the smaller top deck where a translucent tent was added. Even though it was too crowded to see clearly, Pavim and her family were a presence just by the way the crowd opened in front of them and closed behind them as they moved around the boat. They emerged on the stairs to the upper deck where they took seats, followed by a wave of guests who took couches and cushions wherever they stood at that moment. Then came a scramble to organize family and friends. Hesitating, Saina found himself at an opening some distance from Sevrese. He saw her from behind and pushed forward to where he could at least observe her profile. There was no veil this time and he saw the same lips and chin line and nose he remembered from the forest. He drew a quick breath involuntarily.

But his gaze turned on the Sulatin robes on three figures near the Regent, who now faced the gathered crowd. He slid closer to see who had come, but the boat launched with a slight jolt, swaying the hanging lanterns and causing him to go down on a knee. Sevrese saw him and they shared a look. She motioned him to her side. Deserena sat with her on a couch and beyond her Khoroas, and she pressed them to make room.

He had just enough presence of mind to step through the crowd cautiously, fighting to keep his balance. Then he slipped down next to her. At the same moment several more people came as he had, almost dancing among the bodies to find seats. Everyone shifted and Saina was pressed tightly against Sevrese's side.

He apologized and she gave a nonchalant laugh to dismiss it. Their eyes met again, and it was proof of the general's favor. *She does not know that I know. For once in this whole adventure I have an advantage with someone.*

But only for a moment. The boat swayed again and their arms pressed against each other once more. It was clear to him suddenly what really separated a monk's experience from everyone else's. Monks do not touch women—and would not endure being monks if they did.

His beads seemed to drop into his fingers on their own, but he shook them back within his sleeve. He was eager to move into this world tonight, and he did not need the old one undermining what courage he would find.

He ignored his racing heart and leaned his head her way. "I—I am told you are an exceptional rider. Almost as if you could talk to horses."

There was suspicion she could not hide. She nearly smiled, and then she replied, "Someone has exaggerated. Who told you this?"

"Well, actually, it was an intuition. I am a Sulatin, you know—well, I was a Sulatin. And it might surprise you to know I was considered the best horseman in all of Prayadevale."

He waited but she did not give way. Her head twisted slightly with curiosity. "Is horsemanship among Sulatins judged by riding horses or talking to them?"

He nodded. "Mostly talk." He added quickly, "I am looking to enhance my skill as a rider."

"What do you lack?"

"If I could learn just one thing—riding blind—that would complete my training."

She pursed her lips and raised a brow, then nodded sagely and whispered close to his ear, "Yes, I can teach that, but only to a worthy student. Are you also considered the worthiest in Prayadevale? We have Sulatins here tonight. Will they speak for you?"

Now he glanced at the dais. To his astonishment he saw the Intercessor Athayam, the Conductor Luzarain, and a monk he had never seen before."

He swallowed. "Maybe not."

She laughed. He bit back a smile of his own. They shared a look that acknowledged everything but spoke of nothing. Then a gently waggish demeanor took over her face.

"Even so, I will teach you tonight, after the barge docks. In the dark we hardly need a blindfold. I have a wonderful horse for you to ride."

"Well … I hardly … I mean, this is a celebration for your mother. I wouldn't impose—I have no riding dress and—"

She had the command of a Daughter of the Seed. "I will arrange everything. I have clothes at the stable and yours will do as they are. Only, I am afraid about the moons. Horses tend to get spirited on nights like this."

"Exactly. Perhaps we should wait. I want everything to be right."

"No—no. A man who can converse with horse will no doubt want a particularly spirited one, and I have such a one. So, it is decided. You have found the master you seek."

She burst out with a laugh just at the moment the room became subdued, and everyone looked at them. The laugh was swallowed with difficulty. Saina felt a rush of exuberance he had never known—and more than moderate fear.

Next the air was enveloped with devotional songs from the back of the boat. The Regent and Intercessor Athayam sat on separate divans at the same height, she smiling as her gaze traced slowly round the room, he with eyes closed and a smile directed within.

Many evenings Saina had listened to these songs in Prayadevale, and he appreciated how their rhythms lifted the listener to a finer realm. Now they had no such effect on him—his consciousness leapt like a monkey among the fruit vendors. This was a market of the senses, where first he came upon the spicy scent from her skin. Then the strands of gold and brown as her tawny hair fell along her neck. And the fanlike spread of her fingers resting on her crossed legs. And the way her chest rose and yielded softly with each breath.

When the songs ended, the Regent sent thanks and tokens to the musicians and spoke briefly of her gratitude for the affection and fidelity of the large family of Ryadabode. Then she spoke to the Intercessor, formally requesting his blessing on this night and some lesson to be shared.

Behind his pure white beard flowing upon his rust robe the old Sulatin leader smiled graciously. He spoke of the great joy of witnessing such esteem between ruler and people. In a long, rounding way these comments developed into a lesson on sacrifice of the true monarch and the gift of loyalty from her subjects in return.

Still Saina could not follow a word. The cultured expressions of the highest-ranking Sulatin were flying past him with no hope of entering this mind. Indeed, he knew he was so corrupted that he felt not guilty, even quite satisfied about it.

There was next a break and most of the celebrants were excused to enjoy the spectacle from the lower deck and to allow Pavim time with her family and her Assessors and the Sulatins. Deserena was included and thus no one suggested that Saina not be.

Now the talk had his attention, for revealed to him was the side of the Sulatin Order that Saina knew nothing of. At first glance it could prove Panjael's accusation of Sulatin interference, but in this context of Pavim's devotion to tradition, it was a lesson on how the sacred duty of the Sulatin Order was carried out among the Ten Abodes—and had always been carried out for five hundred years. He didn't know any of it.

"Master Athayam," began the Regent, "may we speak of policy on a night like this one?"

"The night is yours entirely. What do you wish of the Order?"

"You have already favored me with as much information about the violent events in Satamabode as I have asked for. And while ordinarily I would not think to stain the beautiful spirit of this evening, there are times when pleasure simply cannot take precedence. I would like you to reveal to us what the Order sees behind these events. What you believe will come of them. What your feel will survive and what will be lost and never regained."

Athayam nodded slowly. "I would be the first to admit, my dear Pavim, that such questions cannot be avoided even as we celebrate a much more enjoyable event. In fact, it was as much my doing to make this night a time of speaking candidly about these same concerns as you expressed. I want to give you, your family, and your advisors some words that promise something very great, although I cannot ignore that we must also face up to challenges very dire."

She took a deep breath. "Well, I don't wish to put off something very great, but the stability of our Abodes is threatened and the consequences are indeed dire. I have concerns even for the security of this Abode. But most immediately I have concerns for the destiny of some of my guests." She nodded toward Deserena and then, to his discomfort, to Saina himself. "On their behalf I cannot be indirect. I hope I am not blunt, but all reduces to one question. So let us begin with it. What will the Sulatins do about the crimes of Hanarabode?"

"Mmm." Athayam gave a slightly pained look. "We are without authorization to do anything, of course."

"In principle, perhaps, but in practice …"

The old man nodded. "Ahh, in practice we have been accorded tacit authority by the Abodes. We have established a tradition of consensus among them that has always answered each crisis. Five hundred years of success as mediators. But no event in all those years matches what we have lived through in these days."

"No, of course not. And do you believe such a consensus can be reached today? Surely there is no Seed Bearer *un*willing to condemn these acts."

"We have known each other too long for me to dissemble with you. There are some who waver, some who wait, some who rationalize, and even some who deny any wrongdoing took place. Since those who witnessed them are either resistant to questions or deceased, there is little chance to achieve consensus. Yours is the one Abode to articulate a stand. What you have done for Deserena will secure her safety against all the shocking and misguided efforts of Seed Bearers Pharmos and the Heir Varanos. That much is accomplished. But it is far from enough." The white beard waved as his head shook briefly. "We cannot sanction patricide, yet neither can we prove it. We cannot ignore the attack that caused to the Seed Bearer's death. Pharmos is certainly to blame. His Assessor Ruryo is certainly guilty. Varanos is culpable by way of conspiracy."

Athayam gave an imperceptible nod to the third Sulatin, who rose from his seat beside the Conductor Luzarain and poured water into a golden cup from a jar set aside for Athayam.

Saina watched the man walk with slight difficulty, as though his feet were injured. When he kneeled and waited for Athayam to take a long drink and return the cup, Saina felt a sudden jolt of surprise from Sevrese. So much so, she unknowingly grasped his arm.

Sevrese shot a glance round quickly, but did not find whomever she sought. She looked at Saina and then whispered right at his ear. "Look at his feet as he kneels. I saw him in Alambarat—disguised as a blind beggar. His feet were scarred. This is the same man. A Sulatin spy—he saved me from the mercenaries. He must have been watching me all the time. I wish Bhalkavar was here to see him."

Athayam wiped his mouth with a small cloth, and then Daiyenso returned to his seat as the Intercessor continued.

"The risk is that Ruryo is justified. That he brings prosperity back to Satamabode or even surpasses what was before. Its citizens will not be blind to it. Nor will those of the other Abodes. Already we are told the relief of the people in Sugorai and Alambarat is palpable that the mercenaries are gone. It was Ruryo who brought the mercenaries to torment them, and Ruryo who arranged their demise. But he is not blamed for the one, and for the second has very cleverly used the first son of Murosaya as the savior to the people. The deception may be ruthless, but the result is perceived as beneficial to most of the people in Satamabode. Thus a question arises. What if the Seed Bearers and our Order are in fact holding everyone back? And if we attempt to reverse what Ruryo has begun, given this possibility, then the benefit would appear to be only to the Seed Bearers and the Sulatins."

Pavim's eyes closed. "It is inconceivable that Ruryo could have this power over us. You cannot let this happen. He is evil. He must be exposed and brought down."

The Intercessor now looked at Pavim's eyes and held them. "We cannot simply say Ruryo is evil. All change must begin with destruction. The fruit must rot to produce the seed. Pharmos and Varanos, if nothing else, provide that. They offer weakness and greed, without which his Assessor Ruryo has no strength."

She was very agitated now. "You speak as if this is meant to be. Destruction in this case has meant suffering of a kind I would not expect you to accept. Brutal weapons and brutal mercenaries. Thievery.

Murders. Yet you are suggesting the Sulatins will sanction it. What became of righteousness?"

He seemed even calmer with her challenge. "Yes, righteousness is the idea to consider now. It is possible that a great change is indeed coming, Pavim. But not the destruction of the Ten Abodes. Something much larger than that." He paused and let his words hang in the air as he spoke them. "There is evidence that the Preceptor has made himself known a second time in our history."

"The Preceptor," whispered Pavim cautiously. "And what are we to make of this?"

"We make of it that life propels him to us again. Knowledge and time are ultimately incompatible. Over time knowledge will be lost. That was the birth of the Sulatin Order five hundred years ago." He raised his eyes to include everyone in his discourse. "In truth, however, creation and destruction are simultaneous and continuous in Goddessoma. We see them as separate in our mortal world. We accept that between the creation of knowledge and its decline and ultimate destruction is time. And just as the nadir is reached—the loss of all knowledge—some Ruryo must come along as the destroyer of the old. Our Infinite Goddess, Mother of All, creates this agent. She in turn answers the destruction with creation in the form of revival of the knowledge in its purest form."

Saina thought, *Pavim was right. If that is what is at stake, then this is the Sulatin's fight. They are the only ones to blame for the loss of knowledge, because it was theirs not to lose.*

The Intercessor continued. "In truth, the knowledge is at once everpresent and everlost. And the Preceptor does not appear suddenly, but is always there—in Goddessoma. In the mortal world we make judgments and take actions and err as often as we succeed—but nothing ever happens to destroy Goddessoma."

Saina saw something in Pavim soften, and she sank into contemplation. She was a believer in her core and could not reject the promise his news held. It gave her hope, but Saina doubted she knew what to hope for.

In contrast, he tried to imagine Panjael hearing of the Preceptor. His skepticism would render these words a clever and desperate ploy to prolong a decaying Order. And why not? To the faithless or the uninformed, this was a reasoned and expedient response, one that at worst purchases time for diplomacy and subterfuge to find their way to success.

"Who is he—the Preceptor?" Pavim asked. "And where does he show himself?"

Athayam spread his hands slightly. "Ahh, there is the very heart of the problem he poses. He makes no claim to be the Preceptor. Nor a claim that he is not. We debate it among ourselves." His hand waved lightly toward his two companions. "Meanwhile he remains a complete recluse, alone in the forest, content with his austerities. Only our Daiyenso here has spent time with him."

She gave Daiyenso a piercing glance. "Suppose it is true. Whom would *he* name as the villain in these events?"

"From the perspective of one so highly evolved, heroes and villains, good and evil, right and wrong, bliss and suffering may not be as clear as you would want. When the Goddess destroys and creates, all is for the good. And that may pertain here. All may be for the good. Even villainy must be commended."

"I intend to continue to hold Ruryo as unrighteous, evil, and the cause of suffering."

Athayam nodded. "Yes. Righteousness is the issue for the Seed Bearers. You alone understand. But unrighteousness may be essential for the destruction and creation of knowledge. And righteousness will be one of the benefits of the creation that comes."

She gazed at him thoughtfully. "Thank you, Athayam, for your candor."

"With you it must be so."

"Please join me now to view the moonlight and the fire upon the water."

Athayam nodded. "In one moment, my friend. I would like first to speak to this young man who comes from our side."

Saina froze.

Pavim regarded him with only slight surprise and much more regard. "Of course."

Three sets of Sulatin eyes were upon Saina as Pavim ushered the others out—trying to leave the heaviness of events behind. Saina's anxiety was made much worse when he felt the separation from Sevrese.

"Saina, my greetings to you," Athayam began, "and my deep condolences on your losses—Murosaya and your brothers."

Saina stammered a series of thank-you's. His tension was deepened by the unrelieved glare of the Conductor who was now standing behind Athayam. He hardly heard the Intercessor's next words.

"I would ask you if you have anything to pass along safely to Prayadevale."

"I do?" *Something like the scroll of Satamabode, I suppose?* "I do—but I have to retrieve it from safekeeping."

The words came out as the weakest possible response, yet they had the strongest effect on his will. Instantly he saw himself back in the Garland Forest, and against all reason he saw success. He would retrieve it. He was sure of it. It was the first thing he had been this certain of since leaving Prayadevale. How it was to be accomplished, he had no idea. But that was his task. Keeper of the scroll. That was his purpose, whether Sulatin or soldier or outcast. Whether Murosaya, Ruryo, or the Sulatins demanded it.

Athayam did not look as satisfied as Saina felt. Even less was Luzarain. "What kind of delay do you expect?"

Saina swallowed but confidence was still within him. "I am unable to predict that. What with all this disruption, there is some danger in reaching it right now."

"Danger," Athayam repeated—with skepticism. "You said safekeeping."

Saina could not answer. His brows arched briefly. *You have no concept.*

Athayam looked long into Saina's eyes. "Ask Regent Pavim to send word to me when you are ready. I will come here to receive it myself."

"May I respectfully ask—apart from the safety of the scroll itself—why it is of such value right now?"

Luzarain stepped forward. "To answer your rather sharp questions, that remains a matter of speculation. Perhaps hidden in the folds is a recipe to neutralize the power of the weapon that has everyone so frightened. Or some other factor we have overlooked to resolve the threat Pavim feels so strongly about. If I may respectfully ask, why is it of such value to you right now—that you would withhold it?"

"I have no excuse to offer you." Saina thanked him awkwardly with a nod, assuming dismissal, but the Conductor made a movement with his hand that Saina interpreted as something more to come. He waited nervously.

In his years at Prayadevale he had taken Luzarain as the highest embodiment of the knowledge they all were supposed to seek. Yet until the day of his leaving Prayadevale, he never had he been allowed to approach him. Now, for a moment, he had the man's attention. And for all his countless questions of the past and the hundreds of concerns arising in the last few days, he did not know what to do with it.

The Conductor helped him. "What will you do, Saina, when this task is completed?"

Tentatively, he offered, "I pledged to act on my brother's behalf, and I cannot give that up even after what I have heard of him since. I am bound to believe he still offers the hope to reclaim Satamabode—at least until he releases me from that pledge."

"Mm-hmm." He considered Saina again for a few moments. "Then you have chosen not to return to our Order. Is it not so?"

Having the fact put in front of him so bluntly made him immediately protest. "No, sir. I—I would not say *chosen*. Had it not been for these events—"

"You stood before me and I told you this was a choice. You could stay with the Order. As it turns out, not much has been accomplished by your leaving."

Saina swallowed. "That may be, but from your earlier words, Ruryo is the only one who can claim accomplishment. The truth is, I feel after all my years there in Prayadevale I have nothing to show for it. Now I am in another current that feels very strong. I want to follow it until I do have something to show."

The flow of tension inside him finally flooded his chest, and he shook slightly. He could not believe he had just complained to the heads of the Sulatin Order that they had fallen short of his expectations. Another example that the impudence of his first year at Prayadevale, so long thought to be suppressed, was actually an irreducible part of his character.

"If I may add." It was the voice of the third Sulatin. He waited for Conductor's look, then said, "There is a parable that might be useful for him."

The Intercessor nodded. "I would like to hear it."

Daiyenso gave Saina a gracious nod. "It is understood that you now have some experience with the ferines, so you may appreciate this tale of one. It happened that, long ago before the Sulatin Order was founded, even before the Founding Seers and the Ten Abodes, when the passing along of knowledge was simply a gift from teacher to disciple, there was one such master who was traveling through a town with his students.

"These students were forever complaining among themselves that their teacher was holding back the deepest knowledge from them. They debated whether it was being withheld because he had a conscious plan for them, or because he kept it for himself and had no intention of revealing it, or because perhaps he did not know these secrets.

"In any case, their disappointment was great for they had committed their lives to this learning and felt, as you do, that they had little to show for it. They did not express this directly, but how can you keep your heart from your teacher?

"Finally, one of them approached the teacher to voice all of their dissatisfaction. *Master, when will you reveal the highest knowledge to us?*

"The teacher answered, *After you have arranged our meal and a place to sleep for the night.*

"Now they were very excited. They went about the town to find someone who would feed and shelter a wandering master and his disciples. At a rich man's house they were called over by of all things a ferine in a cage.

"The ferine actually spoke to them as a person would. *You need food and shelter for your master? Ask here,* he told them. They did, and the owner invited them all to bring their master back to the house, so as they left they thanked the ferine.

"*I have a favor to ask*, he replied. They of course said they would grant it. *Ask your master how I am to get out of this cage.*

"They thought it ridiculous to bother their master with such a self-centered concern—and from a ferine at that. It was not the place of a great teacher to remove ferines from their captivity. So they returned to the teacher and told him of their success, but they ignored the ferine's plea. The master suspiciously asked them if there had been any request for payment. Since there was only the ferine's question, they had to relay it, but they did so with great embarrassment.

"Upon hearing the question their teacher fell to the ground, clutching his heart in the agony of death. The students panicked completely. He had taught them much healing knowledge, but it all fled in that instant. In time, he revived himself, but he was very weak and asked that they return to the place where the ferine lived and bring the food from there. He preferred not to move for the night.

"They were still very distraught when they reached the house to make the arrangements. The troublesome ferine called them over to ask if they had repeated his question to their master. One of the students said angrily, *We asked your stupid question, ape, and it nearly destroyed our master. He fell over with convulsions and all but died. And this was the night he was to reveal to us the deepest knowledge. Thanks to you we will not hear it. Leave us alone.*

"Whereupon a look of great peace came over the ferine, and he immediately fell down just as the teacher had, apparently dead. The students were astounded at the coincidence. The owner of the house rushed out to see and opened the cage to try to revive the ferine. With the door of the cage open the ferine leaped out and up into the trees. Just before flying into freedom, he turned to the students.

"*You listen to your master for years and learn nothing. I ask for one lesson and find the way to free my soul. You should not waste your master's time like that.*

"At that moment the master appeared at the house, saying he felt quite himself again and would take the generous offer of food and shelter there."

Daiyenso looked into Saina's eyes for just a moment, enough to announce the conclusion of his point. Then he let his own gaze drift to his lap where his hands rested.

The Conductor raised his brows with a satisfied smile. "Daiyenso makes many points, Saina. Does the tale suggest anything to you?"

Saina took a deep breath. "That instead of holding Prayadevale responsible for what I do not know, I should apply for knowledge in places I have taken for granted."

"When you left Prayadevale, I also told you that in leaving our path behind, you will find it follows you. Tell me, do you still wear your beads."

"Yes, of course," Saina replied. He had never considered taking them off his wrist.

"Why? What use are they?" Luzarain asked.

The answer was too simple, but Saina followed his lead. "To count the names of the gods."

"So everyone replies. Yet, the beads are one of our great mysteries. You spend all this time—naming, naming, naming the gods of Goddessoma. Then, suddenly, you realize, you already know Goddessoma. The counting of the beads does not bring the knowledge itself. Yet you must count to discover what you already knew. Doing, doing, doing— already done. Your destiny does not depend on Panjael's wishes. Not even yours. It is already accomplished. Your action can neither bring it about, nor stop it. Or else, destiny is not destiny. Yet—inaction is not a choice. You must act. So act. Doubt nothing. Regret nothing. You feel your path is not with the Sulatin Order? Then choose other teachers and give them all your attention. Not a portion. All of it. Understand this. *Do*, but not by halves, by the whole. Then let go of the doing, because it avails nothing. That is the mystery of the beads. Count them devotedly and with joy. But expect nothing."

Saina suddenly saw the Conductor's power. A teacher's power. He had never understood in all the years at Prayadevale. And that was why he had nothing to show for it.

He nodded. Luzarain returned a quick nod and then looked away.

The Intercessor rose. The exchange was over. Saina backed out quickly with a bow, feeling equally crushed and exhilarated, enlightened and mystified. Once out on the deck a sudden, piercing thought of Bhalkavar's offer came.

Saina, come to me. Whatever you need.

The moons were spread across the sky now—waxing, full, waning, reflected in the lake along with thousands of lights. He passed quickly through the crowd. He passed Deserena midway and found her entranced again by Khoroas' charm. She smiled at Saina in a way that allowed no interruption to her pleasure.

When he at last reached the general, he found Sevrese there as well. There was no acknowledgement of the past life of the journey, nor of secrets revealed or hidden away. Instead, Saina leaped into a new experience with them.

"General, I want to take advantage of your offer. Two favors."

"Good," he replied with an expansive wave of his hand. "Put me to a test."

"I am the one with a test. I need another horse and supplies for travel. Is it possible?"

"And where will this horse have to go?" asked the general.

"Back to the Garland Forest."

Sevrese looked stunned.

"When?" the general asked.

"Tomorrow."

"Mmm. I will give you these, of course. May I ask why?"

Sevrese broke in, "To retrieve the package you lost to the ferines?"

Now the surprise was Saina's. He nodded. "That's right."

But the general suddenly distrusted the venture completely. "What does it contain, Saina? There is a lot of danger and little chance of finding it intact. Certainly you should take some men with you or you may wander for many days."

"No, please, General. I have a very strong feeling that I am to do this for myself. It is something the Sulatins want from me."

Bhalkavar rubbed his head and narrowed his eyes. "Alright. Sevrese, do you have a horse that can make friends with the ferines?"

"Yes. We are going to ride him tonight, as a matter of fact. Saina has asked me for riding instruction."

Saina bit his lip as he turned from her to the general. Then he smiled wanly.

The general shook his head slightly in mock disdain. "If you survive this night, I may decide to teach you the martial art."

Saina exalted. "Would you, sir? That is the other favor."

The general had not expected it. He gave Saina a quick appraisal, up and down. Then he nodded back once again. "Alright. Survive tonight's instruction. Survive the ferines. I will be waiting."

"May I give you one lesson in return, General?"

"And that is?"

"You said you do not want Deserena to realize your identity."

"True."

"Then you need to find shelter from the moonlight. Your head is the brightest light on this boat."

Sevrese laughed. The general rubbed his stubbled head uncomfortably.

After the Regent had retired to her palace, the festivities of the night moved from the lake to the city and spread into every tavern and gambling hall and alleyway of Virnipal, the entertainment steadily descending from its elegant beginning to tumultuous songs, droning horns, clashing bells and rumbling thunder of drums. Every appetite was excited, and every opportunity arose to fill them all.

Against the backdrop of the commotion, even in the training compound of the Ryadabode Protectors at some distance, the two horses Sevrese now led from their pens were in a sideways prancing delirium. Their ears spun toward every sharp sound, their eyes widened, their nostrils snorted. To Saina it made them arresting to watch—but folly to ride.

Sevrese tied them for saddling, and then she asked him to introduce himself to them. She made him lean his nose to each of theirs and share their breath. The curiosity of a new human and new breath calmed them for the moment.

"Maybe they talk to you in your mind, but this is how they talk to each other. I believe they respect us if we do things their way. I named this fellow Shade. He is the younger half-brother. Here is Grizzle for you. Bhalkavar bred him—and named him—and taught me as I bred and trained the second. Along with my dark bay mare—my lifetime friend, who is named Tamarind—these two are my treasures."

"He belongs to the general?"

"No. Bhalkavar has virtually no possessions. He gives everything away to people who both need and prize the gifts and asks for nothing in return. Grizzle he gave to me as a test to learn dedication when I was younger—and wilder."

"He is a good teacher."

"So is Grizzle."

Each of the horses was gray but not matched. The older was beginning to fade to white except for his legs, which remained charcoal. The younger brother showed a striking raven-colored shadow underneath gray dapples. In the mixed moonlight the horses shone like enormous silver statues.

"They are so magnificent," Saina observed softly. "And your Tamarind?"

"No. These two are stallions, and in this atmosphere, one cannot introduce a mare. It's near her breeding time."

Saina watched her hand stroke the velvet of Shade's neck and could almost feel the touch of her fingers in his mind. She handed him a brush. He was relieved she could not divine his thoughts. He took her instructions to groom to her standard and to calm them for the saddles.

They next moved to a vast training arena where the warhorses learned their art. The horses took this for drill and were willing to put aside the city noises and attend to the work as they were used to do.

In a shimmer of movement Sevrese was up in the saddle as if lifted on a breeze. Saina struggled onto Grizzle, who gave a sidestep meant to confound his rider. Once up, he felt the horse remaining aloof and cautious, and there was no communication with him for now. Saina knew he was being measured, but he felt the horse to be patient and willing to endure whatever Sevrese put before him and atop him before complaining.

She let them walk the entire rectangle slowly. Though the celebration could be ignored, the horses were unwilling to settle completely until they could inspect the arena themselves. They patrolled it three times in all, starting at every shadow until they were at last ready to work. Quickly they were trotting and their tails rose.

Sevrese stayed by Saina's side, keeping her horse in perfect pace with his, using him to lead Saina through a drill of gaits using only the lightest leg pressure. They all understood the subtleties perfectly but him. She lived up to the role of teacher, observing him carefully, giving instruction that was easy enough for him to follow, praising his progress.

When they cantered steadily round the arena the horses began to reveal their strength. She drew out ahead and suddenly took to dodging and jumping obstacles. Saina panicked momentarily and shouted. "I don't know what I'm supposed to be doing!"

She could not hear him.

Instead the horse answered in Saina's mind. *Of course you don't. I'm the one doing everything. What you should do is—do nothing!*

Doing nothing was not as uncomplicated as it would seem, but Grizzle was true to his word. He took care of Saina—or simply ignored him. His loyalty was to Sevrese and Shade, as was his high sense of honor. He would not disgrace her by mistreating his rider. Even the small jumps she led them through, and the one huge one, did not dislodge Saina as long as he followed his mount's lead by not interfering.

Saina's concern came when he could feel Grizzle grow ambitious and begin to race. The honor of victory seemed to be overtaking the honor of courtesy. Sevrese sensed the danger and kept them on the flat for a lap, still cantering. Next she pushed Shade to a gallop and Grizzle's tail went up with his lunge to be in front. By then Saina did not have to try to do nothing—he had no other choice. He leaned forward over Grizzle's neck, grabbed a handful of mane, and took the wind and sand in his face. There was nothing to anticipate either, for the furthest he could see in the darkness was behind him before he could react to it.

The arena was so large and so familiar to them, the horses could choose their own way to slow and stop. But even then when they settled their feet, their necks continued to thrust into the air as they seemingly blew fire through their nostrils. Sevrese walked them round, ending at a storage shed constructed just outside the railing. There she dismounted and poked inside. When she was up again she held a bow and a handful of arrows. Together they trotted over to a runway in the center of the arena.

"Wait here," she directed and disappeared into the moonlit shadows.

Saina heard the beat of her approaching charge before he could make out what she was doing. Then he saw she had dropped her reins and pulled the bow back across her chest, directing the horse only with her thighs and the shifting of her seat. The bow stayed motionless as the horse galloped by—except for the moment when the arrow flew to a hanging target opposite the runway.

Saina moved in to inspect as she slowed in the distance. Her shot had pierced a ring that hung in front of a wooden board. She returned and he regarded her with intense admiration.

"This," he offered with an appreciative laugh, "is a wonder. I would have never guessed your skills."

She laughed in response. "I was lucky. Not how it usually happens when I try to show off. And it is all I can do. When Bhalkavar trains his men, they must hit the ring as it swings. I have never accomplished that."

"But do they hit it in the dark? I could not do that standing still in front of it. I doubt even in the light I would have a chance."

"It is just repetition to advance to this level. Bhalkavar tells me that beyond that is a profound awareness—when target, bow, arrow, rider, and horse all become one. That is what the true warrior must ascend to. He will be a good teacher for you, for are not such things in the domain of the Sulatins?"

She did not wait for a reply but slid to the ground. Saina joined her. She took off the saddle and bridle and told him to do the same.

They held the two horses lightly around their necks with the reins until everything was free.

"Watch out," she said and released them from their leads.

They both dug in with their back hooves and left with a shower of sand spraying into the moonlight. They kicked at each other with perfect precision to miss. They whirled and reared, straining in mock attack. Soon they rolled in the sand to grind away the sweaty itch from nose to tail and shuddered when they rose. Eventually they drifted back to report and blew fiercely in their riders' direction as if Saina and Sevrese were foreigners they had never seen before.

"The Goddess fills them tonight. It is a reward for them to play where they must work. Bhalkavar makes sure they get that. We should graze them awhile as well when they are cool. And if you can delay your departure until midday, Grizzle will be well rested. Do you mind the time?"

"Mind? The truth is I will need the rest more than he. This night has been an enchantment. It is a privilege to see it all the way through. Does your mother's birthday always bring such excitement and satisfaction to so many?"

"This has been as good as I can remember." She took a deep breath and exhaled a warm fog into the cool night. Saina watched as if it extended her body toward him. Then she added, thoughtfully, "Under the circumstances."

As if that realization must break the spell, he felt the weight of the vast uncertainty of the future. "Yes. This is a night in the spirit of the past. We cannot know if it will ever be repeated."

For a moment they remained still then he ventured a new direction. "May I ask you about something that is personal—about the general? You are very close to him. He is a standard for all warriors. I would like to know more about him."

She hesitated. "Yes, I promise to be more forthright than when you asked me about my mother. I apologize for the dishonesty. It makes me feel"—

"No," he said softly, "all that can be put aside."

She gave him a long look. "Yes, it can. Thank you. Now, let us take care of these two, and then let me speak of it."

It wasn't until the horses were bathed with buckets of herbal water and grazing on a large expanse of grass near the stable that she brought the subject back. The clamor in the city had not diminished, but the horses were now blowing soft sneezes of contentment as their muzzles picked expertly at the grass.

"Bhalkavar is great, of course," she said, but then changed the tone immediately with a distant questioning in her eyes. "I don't know why he has always favored me. With Khoroas he is strict—well, he is strict with me, but he softens, too. You see, he has no family himself. He is devoted to his warrior status. Never deviates from it. He has some quality that I find—well, I don't know how to say it without sounding overblown. I see him like a solid truth walking among shadows. I have to appear to treat him as if he is mortal, but in my heart he is beyond that." She looked deeply at Saina. "I have never told anyone this. No one has ever asked. Why do you?"

Saina scratched at his horse's damp neck before answering. "It is not simply curiosity. Something happened to me when the Sulatins spoke to me tonight. It leads me to the general."

"What did they—I'm sorry, that is not at all for me to ask."

"No, please. It's good. I would like to talk about it. You seem as close to the Sulatins as I have been. More. It is amazing to me how familiar you and your family are with the Intercessor, when we students never get to see him."

"Really?"

"Oh, yes. My life has been very isolated. The Sulatin leaders do not much engage us. You see, we come from such diversity. It seems their first task is to end all distinctions among us. A name, a title, a home in the high country or the plains, skin fair or dark—only one difference ever exists, and that is the difference between the confirmed Sulatin adept and one who is not yet so. One has knowledge and humility, and for the other it is only questions and submission. If the younger students were to vie to receive the attentions of the leaders of the Order, it would provide one more distinction to fight away. So, for the Intercessor to even notice me—let alone know me and speak—well, his words carry more weight than anyone else's could. The Conductor is a little more visible in Prayadevale, but still he is not someone we approach. I have never even known the existence of the third one—Daiyenso." He paused. "To answer you, what they told me was that I need not return to that life."

"Were you contemplating that?"

Saina shook his head and looked at her directly. "No. But as unformed as my duty and ambition might be, in light of the news out of Satamabode, I now have no direction at all. I am grateful for your family's hospitality, but I am too idle. Their release to me was accompanied by the instruction to find other teachers. Like the general. And I believe my impulse to return to the Garland Forest will fulfill that as well."

"Are you willing to tell me what you lost to the ferines?"

He hesitated. "It is difficult for me to say this." Grizzle raised his head and stared at Saina as though he had been listening. "Ahh, you see, I am caught."

"Yes, horses respect honesty—although they do not always give it. They are too clever."

"I see. Well, I am left with the mystery of my father's cleverness. What I must recover is the scroll of Satamabode."

"I thought those were kept in Prayadevale."

"One of them was not. Something my father did many years ago— his secrecy makes the reasons all the more important. Before he died he left instructions that I must care for it and use it to restore the Abode." He shrugged. "Instead, I gave it to the ferines. I believe it still exists. I believe I must retrieve it. And without anything but my belief, I think I can discover how it pertains to restoring Satamabode. Only, the Sulatins want it as much as I do."

"Why?"

"The scrolls contain the cognitions of the Founding Seer, everything that opens the door to Goddessoma and the Sulatin powers. Protecting this knowledge validates everything. The Ten Abodes, the Seed Bearers, the Seed itself. But this alone does not explain their interest. So, I cannot answer your question yet."

She took his arm with her hand. "You have a task I cannot even imagine. But I am impressed you feel confident. And I too believe you can do it."

"You have a lot to do with my confidence. I don't know why yet, but I believe I can discover that as well."

She smiled. Then she looked wistful. "Since you shared something very private with me, I will tell you something about Bhalkavar that I would never tell another. And it pertains to my mother." She leaned lightly against Shade as if she needed support. Her body shook once with emotion. The horse gave short huff.

"I have always puzzled over why Bhalkavar was never made Assessor Martial of our Abode. His stature as a soldier is much higher than the Assessor my mother named. His accomplishments, much greater. In fact, all the Assessors deprecate, though they command him.

"I have speculated—combining these facts with his having no family, as well as this feeling I get when I see them together—that long ago, before my father made my mother his queen, Bhalkavar had a devotion to her. She came from the north, from Navayabode, and visited here—you know, the way Daughters of the Seed are shopped around. Or I suppose you don't. But she loved it here. And the nature of royal arrangements is that alliances come first, emotions follow, so she probably assented to a marriage hoping for the best. But something else happened—that is my notion. The story he told in the forest—about the garland tree—that was about her, I am certain. Of course, it would have been impossible to act upon—even the flowers of the garland tree must have been an outrageous indiscretion.

"It may just be my fancy, but if it is true, would it not follow that she could never ask him for so formal a relationship as Regent to Assessor? If she did ask, he would have to accept for the sake of compliance, and yet he could not accept for the sake of honor. So, she relieves him of it. And so, perhaps as a kind of compensation, to me he can be a friend, more than is usual. And whatever could have been between them—and could not have been—can be ... diverted."

They looked at each other as if each suddenly had some qualms about sharing these thoughts. It occurred to neither of them that talking about an old affair was a way for them to take part in the sensual atmosphere that engulfed the city.

Her horse brought his head up suddenly behind her and playfully with his muzzle pushed her with force. She stumbled into Saina. Her tawny hair brushed the side of his face and ignited an energy that rushed through his chest and churned his stomach. They backed away from each other, embarrassed but laughing to cover it.

For Deserena the night had been a waking dream—so many pleasures strung like beads on a necklace winding about her. But now, as she entered her bathing pool adjacent to her room in one of the royal family quarters she felt as if the string broke and the jewels scattered.

Before her feet reached the bottom step, a tear-filled agony welled up. She settled into the water quickly, hoping for relief, but as the steaming scented liquid rose to her shoulders the flow of her tears broke.

One of the attendants went in beside her clothed in a nightdress. She managed to guide the Daughter of the Seed into a comfortable place to let it out. She held Deserena to her own body as she convulsed. It took some time before she could release her. By then the pain showed only in the grimacing face. Deserena had gone limp in the heat.

Images of her dead father and her dead mother and her loathsome brother filled her thoughts. Her beloved father—no one would tell her of his dying, and she imagined it at its worst. All of her security, all of her possessions, every emotional comfort she had been accorded through her life was gone with him. Her brother was as good as gone as well, but as the probable murderer of their father all emotions for him were instantly choked off. They were hardly close. Her mother was obsessed with him as soon as he was born, and he gladly stole any maternal time, let alone love, that his older sister might deserve.

She gave a thought to her grandmother, the Dowager in her own lonesome chamber in Alambarat. For so many years the Dowager had been the enemy of her son Qurmadi as well as Deserena's mother for reasons never explained, and she was now growing deranged. Affection between them had always been avoided. She would die next, and the last of her family would disappear irrevocably.

And Panjael. His pledges to her had been reversed without any attempt at contact, let alone explanation. Did he ever love her? Would he have loved her enough?

Over and over the feeling beat in her heart. *Tonight I am completely alone. In all the vastness of the universe and for all the length of my life. Utterly and always alone.*

Even as much as the compensations added up here in Virnipal, in the end—tonight—they served only to increase the weight of what was lost. The regent's family was so much more than hers had ever been. The delight of an evening such as this one opened new layers of sadness the more her reflections sought to prolong it.

In the presence of the Regent and Sevrese she had to reflect on her own shortcomings. If Pavim were the model of a queen, Deserena knew she herself had not the force of character for it. Nor did she have the discernment and deep concern for principle that allowed Sevrese to challenge any fact that everyone else took for granted. By comparison she felt herself vain and uncertain, seeking only more gratification and contentment as protection against all that she had no control of.

But why must her needs be wrong? As the Daughter of Satamabode she had always been led to expect a man of highest status would ask for her—a Seed Bearer of course. Though from her side it need not be only that, for none of the Heirs had ever appealed to her—except Khoroas now. Also, she was taught that the day she said yes was the day that her life both began and the day her life would end—for all she aspired to would have been fulfilled. She did not know how else to think about her life or about a man. And without one, on her own merits she feared she was nothing.

Except Khoroas—that thought dallied in her mind. He was certainly all she had ever longed for. His manliness was not as mature as Panjael's. He was not protector, but lover. For the moment, perhaps forever, that quality would serve her very sufficiently. But what was a lover unless he is constant?

How could Khoroas be constant? It was a simple guess that he had made love to every girl—royal or servant—who came his way and that they were thrilled at the prospect of pleasing and possessing, if briefly, such a caring lover. Caring for her alone—each one of them was sure of it. Yes, Khoroas could make them all feel that. If it was true in the moment they gave themselves to him, then why not beyond and why not forever? Until they finally admitted to themselves that each was only one in a long line who accepted his promises into their hearts.

Could she accept at least what he had to offer? No. Not if it rendered her even more profoundly alone, and what other result was possible? *If only he could love me completely*, she cried out in her mind.

She had come to hate all the *if-only's* of her thoughts. They weakened her no less than all the deaths in her life.

More tears emerged. She held them long enough to thank the girl and let her withdraw. Then she floated in and out of misery until the water cooled enough to be noticed.

The girl wrapped her in a cushioning robe and combed her damp hair into a long black mane. She was so withdrawn she was unaware when the one who had helped her in the bath left to see to the door.

The girl opened it with her moist dress clinging tightly against her body, showing the curve of her breasts and the dark bumps of her nipples. She did not hide anything, for she expected to find Khoroas behind the door.

He stood there in a languorous pose, but drew himself up to admire her in the dimness. There was something even more delightful in the way the sheer cloth clung to her, than the many times he had seen her with nothing.

She gave him a look of reproach then shook her head softly. "Your timing is terrible," she whispered. "But then it is not for me you called."

He put his finger to his lips then tapped it there as he smiled slowly. "Don't be jealous. Besides, the scent of this room whispers to me."

"You will fail. Your timing is terrible for her, too. She is in misery."

"Ahh. Then my timing is perfect—if you will be on my aide. She needs all our attentions."

"What is my reward?"

He snorted softly. "You have been credited so far in advance, you are in debt to me for life." He put his finger to the tip of her nose and drew it down to her damp chest.

The girl shrugged and opened the door to him. When they crossed the room Deserena finally became conscious of them.

"A visitor," whispered the girl.

"Khoroas—please, not"—a wretched look spread over Deserena's face.

He floated to her couch, setting aside the small bottle he carried, and with a look of deep compassion spoke, "What change is this? Was the pleasure of this evening so fragile? Well, of course I understand. Deserena, I am sorry. Tell me your heart. I must know what you are feeling. Let me listen and comfort you." The words came out with such honesty, no one would have given a thought to calculation.

She studied the angular grace of his form and his features. His skin was smooth and shades lighter than hers. His hands were tactful but strong. His confidence was like a perfume. Her gaze finally met his and she fell into it completely. Her chest heaved and new tears began. She felt his arms encompass her but did not know how it happened. She felt the hand of the girl stroke her head and neck repeatedly. She heard his whispers in her ear, ignoring the words for the comfort of the sound and the sensuousness of his breath upon her nerves.

When her tears subsided once more, Khoroas kissed her cheek softly. After a pause he pursued it. He kissed the hand of the girl, who drew back Deserena's robe just to reveal the wound on her shoulder. It was bare now, still reddened and scarred and tender. Khoroas put his lips there, too, as softly as petal falling.

This roused her and she edged away slightly. Instantly Khoroas moved off.

"I am sorry. I offer you comfort, but I am clumsy and of no use. I will go." His eye caught the girl, who smiled wickedly from behind her mistress and shook her head softly.

Deserena breathed deeply twice, then abruptly went to her feet to stop him. The girl hung on to the robe just slightly to dislodge it from her shoulder as she rose. Unclothed, Deserena pressed against Khoroas for protection of every kind. She felt as if a wall closed around her and she was within him.

"Don't leave me. Don't anyone else leave me alone." She hugged as tightly as she could until his stroking hand along her spine relaxed her inescapably.

He drew her to her bed and, still holding her, lay down so that he felt every softness of her form melt into his. The servant girl joined them again, behind Deserena, forcing her even more deeply into his arms, adding her own strokes to his.

Then she let her hand drift along Deserena's long hair, across her shoulder, around her breast and into the crevice between the bodies of the two royals. She lingered upon the thigh of Khoroas and lightly brushed in a widening circle against the silk of his pants. She sought the tie at his waist and loosened it, but she felt him very lightly recoil.

He shook his head minutely.

She frowned, pouted.

He gave her a nod to go.

She let her hand tease him once before withdrawing, as if to remind him of what she meant to him, but he ignored it, and she slid away from the bed leaving the sound of silk upon silk and the gliding movement of her silhouette for him to contemplate on his own.

Khoroas lay there with Deserena in his arms, and for the first time in his life he let sensuality pass away from him. He was completely astonished at himself—for had he not attended to the needs of so many women even before his adulthood? Enough practice to accomplish all he wanted with Deserena. Yet, none of their needs had felt like hers. By comparison, he could say he had not felt them at all. And for no reason he felt hers—for love perhaps, but he was unsure of that.

Her need did not pull him to her as he was accustomed to, nor did it capture his loins. Instead he found a deceptive ache behind his ribs. And it was not going away. This was deeper than passion. In fact, love was likely—no, conclusive. This was the vast emptiness of love in search of a worthy object.

He could have held her for days like this, never venturing sensuality. He told her as much, whispered in her ear, and he knew it sounded like a ploy—or should have—but for once he felt it in his heart.

She knew he meant it. And it meant everything to her. Her body was surging for his—not because she wanted to please him in the hope he would say *forever*. But because she knew for her he had accepted *forever*, and now passion was the fulfillment of emotion.

Suddenly she rose up and kissed him with a wild craving. Her arms wrapped tightly round him, pressing him so close to her that movement was impossible. Her lips slid off of his and sought to taste his flesh everywhere—his neck, his ears, his shoulder. She caressed his chest and stomach with her cheek, grabbing his skin between her teeth for an instant here and there. Her hair was loose and still damp and gave him cold feather touches of pleasure. Then she lowered herself so that her breasts just brushed his chest with indescribable sweetness.

He let her have her way, offering soft groans as a display of his satisfaction and gratitude. At the impeccable moment, he took her authority away—just when she might have wondered what he next wanted from her. He did not want to hear words. Words were for another world. Here an uncontrolled murmur was welcomed, but words could only interfere. It was the sense of touch that would be honored in this world.

And he had artistry in it. He gave it all to her. He drove her slowly and inevitably to rapture. For himself he took nothing. He wanted nothing. Never had he ignored his needs so absolutely—never had the perfection of his partner's sensations been so momentous to him.

When they took rest at last, all the peace of the night was to be hers as well. For his part, he lay awake under a blanket of exuberance he had never experienced before. He had at last been overcome by an obsession so massive that it must last a lifetime—he wanted only her.

Once he comprehended that his surrender produced not loss nor confinement nor fear but only wonder and elation, he could slip into sleep. Now—guarding over her contentment—for the first time in his life he felt he could rest.

Except—doubt came. It could not be this simple. He needed to know that she understood. Really understood. Not that he had roused her, but that he had felt love and that love roused her.

He wanted to tell her out loud. To say the word *forever*. And to hear her respond.

But he realized that *forever* aloud would only be false again—practiced, contrived. He had to have faith in his feeling and accept the risk.

As if she felt his tension from her sleep, she opened her eyes, pressed closer to him for the length of her body, and said softly, "I am so happy—for the first time. The loss is over."

He encircled her and whispered, "You will always be happy here. I promise you."

She floated in the gap between sleep and waking. Her body shuddered, and she gave a moan that sounded like a devil banished from her mind.

—∘∘◦❊◦∘∘—

The city of Sugorai was constructed on a diamond-shaped island that rose out of the expansive river in the uncharted past. Flooding slowly cut tunnels out of the solid earth and on top of these the palace was built. No doubt they were occasionally practical for storing Seed Bearers wealth and to hide movement through the city, but eventually their value as a prison took precedence.

Well past the middle of the night Ruryo entered the underground alone and found the cell the turnkey lived in. His service had been constant for many decades, Ruryo learned, and over time he grew too used to life in these depths to leave it. It made him a perfect guardian for the only prisoner Ruryo had consigned to this prison.

Ruryo shook the turnkey roughly and held the lamp close to his eyes to startle him further. The old man awoke with a muffled cry, coming out of dream that left him dazed and uncomfortable. When he saw Ruryo face above the lamp he quivered.

"Stay quiet and listen. Questions first."

"I know the questions, sir. No one has come down here since you were here before. And I have not left, for how can I? I have been down here nearly all of my life."

"Good. How is the prisoner? Sit up."

"Yes, that's better. Could I have some water, sir?"

"Better—a flask of wine for you." He waited while the man gulped it down.

"The thing about the young man is this. In my opinion, if you do not object to my speaking it. He has not been down here so long, but he already shows signs of losing his mind. I know you explained he was harmed in a fall in battle, but so much time in darkness and silence— well, I myself have had such spells just thinking about what lies around in these tunnels after nearly a thousand years. He only gets a lamp with his meal and the oil is finished by the time he is finished. It's not right, sir. A young man like that needs to see the sky."

"It is not only right, it is perfect. Don't bother thinking. However, I am giving you the freedom he does not enjoy. I want you to leave us alone. I don't care where you go but you cannot witness this event. Am I clear?"

"Yes, sir. Very clear. No thinking, no watching. But I don't have anywhere to go."

"If you press me I will have your head watch the sky from a pike. Light several lanterns to mark the way to his cell right now, and then depart. This meeting is none of your business. My being here is not a fact you can claim. Do you understand?"

"Yes, yes—yes, I do. Indeed. No thinking, no witnessing. You should know that my memory is not very good after all these years down here anyway. Worse than him, maybe."

"Alright, then. You give me a different idea. Just do as I said, give me the key to the cell lock, and come back here and wait for the meeting to end. I will see to everything else."

Ruryo pulled the turnkey up and pushed him into the tunnel. The man gathered lamps and spaced them as instructed.

Meanwhile, Ruryo returned to the entrance to the prison where a figure slumped on the steps. He talked him to his feet and acted as his crutch, moving slowly to the only cell with an inhabitant. The figure slumped over again.

"Nacros. Rise up. I have a visitor. Nacros?

"Who is it?"

"Your Seed Bearer wants to talk to you. He wants to ask your forgiveness for the harm he brought to your family. You remember Varanos?"

There was silence. "Not sure." More silence. "I remember ferines."

"It doesn't matter. The ferines probably hit you on the head. Is that what happened?"

"Maybe. I remember fighting them. They pulled me off my horse … somewhere on the road … then I was here."

"Have your eyes adjusted? Can you speak to your Seed Bearer?"

"It is dark here always."

"Nacros, you do remember your enemy? Who was the traitor to your house?

"Not me. Not the ferines. It wasn't them who knocked me out. I hit my head. Then I was here. How long have I been here?"

"It has taken the traitor who killed your father this long to confess. He wanted to beg your forgiveness. Can you name him?"

"Mmm. My father died at the hands of his own Protectors."

"Good. Who turned them against him?

Nacros winced. His words began to slur. "Not sure."

"What would you do if you knew who killed your father."

The slurring became a distant laugh. "Now you are … now that's—that's easy. Where is my sword? Because I will cut him gizzard to gullet." He laughed, stuttered, and fell into nonsense.

"I will bring him in." He threw the sword to the other side of the cell, and quickly opened the lock. Then he dragged Varanos across the threshold and locked the door.

"I know him. He doesn't look very good."

"Lift him up to your bed so you can see. You know him. It's Varanos."

"He's heavy. Hey, Varanos, I know how you feel."

"No, Nacros—you don't. He feels guilty. He wants his punishment. He killed your father."

Nacros took up the blade. "Then this is for my father—my father whose name was ... Murosaya. This is too good for you, Murosaya—I mean Varanos."

"Do it!" cried Ruryo.

Nacros drove the blade into the heart. Blood sprayed to the rock ceiling of the cell. He swore with happiness. "Did you see that?"

Ruryo returned to the turnkey's cell. "My meeting is over. Did you finish your wine?" There was no answer. The turnkey's service and his life were over.

EPISODE 6

Saina was lost. He was forced to ascend the mountains away from the pass to Alambarat, taking narrow trails blazed by animals and water. He spent as much time walking as riding and retraced his progress one deadend after another. When he finally reached the Garland Forest, it resembled nothing of his first trip, and he could not locate the old road. He felt frustrated but knew it mattered little that he was lost—he would not be lost to the ferines.

Sevrese had given him Grizzle for his endurance and his sure feet. But the horse's sense of dignity did not encourage sharing thoughts, so they kept their own counsel for days. Then at the end of the day Grizzle was grazing in a thick grove and raised his head to give Saina some advice.

The air was hot and but the sun was soft behind the peaks. A shadow passed swiftly in front of them on the ground, and Grizzle simply said in Saina's mind, *He knows.*

Saina looked up to find an eagle light on a high branch above him. Grizzle stopped. Saina formed a mental image that asked, *Seen any ferines?*

The bird flapped and rose in the air, then swooped back to a lower branch. Saina looked him in the eye, but got no response. He slowly walked under him and the eagle moved on to another branch ahead of him. There was a trail that passed through the expanse of grass and appeared to enter a dense grove on the other side.

Saina left Grizzle to eat and followed the trail with rapid steps up to the trees. The eagle was waiting in one of them when Saina arrived.

There? The grove is their home?

The bird took two steps along the branch in the direction of Saina's question.

Thank you.

Saina watched him leap into the sky and circle over the meadow. As Saina walked back to Grizzle the bird swooped low and screamed as he broke his flight in the grass. He rose with a writhing black snake in his beak, flew over Saina and held his catch as his wings beat the air to keep his place. Then he was off over the treetops.

Saina brushed Grizzle mane. *It's good to know who to ask. I may leave you here. I'm sure you can get along.*

The horse blew softly through his nostrils. He knew what to do here.

Saina moved him nearer water and tethered him loosely between trees, knowing his knot would be easy for Grizzle to pull apart. He then returned to the grove on foot. The ground was thick with growth and uneven with rotting logs hundreds of years old. He knew his movements could not go undetected.

He found another stream trickling from a ravine at the edge of the grove. It disappeared under several fallen trees and then pooled further along. He thought the trees could give him cover from both the ground level and the heights above. After sunset he heard the ferines' calls. The direction and distance was difficult to judge, for the sound glided through the waving branches and bounced among the clefts of the slopes.

He saw them gathering in the darkness of the forest ground and the branches above. He moved away from the stream cautiously along one of the twisting fallen trunks to get a better view. He slipped on some decaying flowers and thought they must have heard him. He saw the trunk was a garland tree that still had a living arm. He felt it brought him luck even though the scent was turning sour.

He waited and watched until twilight. At that point there was nothing to see, only to hear. His mind drifted with their melodies until the ferines began a chant when the first moon lit the grove.

"*Shib. Shib. Shib. Shib. Shib. Shib. Shib. Shib.*"

Hundreds of ferine silhouettes were illuminated. But it was not moonlight. He realized that one ferine had mounted a huge fallen log, and behind him came the light—covering a man.

The Being Surrounded by Light.

Every sound in the forest came to a stop. Shib spoke to them, but unintelligibly to Saina. He held forth like a storyteller, and they murmured and enthused as the story inspired them. It ended soon enough when Shib held up a bundle above his head. Saina recognized it as the scroll of Satamabode.

This brought the chant to a new height. "*Shib. Shib. Shib. Shib. Shib. Shib.*"

Shib sat and the Being Surrounded by Light shifted slightly as he took the scroll from Shib and slowly unrolled it. Then he began to read. Saina sensed that the ferines were hearing this entity in their own language—their attention was complete and their reactions followed his own—yet Saina at the same time understood it in human words.

The Being Surrounded by Light related a story Saina knew nothing of. It recounted an episode before the Founding Seers established the Ten Abodes, when the inhabitants of this land lived in their city at the foot of these mountains. A demonic foe held the basin in thrall for many years. Over time a few escaped into the mountains, but not enough to return and challenge the demon. Eventually came a young man who befriended the ferines in his exile, learned how to live among them, and saw their fighting skill.

On his behalf the ferines agreed to face the demon and defeated it under the young man's leadership. He became a savior to his own people. He joined with a wife and gave birth to the child who would become the Founding Seer. The Being Surrounded by Light explained this was the reason the ferines were always esteemed by the inhabitants of Satamabode and granted the Garland Forest as their sanctuary— with the exception of much later episodes when they were captured and caged for entertainment by descendants who had lost their knowledge of living. When the end of the story was reached the ferines became excited with cheering that formed into a song to which they danced on the forest floor. Saina edged backward to stay out of the way and settled his head against a huge limb resting on the ground in the darkness.

He could not believe what he had seen and heard. It was like a child's drama and yet it was struck him as the Goddess' truth. He began to feel the ferines' energy rising inside him. He stood and might have stepped into their dance had he not slid again on the wet blossoms below his feet. He tried to grasp tight to another limb. He felt a spinning sensation as if he was falling from a height—but without fear. He was elated—infected by the joy the story brought to bodies swinging a swirling ahead of him. He realized he actually had fallen and stretched once more to grasp a branch that would pull him up. It broke in his hand.

He laughed without reason until the memory of the horse-coper's warning came back—not to handle the bark of a Garland Tree. His hands and every spot on his body they had touched felt hot and raw. He looked at his hands in the darkness, but they were much too far away for him to see them clearly. Luckily the darkness was moving away. He was surrounded by light and incredible happiness.

He felt like singing but gave the notion up with the first croaking note he tried. Then he believed a chant was the right application of his talent. He coughed and breathed deeply and coughed again. He closed his eyes and tried to remember the chant. He didn't think it would be that hard. Then he remembered. Or was he hearing it? Yes, someone was chanting, *Shib, Shib, Shib, Shib...*

It was inspiring and he joined in loudly. The other voices stopped. Maybe he was out of harmony. Yet this was the most harmonious feeling he had ever experienced.

It's not a poison, he told himself. *It's the threshold of Goddessoma.*

He could see the movement of particles of light along his body— then within his body where fluids and particles commingled in waves. And the lights were alive. These were the gods, the devils, the creators and destroyers—making and remaking his life in the form of food and breath and blood and waste. Her divine laborers revealed. His body within the Body of the Goddess. And his eyes could see everything Her eyes took in, making and remaking the air and earth around him—all the outer world was contained within Her and within him.

There is no being that is not me as long as I am Her. There is no poison that is not medicine as long as I am Her.

This was one drop of the knowledge that was supposed to be preserved. This was the truth that lay behind all that senses perceive. The scrolls contained it, hidden in a child's story. But it was just as available from the garland tree poison and present everywhere in finest particles of every object of life.

This was the Seed. The *true* Seed. It was so simple. But without a mind to cognize it—it became as if nothing.

And these ferines understood. The knowledge connected each of them to the ferines in the story they listened to, as if threads of aether bound them. And he saw there must be an identity for himself as well. A thousand years did not separate anyone from anything. The Seers were timeless. Their knowledge was timeless. So, he realized, was *everything*—timeless and perfect and absolute. But everchanging and replaced. If one could know this, then one could know anything, be anything, create and destroy anything.

He felt a hand on his face. Two hands. Hands holding him everywhere. Hairy hands. He opened his eyes.

"You're Shib. You're my new teacher."

Yyyuuurrr immm.

"It's true, I am him. And … welcome to Goddessoma."

He collapsed into Shib's grip. It was daylight.

Saina fought to stay conscious. "How long was I like this? All night?

Shib took Saina's hand in his own and unrolled three fingers then gripped them together in front of Saina's eyes.

"Three days?"

He rose with difficulty. There were ferines everywhere around him, but he was no longer in the grove of trees. This was a field of green grass surrounded by pines. A small lake glistened in the distance. Grizzle had his head down feasting.

"You all took care of me?"

Shib nodded.

"And the Being Surrounded by Light?"

Shib nodded. *Yyyuuurrr immm.*

This was the second time Shib said it. It seemed clear the first time, but now Saina's mind was reentering the familiar world and Goddessoma was memory. "What do you mean?

Shib picked up the scroll where it lay nearby. He took the roll in one hand and pointed to it with the other. Then he hit Saina on the head with the roll and laughed.

—◦◦○◦◦—

"What a story!" Luzarain gave a rare smile and shook his head. "Is Pharmos sane? They discovered Varanos' body in the prison below the Sugorai palace—dead for many days? Apparently killed by a prisoner, who turns out to be a son of Murosaya and conveniently escaped."

Athayam dug his fingers into his beard and sighed. "The letter suggests that Varanos sought redemption and claims he left a note admitting his guilt in killing his father and Murosaya."

"Even more impressive, Varanos abdicated his Seed Bearer status. Ruryo has turned murder into gold. It doesn't even matter if we believe it. All these details are simply distractions. His declaration is that the line of Seed Bearers of Satamabode has come to an end."

"Yes. And his challenge? What are the other Abodes and the Sulatins going to do about it?"

"Well, I see Pharmos makes a generous offer to step into the title. Ruryo must be beside himself with pride. His audacity is unparalleled."

"I would like to know two things before I take a further step."

"You want to know if Daiyenso knows the truth of this event. What is the other?

Athayam lifted his head and gazed at the empty sky from Luzarain's window. "What is in that scroll that might bring some sense to it all?"

Luzarain shook his head. "It is possible he knows nothing and equally possible the scroll will tell us nothing. His Preceptor wants the Sulatins and Seed Bearers to chase their tails."

"Indeed? So have these events at long last convinced you the Preceptor is here?" Athayam gave a dismissive wave to preempt an answer and stepped into the doorway of Luzarain's quarters. "I have another communication for your information. Pavim is organizing a meeting of Seed Bearers and myself to the north. She will not let them avoid action any longer."

"She will leave without action and without thanks. And rightfully so. This has at last risen to a level above the Seed Bearers."

"Mmm. Perhaps. Yet I must go. What else should we be doing?

"Doing? Yes, anything will serve as doing. The result is already done."

"And what is that?"

Luzarain stared at the Intercessor and smiled. "In truth, Athayam, I have always believed the man in the Garland Forest is the Preceptor."

"Then why have you denied it to Daiyenso?"

Again there was a pause. "Because everything in the mortal world must have its opposite."

Ghoru held his hands behind his back, twisting the skin around the wrist of one in the grip of the other. He swallowed, then drew a long breath through his nostrils and met the eyes of Ruryo's deputy who was sitting behind a table in the only shade of the palace courtyard left in the midday sun.

He had to speak in measured words to keep his anger in check. "But I just explained the situation to your deputy outside the palace gate. You have my petition, and you have his commentary. Why do you need a repetition of the whole thing?"

These lower deputies were imported from Hanarabode, but some of the guards nearby were from his own Protectors. He ignored them. They ignored him in return. He had not responded to Panjael's call and had not participated in the revenge against the mercenaries. He felt no impulse to tell his story and was not tempted to hear theirs.

The official scanned the scroll, rolling it deftly, if reading little. "For one thing, the petition is very poorly written. Hardly understandable. In

Hanarabode a petition must be presented in a certain way. Otherwise it is hard to take the argument seriously."

"Well, in Alambarat we have a shortage of the materials required by the court. Something to do with the way your allies sacked the city every night."

The deputy's eyes narrowed. "You won't help your case with sarcasm. We heard your opponents yesterday. Their petition was quite well crafted. And they have an advocate, who has made everything clear from their side. That is the other thing. You do not have one, I see."

"No. These opponents live here in Sugorai, don't they? In Alambarat we have only our word."

"You are a soldier. That is what they said in their petition, yet you make no mention of it in yours."

"I am an innkeeper now. Retired soldier. I paid for the inn in jewels I recaptured from one of your mercenaries. The owner was happy to get them and they were worth much more than his dirty inn. He wanted no more of the business because your mercenaries were threatening to rob him of everything and kill him. It was the last soldiering I am likely to do, but I protected one of my Abode's citizens from your mercenaries. Did his relatives put that in their petition?"

He waved off the connection. "The mercenaries were part of the plot by the traitor Varanos. We were the ones who arranged to remove them. Your own Assessor Martial led the attack. Why were you not involved?"

"I was involved even before you arranged it. I killed several of them who were attacking an innkeeper and his customers. And that is how I earned an inn as my reward."

"But the innkeeper died."

"Not while under my protection." Ghoru's mind went back to memories of his earliest Protector training, when they taught him to stand alert and composed while enduring taunts from young officers who only a year before had been cadets. It used to work, but he was struggling now.

The deputy ignored anything he considered irrelevant. "What do you mean that he died later? It says in your opponents' petition that the owner was killed the very night you claim the inn was transferred to you."

"They offer no proof of this. I was not aware of his death until his relatives showed up to claim the inn. They said he had only just died and that was much later than that night. Now they tell it differently, as if to accuse me of killing him. I am sorry for what happened to him, but I did not cause it."

"Really?" The deputy gave him an appraising look. "They say there was no sign of any attack at the inn. No sign of mercenaries. I have no reason to doubt their story—no more so than to doubt what you claim. And what about these jewels you say you used to purchase the property? You admit they were stolen, and you stole them in turn. For all we know they may have been stolen from the innkeeper's family. It is absurd to say you bought the inn fairly or earned it by acting as a soldier on the innkeeper's behalf. You admit you were not a soldier at that time. You were not within your rights to act on anyone's behalf. And I must point out that according to the family, the innkeeper was killed that night and the jewels were stolen from him. There is a death record. What do you say to that?"

"I say, how did they know the jewels were stolen from him if he was killed before they saw him? They didn't know at that time he sold the inn. If they lie about that they are lying about the rest. It is simple to get a death record that says whatever you want it to say."

The clerk shook his head. "You put your case in great jeopardy with statements like that. Anyway, the death record is irrelevant. I am saying that you had no right to pay for the inn with property stolen from your fellow citizens. That is not honorable for a Protector. Assessor Ruryo is doing everything he can to return Satamabode to its prior status and every citizen with it. Therefore we can no longer tolerate soldiers taking advantage of citizens."

"But I saved a citizen. And I did not steal the jewels from citizens—I reclaimed them from mercenaries."

"Then the proper thing to do was to return them to their original owners, not buy an inn. In fact, you did not save a citizen. Had he not given you ownership of the inn, he would have remained there and would not have been killed that night. So even if you manage to prove his death was not your doing, certainly it resulted from your actions."

"Now that is an unusual point of view. I bring a perfectly valid petition to the Assessor Concordant, and as a result I am charged with theft and murder? That is mad."

"My deputy outside the gate is neither corrupt nor mad. I am only repeating what his commentary here states. It is his job to admit the cases with merit and turn away the others. He listened to your account, read your petition, and added those thoughts. But he did not turn you away, therefore we begin with the assumption that your petition has potential merit. It is my job to discover what merit that might be and how relates to your adversary petitioners. I am listening to your side, am I not? You think you are treated unfairly? It is right here for you to read. You have a right to read it." He tossed the small scroll toward Ghoru's side of the table.

"I know my rights. I served in the Protectors of Satamabode to preserve those rights." Ghoru cut himself off from suggesting Satamabode's rights had been changed. But he did not reach for the petition.

"You have a witness? A woman named—Nymia. Is she here? And her occupation is? Wait—it says in your opponents' petition that Nymia is your wife—and your partner in ownership! And she was involved in the very episode that caused this dispute."

"Being *involved* is what qualifies her as a witness. She saw everything. The innkeepers' relatives saw nothing."

"But she is not impartial. She cannot be believed. If the relatives saw nothing, they are impartial."

"We became partners by being the only ones left at the inn. The owner feared reprisals and wished to abandon the inn."

The deputy shook his head with annoyance. "The threat of reprisal was caused by you."

"I will say this very calmly. Prior to the threat of reprisal was the certainty of the innkeeper's death. I saved him. He was going to abandon the inn. I offered to buy it. He accepted. The transaction was witnessed by a woman who later became my wife."

"Do you have proof of marriage?"

"You see, the offices of the Assessor Concordant are overcrowded with petitioners as you well know. Worse in Alambarat than here. There was no time to obtain a formal marriage record."

"I cannot allow her to testify as your wife without proof."

"And if I have proof we are married, her testimony cannot be believed?"

The deputy stalled, making fussy movements to organize his table, avoiding facing Ghoru's eyes. "I cannot imagine bringing this to the attention of Assessor Ruryo. Yes, his offices are very busy, so imagine his own schedule. Only the gravest of matters go from this table to the table inside the palace door and then to him. I cannot see that this is a matter to take beyond this table." Now he looked up for an instant. "The truth will never be known in a dispute like this, where one side simply contradicts the other. But yours is the less credible by far. Even if we simply look at the principle of righteousness, ignoring fairness for the individual concerns, how could we not favor a family who has owned property for generations—over someone whose claim rests on an entirely spontaneous and probably frivolous gesture? Besides, what is an inn to you? You are a soldier, and it is your duty to rejoin the Protectors. Have you not heard of the amnesty? Do your duty."

Ghoru glowered menacingly over these last words just as the deputy glanced up to give them more impact. He could not hold Ghoru's gaze.

The deputy called to one of the nearby guards. "Go find the Assessor Martial. He was right here in the courtyard a short time ago. And get someone to watch this man—and the woman who is with him—until he arrives."

He exchanged looks with the guards. They showed regret but shrugged. Orders. And guarding a member of the Protectors who did not show up for the amnesty could be a loyalty test.

Ghoru did not move a twitch. Not until he saw the party approaching from the palace doors far across the courtyard. He knew the man's walk.

Panjael simply raised his brows slightly as he came close. He used no greeting or name. He listened to the deputy and then motioned Ghoru away from all other ears in the center of the courtyard. At last he spoke.

"What is all this about? I am told I should take you into custody as a thief and deserter and murderer."

Ghoru smiled. "Panjael, I'm only an innkeeper. Those charges would be difficult to prove." He jerked a thumb toward the deputy and looked at him with scorn. "Now I lost my inn, thanks to him. Tell me, is it true that Ruryo now spreads harmony and prosperity as his title implies? I have a lingering suspicion that everyone in Satamabode is deluded."

He held Panjael's eyes for a long moment. It ended only when he smiled. "But you are looking very fine. Not locked up below the palace like I expected. What about these stories of the mercenaries and the death of Varanos?"

Panjael gave quick glances around. "I have reached an understanding with our new rulers. But not their trust. All I can say is that truth is not what it was. My truth is I returned to Sugorai to prevent the possible slaughter of our Protectors and to kill Varanos for the death of Murosaya. Stupid maybe. I must have been in a bad mood. But by playing Ruryo's game the Protectors are alive and Varanos is dead. I am not complaining about truth."

"Sounds complicated. I should have come to you, but I thought I retired from warfare. I have a woman now. For a short time I had an inn. I wanted only those simple things. I was mistaken about the inn, but I am right about the woman. Want to meet her?" He waved her to him.

Panjael shook off the heaviness that had gripped them both and watched Nymia approach. "You have made the right choice, Ghoru." He introduced himself warmly when she arrived.

She considered Panjael for several moments. "Are we going to get our inn back?"

He shook his head. "I haven't the authority for that. I am sorry."

She bit her lip without opening her mouth. "Then you are going to take him away from me for your Protectors?"

He shook his head again and smiled. "I haven't the courage for that."

She gave a quick laugh.

"Whatever happened to your brother Saina?" asked Ghoru.

Panjael shook his head. "I have had no word." He looked around. "As you can imagine. Why do you ask?"

Ghoru shrugged. "I like him. He has something—the Sulatins must have given it to him. I cannot imagine he has quit his efforts on your behalf."

Surprise showed on Panjael's face. "The mission my father sent him on was doomed. If he still follows it, he is probably doomed as well." He sighed and added in a mumble, "It is certain Murosaya's entire family is doomed." He reached out with both arms to touch their shoulders then he turned and moved off toward the deputy to control the story that would be told to Ruryo.

"Why did he say that?" asked Nymia.

"Mmm. The story is his youngest brother killed the Seed Bearer and remains trapped in the dungeon below the palace. By his own choice Panjael walks a path narrow, steep, and twisting—trapped in a dungeon of his own making. But is wrong about Saina—I am sure of that. I hope it will not be too late for Panjael to benefit."

They turned to watch the interaction with the deputy, but in the interim he had been relieved at the table and the new one listened to Panjael without interest. Panjael gave them a resigned nod. The new deputy tossed their petition into a bin for denials. Ghoru's arrest for murder was forgotten, and it seemed to him murdering the innkeeper's relatives was the only way to reclaim his inn.

"Where does your path lead now, my love?" she asked.

"Well, I just lost another fight because of Hanarabode. Last time that landed me in bed with you, so I think good things will follow. Let's go back to Alambarat and find a new bed."

She pressed closer to him and cupped his cheek with her hand. "Do you want to find this other brother?"

He kissed her forcefully. "Let him find me."

In Arstansa, the palace city of Mesanabode Regent Pavim stood alone on a parapet. She could see the hills in the distance hiding the

Abode of her youth, and the dry wind of the plateau, snapping her hair across her face, brought back many recollections. In one forceful gust her finely boned body actually swayed to the east.

In the distance the ground had dried to gold. Dark grazing herds that had thrived on the thick green fur that came up through the snowmelt last season were now forced to snap off stiff bits of the brush that had not blown away and quickly move on. They rolled across the land like cloud shadows.

She could feel her lips drying—another childhood sensation—and instinctively she felt for a little pocket that was not there inside her coat. It would have contained the balm everyone here carried in the northern Abodes, but she was left to endure the parched feeling.

As apparently we must endure all things, she thought.

She tightened with impatience. All seven Seed Bearers had acceded to Pavim's pressure for this meeting, three had journeyed long to have a voice. Intention was not the problem, once the news that one of the Seed Bearer lines was forever broken was shared. But from the first afternoon session no one accepted more than a few words from another's mouth without contradiction or correction. They were gloomy over their evening banquet and scowled over their breakfast. When arguments were replaced with brooding reticence, Pavim removed herself to admire the single-mindedness of the wind from the castle wall.

At the sound of approaching steps she turned and saw her brother coming to her, Seed Bearer Joseresh of Navayabode. He was a slight man, with a frame similar to hers. His skin was lined by a life in this plateau weather, and when he pulled his light cloak over his head to keep the wind out he looked as if he was ill.

"Not the refined air of Virnipal, is it? The wind no longer carries summer heat now. I hear it always said that when one leaves this plateau as you did, one can never return without suffering. But it looks like I am the one who cannot take this weather."

She waited until he stopped beside her. "Who says I am not suffering?"

"Ahh. Out here? Or in there?" He gave a wave to the meeting and bounced a little to loosen his legs once he stopped beside her.

She offered a wry smile, turned, and leaned forward against the timber wall, her chin resting on the backs of her hands. "I keep going over everyone's words, and I keep going over all of Ruryo's actions. If only he had not done this one deed, then Seed Bearer Renalder's objections could be put aside. Or if only he had not committed that other act, then we could meet Orlear's hesitation. And so on and so on and so on. Until it is clear there is no response that initiates any kind of beginning. Every observation stops whatever movement we started, so there is nowhere to go."

Joseresh sighed. "There can be no resolution, Pavim, because the problems are irresolvable. You must accept that precedents are worthless. You must accept that Athayam cannot bend the strict boundaries surrounding the Sulatins. There is no right way remaining, only the most expedient way."

"That word again." She gave a curse silently into the wind.

He scratched his nose and closed his eyes to wet them. "What word would please you? Some principle or some tradition has to be broken. That is what Ruryo has forced upon us."

She answered without lifting her chin from its perch, and her voice sounded constrained. "I like *righteousness*. That word pleases me."

"Well, righteousness would be damnably simple, if Seed Bearer Qurmadi had picked a wife he could stand to sleep with and produced a few more Heirs besides the wretched Varanos. But how do you do what is right when there is no Seed Bearer to work with?"

Pavim could not help a smile. "That woman. She was like dried fruit. The tart variety. Still, why blame her? He was no pleasure to live with or sleep with, I'll wager."

"Well, what does it take? Two horses manage with a few screams and kicks and its over before you blink. I produced three sons and still had time for three daughters in the same manner. Let Ruryo come after me."

Her smile spread to a light laugh. "You have the great fortune of a wife who bears healthy children and condones you—even loves you, misguidedly."

He took up her position beside her, but rested his elbows atop the wall and put his palms to his cheeks. He grew serious. "Yes, I do. That should be enough. It is a simple thing, really."

She did not respond. She did not think love was simple in the least—in her experience. Nor was the matter of healthy children. She straightened and faced him.

"Joseresh, before we go in, let me test an idea."

He nodded.

"We have talked around Deserena many times. If we are all heading toward expediency, then I would rather bend the principle of the Seed than the verity of Seed Bearer rule."

"Agreed—and you could get agreement on that if Athayam was out of the room. You are obviously suggesting Deserena."

"Mmm. What Athayam has to give up is the fact that no cognitions will ever arise in Satamabode again. But none has come for a thousand years. We are rulers now, not seers."

"Downright blind in some cases." He turned around and leaned back against the wall, wiping his nose against the drying wind. "I am surprised to hear you make such statements, but when I listen to Athayam's suppositions about some treasure house of knowledge encased in my slimy stuff, I really wonder who cares. In any case, Deserena's supposed consort is now under Ruryo's command. I don't see her accepting a boy half her age with Pharmos as her father-in-law."

"But she does have a worthy object of her love now. You must say nothing of this, for I do not want either of them in danger, but she and Khoroas have formed the bond that could solve this."

"Be careful, Pavim. This will not be perceived as a matter of principle. We scoffed at Pharmos merging two Abodes, and there are six men in that meeting room who might forward their own interests once the gate is opened." He stopped and confronted her. "Even I find it hard to hear Khoroas is in love."

She licked her lips and then wiped her finger across them immediately. "That's cruel. It had to happen. I have been hanging on to the Regency in anticipation. Khoroas has changed—because of her."

He raised his brows. "Alright. Apart from the way you have spoiled him, let me accept that possibility for the moment. So what do we have to do? Convince the Seed Bearers that Khoroas is the right man for Deserena and nine is the right number of Seed Bearers for Athayam."

She shrugged. "You miss the point. Deserena becomes the Seed Bearer of Satamabode."

He shook his head. "A long step for Athayam's old legs. Better she had stayed with Murosaya's son for this particular purpose. A consort, perhaps. A merger of Abodes, unlikely."

"Every solution is easy to deny. Meanwhile Ruryo stalks his next victim.

He grunted.

"What's wrong?"

He took the full force of the wind in his face and the wincing expression fit his thinking. "Do you know why Athayam defends the necessity of the Seed?"

"It's no secret. It is in the scrolls."

He nodded with arched brows. "Right. It is an absolute—cannot be broken. Better said, it protects Sulatin neutrality and inaction. Listen, even Athayam accepts there is no going back to Ten Abodes—you can see the defeat in his eyes. Worse, once we make an expedient plan— whatever it is—we are now in competition with Ruryo for who leads righteously. How many men in that room will win that contest? Will I? Will you and Khoroas? Ruryo has backed us into a corner and stripped our authenticity away. For the moment—and only for the moment— Sulatin authenticity survives."

"Ruryo must be punished—better exiled, best executed. Pharmos should abdicate to his young Heir. Immediately. Meanwhile those six men and you and I must live up to the ideal of leadership I am certain the Founding Seers described somewhere in those scrolls."

"We would have to fight for it first. There is the mystery of Ruryo's weapon to contemplate."

"Our numbers would overwhelm any weapon."

He shook his head. "This is not a group that sees generosity where there is a chance of seeing self-interest, my dear. When the prize is

Satamabode, they all have sons they would want to tempt Deserena with. It would be better to cut Satamabode into eight pieces."

"Fine. I admit the expedience of my son's affections are part of the plan. But only because we cannot ask Deserena to mate with an Heir drawn by lottery. I am the one compromising principles here. I am saying a half-truth is better than a lie."

"Forgive me, but if Ryadabode had been attacked and Khoroas played Varanos' part, would you want Sevrese to make that bargain?"

She nodded. "Deserena is like a daughter to me."

"Pavim, you must rely on my bringing this to the table. Your motives are too strong and your rejection of your own principles too suspicious."

She pressed her hands to the wetness of her eyes. "No. Why bother? The six men in there and you and I and even Athayam are not ready to accept what is inevitable. Ruryo must kill us all and all our families. He is patient. It may take years. But if we linger on this decision and refuse to act conclusively and immediately, then we deserve that fate."

"If you say that in that room your cause is lost."

"If I do not say it, all our sons and daughters are lost. Ruryo has a poison for each of us. He waits only the moment when there will be no resistance—no outrage from our people. He wants to be their savior, but he cares nothing about them as long as they agree to his order."

Her brother put his arms around her. She resented it but allowed it.

"Your people will never judge against you. You are the only ruler among us who has nothing to apologize for."

She withdrew and backed up a step. "No. Even if that was true, I will be the first he attacks." She looked into his eyes deeply. "I am not going back into the meeting. I am going home to pursue my own path. I do not want to talk to Seed Bearers again."

He held up his hands in defense. "I will make the case."

She turned and left him in confusion. It was the best she could hope for from him—from all of them.

"Pavim, you can't walk out of the meeting you forced us to attend."

"This is what happens when the Seed is lost!"

Is the Preceptor the only hope? The Goddess is now destroying her creation. And who can oppose that? It is Hers!

—∘○∘❮❖❯∘○∘—

Night was far along when Saina and Grizzle finally approached the long stable yard. The whitewashed stone barn still glowed, but the moons were less generous tonight than his first time here. He and Grizzle were weary enough to be glad no one would notice them. He dismounted and a scream came from horses in their paddocks, which Grizzle returned emphatically.

So much for avoiding notice.

By the time the saddle was off Grizzle heard something in the dark and nickered. Saina knew the person who earned that sound and turned to see her running. She came to a stop a few paces away, unsure of the right greeting. It did not matter, for Grizzle was stomping for treats.

"He's tired but not hot. We walked at the end."

"Walked? I expected a gallop—didn't you miss me?" She laughed at the blank look on his face and came close to give him a soft embrace, but Grizzle pushed Saina with his head to move him out of the way.

"Oh? Jealous?" Sevrese chided and the horse only pawed the ground again. "I'll be back."

She came with a full basket of favorites, but by now the other horses were calling for their share.

"Saina, you should let me take care of this while you have a long soak. You have no idea how keen these horses are about late night parties. This will take some time."

"No, I don't want to be anywhere else."

She gave him a long consideration. He held the look longer than she did.

"How was this horse?"

"Grizzle was a great partner. Thank you for trusting me with him."

"I'm sure you were good to him as well."

The horse stamped a front foot for faster delivery, and a chorus from the stable echoed. When Sevrese had visited all of them, she invited Saina to a late meal of his own on her terrace. The hot nights were finished for the season, but the sky was rich with stars and one moon was still to come. He accepted and claimed her offer of bathing.

Later when he joined her she caught his strong natural scent. "Hot water changes everything. I suppose you spent ten years without it."

"Would you still love to live a Sulatin's life if there was none?"

"I did say that, didn't I? Yes, I think I could take it."

"What if your masters told you the cold water gave strength, when there were hot springs an easy walk away?"

She shook her head and laughed and spread her hands over the side table. "I had this voluptuous assortment of foods prepared for us, but I can have a bowl of millet ready if you want strength."

"It's a beautiful table, and I am hungrier than all those horses."

"What have you been living on?"

"Ferine hospitality."

Her mouth opened in surprise. "You must have a lot to tell me."

"I have been so impatient to tell you everything, I—I mean, I missed you very much. Miss talking to you."

She smiled and ran her hand down his arm, taking his hand and leading him to the food. She picked up a plate and filled it for him, then leading him back to the small table where they would eat. When she had settled herself, she let him eat and held back any questions that were not about the food. Finally when he was drinking tea, he described to her the ferine ways of living and told her about Shib. But he knew she was holding back the one question that drove him to the Garland Forest in the first place.

"You must have noticed when you put away the saddle that I did not return with a scroll."

"Yes, but I hesitated to ask. Is it lost?"

"No, it is in the safest keeping I can think of. I was able to study a good deal of it."

"So there is more than just the birthdays of people like me?"

"Yes, a thousand years of births, but I passed all that by. The other records of the Founding Seer were all I was interested in. Not easy to read because the writing was different then, but still engrossing. I learned that the ferines were allies of Satamabode before the Ten Abodes were founded. They are formidable fighters.

"That I know firsthand."

"Well, they believe that story is repeating. They say I have come like the one they fought with back then—he was father to the Founding Father of Satamabode. They are still loyal by the memory of their songs and are eager to take back Satamabode."

She stared. No words came.

He gave the slightest smile and shrugged. "That is what they think."

"Then you must take instruction from Bhalkavar as soon as possible."

He set down his cup. "You believe it?"

"Why not?"

"I thought I was the only one who would believe it."

"Thousands of ferines do. They seemed very intelligent to me." He hesitated and shook his head slightly. "No one has ever trusted me to do a tenth of what it will take. I don't even know what it will take." He took a deep breath and shivered as it left him. "You are generous to have some faith in me."

"No. On the contrary. Prudent. You would not know that Varanos is dead—supposedly killed in revenge by your brother. Not Panjael but Nacros—who survived the ride to the border."

"That's astounding."

No worry, no one thinks it is true. My mother has just returned from a meeting of the remaining Seed Bearers and the Intercessor. She alternates between fury and hopelessness. They have no answer to this crisis. Someone must find an answer. Why could it not be you?

"You know my thoughts. I will take the general's offer. But I must keep what I have told you—everything—to myself. I cannot give him this explanation. Not yet. Not to anyone but you. I trust you. Not that I have doubts about him or your mother. But they would both dismiss my solution as childish. You are the only one I can talk to." He gave her a glance and quickly looked into his tea as he drank.

She understood. She too looked away. "I gave you reasons not to once, but I will never give you another. You have thousands of ferines and one human friend you can depend on."

They ceased talking for a short time. Then Saina resumed.

"I am shocked that the Seed is gone. Glad to know my brother lives but both of them troubled me. Whatever will happen next to them?"

"That is the question all of us turn on ourselves and none can answer. Be happy you have one for yourself."

"I should tell one more thing. I fell ill—well, I was exposed to the garland tree poison. I was out of my mind. The ferines took care of me. Even though the bark is poison, they make it into a medicine. That is how they brought me back." He paused. "In fact, I was not out of my mind. I had perfect clarity. The tree is a miracle tree. It gave me a vision of Goddessoma. In Her Body there is always war—Her devils and gods, Her creation and destruction exist in eternal conflict, in shifting balance, in which neither triumphs. But because She keeps them in balance, we are used to feeling a sense of peace overall. Now is a time when the balance is lost—lost because we have lost our knowledge and experience of Goddessoma. That causes us to believe we are acting on our own without Her. So no longer is everything born in the right time and everything dying in the right time. And peace has slowly slipped away, leaving us only the awareness of war. We all have to play a role in the return of that rhythm."

She stretched and took his hand. "No, I was premature. You have three you can trust—the ferines and me and the Goddess."

He gave a nervous laugh. "It gets better." Their hands stayed together. She gave a little more pressure. "I also saw a man there—only once and only from a distance before my mind was overtaken by the poison. They call him the Being Surrounded by Light. And that is the truth—light never leaves him. The Sulatins talk of self-effulgence. He has it."

She gave a light gasp. "The Preceptor. That is what Athayam said—that he lives with the ferines."

"They adore him. They don't bother about proof."

"Ahh. Well, that is enough proof of why you did not bring back the scroll. It is yours now. Yours and the ferines. It contains your instructions."

"I believe it does. However—"

"You don't think it will have the same effect on the Sulatins. Or on my mother. Or Bhalkavar. Or your enemy Ruryo, for that matter."

He met her eyes again. "That is why your believing all this means so much to me."

"Saina, when I was with you in the forest even a blind girl could see you were in complete suspension. Lost to the Sulatins and lost in the world away from Prayadevale. Now you have found a spot of solid ground. It may not be in either world, but it is solid ground, and you should move around on it now, a few steps at a time. Get your bearings."

He still felt embarrassment for that time. He looked down at his bowl of tea as a distraction. On its side he saw the image of the Goddess beautifully crafted.

"There She is. You can see on her face compassion and forgiveness."

"That is mine." She pointed at the bowl. He looked confused. "I mean I formed the bowl and painted it many years ago—it is my work."

"Ahh."

"You are not aware of the diverse pursuits of a Daughter of the Seed. I have a lot more than riding to teach you." She laughed to dismiss the claim.

"I doubt even you could teach me to be a potter or painter. Do you have more examples I can see?"

She rolled her eyes, "Years' worth. But to see them you must tour the houses out there in the valley. That is where all but a few are stored. I hope our people enjoy them. Sometimes I wonder if they said, *Here she comes again, put out the pottery.*"

He smiled. "You give them to your people. I don't know anything about the Daughters of the Seed. Only what I saw in Deserena."

Her brows rose. "You say that as though you judge her. Do you know that she and I have made many visits to the families here who have sick ones or who have had misfortunes? She admittedly has not been trained to endure escapes through a hostile forest, but she knows as well as anyone what she owes to people—even those of Ryadabode. She knows the duties and the sacrifices expected of a Daughter of the Seed."

He wanted to crawl away, and it showed on his face. She laughed at him. "Saina, be easy. I am tormenting you. It is no great skill to spread some of our comforts among those who esteem us. It takes no great spirit to be generous when one has been given so much. The test of generosity is to give when one has little. You are very agreeable to admire Her image, but that is nothing to the understanding of the image that you expressed before. That is the test I aspire to pass. And it is the reason I envy your experience."

His throat tightened. He had one sin he felt compelled to reveal. "My experience as a Sulatin student is in fact clouded by one event."

Hesitatingly, he let the story out. She stared at him without replying. She reached for his hand again and took it in hers. "I can see you have suffered years of regret. I see that as these words pour out of you. You shiver at the memory. I am sorry, Saina." She let go, folding her own hands together on the table in front of her, and took a deep breath. "My family cannot avoid responsibility for the fortune of others. It is not a presumption to us but a duty. Since that day you have been able to avoid that duty, but it produced only dissatisfaction. Now you seem to have a second opportunity. Don't be ruled by that event. If you can do anything to resolve the tragedy that you believe is coming, then you must risk yourself. Risk everyone. Risk me. Nothing less will prevail."

He stared into her eyes and caught the reflection of the first blush of light emerging in the sky behind the eastern mountains. Instinctively she stood and crossed to the balcony edge, where her gaze could sweep the valley.

He followed and stopped a little behind her, closer than he had ever been to her without the aid of accident. She threw a look over her shoulder to acknowledge that the proximity meant something to her. Then she spoke to the valley extending below them. "Too late to say goodnight," she said. "Thank you."

As she turned, her hand went up to his face and slid gracefully along the back of his neck before it withdrew. She whispered, "Don't hang back in anything." She went inside into the darkness of her rooms, glancing once more at him with a look as brief as a blink. It was one he knew he would remember forever.

And into that mood walked Bhalkavar. He saw Saina on the balcony from the courtyard below and waved him down. Meeting him could not have been more different from a long and beguiling talk with Sevrese. Bhalkavar slapped Saina heartily on his shoulder.

"Saw the horse was back. I thought Sevrese might commandeer you before I had the chance."

"We had a long and illuminating talk."

"I see. Now, are you ready to learn the art of war?"

Saina felt power in the general's words. Saying yes could never be taken lightly. "Yes. Yes, General—are you willing?"

Bhalkavar's beard was covering his cheeks, but his head was still no more than fuzz, and neither one supported the judicious pose he struck. "Are you qualified for this study?" he asked. Then he answered for Saina, generously. "Of course, you are. Unequivocally. I don't mean have you played about as a soldier like the cadets I get from the first families. You know something about how to learn. But this is a late start. It takes years to perfect battle skills. You are willing to put in years?"

"I do not require perfection for what I have in mind. Just a competence—and knowledge of tactics." He paused to think. "And, I must know the art of leadership. I have had no success at it in the past. And I am not sure what to learn from my failures."

The general gave him a long, thoughtful gaze. "All right. Not years. But how hard will you work to shorten the time?"

"This will be my only task."

"Well then, we can begin this morning. Don't look surprised—the rains will be here soon. I have something special planned for you then."

Saina let out the air he was holding. He feared falling asleep in his first effort. But he nodded with gratitude and managed a look of conviction. "But, sir, please tell me—am I going outside my bounds? I don't really know what arrangement the Regent has made with Deserena and I have no compensation for what you are offering? I am not certain how these things are done. I have absolutely no means."

Bhalkavar held up his hand and thought a moment. "You need not think of these things, for hospitality has no cost. But perhaps it makes you uncomfortable to live in this palace, after the life you have led. You will be my guest. At my quarters. I have a few rooms, cold water, and a cook that would never be accepted in the palace. Forget all those pillows. You will not feel under any obligation—no need to have armor forged and expensive weapons—and you will live like a soldier. Free your mind." He laughed. "You will not find it much different from living like a Sulatin. And if you put your attention where I tell you to, you will learn what you need to know. You need trust and surrender. That is a Sulatin teaching, isn't it?"

Saina nodded. "Yes, and the second time today I have relearned it."

"Mmm. Then join me, so that we may be friends."

Saina did not mention this was his second offer of friendship as well. "General, I could not have a greater wish fulfilled."

Regent Pavim excused her Assessors just as she saw General Bhalkavar enter the hall from a side door. As they rose, she gave a series of instructions, so that they drifted out one-by-one. Even when the last of them withdrew, the general did not take a step. It was a ritual, understood by all, that he would take no precedence.

When the hall was empty but for the two of them, she rose and poured him a strong amber-colored wine from a closed jar, adding water by half. He came to stand near her but did not take the cup.

She turned from him to pace slowly. "Please, take some. Do you not recognize it? It is from my own birth Abode."

He stared at the cup and took in her disappointment. "Is it an apology?"

She sighed. "They are all cowards. Either that, or simply so shortsighted that it comes to the same thing. My storming out seemed to have very little impact. I've received apologies from all of them, but they take no responsibility beyond their concern for my tranquility. How does tranquility matter in these times?"

She set the cup down as she passed the table again. Her turns brought a flutter to the soft drape of her dress, which distracted him pleasantly.

"When I came to Ryadabode, I was fully aware that it could boast no particular stature among the Ten Abodes. But I should think after so long of my regency—when I have devoted my energy to making certain Khoroas would lose no ground by the death of his father—that I might have earned their consideration. Yet, I sway no one. My brother sends me wine and is glad to be rid of me." She stopped and smiled for an instant. Her hand gestured to the cup. "Please, Bhalkavar, I have no doubt it is good. I am only ranting."

"Nothing will happen until the rains are over. It is fortunate for us that Satamabode is the most vulnerable with a river that size. Ruryo cannot claim to bring peace and prosperity while the basin floods. But we must make ready. He will attack another Abode, and the longer the Seed Bearers wait, the less power they have."

She shot a glance to him and their eyes held each other. "I can see you think the next will be ours."

"Of course. Hanarabode, Satamabode, Ryadabode—we are a belt across the Ten Abodes from the western plains to the sea." He paused. "Not to mention you offer the only threat of reprisal and hold the last living member of the Seed of Satamabode under your protection."

She paced again to relax herself. It had no effect. "I believe I know what you are going to recommend."

"Attack Ruryo immediately after the rains."

She nodded. "Of course." She winced. "We haven't the martial strength to defeat the Satamabode Protectors and the Hanarabode Protectors combined."

"They are not combined. That's why we need to act quickly."

"What do you mean?"

"No son of Murosaya is a traitor. Panjael still works for the future of Satamabode. Of course, he is not fooling Ruryo, but he will come to our side against Ruryo at his first chance. So will his Protectors. Ruryo is no leader, only a storyteller. Right now everyone is going along with the story because there is no alternative. What if Panjael has a story of his own in mind and we are part of it? The other Seed Bearers have proven they will not challenge any change."

"Can you expand our Protectors by then?" She took several steps toward him. "Of course you can. I will appeal to all the first families to give you the rest of their sons and ask all citizens to volunteer as foot soldiers."

"And you can guide your own son into marriage with Deserena. That would help inspire Satamabode to rally to us." He looked away. "In fact, it would be all the better were he to be given his Seed Bearer status."

She blinked repeatedly at his boldness. "You think I would thrust Khoroas into this as Seed Bearer?"

"Pavim, we cannot enter this fight without accepting risks or consequences we cannot control. You will decide about your regency, not I. But he gives us the power of a Seed Bearer."

"What am I giving?"

"The love. No other Seed Bearer has the gift."

She tightened her lips and shook her head. "You ignore the weapon. And if that weapon defeats us, we will have given Ruryo that belt across the Ten Abodes more easily than if we had done nothing."

He nodded. "But we will have achieved righteous action—win or lose."

She stood very close to him, meeting his eyes. Her chest rose and fell with emotion. "You are the only one who could inspire me. Why have you waited? I needed to hear this."

He gave a careful smile. "You needed to see the others fail you first—Seed Bearers *and* Sulatins."

She turned away. "You resent that I put you last and then tell you I depend on you."

"I never go that deeply. But nothing is hidden from you. You have always seen me to the marrow."

She nodded very slowly and circled the room again. He regretted saying that. It was not the time to recall old wounds and weakness. He waited, knowing she would turn with a new face.

"You have your first recruit for this effort. What is his progress?"

He accepted the change. "It has only been a few days, but he learns in a day what takes others a month. I never correct him twice. He makes the change and the skill belongs to him. It is a good thing these Sulatins do not take up arms. They would be formidable. They understand the power of attention. None of the first family boys have any idea."

She smiled carefully herself. "Indeed. This confirms what Sevrese tells me."

"Yes, I have seen her interest."

They shared a look.

"Have you been able to discover what his success in the forest was?"

"He went to recover something stolen by the ferines. I have not asked him about his success. We shared an experience with a ferine before, so he has told me more about how they live."

"Of course. I am sure he told Sevrese, but she keeps still about that. He sent a message to Athayam, and there must be a connection." She began pacing again. "I am aware he lived among the ferines. Hard to imagine, but maybe preferable to living among the Seed Bearers."

"Did she tell you he was poisoned by a garland tree, and the ferines nursed him back?"

This brought a look of surprise. "Athayam said something to me on the boat. It seems long ago. I took him for a courteous but feckless young man. The Sulatins spoke to him at length that night, and afterward as we left the boat together we passed Saina and Sevrese. He whispered, *Take care with this one.* She remained silent for a moment. "Does *take care* mean to nurture or to beware?"

"It will be difficult to succeed at both," he replied.

She drew herself up and nodded. "Thank you for your counsel. You know your charge better than I. Meanwhile I will push Athayam for the Sulatins' research on a weapon to counter Ruryo's." She turned to leave and added. "Take the wine, if you wish. Perhaps your officers will value it."

When she left he picked up both the cup and the jar of wine and carried them outside the palace. There he poured them into the gutter of a side street.

Luzarain and the Intercessor walked astride into the knee-deep parched grass that stretched from the monastery to the forest. Daiyenso stood at the edge of the first stand of trees and folded into their wake as they arrived. When they stopped, Athayam spoke without his usual delicate opening.

"Has the Preceptor instructed you to come here then?"

Daiyenso spoke flatly. "He has. It is possible he understood your desire to talk."

"I see. It is true we are curious about a communication we received from Saina through Regent Pavim. Luzarain continues to question your methods and your allegiance, and I am losing my resolve on the other side of the question with this latest news."

Daiyenso gave a quizzical look. "I have not changed from anything I told you in the past."

The Intercessor came back instantly. "But your master has. In the past he showed no inclination to take action in events. Saina writes me a letter through Regent Pavim that says he will not deliver the Satamabode scroll to us, because he has decided to leave it in safekeeping elsewhere. He has been in the Garland Forest in the company of the ferines, which means he has met with the Preceptor. We both assume you were a party to that meeting."

Daiyenso shook his head. "There was no meeting between the two of them and no conversation. Saina did come to the forest to retrieve the scroll. He did not tell you in Virnipal that the ferines had stolen it mistakenly during the escape of the two Daughters from Alambarat. When he came back the ferines gave it to Saina and he studied it for a few days. Hard to learn much in that time. But he made the decision to return to Virnipal without it—leaving it in their care."

Luzarain cleared his throat. "Extraordinary. You were a witness to these events?"

"Not to anyone's notice."

"Well, yes. But it is abundantly clear that your man in the forest has assigned Saina a role in this drama—if not directly, then through the ferines. Which recalls your own efforts to retrieve the scroll when it was lost in Sugorai and then to put it into Panjael's hand so he could deliver it to Saina. All along your Preceptor wanted to keep it from us."

"You both seem more than curious."

"Certainly," answered the Intercessor impatiently. "We work tirelessly to bring some relief to the Seed Bearers and negotiate with Pharmos. We depend to a great extent on your observations. But if Saina has been propelled into these events by the Preceptor, then your counsel becomes questionable. You may have reached a limit in your ability to balance the two."

Luzarain added, "You give us what you see everywhere but in the Garland Forest. And that is the only information that can possibly break this deadlock."

"Deadlock? Ruryo seems to have all the advantages and all the will." Daiyenso spread his hands slowly. "In my few direct experiences with the Preceptor, I have seen no evidence that he has taken any side in this. We are not adversaries, Intercessor."

Athayam took several paces and turned to face them. "No, not enemies, but surely on different paths."

"But not different goals."

"No? I recently spent several days with the Seed Bearers, whose direction, excluding Ryadabode, is nothing more or less than to preserve their own governance—in spite of Ruryo's likely intention to end it. They care no more for the legacy of the Founding Seers than Ruryo does. Our Order has to defend the Seed Bearers' connection to the Founding Seers, while at the same time preserving the knowledge given us by the Preceptor five hundred years ago—as well as protecting our tradition from Ruryo's intention to end it. We cannot give up one for the other. Now the Preceptor appears to put the hands of a young and undistinguished Sulatin student on the reins of a vehicle the direction of which we have no understanding." He sighed. "I am not talking about enemies. I simply want to know once and for all what action best serves the highest goal. That would be the Preceptor's goal. And if I interpret you correctly, Daiyenso, that would be to do nothing."

"I see no reason to void one of our most compelling teachings. Doing-doing-already done."

Athayam gave an exasperated look.

Luzarain laughed darkly. "And if you are mistaken about his status, Daiyenso—then *done* will be Ruryo's doing."

"What would you rather have from me?"

"Instruct Saina to return the scroll, that we might discover what is contains that will resolve this impossible dilemma." Athayam's calm was lost. His hands were waving as he spoke. "What if there is an antidote for Ruryo's weapon there? The key to this lock is obviously not talking among Seed Bearers or dueling with Ruryo and Pharmos. Everything points to the scroll."

Daiyenso countered, "Luzarain, no one knows the content of the scrolls better than you do. You must have seen it before Murosaya withheld it. What do you think is contained in the scroll that could possibly give Athayam what he wants?"

Luzarain closed his eyes a moment. "A way to revive the Seed of Satamabode. I will achieve a way to counter Ruryo's weapon. That is a small thing. But if we lose the Seed of one Abode, it is as good as dismantling them all. And that is why Ruryo holds all the advantages. Not his weapon."

Athayam held up his hand. "If you are right, then what is the purpose of putting the scroll into the hands of Saina? That is not a very economical solution."

Daiyenso added, "It is not in the hands of Saina. It now resides with the ferines."

Athayam gave a long look at Daiyenso's face and a slow knowing nod. "You confirm my fears. Your service to our Order is compromised. And we are compromising your service to the Preceptor. You cannot serve two masters—even if you claim the goals are the same. You are freed of your responsibilities to our Order. If you come to us, of course I will assume the Preceptor requires it and welcome you. I wish the Preceptor would address us directly—for the least reason that I should not have to tell you this. It embarrasses me."

Daiyenso shrugged. "There is nothing in this world that can endure forever—or even for a moment. This fence you erect between us is necessary, but it will blow down like lace for all our efforts." He looked at Luzarain. "You think the same way I do."

"Yes, I always have."

The man mystified Athayam. He watched him disappear into the shadows and turned to Luzarain. "I am of a mind to go to Virnipal to confront Saina." He glanced at the sky and the clouds clotted against the mountain. "I should hurry to miss the start of the rains."

Luzarain nodded. "I believe that is prudent. However, I am inclined to confront Ruryo."

Athayam blinked. Luzarain mystified him no less.

—∘∘⊹∘∘—

Heavy clouds were creeping through the mountains of Garland Forest and down from the higher peaks where Prayadevale stood. Freed over Ryadabode they scattered and rapidly rolled over the valley sky. Heavy rain was already falling on the basin beyond, and in a few days Ryadabode would receive its share. At first the season was welcomed as relief from the summer burning of the land, but that benefit would later turn into biting cold nights, bleak snow on the high mountainsides, floods in the basins and gray days from morning until night.

In the Protectors' training compound heat of a different kind came from within. Saina dripped sweat from his helmet until he could barely see. The leathers he wore were soaked. He struggled to hold his slippery grip on the sword—long saber of the Protector officers. But he felt elation. He had bested two simultaneous attackers—only cadets like himself, but they were far ahead of him in training. And they did not lose on technicalities as most opponents in these early stages. He was quicker in body and mind.

He acknowledged them with a left-handed fist to the shoulder as was proper. And he felt a swell of victory as he did it—Sulatin training was to bow low as a denial of any competitive impulse. When his moment was over, he left the circle to watch the others. Later they would all commend and critique each other in the group. He knew he would get few comments, because he knew his defense and attack had been perfect.

At the end of the session when the day's training broke, Saina looked round the arena with the same pulsing curiosity he was used to feeling—to see if she was there.

She was. He saw Sevrese watching from a bench in shade in the distance. That made five times now. She did not stay to speak afterwards, but he was very gratified when she waved.

This time Bhalkavar was beside her, but he turned and walked away. She motioned for Saina to join her in his place, and he looked around quickly to see if it was noticed. Of course it was.

"Some progress, eh?" He shrugged when he reached her.

"Do you want to know the truth?" she asked. Her eyes bore into him.

He wagged his head equivocally. "Tell me. It is sad?"

"Your instructors are amazed at what you have shown even in this time. They have a saying about you."

"What do you mean?"

"They say you are a two-lesson cadet—one for mistakes, one for corrections. That's all you need."

His lips spread between a smile and a wince.

"And the general told me that in all his teaching, you are the only one who actually understood your own body."

He gave an embarrassed laugh. "You mean the drills about the body—first know the feet on the ground. Then the ankles and the muscles in the leg and on and on. Yes, I knew that because of Sulatin training. They teach how to move your attention to every detail, inside and out. It is part of the healing training for them. Here it is part of the fighting training. They seem to reflect each other."

"Yes, I can see that. The general said he always expected that the warrior mind is also the Sulatin mind."

"But you made me realize that first."

"Did I?"

He nodded. "You remember our riding lesson? You told me Bhalkavar says that the awareness of weapon, warrior, war all become one."

She laughed. "Yes, and I am still ahead of you with the bow."

He watched a tear of sweat release from her hairline and slide down her cheek. He wanted to wipe it away but the thought embarrassed him and he blurted out, "I think you are ahead of me in much more than that."

Her eyes widened slightly, thinking he meant to flirt. "Maybe it is just that you are still holding back."

He realized his effect and his gaze turned sideways, where Bhalkavar was watching them from a distance. For an instant Saina felt culpable—that perhaps he had caused offense in his familiarity with her.

She laughed lightly at his confusion. "There is another party you must attend tomorrow evening. My mother's. Once again Athayam will be there. He asked to see you. You wrote him, as you said you would. I wonder what you could have said to bring him so quickly."

He met her eyes earnestly now. "You know, of course."

"Yes, he will ask for his precious scroll. And what will you say?"

He just smiled cautiously. "Are many guests coming?"

She nodded. "The heads of the families that were on the boat. Athayam surely would not expose anything intended for you alone to such a group. I expect you will have a separate session."

Saina felt the beads under his wrist guard—grimy with sweat and dust. They were no help. Instead he heard himself say, "He will ask for the scroll. All I can give him is my reason for withholding it. That, he cannot accept. So—how will it end?" He felt a sinking sensation in his body. Not one he was taught to recognize as a warrior or a healer. Nevertheless it spoke to him clearly. He knew the challenge would compromise Sevrese with her mother. More so than any affection or urge he had for her.

She opened her mouth to speak, but did not. Instead she gave him a touch on his arm, and they left each other.

Saina took a long breath and watched her go. Then he looked up to the sky above the mountains. In Prayadevale, he had always lived above the final surge of summer heat and the release of the soothing rains. His summer ended with days of mists that one day simply turned into snow. The change was so natural there was nothing to anticipate, but he could appreciate how waiting for the first covering on this brilliant blue sky and the downpour that would come made people very tense.

He started toward the baths of the training compound but in the glare his eyes caught a figure coming toward him from the distance. He watched as if he could not move. His mind was not entirely his own.

He realized soon enough who it was. The Sulatin who awakened him to the wisdom of the ferines with his story on the boat. Daiyenso.

And why Saina's feet were fused to the ground suddenly made sense. A Sulatin adept was near.

"We must talk, Saina."

"Will we not be seen?"

Daiyenso shook his head. "We will not be seen."

Saina glanced around and no one was paying any interest.

"You know the one the ferines call the Being Surrounded by Light."

"I saw him. The Preceptor, you mean."

"His knowledge is limitless. You realize his awareness of you is the same. But, even so, all your actions and all your decisions are yours."

"What does it mean—that you come here to tell me this? Does he have some instruction for me?"

"No. I come on my own impulse. Since you left the Sulatins, I believe you have found a voice inside you growing stronger. Telling you what to do and what the doing means to you. It will grow much stronger much faster. But even now, you must listen to that voice. Pay attention. Trust it. Just now it came to you?"

"Yes. When I found out Athayam is coming, I knew what must happen."

"That's right. That certainty"

"You are telling me it is not the Preceptor's voice."

"It is your own. It comes to you as all things come to all of us. Through Goddessoma. That is why you can trust it. The Preceptor's voice, your voice, the Goddess' voice—all one. Do you understand?"

Saina held back. His eyes closed from the glare, and his mind suddenly remembered the rooftop, the boys. An inner voice he could hear even now as it dared them—his inner voice that spoke aloud and killed them. But those words did not come from the Goddess. They came from his anger at his father who had sent him away and his mother who had died. Yes, he understood the difference.

He opened his eyes. He was not surprised that Daiyenso was gone or that his limbs moved freely again. Shouts came from across the field. His fellow cadets were heading to the baths. Now they noticed him alone. He waved and ran casually into the heat waves rising on the training ground to join them.

In spite of Daiyenso's assurance, once Saina approached the palace dining hall he found his inner voice was annoyingly silent. Bhalkavar cancelled the training, and without that to concentrate on throughout the day Saina's mind was buffeted by questions and answers, challenges and rebuttals. But the more he projected, the more rigid he felt—not how Bhalkavar taught him to duel.

Most the rest of the guests were mingling in an outer room. Saina drifted to the edges. Pavim arrived with the Intercessor and her family. The doors of the hall opened for their immediate seating. Saina followed at the end.

To the guests the atmosphere of the evening was little different from the boatride. While the Regent and Athayam were conversing privately at their table, the guests managed a buzz of their own concerns and pleasures. This time Saina was denied seating next to Sevrese, and they watched each other at intervals from a distance. Ironically he had an empty seat beside him, which was filled by Bhalkavar just as the servers began. The two talked of training—but more awkwardly than in the general's quarters.

Even as he convinced himself that the test would come after the festivity, Saina could not contain the doubts that a potential disaster lay ahead. At the end of the meal Pavim asked for quiet and announced the betrothal of Deserena and Khoroas and the marriage to take place as soon as the rains ended. The announcement created a wave of happiness, and volume of excited conversation increased. Saina relaxed—the Intercessor would not mar the pleasure of this moment.

When the servers cleared, he saw Pavim prepare to engage Athayam with a question as she had done on the boat. Her mouth opened, but Athayam held up his hand without his usual gentleness. He gazed directly at Saina, who felt dread rising through from deep in the earth, through the palace, into the cushion below him, and rattling through his spine.

"I wish to say something," Athayam began, "about the scrolls of the Ten Abodes—something to enliven the understanding of one of your guests here tonight. Others should hear it, because today no one can be protected from the changes that may come."

If the watchers had intended to be politely attentive, now they were transfixed. Save for Sevrese, there was no awareness of the topic, and certainly no precedence for the Intercessor's attention upon someone like Saina. Yet he proceeded as if no one else were in the room.

He moved his long hair back from his cheek momentarily and fingered the thin strand of beads that hung down below his chest.

"How well is the scroll of Ryadabode known?" He looked around at the blank faces. "Not at all. Should this not surprise you? Your own Founding Seer—and yet, his words remain closed away from you?" He smiled. "When our Order was founded five hundred years ago, the scrolls were all sent to Prayadevale with the belief that the knowledge within them would from then on be entrusted to us. Each scroll is vital. Each one is a creation of its own. Together they make a powerful whole. And this whole knowledge, when—let us say—it is properly understood and expressed, can give rise to the highest states of mind. States when pure knowledge dawns in the awareness. When the forms that govern our life—what we call our gods and devils dwelling in Goddessoma— themselves manifest to our senses. Then the Body of the Goddess is open to us—from which we came and in which we live and to which we go when we die, for Goddessoma encompasses everything. In that realm all desires arise, and with only a whispered asking all desires are easily granted. In short, with the scrolls the divine world ceases to be hidden from human minds."

Saina hardly felt he inhabited his body—but he was far from Goddessoma. Now Athayam drew a mark on him to aim his words.

"One scroll has been withdrawn from us. Only one. It is only a tenth of the sum, yet without it the whole will never be realized. As a result, we Sulatins have lost our status as custodians of knowledge. Now one Seed Bearer line has been withdrawn from the Ten Abodes. You feel the confusion and anxiety. It is no different for the Sulatin Order to lose one Abode scroll. When ten is the whole, nine are nothing. The realization paralyzes us.

"We have attempted in every way to compensate for the shortcoming, but inevitably failure lies ahead. Knowledge is destined to remain incomplete. Life will fall out of balance. Conflict is inevitable. And here is the time when the Sulatins fail to perform their sacred office. Everyone here—everyone in the Ten Abodes—will suffer as a result."

He paused and broke the gaze with Saina, but now everyone in the banquet hall was drawn to him instead. The Intercessor then scanned the room and ended with Saina again.

"We may say the unfortunate action that removed the scroll transpired when Seed Bearer Qurmadi and his Assessor Martial Murosaya refused to return the scroll to us twenty years ago. It was taken to Satamabode to record the birth of the Varanos, Heir of the Seed. But our members were not allowed to bring it back. Nor was any explanation given.

"Now, so many years later, when I learned that Murosaya released the scroll to return it to its natural home through you, Saina, I believed that at least one good could come of this tragedy we currently endure. It seemed, in the face of defeat Murosaya admitted to himself the jeopardy he had placed the precious scroll in—not to mention the knowledge behind it. But it turned out I was overconfident in that belief. First report was that the scroll was left in safekeeping during your escape through the Garland Forest. The second report was that you recovered it but would not return it to Prayadevale—in defiance, like your father. I came here tonight not to enjoy the hospitality of Ryadabode, or to appreciate this comforting news of joining an Heir and a Daughter in marriage, but to confront you in the hope that I have misunderstood these unusual facts."

He stopped and Saina twisted. The rest of the guests were overwhelmed. Every eye was upon him with confusion, shock, and accusation growing rapidly. He had to stumble ahead. He had to measure out his resistance even beyond his father's so all would see his intention. Yet he did not know his intention—only the surety that he must trust himself. He realized that was not an answer acceptable to anyone in this room save one. And she was the only one not looking at him.

"Intercessor, you ascribe sinister motives to my father. In fact, no one alive knows why he did this. Can you expect me to believe that he wanted to set in motion an era of destruction? It casts a foul shadow over my father and the late Seed Bearer and insults them both—based only on supposition."

Some of the guests clutched their chests.

Athayam waited, as if he could be more interested in rearranging of the folds of his robe. He began speaking before he had settled it. "If a warrior of Murosaya's stature takes such a position, it cannot be other than an insult to the Sulatins, to the Seed Bearer of every Abode, and to all the people who live within the boundaries of the Ten Abodes. But let us ignore the past, where cause and effect are now impossible to account for. We must look to the future. The only relevant concern is the scroll—and the knowledge it holds—reaching its safekeeping. And it is you who commands cause and effect for the future. You have replaced your father. A noble act usually. But is it your intention to make everyone endure an era of destruction?"

Saina took heart. This was artifice. He did not accept it. He must challenge it. Athayam was asking Saina to defy him. But was it a trap, or some symbolic act? He felt more lost than in the Garland Forest. In the pause, he leapt.

"Forgive my persistence, but you have quite clearly concluded that without my father there would there have been no Ruryo. That without his act the Seed of Satamabode would not have ended. And you are now implying that without me, there can be no resolution to this conflict and all the disruption and suffering it will cause. Do you expect anyone to believe that with the scroll you can restore the Seed of Satamabode?"

"It is possible—no, I believe it is probable that the scrolls contain a way to restore what the Seed of Satamabode contains. The scrolls record the cognitions of the Founding Seers. Just as their cognitions pass through the Seed, we can conclude that understanding of the cognitions may also cross generations by their words. The hand of the Seer touched the brush that touched the ink that touched the fiber of the scroll." He paused a moment to let the image sink in. "But we can only prove that conjecture when the scroll that is missing is returned."

He may be right. It was in my vision in the forest. I saw the knowledge is everywhere, behind everything, within everything. And it really is there in the words, in the ink, in the cloth. So, yes, perhaps the Sulatins could perform this miracle of resurrection.

But the inner voice stopped him. The thought came into Saina's head, *Don't hold back!* And what he could not hold back was his impulse to attack Athayam.

He shook his head. "So little. So late. Soon half a year will have passed, and the power of the Sulatins has been so slight that they cannot act against Hanarabode. They cannot bring concerted action by the remaining Abodes. They have let a Seed Bearer line expire. They are fearful that Ruryo intends to destroy the Order. The only conjecture to be proved is whether Ruryo is right about the governance of the Ten Abodes. Whether the Sulatins should even be granted a look at the last scroll. Whether they would even have the knowledge to find what they hope is there."

Tension froze every hand round the table. Saina did not look at any of them. But he saw all around him in the air—in the aether behind the air—spirits and devils and gods agitated like a pride of montane cats choosing a leader. This meeting was far more than words waged between Athayam and himself.

The Intercessor merely smiled. "I wanted to hear you voice that opinion. I hoped to inspire it in you. Your challenge requires we examine a greater truth—beyond the Seed and beyond the scrolls." He nodded for a few moments. "That truth is, over time, all knowledge becomes weakened. We see it happen through the abuse of knowledge by mortal man in countless ways. One man expresses a thought that passes to another and again to another. Even in a short chain of interactions, the meaning the first man took from the thought is no longer his. Because of the pattern of all life—creation is followed by dissolution. And preceded by it—all destruction gives way to creation. We need not look for individual causes, when in fact that is simply how life itself moves. It is all the play of the great Goddess, expressed by Her eternal Body. Thus, to our shaded human sight, it appears that some events form the beginning of a chain, the links of which add one-by-one, until the chain is finally capable of binding its own creators. If this act with the scroll can be seen as the beginning of a sequence of destructive events, then we may feel secure that life will respond. Perhaps in this case, with the reappearance of the Preceptor our knowledge will be reborn. From that perspective, Satamabode takes a heroic stance, and Murosaya has offered the most complete sacrifice possible."

Saina weighed this. He had some difficulty imagining Murosaya knowingly serving as an instrument of divine purpose. "Then it follows, does it not, that when the Order was founded the very plan that established its existence contained its destruction. It was the Preceptor five hundred years ago who created the plan. And must we not conclude he did so consciously? In which case Murosaya's deed was unconscious. And mine. We are flaws placed within the plan by a greater mind."

Athayam showed no impatience. He now seemed to enjoy the discourse, however uncomfortable and utterly confused it made the rest of those present. "It is inappropriate to speak of conscious action. The Preceptor functions from the level of Goddessoma. Life itself organizes his actions. Life is perfection. Her perfection. Yet to us Her perfection is unintelligible. In the mortal world how can creation and destruction equally bring bliss? We can see only comparison—perfection is defined as no flaws. You would have it that Murosaya's act was a grain of sand in a shoe. Eventually the wearer must take off the shoe. But on a perfectly smooth surface the only way to walk is to spread grains of sand so our shoes will grip. The unbounded, eternal Mother is smooth like the finest polished stone. Without the sand, we cannot walk upon Her creation. You are the sand." He held out his palm as if the sand was there. But his hand pointed at Saina. And everyone saw it so. "You must decide if you are the grain of sand in the shoe or the sand spread of a perfect surface."

There was a silence the likes of which none of the guests had ever experienced. It took every measure of Saina's self-control to prevent a convulsive shudder. What was this destiny that so absorbed him? He felt absurd—unready to assume the role. It was too great. Visions or not, he backed down.

"All right. Sir, I will retrieve the scroll. Who am I to presume upon this flow of eternal events?"

"But," the old man's look bore down even closer, "from what I see and hear from you, I think you have seen these eternal events."

Saina wondered urgently, *What did I really see in the grove with the ferines?* He was so certain—the seed of all knowledge, his own destiny, the mechanisms of his action. These did lead to Satamabode's restoration, which then led to a reformation of the Ten Abodes altogether, which must then lead to ... the Sulatins. All of this certainty based on taking poison in the Garland Forest. His breath quickened. His will was draining from an open wound in his soul.

"What is a vision but the most arrogant form of sight? As easily illusion or delusion."

"And what if you ask instead—who am I to refuse this current that carries me?" Athayam drew back slightly. "I came from Prayadevale to tell you myself. Do not return the scroll. If you have vision, trust it. Understand that your action begins in Her."

Saina at last saw Sevrese meet his eyes. *Don't hold back!* Then she looked away again.

The Regent could not restrain herself. "What are you saying? Forget this business of a scroll or the actions of this young man. The Sulatins will countenance this outrage by Hanarabode? They will abdicate their authority? Because righteousness has an opposite in the mortal, we cannot perform it? We simply wait? I know nothing of Goddessoma, only this world. And in this world, where Ruryo ascends, righteous action can restore the knowledge, the Abodes, the Seed, and the Sulatin Order. To wait is to die."

"My dear," went on Athayam, "What you take to be my aloofness is simply an understanding that the Goddess' nature will organize better than does man and woman. After all, it has given us a new incarnation of the Preceptor. There is no more fundamental sacrament." Then he looked at Saina. "You go ahead as you plan. To do less is to insult him."

She shot a look at Saina, but a much different one from Athayam's. In hers he saw fear—fear that Saina had become another troublemaker, perhaps more promising than Ruryo but lacking any of his potency.

A scroll did not stop a demonic weapon or a murderer. Saina was not going to stop Ruryo.

The dinner ended abruptly when Athayam smiled and urged everyone to rest. They left in fits, not knowing how to be polite.

Saina wanted a moment with Sevrese, but the room was too full of confusion. He did not want to antagonize Pavim. He felt morning would bring them together. When he gave up and turned he was confronted by General Bhalkavar.

The general blinked, his lips spread short of a smile. His head cocked almost immeasurably. Saina thought against all odds his friend was proud of him. But the look fled when he spoke a command.

"I have not announced it, but tomorrow all the cadets will be marched over the eastern slopes to our training facility on the coast. Get some sleep. It is not an easy descent—in fact we pick the hardest way we can find."

He put one hand on Saina's shoulder and quickly removed it. Then he turned and left the room.

—∞◦◦◦◦—

Sevrese slammed a cushion against the wall, dislodging a stone carving that split upon hitting the tile floor. "You betray me!" she shouted, and turned her furious eyes on Bhalkavar.

He took her attack with somber steadiness. "Sevrese, you cannot see that this is in your best interest. Certainly, you can see it is better for him."

"No. No, that is not true. You use that to justify your own meddling. You ignored me. If you have no consideration for my feelings, then let them be my affair and leave me alone. You acted only on your own sanctimonious impulses."

The general matched her. "I believe there would be common agreement that, whatever this attraction between you and Saina may lead to, it will cause more suffering than happiness."

"Thank you very much for your concern!" she spat out, and then she let the next statements each rise in intensity by measures. "But I believe you have far exceeded your authority with me. You have dishonored our own friendship with subterfuge. And you have lied to him—who trusts you far beyond even his Sulatin teachers!"

She was shaking to hold back her tears. He reached forward to her, but her arm cut at him like a sword.

The general's patience would not admit much more. His voice grew sharp. "Sevrese, surely you know it is part of the training he asked for. Every year the cadets spend the rains on the eastern shore. You make it sound as if I sent him into exile. It is no more than a day's journey. Why is this such a surprise? I could have delayed, but the rains are heavy in Satamabode, already flooding the great river. It would be deadly to climb with that pouring down a few days from now."

"You continue to deceive even now. If you had planned to send him, you would have told him. Of course it is exile! It comes a moment after his performance before the Intercessor. Do you think me so stupid as to not realize the effect his words had on you—and her?" She flung a glance at her mother who sat upon a couch on the other side of the small audience chamber. She had her legs drawn up and held them with her arms loosely. The position made her look delicate and unsteady.

"But that is not the worst of it, General," Sevrese continued. "If you knew my feelings and cared about me, you would have given us at least some time to part. You instead constructed this move in haste because you presumed my friendship with him to be more than it is. And that insults me. You made it happen as soon as you misguidedly saw signs of our affection. So do not cover the truth with *only a day's journey away,* when you know very well the trail is impassable until the rains end!"

This time his own anger broke, but he buried it within and turned to the window. At last the Regent spoke. She loosened the hold on herself and sat very straight.

"Do not exceed your own boundaries, dear Sevrese. And do not dissemble with us in your turn. In fact, it is obvious your friendship with this young man goes beyond what I or anyone else can consider salutary. Even if your accusations against our general were correct, I would respect Bhalkavar's judgment and thank him for his intervention."

Sevrese whirled in response and narrowed the force of her emotion on the Regent. "Mother, do not dare to do this to me. You think that an absence of a long season will temper my feelings, but you badly miscalculate. If I had any hesitation in my affection for him before this, I assure you, in simple defiance of your intrusion, I have now rooted it forever. When spring finally comes you may banish me or prevent his return, but it will not move my heart away from him."

The Regent let her head drift upward in her aquiline way, yet kept her gaze upon her daughter during the movement. Then she added a long regal breath, in and out. "Sevrese, before he renounced his heritage for the Sulatins, his family line was worthy of you. Yet his father is now blamed for the destruction of the Ten Abodes. And he himself is at this point apparently the destroyer of the Sulatins. Athayam sanctioned it, but let's admit most of that argument took place in the aether. Nothing I heard denies questions about the appropriateness of even a bond of friendship at this time. You are a Daughter of the Seed. The attachments of a Daughter must follow precedent. Set policies. Create alliances. It may be the same for every farmer in the valley, but for you it happens on a higher scale. Your world and theirs do not intersect on this point. You lead a privileged life, known by at most a score of girls at any time, and no one ever suggested that among those privileges was a promise that your emotions were free. Athayam shocked us last night. He displays to us that Saina is not what we think him to be. What is happening among the Ten Abodes is more profound than the happiness of one life—anyone's, yours included. We are in danger as grave as any we have known, and, amazing as it is for me to hear, Saina has a role in it. Perhaps a central one. I suspect Saina does not comprehend it yet either. Until what he really is becomes known, a Daughter of the Seed cannot commit herself to him. She would not know what her commitment would mean to the other Abodes. Surely this is not lost on you."

The first tear broke loose and streamed over Sevrese's cheek. "You are so certain of your belief and your authority," she snapped.

"I am."

"Well, I do not accept your speculations as reasons enough. You cover up like Bhalkavar does. Must you require me to relive your own mistakes to prove again you two were not the most misguided of all?"

"I beg your pardon." Pavim's tone was forbidding.

The general kept his back turned to them both. Sevrese saw it stiffen. She kicked the broken piece of sculpture away and stormed out the door.

After a long silence, Bhalkavar turned around and met the Regent's eyes. They had been waiting for his. Neither of them was going to say, *She'll get over it.* They both knew it was quite possible never to get over it.

"She is smarter than us," said Pavim sadly.

He sighed and nodded. "All the more painful to see her not win."

"Mmm. Your confidence is misplaced, I am afraid. We are too late. Our best hope is that his destiny is so profound, a new order replaces this one and they can have each other without censure. Our sort is bound to be powerless in whatever comes anyway."

He gave one quick, soft breath—hardly registering as a laugh.

Her eyes went to the window beyond him, not seeing at first. "Is that rain?" Then, quietly, "So beautiful."

"Yes. There is irony for you. I told you I should have sent them off days ago, but I delayed for this this damned dinner. I thought he would want to hear his old master, not duel him."

"Well, that brought everything out in the open. This is no longer about Sevrese's attraction and her penchant to rush every passion to completion without a second thought. She was as confused as we were last night."

He shook his head. "This talk of destiny throws everything and everyone off. I cannot accept it. He intrigues me. Perhaps he has something great within him. But there is no possible way he can even affect the state of things, let alone transform them. Training—certainly it pleases me to help and he is an excellent student. But for what? He has no stature, no influence, and nobody to follow him. What am I failing to understand?"

She shrugged. "Tell me when you have seen a performance from Athayam like last night's. In less than half a year, the world we know has been tested and fails. How do you think Athayam feels, contemplating his place in history as the last Intercessor? Under whom the Sulatin Order dissolved—was that not what he was talking about? And then, we are to leave it to this Preceptor to resolve our catastrophe, but he does not seem to take any interest in it. I have never been so bewildered in my life. Last night was a blunt reminder that it has taken me a very long time to appreciate just how addled I can be. And now I want only to gather my children together and hold on to what I do know." She lifted her knees and let her feet down to touch the floor. "In a few days I will go to the mountain retreat for the first snow. I invited some of the families last night. Khoroas and Deserena will enjoy it. Sevrese will come because I require it, and she will sulk and glower at me."

He nodded. "Hers is a mind as hard as granite—but burnished to a knife's edge."

"Yes, well"—she stood and walked to the window to contemplate the rain falling—"perhaps that equips her to deal with whatever may come better than I can." She gave a delicate wave of her hand to the sky. "You see? In the past I would have simply said, *Ahh, here it is—with the rain another year now washes away until renewal comes.* Today I look at that and wonder whether at this season's end everything I know will be washed away. Irretrievably."

They looked at each other. Both could have spoken the same thought, but each hesitated. She let it out obliquely.

"I apologize for her insult. Her—false accusation."

He nodded.

She waited a moment, turned to go, and then he uttered the words that had never come in all this time.

"It was not false."

Her eyes turned back to him very deliberately, as if she did not want to pursue it, but how could she not? "No, it wasn't. But we will speak of this now? After a silence of twenty years?"

"For me it is yesterday. It is today. It is always. It haunts me—what we could not fulfill. What we failed to fulfill. And when I see it again in her, I cannot stand to add more of that pain to life." Pressure rose on the surface of his skin, through his neck and into his temples.

She stopped. Her body was rigid. "It was you who said life would not support what happened between us—or else it would have happened, naturally. Yet, I was ready to give up everything."

He turned away. "It was not right that we should just flee. Were we to end up in some nomad camp? Your father, your whole family devastated. Two Abodes at each other's throats. I could not presume to put my feelings above that."

"Then you chose propriety over love, Bhalkavar. And presumed upon my feelings. Because I would have lived in the basest hut for our love."

His fists clenched and released. "*You* are the champion of tradition—and propriety. I was guarding that."

"That is the only choice you left me with. I am your creation."

After a long silence, she turned and left him with a solemn walk. His own gaze followed the movement of her body meticulously. His mind relived the one time he had known it intimately, as if it had just passed.

Now I know how Saina felt before Athayam—I am the cause of the destruction of our love and Sevrese's on top of that. Yet, like him, I was just trying to do the one thing to make it right.

EPISODE 7

As the alchemist followed Ruryo into the dark corridors under the Sugorai palace, he could not hold back his criticism.

"Assessor Concordant, I returned because I am extremely disappointed to learn you place so little value on these works of mine. Instead of trusting they would act precisely as I described they would, you added a poison to unnecessarily kill many worthy people. You cannot conceive of the destructive power of the Goddess. That was what I gave you. And with your inflated sense of your self-importance you thought you could improve the weapon."

"You have a lot of nerve, since what you gave me has proven useless. If there was so much power, explain why all of the remaining arrows were dissolved by a little flooding."

"You stored them underground in a flood basin during the rains, and you fault me?" The alchemist sneered. "Everyone fears you for your incisive judgment and faultless execution. You are laughable. You have thrown away the only real advantage you held—the difference I gave you. Do you think your enemies will hold back if you have no weapon?"

Ruryo reached the cell where the cartons were stored and held up his light for the alchemist to inspect his creations.

"The first rain of the season is never as hard as this was. Nevertheless if you had not made them so fragile ..."

The alchemist picked through the remains carefully, and then declared, "Not one remains."

"What?

"They are designed to break on impact so that the separate elements will mix effectively."

"I am aware of that. But a bird landing on them apparently would have done the same."

The alchemist pulled the lantern from Ruryo's hand and inspected the stains on the wall. He went into the corridor and did the same, following the walls several paces in each direction. When he returned to the cell he thrust the lamp back in Ruryo's hand and laughed.

"Do you see the watermark here? It is higher than on the walls out there."

"What difference does it make? You have only one use to me. Replace these ruined specimens. I will find another storage area."

The alchemist looked amused. "What power do you think you have over me? You will lock me up here? You had no promise from me, Assessor. You paid me nothing. I offered to help you. You blundered. You killed unnecessarily and wantonly. You executed your mercenaries whose loyalty I brought to you. You abused the Heir of the Seed waiting for the right moment to eliminate him—yet you could not wait and contrived another killing. You rely on a claim of bringing prosperity and tranquility to your citizens to earn their loyalty, but as the memory of the invasion drifts away they experience nothing that has not gone before you. Finally, you have mishandled and lost the weapon I gave you. You credit yourself a master of strategy, but you have stumbled over every advantage like a drunkard."

Ruryo felt fear for the first time since the gates of Sugorai fell. *How does he know this much?*

The alchemist laughed. "You are finally reduced to earning victory in an honorable way. Or do you have plans to poison everyone in the Ten Abodes?"

Ruryo recovered. "I have other weapons you know nothing of. Do you think I am dependent on you?" He shook his head. "It's like talking to a Sulatin."

The alchemist stepped close. "If you are too arrogant to understand how to win, then let me tell you how you can easily lose. There is one other who can destroy the Seed Bearers, the Abodes, and everything you wish to destroy. Because he understands the power of Goddessoma. Now, what if this contender brings about destruction more quickly than you can."

"You don't know what you are talking about. Who are you? Some itinerant master of dark science. By what authority do you condemn me?"

"Here is some science you may want to study yourself. If the watermark here is higher than the watermark out there, a flood did not cause this."

Ruryo swore at him. "A wave rose—that's all."

"No. This dungeon floods because the river rises too fast for the ground to absorb it. In this closed space there were no waves, only a steady rise. You can see it on the wall outside the cell. Inside the cell there was a surge of water caused by someone who has mastered *The Control of Elemental Forces.*"

"What delusion is this? You claim someone came down here and pushed the water higher. No one knows the weapons were here. No one has keys to this floor. Ohh-wait. Foolish me. If he can control elemental forces that probably means he is more powerful than locks and keys. Ha!"

"Fine. Commend yourself. That is a power you have mastered. But I know who did this."

"Tell me or you will die."

"I will not tell you, and I will not die."

"You are talking about Sulatin powers. Don't tell me you believe the son of Murosaya mastered those. He is only a hapless student."

"You have an ally in me. Perhaps he has an ally. Now that you have lost your precious weapon, the two of you can start even."

"Take care what you say. I can have you killed before you reach the Satamabode gates."

"If that was true, you would have had the power to conquer all the Ten Abodes by now. But you disappoint me, so find another way to secure your victory. Don't bother about the gates. That's not the way I come or go."

The alchemist swept out of the cell. From the darkness he added, "Understand one thing, Assessor Ruryo. The Goddess' destructive power contained in the weapon was not diluted by the rising water. When the chambers broke, the power inside was released here, and here it will stay. Anyone down here will be transformed by my part of the weapon—perhaps poisoned by your modifications."

Ruryo's head turned involuntarily in the direction of Nacros' cell.

He called, "Nacros!" No answer came. He called again, certain his prisoner was out there in the darkness.

There was a sound. Impossible to track, more the yelp of a dog than the words of a man, echoing twice then dying. Ruryo waited but no one came. He nodded to himself.

This will take time. Nacros has been reduced to a rat in the night. If the alchemist is to be believed, he is possessed by devils. But I will tame him and train him to one trick.

Saina watched the rain beat upon the waves churning toward him. Two moons came through the clouds and gave enough light to color the sea with a silver and ivory sheen. More importantly he could survey the climb ahead of him. He pulled his feet out of the sand and turned around.

The face of the bluff looked very difficult, and he had to complete that before his fellow cadets and the officers rose. Then remained the much higher climb to the peaks beyond. Another rush of foam hit the back of his legs, and he sunk further into the sand.

I can hold back and sink into this sand forever or risk everything—my life, my so-called destiny—to reach her.

His status among the rest in the camp was also at risk. To these cadets there was no Virnipal, no comfort, no family until the rains were finished. Survival must be achieved without aid of any kind. And when spring came, which was still twenty days ahead, it would be the task of these cadets to cut a new trail back over the mountain. By then they will have realized they could depend on each other—without doubts or hesitation. To fail—to incur a rescue team—would make this group the target of jests for years.

He was deserting them—only for a day. Yet he was also lying to them—a feeble story of a Sulatin practice he wished to devote a day to in solitude. If the lie was revealed, his reputation would be crushed. However he might fulfill his role in the redemption of Satamabode he would have to ask the Ryadabode Protectors and General Bhalkavar to support him—knowing he had broken the code.

Risk everything—more like throw away everything.

For what? For the ache that would not be relieved until he could see Sevrese—not even knowing whether she too felt the pain.

By the time he scaled the vertical bluff and climbed less than half the mountain he was spent. The rain roared down and ruined every possible trail. He was caked with mud. He slipped back half of every advance.

He knew there was nothing of the romantic in the effort anymore. All that was left to drive him was the fear that going down was by far more difficult than going up. When fatigue swept even that thought aside, he collapsed on a flat rock and closed his eyes. The rain beat on his head and rolled off his nose. He took a long breath and felt his mind give up thinking altogether.

The middle of the night was approaching quickly. He lay in the beating rain with the image of Sevrese in his sight, the sound of her voice in his ears, and a longing for her presence in his heart. Then the vibration came—out of the long habit of nights in Prayadevale on a rooftop with two spirits in Goddessoma.

Everything is possible in Goddessoma. He did not know the name of the power, nor the formula to initiate it—but none of the minor powers he had experience with came to him through that knowledge. They came from simply remaining settled enough to slip into the Body of the Goddess and having a simple desire upon arrival, and what could be simpler than desiring her company—comprehending it was in truth Her company?

The Goddess is everywhere. Once in Her realm I can be anywhere.

He felt his exhaustion moving off into the distance. He thought he had fallen asleep but his eyes opened to lamplight. He rolled onto his back and stared up at the tower of the Virnipal palace. He was surrounded by branches of delicate plants waving in the rain. He sat up to recognize the garden he had glanced from above when he wandered the palace in the first days of his residence. He never found the entrance to it, but he guessed it would be placed under the royal apartments. Sevrese was doubtlessly just above him.

He whispered a deep thank-you and gave a shiver. He stepped into the palace entry and made speed to find the family floor. The corridors were nearly dark. There were no guards or attendants to be seen. But having no idea who could be in these rooms, he stood forlorn facing several doors that promised his goal. He moved close enough the each to listen, but learned nothing. Then just as he left the last door with no idea what to do, it opened and a figure nearly bumped into him.

He found himself staring at Khoroas.

"Saina? What a mess you are. I thought you were sent to the training camp over the—what have you done? You crossed back? In the rains? What would possess you to do that?"

"I came to see your sister."

A slow smile crossed his face. "Really?" Then with depth, "Really?" He swallowed a laugh of satisfaction. "This will prove too good."

"What do you mean?" But Saina did not want his answer. With so little time, he could not imagine investing it in Khoroas. "I'm sorry, can you tell me which is her room? I don't want to disturb anyone else."

"Yes, yes. Saina, trust me. I am very happy you have come. She needs this. But, ahh—you cannot go like that. Come with me, and I will see to your clothes."

"I don't have time," Saina protested.

Khoroas only held up a finger and laughed softly. "Trust me. I know what must be done here. It's just midnight—time enough." He took Saina by the arm.

Khoroas' calm handmade Saina realize how fast his own body was racing. It was true—he could not arrive like this. Suddenly he believed in Khoroas. "All right, then. I am grateful."

Khoroas did not go back to the door he had left but pulled Saina away, whispering, "My room is just over here." He gave Saina a knowing look and nodded toward the first room. "Deserena."

"Then you are already married?"

Khoroas was letting hot bath water into a small bathing pool from a tank above when he laughed. "No, not yet. Tell me, are the Sulatins in truth utterly chaste?"

"Yes. Why?"

"You, too? Even now?"

Saina had never felt embarrassment about the idea before now. "Well—yes."

Khoroas smiled and ordered Saina into the water. "Some believe abstinence increases power, though in my experience so does its opposite. But at least you can avoid that inevitable challenge about the number of beds you've known. If they only knew the value of it for themselves. But their hearts are fragile, and what can we do about it?"

Saina gave a muffled complaint. "I wonder if I want to know what you are talking about. What do you think I have come for? I just want to see her. To talk to her."

Khoroas gave a look of pity. "No. Tonight you go beyond talk. She does not need a monk. She needs you. Don't hold back."

Saina shook his head in wonder.

"Do you have any idea how lucky you are to have run into me?"

"Yes, I suppose I was quite a spectacle"—

"I don't mean that. You actually don't know, do you?"

If his suggestion of guile was not so compelling, Saina would have found him extremely irritating. "What are you saying? Is something wrong with your sister?"

Khoroas rolled his eyes. "Saina, let me be your friend tonight. Your ordeal might have been entirely wasted, for Sevrese was not to be here at all. We were all up in the mountains hosting some of the families at our retreat—she and Deserena and my mother. My mother remained but we three returned this morning. Sevrese has been a dark soul for the whole time. She needs this now. And you need me. You are playing in the game of love, and you have stumbled upon weighted dice. Accept the gift and roll."

Saina wondered why he was listening to this. He did not come to make a wager in a game. He hoped for higher sentiment from himself. Yet, in fact, he *was* listening, and he knew he wanted to win. Here was a player who understood it and could be learned from. Not exactly the master Luzarain told him to find, but very well the right one for the moment.

Khoroas disappeared. Saina dressed in what he had laid out for him. It was finer than anything he had ever worn, but even so, Khoroas had taken care to choose something simple. He was gone long enough for Saina to begin to feel tense when he suddenly burst in, animated by some intrigue.

"Everything is arranged. Servants are outside to take you there. They will bring some refreshments just after, which you should acknowledge as if you ordered them. Don't even mention our meeting. She is asleep right now, but believe me you will awaken her like a bolt of lightning. Say little, leave before dawn. She will never forget." He put his arm around Saina. "Stop by after—I will have your uniform cleaned. Wouldn't want you running into the general looking shabby."

At the door two female servants gathered him up and escorted him along the hall to Sevrese's room. They entered the darkness with lamps, and then returned to draw him in.

There was a timeless moment between Sevrese's waking and her recognition of him. The innocence of a child. Dazed disbelief and a moment's paralysis—then acceptance and a flow of pure joy.

She gestured him to sit beside her on the bed and all in one motion her arms went round him. Her chest heaved a sob against his own. She cried excitedly, breathlessly, for a short time with her face wetting his cheek. Then the tears stopped, and it seemed she whispered a dozen questions before he could reply to one. The servants brought in the tray, and Saina managed to dismiss them with just the regal courtesy they expected.

He started to answer, but Sevrese put her finger to his lips.

"No, forget my nonsense. Oh, Saina, just in coming tonight you have told me all I ever needed to hear. I know what you risked. And you don't know what it means to me."

He soared. A wide smile spread uncontrollably across his face. *How,* he wondered, *could Khoroas know so much and I so little?*

His eyes took in the white and gold silkiness that wrapped her body and the sliding sounds of her movements within it. They drank whatever Khoroas had ordered but did not eat. He ventured to hold her hand in his two.

One last time he pondered what Khoroas would have him do. It did not matter now. Saina was certain what would make her happy would become clear to him somehow.

She moved just enough, without making much of it, to let him find a way to slide into the bed beside her. She put her head on his shoulder, her body pressed alongside his, her foot occasionally, enticingly, found a way of stroking across his own. The warmth, the softness of her form were sensations he could never have imagined.

Her hand slid over his shirt, as if recognizing its pattern. "You have seen my brother? Now that is odd."

"Well, I came a mess and he kept me from making a fool of myself."

"That was unaccountably nice of him."

She laughed sensuously and pressed against him. His arms tightened around her. His hands drifted on a course of their own, coming to rest at her side, between the firmness of her ribs and the subtle rounding of her hip. It was as if in that one curve he found everything that made a woman so unlike a man. He did not intend to analyze, but something deeper took hold of his mind. Ironically in the softness he felt the power of the Goddess. He wanted to follow it to its source.

"Your hand is shaking," she whispered.

"Sorry. You know I—"

"Mmm. Of course I know you have never had this experience." She smiled. "I have."

"Well, yes. I mean, it makes sense."

Her smile relaxed and with a sharper voice. "Does that concern you?"

His eyes squinted, as if looking inward. She did not want this answer to bring the rising displeasure and disappointment to her lips and offered him more moments than she would have given any other man.

He blinked and replied as if she were one of his teachers in Prayadevale. "I can't find any reason for concern." His face showed the satisfaction of reason.

A laugh bubbled in her throat. "Dear Saina, a great many very good things were withheld from you all these years, but you missed completely a great many very distasteful ones." She looked into his innocent questioning eyes and brushed them with her lips before taking his mouth with hers again, more forcefully, until the slick warmth of their mouths could not disconnect.

At length she drew away and took a long breath. "You're smiling," she whispered.

He heard himself answer, as if in the distance, "I am delirious. Every sensation …" he could not speak."

She loosened the top of her nightdress and slid it down to her waist. He saw there what he had seen in paintings and stone only. His hands melted into the comfort of her breasts. She spread apart his shirt and came up to press against him, pushing him gently onto his back.

He watched her hair surround his face with darkness and felt it stimulate every nerve of his skin. She rose to look at him again, then closed her eyes and rocked her legs and hips against his. She slowly lowered back down so that her breasts brushed delicately against his chest before he locked her in another embrace.

He hardened against her, and their breaths came in long, deep pulses, disappearing while their lips met again and again. She broke off to tug away her clothing entirely, and he followed. Then she lay down with arms stretched up to him. He was lost. His body acted without his mind. He found his place within her, felt her liquid warmth surround and invite him, heard the welcoming murmur awaken deep in her throat, and discovered the compulsive rhythm that would not stop. Nothing could contain him. He was flooded with gratitude.

Are the Sulatins mad? What is a life without this?

She asked him in a muffled voice, "Can you feel my pleasure? You are perfect."

He let his hands pass from her thighs up along the curve of her hips, beneath her arms, and into her hair.

"Tell me of yours," she demanded in a whisper, increasing the movement of her hips against his. Her look was more intense. "Tell me." She seemed to be drifting off on a cord and wanted his words to pull her back.

He struggled for coherence. "I know ... that I will keep this moment forever ... as the time I felt divine."

She smiled, opened her eyes briefly, and moments later slowed her movement on him with a series of groans, at last coming back down to him with her breasts once more caressing his chest. The change charged him with his own burst of intensity and elation. He pushed and she absorbed him, sated yet hungry at once. A long slow blowing breath came through her lips and she sank down on top of him.

It took a long time to come back to the present, but when they did they slid apart and then sought the comfort of each other's bodies in a quiet embrace—pleasure giving way to contentment. They kissed with appreciation, not fervor. Each expected the other to talk, but they were capable only of the talk of hands stroking softly.

As he held her head to his shoulder, he felt her consciousness depart and heard the breath of sleep take over. His own mind played back through all the images of the night until thoughts became intertwined with meaningless untroubled dreams.

Khoroas came to the rescue again. They would have slept until the afternoon had not his servant and one of hers appeared before dawn with the Heir's instruction that Saina must be gotten out without a question from Sevrese or himself.

Sevrese knew better than to resent the gesture.

"It is everything to me that we had this—at last. And that you endured so much to get here." She breathed deeply and shook as she exhaled. "Everything, Saina."

He put her hand on his chest. "I had to. Something has been unraveling here. Something let loose like your horses in the moonlight."

She managed half a laugh. It could equally have been a flood of tears. "You say it sweetly. But you must go. You will hurt Bhalkavar if you neglect the training he gives you. Be safe. I will depend on you."

Saina waited at the door after it closed. He heard her break down and wished that love was only happiness.

It was the end of day when Panjael strode from the Assessor Martial's private stable to the palace, having spent twenty days along the river, leading his soldiers through the annual work to repair damage from the floods. The rains were dissipating now, and the skies were broken as the clouds moved more rapidly across the basin. The sun flashed between them, turning them golden instead of gray with rain. It was a false relief. The snow melt would double the flooding.

As much work as they caused, these rising waters were the Abode's divine favor. They slowly stripped the earth from the surrounding Abodes to deposit fresh and fertile soil for the new year's planting—in turn making the Seed Bearer and the first families richer every year. The price paid by the soldiers who faced the toil each year was taken for granted.

As he entered the inner courtyard, Panjael looked down at his filthy uniform. He felt nothing of the benefits of floods, only the exhaustion they caused him. He had no intention of acting his part in Ruryo's vision tonight. He wanted to be alone. However, a glance up at the window to his rooms told him his intentions were irrelevant. Ruryo was looking down at him from Panjael's own window.

He swore and walked a little more deliberately to delay the meeting. But when he finally came through his doorway, any small relief was utterly lost.

"You got my reports?" Panjael wanted the first blow to be his own, but did not expect it to hit.

Ruryo was leaning his back against the sill, arms folded in front of him. "Of course."

"Is something wrong?"

"Not at all. I had water drawn for you. Beside the bath is a new robe to relax in. You see the tray of food and drink. I want to talk. I have a bold idea to tell you."

"Your ideas can always be characterized that way."

Ruryo gave his wry smile. "Bold to me. Challenging to you?"

"Yes, rather like that." Panjael slumped onto one of two facing couches. He was not about to bathe while listening to Ruryo. Instead he took off his belt and unsheathed his sword. Mud had slipped into the scabbard and dried on the blade. He reached for the cloth covering the plates and began to clean with it. Ruryo was simpler to listen to if one ignored all the nuances in his look.

"Here are the facts. After half a year the Seed Bearers have lost their will utterly. They remain all agreed in deploring the havoc wreaked by Pharmos. They all protest what has occurred, but the finality of one Seed Bearer line leaves them without any response. Nothing will bring Varanos or Satamabode back to life." He opened his palms as if to appeal. "Their only concern now must be that I could end all the lines." He rested on that thought for a moment. "Meanwhile the Sulatins cannot find a *power* to oppose us with. They rejected any solution with the remaining member of this family—the Daughter Deserena—sustaining the Seed. 'This I expected—even from you. It was a convenient distraction to undermine their decisions. For a time the old Intercessor dithered about retaliation, but nothing comes of that. So, his only concern now must be that I could end the existence of the Sulatins. Life is in perfect order—my order."

Panjael still did not look up from his task. "The Seed Bearers may be blind and deaf, but the Sulatins should be clever enough to know that is a certainty."

"They all cling to their fantasy of a birthright of eternal leadership or knowledge. Save one of the lot in Ryadabode."

This brought Panjael's gaze to his own. Ruryo gave a short breath as a laugh. "And she is not even a Seed Bearer."

Panjael slowly stroked the blade with the cloth. "Ryadabode is the smallest of the Abodes. Not valuable for anything beyond its own borders. You can't think she is an obstacle to anything you have planned."

"True. But she is a symbol of the ideal Seed Bearer—without the anatomy. And she can puff herself up around the Sulatins. What's more she will never bend on her knees asking for terms, even though it might inspire the Seed Bearers." He paused. "Were she to pass on to the realm of Goddessoma the Sulatins have convinced her of, she would inspire no one."

Panjael stopped his hands again. "Do not tell me you are going to kill her."

"Why—you would not?"

His hands returned to work. "It more reckless than bold given your assessment of her power over the others. It is sometimes easier to inspire when dead."

"True. But there is one way to kill her that kills only her spirit. To kill the Heir is to end Ryadabode and at the same time utterly destroy the Regent's will."

Panjael gave no reaction. But in that moment boldness entered his heart. He felt the blade shining in his hand. Ruryo had no protection here. He could save nine Seed Bearers and be treated as one on the arm of Deserena. So much more efficient that way than Ruryo's.

Never had Panjael been alone with Ruryo with a blade in his hand. The ease of it was unbelievable. Never would another opportunity come. He felt the muscles in his legs ready themselves for the leap he would have to make. The sensation of the blade entering Ruryo ribs was alive in his fingers already. It was just a matter of irrevocable decision.

Ruryo suddenly shouted, "Now!" At once a warrior burst silently from the cabinet beside the window. Another rose from behind a second couch and leaped to the table towering over Panjael. A third dropped from the darkness of the rafters with a blade pinned on Panjael's chest.

Panjael scrambled back, slashing. Ruryo cried out.

"Stop! Panjael—it is a demonstration!"

The three warriors melted back and stood still. They were dark-skinned, black-bearded, naked but for a black loincloth. They hardly seemed to breathe. Ruryo moved in front of them and showed rare excitement on his face.

"I knew what you were thinking just then."

Panjael was speechless. His stomach lurched with cold fear.

"You were questioning how Khoroas could be killed. I have been training a group of our Protectors for more than a year now. Blacksnake warriors—have you seen a blacksnake race across a trail? They can wait in silence in any dark corner, emerge silently, kill their target and slip into the night. Which is exactly what they will do in the palace at Virnipal."

Panjael was still stunned at the relief he felt that Ruryo did not know what he was thinking—yet still got the better of him. "Amazing," he whispered blandly.

"They were here the whole time we spoke, in a well-lit room, never making a sound, waiting for my signal. To notice them you have to be looking for them. Even then it would be guessing. Imagine how easy to eliminate a Seed Bearer now. I have kept them in complete secrecy. Now all their practice will be put to work."

Panjael stared at him. "How many do you have?"

Ruryo gave an exaggerated scowl that said, *Why would ask?* He paced behind them. "When I send these first three you will go with them. You four will cross the mountains to Ryadabode as soon as the rains allow. You know the Regent's palace. I know you went there with your father before."

"A few times. Years ago. The Heir was just a boy then. I have no way to say where he will be found in the palace."

Ruryo looked impatient. "How hard can that be? These men will get you into the palace unnoticed, they will do the waiting and the killing, but they cannot find him if they do not know him. You do. It should be done in one night. Then get out and back over the mountains. I am sending a large force of Protectors to Alambarat. Your men. My officers. You will meet them. The Regent will surely attack us. You will meet her famous general at Alambarat and destroy them. She will have no Heir, no army, and no more conscience or voice for the Seed Bearers. It is a perfect plan."

"You would not murder Deserena."

"Why not? She is bound to be with him. Ahh, look at your face. You have been gone so long you never got the news that she weds Khoroas after the rains. About the time you arrive, I should guess." He laughed. "She was never going to be yours. It was never part of the perfect plan."

Panjael could not think. But he knew it was not a perfect plan. It was not even a good plan. And it was going to ruin him. That was probably part of the plan. But all he really cared about at this moment was the scene in his mind—Ruryo accepting Panjael's blade in his chest—that was now torn up and cast aside.

One instant away! One moment earlier!

Saina sat perfectly still in front of the table of officers who would pass judgment on him, like any cadet of the Ryadabode Protectors. The modest military room was dank after the rains, but the sky outside was bright, and shafts of light cut through the open windows. In the glare he watched dust particles fall like a celestial shower.

Unlike his comrades who had been reviewed before him, Saina felt no anxiety facing his judges, no weight of family honor or public pride. But against the wall in the shadow behind the streaming light sat Bhalkavar. Saina had not seen him since the extraordinary night with Athayam, and there was no knowing his thoughts now. He could not acknowledge him without seeming to claim a privilege, and the general would not allow that.

The officer giving the report of his progress was now describing the final exercise of the camp in which one force attacked a stronghold held by the other. Saina had been given no command position in the battle game. His leaders had blundered badly in the beginning, losing a third of their force in a direct attack, and fled into the tidal marsh out of range of the stronghold.

"It was there," continued the officer, "that Saina took initiative from his commanders who yielded their leadership to him, as they were dispirited and vacillating. He split the force into a main one to be used as a decoy, keeping only six cadets whom he led into the stronghold without notice and took full possession just before the dawn deadline." He paused and finally nodded at Saina. "Regrettably, he lost his own life in the effort."

The second officer on the review panel took up the report. "That concludes a very impressive record of martial skills and leadership growth. If Saina of Satamabode were a citizen of Ryadabode, we would without hesitation graduate him to a command in the Protectors. Is that not the unanimous conclusion?"

The others assented, but one raised his finger slightly to take over the report. He was not one of the officers who attended the camp. "Your summary omits a curious detail in the attack Saina led. You did not just slip into the fortress. More accurately you spent the night with feints and diversions. When you finally attacked, you met sleeping defenders."

Saina nodded, relieved the curiosity was not about his so-called Sulatin exercise in Sevrese's bed.

"Tell me then—this tactic you used of exhausting your enemy through the night. What was the source of that?"

"Our losses left no alternative. We needed help—it seemed that darkness and fatigue were the only allies left. I sent the unit that was to attack in the morning off to the rear and ordered them to rest, while the others kept the defenders alert through the night and attacked only when they were dozing at their posts."

"So you risked all of your men to bet on six."

"Yes, sir. After our initial losses, the defenders could defeat us no matter what we did. But no one can defeat sleep."

The officer rubbed his chin. "Is this a Sulatin principle?"

Saina shook his head. "I learned it from the ferines in the Garland Forest. General Bhalkavar will tell you that this is how they fight."

Everyone looked the general's way, but he sat gazing at Saina with perfect patience. He gave only the slightest smile behind his now-grown beard.

"Then let me ask one more question of you. When you were inside the fortress, it is in this report that you exposed yourself to the deathblow while in front of the attack. Should a commander sacrifice himself that way—the glory of combat versus the responsibility to direct his force to victory economically?"

Saina shook his head intently. "In fairness, the limitations of the game were the cause. If we had had real weapons, none of the sleeping defenders would have been able to wake his comrades. The one who cried out actually had his throat cut, but the mock blade across the neck allows a shout. We lost our secrecy and I fell. Had not the judges fallen asleep, too, I would have been credited as a survivor."

"Ahh. But why were you first?"

"Because to lead, one must be in front. You cannot say, *Follow me*, from the rear. That is what I think, anyway."

The officer nodded. "That is one lesson on the sacrifice of the leader. But a reckless leader just as easily sacrifices his men by being killed. What he must surrender," replied the officer, "is his hunger to fight and to win the fruits of victory. Every decision is for the good of others—his soldiers, his people, even his enemy. All else is craft. That is the character of the warrior leader. Do you see that?"

Saina nodded, but as he did so the officer's eyes shot toward Bhalkavar, and he realized that the man was expressing the general's thought—the general's lesson—for him.

But now Bhalkavar stirred in his chair. "If I may, there is one entry in the report about your disappearance for two days. You did not seek permission from your senior officer. Instead you gave an explanation to one that you believed would agree—and in the middle of the night. Sleep served your goal there as well. But in this camp, as in all martial acts, all were bound together. You broke the bond. And for the sake of a Sulatin ritual? Do you still follow their teachings, or was this something outside the Sulatin experience altogether?"

How could he know? Saina felt a wave in his stomach. "I apologize to all of you. That was an act of necessity for me. Something I was unwilling to sacrifice. It makes me unworthy of your praise today, and I accept that reproach."

Now the general stood and crossed the room into the light behind the officers' table. Everyone remained silent, avoiding watching the movement. Except Saina. But the general did not face him. His gaze remained steadfast on some point outside the window.

"No one's sacrifice will ever be as perfect as the ideal you just heard or what you might have learned from past teachers. We live in a world quite below ideals, I find. It may not be everyone's impression, but I believe that good came of the event." He paused to give Saina the full weight of his look. "I am willing to simply note it and move on. But learn this—you cannot speak other than the truth to your soldiers or to your commanders. There are times when it may not be the complete truth, for you are responsible for their morale. But what you say cannot be less than truth."

There were gestures and murmurs of assent among the others. They made concluding remarks, and the Assessor Martial closed the meeting, but the general stayed, now leaning against the windowsill with his back warmed by the sunlight, blocking the golden shaft.

Saina looked at him to see if he should depart or stay. He received a nod that told him to sit again. They remained without words for a long time. Saina's gaze went to a space in the air between them. Bhalkavar's rested upon Saina's form, tracing it up and down absently. Then he shrugged. "What now?"

Saina leaned forward and took a deep breath. "General, I have a plan to regain Satamabode. I had a vision of the possibility in the forest, and now I can thank you for giving me the training to make the possibility to the next step happen."

"Mmm, I see." Bhalkavar's face remained even. "Well, I wish you well with it. But if the next step—"

Saina interrupted. "I do not have any need for Ryadabode's Protectors—not for my initial plan. I have an army for the first campaign. I may call upon the Regent after that. When I have proved myself to her. The more important gift you have already given me is conviction. Before your training I could not put the thousand doubts out of my mind. The training, the exercises here"—he faltered for a moment—"even my reckless indiscretion, have showed me that I should and can trust what I have been given, no matter what challenges may come. I can act now, and give up the rewards. I did not learn that in Prayadevale—only here, with you as my teacher."

The general straightened and paced, looking agitated.

"Conviction." The general swallowed slowly and ran his hand over his beard. "Listen, leading a handful of men in an exercise is distinctly different from leading a large force of men into real death. You have done very well, I say it again, but you have not been tested enough for what you propose. Surely, there is time in the future for this plan of yours." He stopped, then calmer, he added, "Much can happen that might aid your Abode, and you will lose the advantage of it by acting in haste."

"I understand, General. I don't mean to overestimate my ability." He breathed deeply. "But I believe this is the perfect time. Everything is to my advantage. If I wait, some of the elements of my plan may be lost to me." What he could not say was that in the ferines' world spring was for propagation, and they could not fight once they had mothers and young to care for. Something had to be made of the possibility now.

Bhalkavar puzzled over the statement and what was missing from it. "This force of yours—may I not know? It is not found among the Sulatins, is it?"

"No."

The general breathed deeply. "Good, I would have thought you mad." Bhalkavar was not even looking at Saina now. His words carried him off. "So what is left? Is it possible you met with your brother while you were in the Garland Forest?" He darkened for a moment, as if to speak more seriously. "Saina, I do not mean to trample your eagerness. If it is Satamabode's Protectors you hope to lead, your risk is too high. They are led by your brother, but they now belong to Ruryo. And so does he. If you wait a short time Pavim will order an attack by her Protectors. That gives Panjael his only chance to break free of Ruryo and join you."

Saina closed his eyes and breathed deeply. "General, I do not mean to offend you, but secrecy is a great weapon to me now. Out of consideration for you I cannot speak of it—for were you to have knowledge of my plans, then you may not be able to serve your Abode without compromise. Truth, in this case, is second to silence. If I succeed, then your attack will succeed."

The general stared at him with obvious frustration, but then he nodded. "You are right about that. Not another word." He stopped his pacing at a window that looked out upon the riding arena. "Here is a change of subject you will no doubt enjoy." He jerked his thumb for Saina to exit.

Saina walked out into the light with the general a few paces behind. Sevrese was riding in the arena. He turned to the general. "You meant what you said about…" he did not finish but Bhalkavar knew what he meant.

"A temper worse than her mother's—yet she changed overnight. Yes, I meant what I said about your effect on her." He folded his arms over his thick chest, as if the subject was now banned forever.

She was on Tamarind. She rounded her neck and turned her into a canter. They crossed the arena to meet Saina. The general walked off enough paces not to hear their greeting.

"Beautiful," he said.

"I could tease you and ask which one of us you mean."

"When you ride, there is no difference between horse and master. That's what I mean."

She laughed quietly and added, "I don't think Khoroas could say anything more gallant." Then she asked loudly, "Did you pass?"

He turned and looked at the general, who was now approaching slowly.

"With points off." Bhalkavar came up to her, and Tamarind used his broad shoulder for a head scratch. "Sevrese, our friend is going to war. He needs a horse. Your big grey would do nicely again, I think. Are you that generous?"

She hid the look of concern and composed her face. "Saina, I give Grizzle to you. He is a warrior and he is pleased to serve you."

"He is a friend, too. Thank you very much."

Sevrese smiled, nervously. "Well, if you are leaving soon, will you join me for your meal? Both of you?"

Saina would have accepted, but the general cut him off. "No, he departs tonight."

Now her look of concern could not be withheld.

Bhalkavar waved it off. "War does not start with a leisurely dinner, Sevrese. Besides, when you mother learns of this she will question him for days and debate him out of it."

"Is that so bad?" implored Sevrese.

"This war is his destiny. Don't hold him back."

Saina and Sevrese shared a glance at his choice of words.

Tamarind stamped repeatedly with a regal arch of her front leg. "Follow us, Saina, and we will get Grizzle ready together." To the general, she said, "I am afraid my invitation to dinner is withdrawn. Unless you want to see my blackest mood again."

"No, I only wish Saina had weapon as powerful as that."

Khoroas and Sevrese walked in silence through the heart of the sprawling walled garden adjoining the Virnipal palace. The morning air was moist but the scent of spring had replaced the soggy decay of the rains.

Generations of tenders had sculpted the contours of ground and rocks and trickling water, the low creeping vines and mosses, the shadows of sunlight and moonlight—all combined to trick the senses into a miniature serenity.

Sevrese sat down upon a bench surrounded by early blossoming trees with a crisp perfume. Above the garden walls gusting wind bent the top branches of spreading trees on which the first leaves were appearing. They rapped and fluttered, sending shadows to dance at her feet.

Khoroas watched the display with an introspective fascination. He wondered why he had been here so rarely. There was so much beauty to have taken it for granted. Not only for the eyes and nostrils—he was seduced by the sounds of the dripping rivulets filling and emptying the rock pools and the windsong of the pines around the perimeter.

He looked at his sister with compassion he rarely showed. "He was here for a night and left and here for a day and gone again. I am sorry." He watched her attempt at a smile. "Where did you find such a busy young man?"

She rolled her eyes. "I spent a long time angry and depressed in the mountains because Bhalkavar sent him away. But then he gave his approval and all was forgiven, and what does he do? He sends Saina off on this solitary and mysterious mission without giving me more than a few moments with him. Now I am not angry but just as depressed. It doesn't matter how they feel about Saina, they still separate us."

"I think the general was being protective. He wants Saina to have his chance but he doesn't really give him one. All the better for Saina to return quickly before Bhalkavar starts our own war with Ruryo."

"Meanwhile a wedding and Mother's renunciation of her regency."

"Mmm. I can count on the wedding, but I think she is stepping back on the regency. I respect her hesitation."

"Well, the wedding is the greater accomplishment—given your past."

He winced. "Will you always judge me that way?"

She took his hand. "You have always had my love, Khoroas. But, I admit, I expressed my censure too easily, and it probably wasn't worth a lot to you. It always seemed that Mother made such sacrifices to assure your success as Seed Bearer. You always cast them aside in favor of all her indulgences. And I worried that you might grow addicted to the pleasures of women who adored you, but who got nothing in return from your heart."

He pressed her hand a little. "Can you move on to the generous part I thought was coming?"

"It's here. Deserena has changed that, I can see. For her, you make sacrifices of your own, and that has brought you strength that was not there before." She let go of his hand and folded her own together, raising them to her lips. "Yet, it is also clear that her regard for you has only loosened a stone that blocked the path. The rest of the change is yours. As Seed Bearer. You feel that, don't you?"

He shook his head and gave another light shrug. "She can have all the credit. You may not trust this, but I just don't feel my licentious urges anymore. It seems I want to mature at last. And, I admit, in return I want you to respect me—not because I am your brother, but because I am worthy of it. Seed Bearer? Yes, I see what you are saying. That brings a different level of respect to earn."

She rose and led him on through the garden. Her pace was melancholy even though his words made her feel a sense of pride. "When Mother met with the Seed Bearers in the north, her report made them all sound self-important and deceiving. It's probably not the whole story, but it is enough to make us value what she stands for." She swung around to face him for a step. "Responsibility. Selflessness. Compassion. You will be worthy as Seed Bearer. I am not worried about you any longer. I am more worried about me."

He gave a quick laugh, "How are you unworthy?"

"Oh, I don't have to be worthy. But I am cursed. Judgmental, critical, willful."

"Well, I wouldn't stop there."

She stared at him with a wry smile. They crossed a bridge and took up the water's course off the path. A small harmless snake slid through the undergrowth and they stepped back until it settled.

"You have always battled Mother, Sevrese. But now you have both changed. She has turned pessimistic. You are forever dejected. You need each other but neither of you will shake away the mood. Now that the rains have ended and here we are surrounded by such beauty—I mean, there is so much else to think about."

Sevrese laughed at him. "You are in love, you fool. You see everything reflecting your bride. Of whom she approves—as your luck would have it."

"Did you ever think you and Mother are both made of the same material? Maybe that is all that is wrong." He pulled her around to face him. "You can see the strain has been enormous for her. The hopelessness of the Seed Bearers and the Sulatins. The weight of her standing alone with only her own conviction and her honor. Now she is willing to risk everything they will not. Then to see you turned against her as well. You say you are not angry, but you do not show her that has passed. It is not right, Sevrese. We need to be together now. Irrevocable actions are about to occur for our Abode."

The light and shadow swept her face from another gust in the treetops, and he could not read her eyes for the glare. But he knew he had cut into her, and he did nothing to soften it.

"I don't condemn you," he went on. "I don't even judge you. Personally, I like your choice of lovers. He is intriguing. But circumstances conspire against you. It may be unjust, Sevrese, but your hostility has hurt all of us—not only her. Myself, Deserena, Bhalkavar. My good opinion was never worth so much as yours. I make a small change in my ways and everyone seems to think it a miracle. But you have always had her strength and her uprightness. Your anger hurts her more deeply than my offenses. She does not need any more defeats. Make peace. Even if it is only to agree to ignore the problem for a while."

"Principles are not supposed to change, Khoroas. She decries the Seed Bearers' expedience and delay, but she just as guilty when it comes to Saina."

He laughed. "For all my dissolute ways, Sevrese, at least one talent has come to me and passed you by. I learned how to bend. If the goal is good, then bending is not bad. What principle is at stake here?"

She turned and gave a long throaty groan. She had no answer. Was it truly principle that held her back? Or was it that bending was an admission of defeat? And defeat was the acceptance that Saina was lost to her. How would his quest ever lead him back to her? He faced certain failure. And he faced it alone. But what if he succeeds? He cannot restore Satamabode. No one will thank him once Ruryo is forgotten. Yet none of this could be her mother's fault. More important, her mother had done nothing to block him and gave her consent to train him. Sevrese confessed to herself that she had not honored those indulgences in any way.

"I cannot excuse my ill temper." She gazed into his face. Her mouth gave a weak smile as her brows rose together. "I'm sorry."

He put his arm around her and drew her to him for a moment. She turned her head to him and asked, "Perhaps you could persuade her to join us here? Describe to her how the garden is entirely reborn. It offers balsam for peace. For all of us."

He placed a hand on her cheek—meaning tenderness and gratitude and the appreciation of a moment. "I will do that." Then he withdrew to find their mother.

Alone, she let her mind slip back into the illusion she had created of a life with Saina.

Why—if these feelings are manifestations of love—why should they make me seem so impoverished? So empty of my own happiness and in need of filling by his. There must be another kind of love, she reasoned, *a higher love—the love of the Goddess. I must surpass the pitiful love Sevrese feels, and find Her love with him. Otherwise love is paltry.*

As if by guidance, she turned on another garden path to find a head of the Goddess staring at her from its pedestal—one that she herself had sculpted years before. The eyes seemed sad to her now, and she could not remember that as her intent.

Did I make You so, Divine Mother? Or do You inhabit the clay and transform it into Your image in spite of my hands' work? She put her fingertips upon the head of the stature. She leaned forward and pressed her breast against the face. *Is Your pain as great as Your love?*

In time she heard footsteps upon the garden path and wished agonizingly that they could be his. But he did not come. He would not come. No matter what she felt, he would not come.

She looked up along the path where her mother was walking just ahead of Khoroas. She wiped the wetness away from her eyes, but her mother saw the remains of tears when she came beside Sevrese. She gazed into the face and felt the pain like a mother would. A subtle sigh of sympathy escaped her.

Sevrese felt it and softened. She took her mother's hand. "I am sorry I have not been attentive to you. No, I mean, I have refused you. It is horrible of me. You have gone through so much frustration. I have been so selfish."

Pavim gave a tired smile. "Let's leave recriminations behind. For each other. For ourselves."

Khoroas put his hands on both of them as if to connect them through him. "We have a wedding only one day away. I want more than just a ceasefire."

Sevrese laughed. "If Satamabode had not been attacked, this would be the most impossible event in a thousand years."

"Nonsense," protested her mother. She gave her son a kiss. "You would have found each other. Anyone would know there was one woman out there perfect for you." Pavim took a long breath. "We don't know what will happen to our world. We don't know if the ideal of Seed Bearers or of leadership of any particular kind has any value right now. But whatever door we must all walk through to get into the world that is coming, if you have love, then you can have happiness there." She paused and looked inward for a moment. "Join with her for love alone. The rest may prove to have been a thousand-year illusion."

Sevrese surprised herself—feeling no loss in her mother's words. Instead, she realized she believed in Saina's conviction.

Panjael, disguised as common soldier of the Ryadabode Protectors, waited behind a curtain outside the apartment Khoroas had entered, wondering how any mission could have been easier. Two days to cross the mountain. A few moments to obtain a uniform and dispose of its owner. Waiting a day while all of Ryadabode was celebrating something—which left the palace virtually unguarded. And now only to wait until Khoroas was asleep to insert the attackers.

The moment Ruryo had forced this task upon him, he had hardened himself to the killing. It took nothing but a few practical truths. His opportunity to kill Ruryo vanished, never to return. His Protectors drew arms only at the discretion of Hanarabode officers under imminent attack. As long as he followed Ruryo, the killing of the Heirs and the Seed Bearers was inescapable.

He waited long enough and peered out from his curtain. He stepped toward the door he had seen Khoroas enter. Out of the darkness the Blacksnakes silently joined him. They opened the door without a sound from the latch. Khoroas was not asleep. No one was in the bed. There was a lamp in the bath chamber beyond—and low voices.

The assassins immediately chose their hiding places, but Panjael walked over to the bed and saw the flowers wrapped in the colors of Ryadabode. He saw signs of a Seed Bearer marriage ceremony.

One day late. I don't suppose Deserena would come with me after we watch her husband killed?

He heard their play in the other room—water splashing, muffled laughter, lips releasing. They were getting out, drying themselves. In moments their lives would end.

He looked for a hiding place that would cover his Protector uniform. The couple appeared suddenly through the door. They were both clothed in silk that clung to their wet bodies. He stared at her beauty, and watched Khoroas' arms encircle her. But even a wedding night's pleasure could not blind them to a Protector crouched at the head of the bed.

Khoroas pulled Deserena behind him.

"What is your meaning? Has Bhalkavar sent you? What is this intrusion?"

The Blacksnakes leaped from their cover, but not quicker than Panjael's sword. He swept a blow to his left and the attacker throat gurgled with blood. A slashing blow down the chest opened the second one's heart. The third attacker flew at the couple, and Panjael slid under him and planted the blade in at the bottom of his ribs pushing it through to a finger's length from the Heir's crotch.

Khoroas and Deserena fell backwards to floor, calling for help. Panjael crashed through the balcony door and fled. As if he had mastered the Blacksnake training he slid down a column and into the night. At the same time the next night he was back in the Garland Forest.

He had recovered the clothing and food they had stashed. And he concocted the story he would tell Ruryo. Intervention by Bhalkavar was the only possible obstacle Ruryo would accept. Aided by a claim of failure in the training of the three dark warriors, it sounded plausible. And because Panjael was not expected to participate in the attack, his escape could be explained. For good measure he decided to add an episode of being hunted for a few days which would allow him to arrive much later to Alambarat and join the forces due to arrive there.

But more obsessive than making the right excuses was his confusion about his feelings at the sight of Deserena with Khoroas. The jealousy he expected did not come. To stop the murder was a decision forced by his regrets for all he had done that cut him off from her. In fact, he realized he was capable of feeling happy for her—relieved that she and Khoroas were lovers and relieved of the remains of responsibility to her and judgment for abandoning her.

I have lost all my ability to feel like a lover... like a warrior... or like a man. But I will not be a Seed killer. And it will cost me everything.

He slept in the afternoon under an outcropping of rock. It was good cover but the ground was still soaked from the rains. He awoke stiff and muddy at sunset with the intent to descend to the ruins where he had last seen Deserena—and where he last had his freedom. From there he would walk the foothills to Alambarat.

Even in the moonlit darkness he chose the rough ravines and draws and avoided the old road and even the animal paths. He was suspicious that Ruryo had spies placed in the forest to intercept him—deservedly.

Eventually he saw from the shafts of moonlight that the canopy was thinning, and he took some rest before emerging from the forest to the lower hills. He lay back in the cover of tall grasses at the edge of a small meadow surrounded by the lower altitude leaf trees.

His mood remained pensive and dispirited, until his meditations were broken by a sudden and dramatic sighing of the treetops. There was no wind to cause it. He kept perfectly still, guessing what this must be. When the loose clouds opened to the full force of one of the moons, he could see ferine silhouettes gliding across the canopy.

He estimated hundreds—but then he changed it to thousands. And near the end of the migration he heard the hoofs of a horse. A gray in the moonlight coming very near where he lay. He could not see the rider clearly until a shaft of moonlight caught the profile and he recognized with many blinks that it was Saina passing by him. Behind him, sitting faced backwards on the rump of the horse with his knees up to his chin was an old-looking ferine.

Panjael would have sworn the animal saw him—even that their eyes met. Or surely he would have picked up the scent of one human so close by. But the ferine showed no sign of fear or even interest—just a benign stare.

When the rear guard passed and the trees came to rest, he struggled with every why and how that came rushing into his mind. In the end there was only one conclusion. They were moving on Alambarat. He gave up his circuitous route and decided to follow them.

Saina could not bring death—not even the fear of death—to his enemy. His plan was only to make his enemy fatally incompetent.

He launched his first attack halfway between midnight and dawn. With a nod to Shib came a sound like a demonic wind, creeping through the chilled black air over the city and then thundering over the rooftops and descending onto the doorsteps. Three thousand ferines ringing the city of Alambarat and the camp of the Protectors outside the walls began their campaign of song and chant.

The source could not be guessed by anyone in Alambarat. No one imagined ferines. No one knew what they were capable of. No one conceived of their numbers and no one realized this was an attack. To one ear it seemed to come up out of the earth and to another it descended from the firmament. It grew. It faded. It turned round again and again. It would not stop. It awoke everyone in the city into a nightmare dread. It kept them up until the first light showed in the sky.

What only the ferines knew was that the song was simply from tale of ancient days of distress and rescue. It was commonly sung by a lone storyteller, helping his comrades settle for the night in a mood of triumph and security. No different from a story told to a human child at bedtime. Yet its effect on the Protectors and the citizens of Alambarat was shattering.

By morning in the relative silence there was talk of nothing else among the citizens and warriors. The forest was cautiously searched. Nothing was found. Through the afternoon the edginess wore off, but guards were multiplied around the city and no one thought of settling into sleep early.

The second night another outburst rose in the clear night sky much earlier, for Saina wanted not just to break their sleep but to preempt it. The effect was even more pronounced—lamps lit up throughout the city and people peered from windows to inspect the skies and console their neighbors.

The next day brought hordes of humans into the forest and the foothills above the city. They went everywhere round the perimeter. The ferines were so masterful at escape and concealment, the search was again fruitless. But Saina did not imagine that would last. On the third night the song began before midnight, and even in the darkness it brought Protectors out, crashing through the brush with the anger of deprivation. The singing stopped as soon as they neared any of the ferine positions. It was like chasing crickets.

In the morning everything in Alambarat shut down. Citizens and soldiers were falling asleep wherever they sat. And Saina responded with a sunset song that moved through the ferine positions like a twisting serpent. No one came out to challenge it. But it stopped on its own. And just as sleep came, it started again. And again. And again.

"More songs, but tonight we go into the city," Saina told Shib. "On the rooftops and at the windows. One section after another. He acted out what he wanted and then added. "You watch them all with your scouts. See that none of your people are cornered or trapped. These soldiers have a weapon that is very dangerous if you are caught in a group. You understand?"

Shib nooooss.

Once it began the screams were louder than the songs. No longer were they disembodied somewhere in the distance. Silhouettes racing the rooftops and growling against doors confirmed everyone's deepest fears. The Protectors stayed in the streets but never came close to a ferine.

Before morning Saina withdrew all of his army back into the forest. The city slept but could not rest. Dreams were filled with anxiety and fearful confusion. The absence of the threat was now itself a threat. *What next?* was on everyone's lips.

After sunset the ferines returned silently, and each one carried a fashioned branch from the forest—part club, part lash. Again a large party entered the city in the darkness, but this time they took great care to be seen or heard or scented by no one. A larger party circled the Protector's tents outside the walls. All of them waited for the word to spread.

Inside the city ferines began making random sounds—a broken window, a thrown pot rolling down the street, pounding on doors. Every citizen huddled in their darkest rooms.

Then came the most dangerous part of this battle. Saina sent his army through the Protectors' camp, stripping away weapons and forcing every soldier out into the cold night with as little clothing as possible. They were herded by the club-wielding ferines through the city gates to the largest of the buildings inside the wall—the armory—which had been emptied of weapons by Shib's teams. They were pushed inside until they were on top of each other and could not attempt to force their way out.

Saina made a thorough search of the camp afterwards, looking for the weapon he had heard about, but he found nothing that could have been so threatening. He was relieved, but he felt in truth the ferines would not have been afraid of a cloud of demons. They already faced such an enemy in the story in the scroll.

When dawn came, the city was completely within the control of solemn ferines in the streets with fierce and watchful eyes. When the sun rose and brought warmth to the air, Saina had them draw everyone out of their dwellings and guide them to the center public square.

The ferines led Grizzle to Saina, three of them riding on his back. The horse was snorting hot breath into the cool spring morning air. Saina mounted one street away from the city square and entered it surrounded by a joyful entourage with Shib in front easing Grizzle into the crowd.

Saina knew there was little chance that his army would be taken for liberators, having already paralyzed his subjects with fatigue and fear. He watched their faces as they spread out for Grizzle and realized that in all his life he had never convinced any human audience of anything. But for the two boys on the roof.

He let the beads slip down to his fingertips. One last time his mind began the names of the gods—instinctively. Then, abruptly, he shook the cord off. He looked at the beads, weighing them briefly.

Doing, doing, doing, he thought. *All along, it was done. This is just another doing. We have to eat, to sleep, to lay our plans and to win our rewards. Whether we stand before a multitude as liberator or before a mirror as a fool, none of the doing makes a ripple on the still ocean of Goddessoma where everything is already done—over and over again.*

Saina handed the beads down to Shib. Shib took them with curiosity and spun them round his fingers. Saina never saw them again.

Grizzle continued his high steps but then halted on a command Saina did not give him. In front of him stood Daivenso, anonymous in the crowd. He gave a barely noticeable smile, and turned to lead Saina forward. Grizzle followed immediately and calmly.

Saina reached the flattened mound at the far border of the square and turned Grizzle once so that everyone had time to make their estimate of the young man in their midst. With all eyes on him and whispers flying through the crowd he dismounted and went up the few steps to stand over them. He had just executed a battle plan with perfect success and won a victory without a serious casualty. He felt he earned their complete attention.

"Friends. Citizens of Satamabode." Saina paused after his initial shout, searching the faces of those in front of him. They were all silent now. He spoke in a quieter voice, but it was just as commanding. "I apologize for what you have been put through. We—my fighters and I—are not here as your enemy. We are your friends. These valiant ferines have sworn to help you regain your Abode. With me. I am Saina, son of Murosaya, who was Assessor Martial of Satamabode and the last hero in the defeat of your Abode. Lost to treachery by the very Heir himself and his master Ruryo. Now I come to help you reclaim your Abode and your honor."

It appeared to relax them—a little. A murmur washed over the crowd as they turned to each other, letting out their vexation and astonishment.

"My soldiers will not harm you. Unlike the last invaders of your city, they want nothing you own. They have given their service to me selflessly. A thousand years ago, they fought in a war that established Satamabode. The story is recorded in the sacred scroll of our Abode, begun with the teachings of the Founding Seer. All of us have forgotten those events. The ferines did not. It was my great fortune to discover their willingness and their zeal to repeat that act today. And it is your fortune—for you will owe your freedom from Hanarabode to them."

"We know we caused great tension in Alambarat. But this was the only army whose loyalty I could trust, and I had to use their skills as I could. The alternative—had I come with an army of your expectations—would have made the streets red, and all of you would have suffered ten times more. I know you do not want to go back to that.

"Soon we move on from here to our next victory. I need you to take up your work so that the city functions again. I need you to be what you were before our Abode collapsed. And I want you to have confidence that we can restore it. We can trust each other and from this trust comes resolve."

He waited for a response but there was only silence. He took another long breath. They were so stunned, so exhausted, they could not yet register the meaning it had for them. Or even whether what had happened was good for them. They stared at him without knowing what to say.

He saw a man in front with heavy bandages upon his arm, and felt a sudden and urgent inspiration. "Is this from my work then?" he asked.

The man looked round in disbelief that he had been addressed. He nodded at last.

"Broken?" Saina still spoke so all could hear.

"Yes. I think I will be crippled the rest of my life."

"So, even in my way of fighting there are casualties. Well, come up here," Saina ordered. "Let's start the rebirth of Satamabode by restoring your arm."

By the time the man reached him, Saina felt the source point of the healing energy begin to vibrate in his spine. He knew She would guide him. "What happened?" he asked quietly.

The man whispered so that no one would hear. "Well, truth be known, I fell out of bed. I was so sleepy. I cannot feel a break. Maybe just a crack."

Saina gave an ironic smile. "Just the same, it hurts."

"Ohh—Mother Goddess. No relief. What are you going to do?"

"You called out to Her just now. I will let Her set the bone to mend. That's all."

He closed his mind away from the scene in front of him, and sought the healers of Goddessoma inside the man's arm. A thousand of those gods were coursing through the veins and nerves and bone. But ten thousand devils of destruction. He asked the Goddess to stop them, and let Her creators take over—not a plea but a quiet desire.

It failed to work as well as he had hoped. It wasn't the Goddess's weakness, but his—his excitation was in his way. Suddenly he felt another hand beside his. It was Daiyenso's, and with it came a surge of Her energy. The break was mending. For an instant he opened his eyes to look upon Daiyenso's face, but he was not there. He had not moved from his place among the ferines.

There is no distance in the Body of the Goddess.

The injured man waited with a face full of suspense. His arm jerked once, and then he began to give it movement of his own. A stretch at first. Then he raised it above his head and let it rotate completely in a full circle—first one way, then another. His mouth opened but he could not articulate his feelings.

Saina imagined the joy of a gambler favored in a bold bet. His winnings he offered to the crowd. "Join me to heal Satamabode."

A hum began building around the crowd. But they still hung back. Just as he began to wonder that they would ever accept liberation, a single cry went up from a faceless voice in the middle of the crowd.

"Satamabode!" was all he shouted. He repeated it twice. Someone was there, someone whose losses in the conquest could not be swept away by the return of a few comforts and a credible excuse from Ruryo. And with him, more were remembering. There was another silence after the shouts. Much more and the cry could have faded to embarrassment. But in the moment something took hold in their hearts. The dignity, the anger they had felt months before, returned for all of them at once, and the shout rose like a thunderclap.

Even the ferines joined in. They did not know what the humans were saying. None the crowd understood their call. But the majestic way it spun out of them and flowed over the common was like an enchantment for the city. Saina listened, in part swelling with a sense of completion, in part relieved that they did not all come forward to be healed.

When it died down there was emptiness. Saina scanned the faces in front, idly thinking he could find the face of the first voice to shout.

To his surprise he saw Ghoru approaching. The man smiled at him and arched a brow to confess it had been him who shouted first. Beside him with her arm upon his shoulder was a voluptuous woman. Ghoru, looking proud, said, "Nymia."

She called out in the same way Ghoru had, "What about Sugorai?"

Others repeated the question. Saina knew it was meant as inspiration, but they might hear it as a fear of retaliation.

"We move on Sugorai immediately," he shouted. "We free any of our Protectors here who pledge their loyalty. And I will soon be joined by General Bhalkavar and the Protectors of Ryadabode." He did not mind speaking ahead of the facts. He had to pick the one outcome to hold on to and make them believe in it as he did.

There were other cries coming. Too many now to separate, and the hum rose to a tumult. He looked again to Ghoru. The captain pointed behind Saina toward the top floor of the old wing of the original fortress building from which the square spread out. This was where the dowager lived. And at an open window stood a white-haired figure, staring at the scene below her. The crowd fell into silence again.

"Who is that?" Saina asked Ghoru.

He called back softly in the silence. "Calivara, mother of the Seed Bearer Qurmadi."

Shib rushed up—guessing ahead of Saina's thoughts. *Wannnerrr here?* He was ready to bound up the walls himself.

"No. I will go to her." Saina wondered how he had forgotten her completely. Thankfully, the sweep of the city had left her unmolested in her isolated tower. Shib escorted Grizzle through the crowd with a contingent of ferines around him. Everyone stumbled backward with their eyes upon the balcony. On the way Saina motioned to Ghoru to follow. Nymia came along. Daiyenso trailed behind.

From her perch, the dark piercing gaze of the Dowager met Saina's for every step on the way to the tower entrance. When he was close enough to judge the look on her shrunken face, he could see no indication of her thoughts—only the fierce intensity of her gaze. *Surely, she must rejoice,* he thought. *Or perhaps she is senile and terrified.*

He rushed up the stairs led by eager townspeople, who were seeing her for the first time in years. The occupation forces had left her alone, out of indifference not respect. The only word anyone had expected from her quarters was the inevitable news of her death.

Two servants, a couple almost as old as the Dowager, waited at the door. They motioned the others back. Shib would not let Saina in alone, so Saina pulled him in with him. Ghoru and Nymia squeezed in, and Daiyenso followed, against the servant's attempt to close them off.

Calivara sat to the side of her heavy wooden bed on an enormous archaic throne completely at odds with the low ceiling and cramped space of the room. There were tables covered with a dusty jumble of relics. Cobwebs draped to the floor in the corners. Taken together the confusing disarray formed a single path from the bedside to the door. Saina could see that much had been thrown aside just in the moments that passed, so that she could make her way to the window.

She waved him forward and as there was no place for him he knelt. He looked into the deeply sunken lines of her face, which seemed to fix her mouth in a permanent scowl. Her body was a fraction of what it must have been when she had her health. It sat nevertheless with much of its former grandeur.

"I know who you are," she said as his mouth started to speak. "Don't bother telling me anything. I know. Come here and let me look."

He leaned close. Her hands cupped his jaw and then stroked his hair twice before releasing him. He went back into his kneeling pose at her feet.

There was an uncomfortable silence for all but the Dowager, who was smiling at some inner triumph. "You bring good news about Satamabode."

"I do." He had no idea if she was even aware of what bad news had preceded him. Whether she knew of her grandson's fate. Yet she seemed more alert to him than he would have given her credit for. "You are aware of the victory today over Hanarabode?"

"Is that what all this has been about every night?"

"I am sorry for the disturbance, but my army and my tactics are unusual in the traditions of war."

When she looked into Shib's eyes behind him she smiled. He took the sling off his shoulder and dropped on the bed the Satamabode scroll. He came close to her and she invited him onto the bed.

"When I was very, very young, we used to listen to your people's songs in a little courtyard garden, left for my privacy." She sighed. "I remember the most celestial melodious notes that guided the sun down each evening. Not all of us were cruel masters," she said with a slow nod to Shib, "but I appreciate why you rebelled. Are we friends again?"

Saina could not tell if Shib understood her words or merely read her heart, but he placed his hand upon her shoulder, seemingly without emotion at all, and she topped it with her own. He leaned against the throne and stayed there while they spoke, appearing for all the world like the counselor behind the sovran.

"What do you believe will happen to Satamabode?" she asked Saina sharply.

"We will regain Sugorai. We will push back Seed Bearer Pharmos and his army to the border, if not to extinction. We will accept your own rule, or the Daughter Deserena's. The two of you are all who remain of our Abode's Seed Bearer family."

Calivara smiled again, nearly laughed. "No one will benefit much from either of those choices. What about yourself? Can you lead people as well as you have these beautiful creatures?"

Saina was taken aback. "I have no to claim to lead. I am simply an instrument of"—he could not decide where to go with the thought.

"No, Saina, you are ill-informed." She stared at him as if to close the gap of a long, long life. "Now I will greet you as it should be. As my grandson."

To see her shift from sentience to delusion was too much for him. He felt his mouth open but could not make words come. Was he to humor her and play the part of Varanos? But had she not just called him Saina? No, he decided, he must disabuse her immediately.

"No—no, great lady, you have forgotten"—

"Don't contradict me. I forget nothing. I will tell you quickly, for the story is very, very simple. I need not dwell on anything. You suppose you are the son of Murosaya. But that was a convenience that I arranged. My own son, your father, had his reckless obsession with your mother and left her in an impossible situation. I acted for everyone's best interest at the time, pushing her to Murosaya, whose wife had died. But your father's queen was not to be appeased. She put her hatred to work with her son for the rest of her life. I believe she was responsible for your mother's death. I have no proof. I was banished to these rooms by then. But I feared for you and told Murosaya to send you off to the Sulatins where she could never reach you. He agreed, but then he confessed to me that he had refused to return the scroll they brought to record Varanos' birth. They were not happy but your mother had not yet given birth to you, and he intended to put that in the scroll. Once he did he hid the scroll so no one could take your birth away from you."

Saina's mouth opened but words came hard. "What are you saying—I am ...?" words faltered on his lips.

"Apparently a little thick. You were second Heir of the Seed of Satamabode until Varanos died. Then you became the first Heir and Seed Bearer. Don't think the matter of legitimacy means anything. It is not like women count for much in the Seed Bearer families. Wives, lovers, mothers, servants—we are all in the same condition in the end.

We don't carry the Seed but we carry everything else. The Abodes would have crumbled generations ago if legitimacy were a test. If you want proof, unroll that cloth on the bed. What have you been doing with it all this time?"

With his wits returning slowly he replied, "Actually, I gave it to the ferines for safekeeping."

"The scroll of Satamabode? In the forest? In the rains?" she said in disbelief. "You are lucky, at least. Give it to me."

He instructed Shib, who handed it to her. She unrolled it furiously.

"I read much of it. Not the lineage entries."

She snorted. "That is the only important part. The rest is all mystical ravings of the Founding Seers. Can't make sense of any of it. Here. Here it is."

She slapped at it and pushed it to Saina. "So this changes your plans, does it? Gives them something besides one useless victory? You should thank me for living so long." She laughed kindly at the look on his face. "You see, everyone thinks I am shut away up here in some cloud of insanity. It's just that you come to appreciate in time how wonderful it can be to have some lonely leisure to think. It doesn't take much to stay informed. Most of what passes for fact is nothing but gossip anyway, and if you ignore it you can live as long as I have. If that appeals to anyone."

Saina pulled the scroll to him and studied the page. He saw the name. He knew the truth. His first thought at seeing the true date of his birth was relief that the Sulatin astrologers' dim view of his prospects were wrong. "This makes everything different."

"I should think so." She held out her hand and he took it.

He took a deep and shaking breath. He felt weird to suddenly be given a relation of her stature, but he felt amazing consolation as the threads his story wrapped around him.

He also now had another dead father to mourn. A half-brother as well in Varanos. Not to mourn but to revile with some regret. And Deserena, his half-sister? How to swallow it all?

But most important—and here this new grandmother hit the mark perfectly—he perceived a power flowing through his plan that could never have been there before. No longer a fight over abstract principles, it was now invested with personal motives. He could allow himself to be driven not only by a visionary conviction that he was chosen for it, but he could feel complete justification. There was no one else. It was his fight. If it was all a design woven within the mind of the Goddess, then he was in the fabric deliberately. He gripped himself for fear of the overflow of ecstasy and anxiety.

He looked at Daiyenso. "Did you know?"

Daiyenso shook his head.

"But do you know someone who knew?"

Daiyenso smiled and let his brows rise.

"Now," Calivara ordered suddenly, "someone must take a place at the window and tell them all. You"—she pointed to Ghoru—"just repeat my words. I could never be heard."

Calivara pushed Ghoru to the balcony while she and Saina stood there together overlooking the throng.

She spoke so only he could hear it. He then shouted it line by line so that everyone could hear it exactly. After some acknowledgments it came down to this.

"The Dowager says this brave boy who addressed you today is not who he seems to be. Even *he* has not known the truth until now. I have been waiting for him since his conception more than twenty years ago. He is my grandson. He is now the only Heir who can perpetuate Satamabode. It has all been recorded in secret in the scroll of Satamabode. It is proof. If you care about the honor of your Abode. If you care about a legacy spread across a thousand unbroken years. If you are insulted to your very being at the thought of another Abode defeating you, deceiving you, procuring you with a promise of prosperity—then you should throw your bodies and souls behind Saina of Satamabode. He will be the destroyer of all that is unrighteous. He is your Seed Bearer. You are his people. May your sacrifices for each other make you one."

They listened. They wondered. But they did not doubt. They thought with a single mind. There came a cry from below louder and more wondrous than even the ferines' songs. It was the sound of his name in thousands of voices.

Ghoru turned to him. "I will raise you an army from the Satamabode Protectors locked up in the armory. May I free them?"

"Yes—and will you lead them, General Ghoru?"

Ghoru laughed. "What do I do with the Hanarabode Protectors?"

"Send them back to Sugorai so they can tell Ruryo how he will be defeated."

Daiyenso came to his other shoulder and whispered. "I am going to Ryadabode to get you a second general."

The Dowager turned to go back inside and slipped her arm under Saina's. "Well, that's done."

One figure in the crowd below was not cheering, only staring in wonder. Panjael had slipped into the city after witnessing the battle from the beginning. He had no notion of what he was to do about it.

Regent Pavim was surrounded by her Assessors, her children, and her ward. Bhalkavar stood off to the side, breaking the evenness of the wide circle, in his deference to the Assessor Martial.

The Regent looked across the circle at her daughter, who was pressing her lips and holding her arms tight to her sides. Pavim's eyes narrowed. "You have something to say?"

A peal of laughter broke from Sevrese's lips. She rocked backward and nearly kicked her feet in triumph. Finally she pressed a pillow over her mouth to try to gain control.

The Regent shook her head. "Of all the qualities of youth that aggravate someone of experience, it is the smugness that comes over you when you get one thing right."

"Heir of the Seed!" Sevrese crowed. "We had a prince here and we treated him as if he were an attendant. Well, I for one am shamed. I will send my apologies immediately." She laughed with satisfaction.

"You might begin by apologizing to Deserena," her brother cut in roughly. "And show some tact."

Sevrese sobered. "Yes, you are right. I am sorry. This news must be very disconcerting for you."

"I understand," Deserena whispered. She glanced at Khoroas. "Of course, I know your feelings, and I know I should be as happy as you that my Abode has hope. It's just one too many shocks right now."

Khoroas interrupted. "What does all this accusing mean, Sevrese? We treated him perfectly. Generously. He would never complain. If he had been aware of how things sat, then you might have a point. But I imagine he got more than he expected by far from Ryadabode. You are just trying to dig at Mother. I thought we were past that."

"No, Sevrese is right. It is not in our actions, Khoroas," continued Deserena, "but in our hearts. In my heart. To have a brother suddenly made out of someone I had given so little attention to, I feel I owe him very much." Then she gave a slow look to Sevrese. "It would not be the first time I lived under a misconception about the kindness of another."

Sevrese felt her own mouth open and close. *So the Cheki deception is finally revealed, no doubt by Khoroas—or did she know it on her own?* For the first time in their relationship, Sevrese was at a loss. To her credit Deserena handled such a delicate knowledge with dignity. Sevrese gave her a nod as if to admit a defeat, then smiled quickly with respect.

The Regent cut in abruptly. "Is anyone willing to discuss the more practical points of this news? Bhalkavar, you know his abilities better than we do. Give me your assessment."

The general let his brow rise. "My assessment? That my place in history will be to have trained the man who then assembled the greatest army of ferines the world has ever known."

"Have no fear of irony," Pavim added, "for according to Athayam Saina will probably destroy history before he is done. But how do you consider we should support him?"

The general cleared his throat. He was pleased to see Pavim in good spirits from this news. He suspected it came more from learning Hanarabode had a good beating, than from affection for who accomplished it. But clearly she was elated beneath her mask.

Bhalkavar expanded his chest. "He has tipped the rules of warfare off the edge. I keep going over what the Sulatin told me of the battle.

So extraordinary. To have as good as drugged your opponent before the battle. Attacking with nothing more than clubs. Locking the Protectors up in an oversized closet. You know, he tested it in the mock battle at the sea camp?" He paused as he reflected on Saina's admission that he learned from the ferines. "However, for Ruryo that drug will no longer work. Saina's next battle must be conventional. With what he picked up of his own Protectors in Alambarat and our number from Ryadabode, he will have a superior force. But we have nothing to counter Ruryo's weapon, which we know can destroy a force of any kind or number. Most important, we mobilized our Protectors since the attack on Khoroas and Deserena. They can be in Alambarat tomorrow."

Pavim made a restless motion, her fingers played against each other nervously in her lap. She shot another glance at Sevrese. "The restoration of the Ten Abodes is now upon us, thanks to his effort and thanks again to this news of his status. We will do everything we can to help restore Satamabode. But there is another consideration."

Sevrese stiffened.

"If he is successful, I want to know immediately what he plans beyond it. I remember every word of his challenge to Athayam. He first means to restore Satamabode. But I cannot help him take his fight to the Sulatins—Preceptor or not." She inhaled slowly and completely. "Perhaps his plan may change. But if not, we may be fighting against him as soon as we establish him in power. You understand this, general?"

Bhalkavar gave a single nod.

"And Khoroas and Deserena?"

They gave her their assent in unison.

"And Sevrese?"

She shook her head. "Saina's intentions are not like Ruryo's. With him we only need to ask, *why?* I believe his answer will make sense for the Ten Abodes and for the Sulatins as well. Without hearing it, I will not go against him. He is more to me than the Sulatins or any tradition. And do not forget, he won a battle without any casualties. Do you really fear a bloodbath in Prayadevale?"

Her mother let her gaze fall and let go a quick breath. She nodded slowly. "As long as you are aware of what you may sacrifice."

Then she looked up and turned to her Assessors, who were quick with recommendations for a general call on the seven neutral Abodes and the Sulatins.

Sevrese listened briefly, but she knew all this would be too late to help Saina. She glanced plaintively at Bhalkavar and found him staring at her. She rose and crossed the room to stand beside him.

She threw her head back and closed her eyes. A trembling sigh came out of her. Then she hugged him. "Take me with you."

He snorted. "He is at war. It is not love he needs his mind on. He needs to think of death—making sure it comes to the right people and not to himself."

These last words disrupted the others. The Regent's command came down on them. "If you please, Sevrese. Whatever you have to say, stop abusing the general's kindness for you." The Regent looked at her daughter as if tapping a finger to her chest from across the room—driving her words into Sevrese's heart. *Satisfied? Now leave it alone.*

It brought a smile of regard to Sevrese's lips. She turned and leaped to the door.

"Where are you going?" her mother demanded.

"To write a letter," she shouted back without turning round.

EPISODE 8

Saina sat with Daiyenso in a simple room in the Dowager's wing under the light of a hanging lamp. They extended their legs across cushions, eating a meal of crushed grain cooked into a rough paste with spiced vegetables—an old woman's meal that also served as a Sulatin meal. Each of them mixed the food together with his fingers and brought small portions to their lips slowly. Ghoru had just departed.

"He is very dedicated to you."

Saina held back a mouthful. "When he met me in Prayadevale, he took on the manner of a nurse—with a sword."

Daiyenso nodded. "For one like Ghoru, without honor there is no living. Satamabode left him none. Loyalty to you became his measure of it."

"He said he was expecting something important of me—but Seed Bearer did not occur to him." He shrugged. "I know that feeling."

A soft laugh came from Daiyenso. "But now he accepts the two as one—more than you?"

"In time, I hope to." He took the handful of the food. "It was hard enough to accept I am no longer a Sulatin student. Later I had to accept some skill as a fighter and take command of an army. I can only change so many times in one year."

"You have to be quick about it this time. They all want to give you their loyalty, and you have to show them you accept it.

Saina exhaled slowly. "I could accept the loyalty of the ferines, because it was recorded in the scroll—a partnership that remains in our memory. If I had seen my name there, then it would be easy."

"It is not true because it is written. It is true because you accept it as a matter of will. That is one of the sacrifices of leadership. As a sovran you will yourself to exhibit a profound attraction to those you rule. And then you must be prepared for what it attracts. It is an agreement between sovran and the people that has been devalued. And now both sides have become immune to its power. That is one reason why Ruryo succeeded. In the absence of love and sacrifice, he offers largess. Ghoru understands the promise. He sacrifices his independence because you sacrifice your self-absorption."

"I should study Regent Pavim. She honors the contract."

Daiyenso nodded. "Study Ruryo as well. His contract is masterful—one that brings peace and prosperity back to the very people who should have hated him. They let him think for them. He imposes his will upon them. And it works as long as they remain satisfied."

"But then, he depends upon his subjects being greedy or simply fools."

"The same people who answered your call this morning had acquiesced to his."

Daiyenso took some tea and the lamplight flashed in his eyes. "I have been far beyond the Ten Abodes in my travels for the Sulatins. Once in the Aurean Passage, north of us and inland from Grezana, I was challenged to show my mettle by walking on fire. There are warriors there who do it to demonstrate to their people that they will endure anything to protect them. I got these for my efforts—he pointed to his scarred feet. Their leader is called the Deathless Mother, and her role is to embody their goddess in the mortal world. That is the highest leadership. Since I was there others have assumed the title but not the embodiment. That begins the descent into destruction. It happened to the Seed Bearers once and the Preceptor created the Sulatin Order. Now both the Seed Bearers and the Order have failed. What happens here will be repeated for those people as well.

"You set a high standard for me."

Daiyenso shook his head. "Not I. The Seed is a gift and a weight."

Saina stared at his companion, realizing how little he knew of his life and how strange it must be. "I want you ask you a question."

Daiyenso shrugged softly.

"As a student I accepted the verity of the Seed. Now it has been given to me. But I feel no different having accepted it. Sevrese questioned why only males carry it, and I could only give her an anatomical reason, which she scoffed at—rightfully, I think, because the Sulatins cannot discover let alone prove what the Seed is. Yet this upheaval could have been solved much earlier if the Sulatins agreed to make Deserena Seed Bearer. The Seed Bearer who comes closest to the standard is Pavim. I fear if I believe that possessing the Seed makes me superior to others, I will fail."

"That is what holds you back?"

Saina blinked at the words. He nodded.

"Then you should ask the Goddess. She knows. I don't."

A call started from the ferines out in the mountains, passing along voice to voice. Saina listened and waited until Shib rushed through the darkness of the open window and leaped to Saina's side.

He waved his arms to the road from Ryadabode. *Riderrrr.*

Saina stood up quickly. "The general has come."

The three left for the gate to the Virnipal road. Ghoru joined them.

In the flourish of dust, Bhalkavar halted his cantering horse and casually dismounted. He took an appraisal of Saina in the lamplight while he tended to his tack and laughed. "Saina, we need to get you a monarch's clothes."

Saina swelled at the general's voice. "I have been scavenging and borrowing for all these months since leaving Prayadevale. All I possess is the charity of others."

"Regent Pavim sends her greetings, her congratulations, and her consent to your use of her army."

"In your first reports to Regent Pavim, please say how grateful I am. She must be given all the credit for what we accomplish. I will send to her formally as soon as possible. Meanwhile all the Protectors are eating with the citizens of Alambarat tonight. The city celebrates the beginning of liberation. I hope you do not mind that we included your own army."

The general gave an approving gaze around but brought a questioning look back to Saina. "I will tell her. And it would help if you explain to her your goals and your next actions, so she feels secure in what she has committed to."

He nodded to confirm it. "I must introduce three of my teachers— like yourself. Ghoru guided me in my reentry into the world of the Ten Abodes and is now general of our Protectors. Daiyenso you have met, but you would not know he is a Sulatin who lives in and out of the Order, and he has made sure I do not forget what I learned from them. And this is Shib—my model of grace in battle."

Bhalkavar held Shib's waving hand first. "I met you in your forest. Your Being Surrounded by Light brought the fog that saved us." To Daiyenso he bowed slightly. "You saved our Abode's Daughter here in Alambarat." Then he took a measure of Ghoru. "General, I place myself and my army under your command."

Ghoru shook the compliment off. "No, General, it must be the other way round."

Bhalkavar took the responsibility with the slightest nod.

Saina drew himself up. "So, we move on to Sugorai, and to avoid any traps that Ruryo may attempt, we will move in three sections through the hills east of the city, not the road. Half of Satamabode's Protectors are leaving tonight. If you agree, your force will leave before dawn. Ghoru and I will follow with the rest late in the morning. The ferines will be our guides and scouts, and in two nights we will join outside the city for an attack the following day."

Bhalkavar nodded. "Fast work."

Ghoru asked, "Will you test our battleplan?"

"With great interest." Bhalkavar looked at Saina for a dismissal.

Saina was surprised by the look, realizing again his status was like a new skin. Hastily, he added, "First, there is something I want to offer you. It was Daiyenso's idea. I will let him tell you."

"General there is a man you know in this city, and I told him of your return. Let him explain."

Daiyenso disappeared into the shadows and returned with the theater artisan who had aided the general's escape from Alambarat.

Bhalkavar became expansive. "Why it is you? How many thanks we owe you. This fellow made up our disguises for our escape last summer, wrote our roles—did everything. And fooled everyone—even your new Seed Bearer." He jerked his head toward Saina. "Well, it is good to see you looking sound."

The man was too flustered to make sense.

Daiyenso assisted. "It came to my attention at that time that you were forced to leave your arms behind, General Bhalkavar."

The general gave him a sidelong look and repeated, "It came to your attention? You should know that Sevrese picked you out later in Virnipal."

"Ahh. Well, her mind is acute—no doubt thanks to you." His hand spread to gather in the artist. "This is now returned to you after a long safe-keeping." The artist released the bundle to Bhalkavar.

"Your sword, General. I kept it just as I said."

"I am in your debt forever," replied Bhalkavar, as he opened the bundle. He drew the blade part way with a slow, scraping warning. All eyes were on it. The general checked the edge. The artist's courage returned and he wanted to explain all the care he had taken in the general's absence. But he saw in the others' look that they were moved by something deep and mysterious, and he decided to hold fire.

The sword flashed reflections of the fires lighting the city. Dramatically it called out the reality of war—not a ferine's war, but a bloody human one.

Saina saw the beings of Goddessoma swarm around it, enter it, and slide down its gleaming edge to enter Bhalkavar's arm. All of them—devils, gods, souls—were in this fight. The outcome was in the hands of the Goddess.

Bhalkavar then thanked the artist for saving Sevrese in particular and expressed her gratitude. He recalled details of that day for a short time, and then the man withdrew to spread the story among his theatre fellows. The blade went back into its sheath and into the general's belt.

He thanked Daiyenso and added, "I will walk with Seed Bearer Saina before I join you, General Ghoru."

Ghoru and Daiyenso took a few steps back to wait. Shib called out an order to a small force of ferine guards who he assigned to always accompany Saina, and they swiftly took places where they could scan every space ahead and behind him.

The general watched it with deep amusement and regard. After a few paces he turned to Saina. "You no doubt want to ask me something."

"I have been afraid to ask." He stared at the ground and then took a deep breath and glanced at Bhalkavar. "What does Sevrese think of all this?"

"First I will tell you what your sister thinks."

"Ahh. Yes. But you must know how awkward it feels to hear that."

"No more so than for her. I am certain she regrets some of her behavior."

Saina dismissed any expression of that with a wave of his hand. "Nothing hurt me."

"She has Khoroas now and he makes her very happy, but I sense that the surprise that she has family once again multiplies her happiness. She understands the value of that, having lost it so completely."

Saina nodded many times, thinking of her as his sister. "It was Sevrese who made me see the truth of Deserena's character. I had not been very charitable until then. My regrets deserve to be stronger than hers. I am looking forward to enjoying her. And Khoroas."

"Khoroas is your ally. And thanks to her, a good one. Now..." he paused for a few steps and fell behind as he searched his shirt "... as for Sevrese...." He held out a small packet.

Saina turned and stared at Bhalkavar's hand with excitation in his chest.

"I will join Ghoru now." He pushed the packet into Saina's hand and gave his back a hearty slap.

Saina continued walking until at last he stopped in the faint light of a window on a narrow lane just off the street to the gate. No one was around and no sounds penetrated. He unrolled the small paper slowly. But he did not read it. He did not even look. Instead he called her to his mind in every detail of their times alone together. All his senses came to his aid. He could hear the perfect comfort of her voice speaking in the stillness of her balcony. He could touch the delicacy of her skin in her bed. He could see the moons' light upon her face at the stable. He could taste the warmth of her lips and smell the persuasive scent of her tawny hair.

Thoughts that made war trivial. Monk to Seed Bearer was nothing compared to monk to lover.

But at least, he thought, *if something in this adventure should go wrong, and I could not return to her, I would say that for just the few days and nights of her company I had lived a life.*

With that he began reading.

My adored Saina,

I have had but a few days and nights in your company. Yet if something were now to deny your return to me, I would tell anyone my life was filled with love.

I am overwhelmed at your achievement. There is nothing to compare to what you have done, nor what you will do. I believe the Goddess has named Her champion.

But you must be prudent in the face of all that lies ahead. While I have no doubts on your cause, we cannot rely only on destiny when we do not know the destiny of others.

Though this separation brings me pain I have never felt before, my thoughts, my feelings, my spirit remain with you always. Soon, Saina, at the first moment of possibility, let me be with you.

She signed it simply, without title or seal, as a friend. He read it one more time. Then he rolled it tightly and placed it on his skin under a bracelet his grandmother had given him, where the beads used to hang.

Panjael waited with eyes closed to the early sunlight streaming into the treatment room of the Protectors training compound. The table's aged oil-soaked wood offered familiar relief against the fatigue of his misadventures in Ryadabode, the Garland Forest, and Alambarat.

The attendant wiped a huge handful of a gritty herbs and oil upon his chest and then rubbed with increasing vigor in elaborate patterns.

When he came across some obstruction in the tissue below the skin, he dug freely into it, giving rise to a series of submerged groans from Panjael. Gradually more and more warm oil was added to the mix until the massage became silky and sublime.

Neither of them noted Ruryo's entrance.

The attendant worked with his mind in a separate, contented place, having prepared more than a generation of the officers of Satamabode in this manner for match battles and for combat with the tribals on the plains. Not to mention reconstructing the wounds afterwards. He went about choosing the oils and herbs from among the dozens of jars on the nearby workbench, adjusting the heat that prepared them, letting his robe grow heavy and yellow-red with smears as his work progressed.

The assessor stood and watched the therapy from just inside the doorway. Only when the attendant curtly ordered Panjael to turn over did Ruryo come forward. Panjael looked at him as he rolled, but did not interrupt the treatment. With Panjael's face now down upon a hole in the table, Ruryo spoke.

"Does this treatment really produce some special result?"

Between the quick breaths that escaped him with the pressure of the attendant's hands, Panjael replied. "It is one of the few secrets of the Sulatins that I am aware ever got out of Prayadevale."

"What is the intent?"

"For us it forms the armor beneath the armor. One protects from the outside. The other from the inside. I suppose it is a luxury that few of the Abodes would indulge in, but my father respected it, and we have here a practitioner whose family has served for generations past memory. He knows what he is about. The fate of this body is in his hands."

Ruryo watched the man's face, but received no acknowledgment still. "Armor, really? And can he can keep an arrow from penetrating your chest?"

"No, the outer armor must do that. His art is to keep the penetration from doing fatal damage."

"Perhaps someday in future you will have him introduce this to me."

That took Panjael by surprise. He did not respond.

"Will it disturb the effect if we talk?" Ruryo asked.

"No." The answer was not true, but having Ruryo wait would be an even greater intrusion. Panjael lifted his head from the hole and turned it to the Assessor.

Ruryo began to wander round the room. He passed in and out of the shadows, his expression never fully apparent.

"My messengers tell me that a force of Protectors left Alambarat this morning. Uniforms of Ryadabode."

"The attempt on Khoroas must have pushed the Regent past her usual prudence."

"Mmm." Ruryo sniffed a bottle and wrinkled his nose. "Yet had it been successful, she would not have the heart for it."

"Or the opposite. We can speculate forever. I will still need to meet this force of Bhalkavar's within the next two days."

Ruryo stopped pacing at the head of the table. "I find it strange that while you were escaping Bhalkavar's pursuit in the Garland Forest, your brother was attacking Alambarat. Bhalkavar was clearly readying his Protectors to join him."

After a straining groan Panjael answered. "We saw nothing in our time in Virnipal to say Bhalkavar's men were ready for anything of the sort. Question whatever you want, Assessor, but I can assure you if Saina told Bhalkavar to prepare his Protectors to join thousands of ferines, Bhalkavar would have locked Saina away for his own safety. I was there to see the victory, but too late to do anything about it. Only to know of Saina's true identity. That is the only reason the Regent would have committed her Protectors. The Seed is all she cares about. Bhalkavar saved the Seed for Ryadabode. Saina resurrected it for Satamabode. She must be in ecstasy."

"A good mood for her to meet death."

Panjael still did not look up at him, and perhaps could not have asked the question if he had. "Why did you withhold from me the fact that my brother Nacros was in the prison?"

Ruryo laughed softly. "Don't tell me you need him for victory."

"The only thing I need is your answer."

"For victory?"

"If you like."

"I don't like my orders challenged, as you did with the attack on Khoroas. I don't like my plans to fail, as they did in Ryadabode. I don't like incomplete information that does not add up, as you have given me about the days between that attack and the attack at Alambarat. I did not tell you about Nacros because I had plans for him that did not require you."

"I see. Regicide. Knowing I would have done it without hesitation. And what has become of him? Is that also to be withheld from me?"

"He escaped the dungeon. That is all. I am going to ask the rest of the questions now. Will your Protectors that remained here fight for you?"

Panjael smiled. He could have said, *Yes, but not for you.* "They will fight for me but not against their comrades on Saina's side. They will face Bhalkavar. Your own forces must face Saina."

He raised himself and met Ruryo's gaze. "Are you concerned about the outcome of this battle? How can you contemplate taking over all ten Abodes if you cannot defeat one of the smallest of the lot? With the first release of that vapor or whatever it is in that weapon they will all withdraw. You have all the weight on your side of the scale just from that."

"The weapon is no longer available."

Panjael rose and sat upright. The attendant stood back and waited.

"Did I hear you?"

Ruryo started to pace again but more quickly.

"No one knows that—and this attendant will die if anyone does. If you act swiftly and boldly, you will win just because your enemy expects the weapons to come with your charge."

Panjael took a deep breath and sat in silence. At length he replied, "I will tell my men that I refuse to use the weapon."

"How does that pertain?"

Panjael gave him a stare. "There is a code among Protectors about the nature of battle. They will understand and fight the harder because of it."

"Very well. That sounds preposterous, but I have other matters. As you say, this is the first of several battles to defeat the Abodes. It was not necessary in my plan, but not unanticipated. I am always ready to adapt to challenges."

Ruryo gave a dismissive gesture and started for the door.

"Tell me, where will Pharmos be in the battle?"

Ruryo did not look around. "In flight back to Hanarabode with wagons of loot from the palace. He left this morning in tears and panic."

Panjael held back a smile. He did not lie back on the table to let the attendant continue. His mind could not settle. He knew Ruryo did not believe him about Virnipal. The story could not be broken because for once Ruryo did not have anyone watching him. Nevertheless, even if the next day's battle went well, there would be no trust left between them—though Panjael was certain there never was any.

The attendant asked, "Why do you not want more? The treatment is incomplete and leaves your energy fractured. Let me repair."

Panjael shook his head. "Too late."

"No, never too late. These hands have miracles in them. I can make you whole."

Panjael shook his head. "No one can make me whole anymore."

The man smiled for the first time Panjael had ever seen. "Alright. At least you are much better off than that one. There is no oil or hand that will ever make him whole, I can tell you. A huge knot inside. It will unwind someday—and so will he."

Out among the fields in the Satamabode basin winds were whipping the afternoon air. The Protector banners snapped and their cloaks rippled across their horses' rumps as the last contingent of the new Seed Bearer's forces crossed the farmlands toward Sugorai.

A dozen farmers stood at edge of the field ahead, hands rigidly on their hips and discontent on their faces. General Ghoru reached them first, and Saina watched their arms take to the air to express their anger. He nudged Grizzle to a canter to intervene and heard the last of Ghoru's limited patience.

"Look," he said in exasperation, "I am sure you will receive compensation for this. But even so, your fields lie directly in the line of the resurrection of Satamabode. Don't you think that should be reward by itself?"

"Easy to say. What if you don't win your battle? Hanarabode hasn't been cheap with us, you know," challenged one of the farmers. "We have been promised premium prices for our crops if we deliver on time. You are putting us back enough to lose us a fortune. We want what is due us. Will you back that contract?"

"Listen, you greedy little"—

Saina cut in from the side. "So what damage is done?"

They turned to look at him, but the sun was behind him and they had to cover their brows to see his face. Their answers toppled each other.

"Well, look around. Have you never been on a farm before?"

"You see the fields you missed over there? Those belong to the family that owns this land. They live in Sugorai. We are granted ownership on this field, but their ploughing is done first, then ours. We just ploughed ours and have to seed them now to meet our commitment. You have ruined our field."

"Typical. You protect first families. You avoid the fallow fields and the parcels for the cattle, while you parade over the arable land. What were you thinking?"

Saina heard metal—a sword coming out of its scabbard. A voice called out from somewhere else, "Doesn't he know who he's—" but Saina waved them all to silence.

"No," Saina answered, "I wasn't thinking. I never worked a farm."

"Well, I'll wager you got through your twenty years by eating my grain more than once. So at least you know that we work them," the farmer added contemptuously.

"Have you ever stood in battle?" asked Ghoru. "No? Well, then you have enjoyed the security that our wounds won you in your own fifty-some years, you impudent yokel." Ghoru gave Saina a quick smile before forcing his cruelest countenance upon this poor fellow. "We never came whining to you for recompense, did we?"

"The Assessor Nummary sent his collectors, and we paid, didn't we? So today *we* are the collectors," another one countered.

Escalation was imminent. Saina intervened. "Will you still be able to plough it over again, if all these neighbors work together?"

"We always work together. What about *you* working together? Ohh, you have no plough. No team. So it is up to us—twice."

Saina gave a sigh. "Good. I will work one of the ploughs."

Ghoru spat his opinion. "Mewlers. We must move on."

"No, that is what Ruryo would do—or worse. We can admire their boldness. Besides, fighting on our own land is rightly more complicated than invasion."

"Show me," Saina ordered the farmers as he dismounted.

He made the farmer give him a short lesson in the reining of the horse team and the balance of the blade.

"All right. Let me." Saina gave the horse a nudge with the straps. The animal did not respond.

"Grizzle, help me," he called, along with a mental image of his horse leading the team. Instead Grizzle wandered up to the other horse, sniffed breath for a moment, then bit one of them on the rump. The farm horse kicked but moved out quickly. He knew his work so well that Saina managed the first part of the field easily enough. But then he began to veer as Grizzle had other ideas for a bite of grass here and there. Saina heard the farmer complain in the background as he struggled to keep the lines together.

"No-no-no-no! Agghh—he is useless."

Now there was laughter. A few soldiers rushed to aid Saina. With four men they could control one farmer's work. By the time they had crossed the field four times, they made it look effortless. One of the escort replaced Saina and he joined the farmers.

"Unfortunately, my men cannot spare any more time. But I will send men back to make up the work in a few days. Get as far along as you can. Perhaps the Goddess will keep the weather for you."

They were suspicious. "You have authority to make these statements about sending more workers?" asked one. His eyes surveyed the work going on in the distance and then searched Saina's appearance for any sign that he was in command. "Who are you?"

"My name is Saina."

"I don't know that name. What is your father's name?" His inquiry was less than cordial. Saina had not earned an ally yet.

Ghoru stepped up again. "Do you remember the name Qurmadi? Does the Seed of Satamabode bring back anything?"

"What of it? The traitorous Heir sold it for nothing. The Seed is dead."

"To you and your faithless friends. But another Heir lived in secret. The Dowager revealed it. It is recorded on the Abode scroll. His name is Saina. He will restore your Abode and banish your enemies. Just try to remember who your enemies are."

He looked between Ghoru and Saina with such hopeless confusion, it seemed he might run. Then came deep emotion. Tears streamed over his sunburnt cheeks. He tried to speak but could not. Saina saw him about to go to his knee.

"No-no, you are my teacher," Saina cried, grabbing him. "This morning I knew so little of the farmers of Satamabode. I have not lived here with you as I should have. I have been in exile. This afternoon you have taught me to plough. You taught me the people of Satamabode should weaken to no one—most of all, not to their Seed Bearer."

The man was so flustered now the tears turned to sobs. Saina found himself completely embarrassed.

"Please, sir, sometime in the future after the field is ploughed, you and your neighbors bring to me an accounting of what our movements through your land cost you. I will provide an accounting of what I think you gained from our victory. If it does not balance, we will negotiate from there. Is it fair?"

He nodded, dazed. He could not recover to talk. Ghoru laughed at him and pushed him along.

Saina mounted Grizzle, and Ghoru said to him, "These rustics will spread this story everywhere until it is told in a hundred variations."

"Ahh—I hadn't thought of that," Saina replied. "But our movements will not be compromised."

A look of amazement crossed Ghoru's face. "No, not your *security*—I meant your *glory*." Then he muttered contentedly, "Perhaps not so much has changed since our first ride." He laughed.

—∞o⊱✦⊰o∞—

"Nacros! Thank you for coming." Ruryo gave him a pat on the shoulder. "Looks like you enjoy your meals."

Nacros rubbed his beard and found crumbs falling into his lap. He swallowed with difficulty and looked distressed.

"The light." Nacros' voice creaked, as if he were an old man.

"Yes. Every day for some time now I have put a meal and a light out for you. You found my gift very quickly. And you have returned every day since. I wanted you to do this, so I could speak to you. I have a proposal to make. I want to take you away from this darkness. I will set you free. You just have to do one thing for me. One task. Something you will like to do. I am certain we can come to an agreement."

Nacros walked into his cell. He crouched and jumped, catching the bars above him and swinging slowly while he watched Ruryo.

The alchemist was right about the power of that vapor down here. He looks harrowed and demented.

Suddenly Nacros spoke. "Assessor Ruryo? Please, come in! Welcome—welcome." I can see. I like the light. It's been dark a long time." He pulled himself up and fixed his feet into the bars, dropping to swing upside down.

Ruryo came forward to slowly and carefully close the cell door. He was heartened to see that his prisoner was not as bad as he looked.

Nacros saw what Ruryo did, but offered no objection.

"Do you remember your brother Saina? I want to talk about your brother Saina."

"Ohh. Not Saina my brother. You said that wrong. Saina is not my brother."

Ruryo started. *How could he know?*

"You see, Assessor, my father explained that to me. I forgot him. I was angry at him for putting me in here. I was going to kill him—but then he explained it all to me. And he said he was glad I killed Varanos. He didn't say anything about the ferine I killed before that." He took a long breath again and seemed to be thinking deeply. "You can see everything in the dark—sometimes. Things that are in your head but don't come out in the light. Like my father. He is here. A lot of people are here

"Yes, feel I sure that must be true. Your father was right about Saina after all. Saina is an imposter brother. And I want you to have the honor of punishing him for his lies. If you agree to my plan and pledge your loyalty to me, I will release you very soon. Not only that, I will be needing another Assessor Martial, and I believe you are by far the best man for the job."

"I fought ferines in the Garland Forest." He flipped and landed on his feet in the cell. Then he took a big breath as if this memory awakened him. Then he bent down and spoke low. "Kill Saina?"

Ruryo hesitated. "I am happy to see you grasp my plan so quickly. Yes. But I have to tell you how and when to do it."

Nacros shook his head. "After I kill Panjael. He was the one who got me in here."

"No, Saina first. You have my permission to kill Panjael after you kill Saina."

Nacros turned angry. "I am going to kill the person who put me here first."

"Yes. I see that. It's a good plan. Panjael put you in here. I didn't want this, but he said you will kill him and he was afraid of you. He said your skill was far beyond his, and he feared you would kill him. But then I want you to kill Saina. Do you understand? You must get this clear."

"I understand you, Assessor Ruryo. Now if you will just take me to Panjael."

Ruryo made an elaborate gesture of regret. "Panjael is not available tonight. But Saina is. He will be camped across the river and in the hills. I have men who will take you to him in secret in the dark—just as your prefer. One thrust and it is over. Then they will take you to Panjael tomorrow. All your desires fulfilled."

Nacros smiled and bent his head like a conspirator, whispering. "I found light down here. Not this light. Another light." His hand waved toward a dark passage. "The river, too."

"That's good. I want you to stay here. My men and I will come down and guide you to Saina. Do you understand?"

"I should talk to my father."

"Excellent idea. Look him up."

Ruryo reached for the key in his pocket to secure the cell. Nacros watched the key turn in the lock. Ruryo slowly repeated his instruction.

Nacros smiled and nodded. A madman smile. A nod that came too fast.

"I will show you." He leaped again to the top bars and began swinging all over again this time toward Ruryo. "It wasn't you who locked me in here, was it? You can't even get that right!"

Ruryo jumped back and watched Nacros kick the cell door. The hinges crumbled and the door fell flat to the ground. He jumped and landed with a roll, leaping to his feet and disappearing into the darkness.

It took Ruryo some time to settle his heart and breath. Then he swore and sighed.

Every son of Murosaya and Qurmadi is either useless or infuriating. It would have been a story for the Seed Bearers to contemplate, but so is the efficiency of my blacksnake warriors. And they can have revenge on Bhalkavar as well."

Saina's force reached the camp during a lingering sunset that painted the skies over Satamabode in war hues. There was little to call a camp. Even though they were hidden in low hills out of direct sight from Sugorai, the generals knew there was no secrecy. Ruryo must have observers and messengers all over the Abode. Still Saina's soldiers cooked no meals and pitched no shelters and lit no lamps. When darkness fell there were not even silhouettes.

Saina, Bhalkavar, and Ghoru sat together on the damp ground. The battleplan left only one question unresolved.

"All my Protectors are talking about it—they remember once you see one of those arrows coming you are bound to go mad with fear and then quickly die." Ghoru shook his head. "There is no denial or softening for it."

Bhalkavar grunted. "And they have infected the Ryadabode Protectors, who have embellish the stories."

Saina tried to dismiss it. "To Regent Pavim Ruryo is a man of expedience. The expedient man would hold back his weapon. Ruryo's true power is not the weapon but the strength we accord it. With that strength the expedient man would negotiate."

Bhalkavar gave a long breath. "He must win this battle decisively. As powerful as the weapon was the fact of the end of a Seed Bearer line. You took that away from him. He starts over here tomorrow. He will use everything."

Ghoru nodded. "You trapped him like an animal when your name appeared in the scroll. This battle is all or nothing. Return the Seed Bearers and Sulatins to their knees with victory or lose everything he has constructed and every threat he possessed. Victory is measured by one outcome only—your death. Not only will he use the weapon, but he will direct it first at you. We must stand before you and keep it at bay."

"If I cannot reveal myself, then he has killed me."

Bhalkavar gave a satisfied murmur. "Well said. But your general is right. If he had succeeded in his attack against Khoroas, then your restoration of the Seed of Satamabode would not impede his plan. But—it follows that for your victory it is enough to live through this battle. With that and our ability to diminish his forces, we win."

Saina fought against their words in his mind—they did not match his visions in the Garland Forest. "In his attack on Sugorai, the weapon was used only in tight spaces. Am I right?"

Ghoru considered and agreed.

"The vapor you described is heavy and settles quickly after it is released. The winds in the open air will disperse it. We must have men all along the line whose only concern is watching for the weapon. When their warning is sounded, all the Protectors in that area spread out and back out of the vapor's reach. That is how the ferines fight. Tell our men that we know the weapon's flaw. Even so far as to invite its use in order to prove its failure."

Ghoru and Bhalkavar each gave a murmur of approval.

The general laughed. "Saina, you twist things like a Sulatin. Let us hope you are right."

Ghoru added, "If you can guide the weather with your Sulatin training, gives us a strong wind."

Saina rose and stretched. "I want to walk among the men with you. But you offer this tactic—you carry more weight than a Seed Bearer or a Sulatin tonight."

He wandered through the camp, drawing away from the generals as they stopped to talk. Nevertheless the men still surrounded him. Ghoru was right about the story of the ploughing, which they parodied for his amusement and congratulated him for defending the Protectors. He traversed the length of the camp and moved beyond the outskirts to stand in the starlight and the pale glow of the first moon. He was still inclined to being alone in the night as in Prayadevale.

He stopped and closed his eyes to feel the air on his face—thicker with moisture than in the mountains. He felt the wind whirl suddenly and when he opened his eyes dark forms were all around him. He caught the moon glinting on a blade and dropped to the ground. But nowhere was safe. An arm circled his neck and pulled him away.

It had hair all over it. Ferines were everywhere, tumbling over the ground and into the air above him. Then came cries from all around, and finally a body fell upon him, pinning him to the ground. In his arm he felt the Goddess' power—not the healing gods, but the destroyer devils. He broke free enough to pound his fist into the attacker's head. The blow was close to deadly.

The confusion cleared moments later when Protectors swept in and Ghoru and Bhalkavar were at his side with appeals for his well-being.

He stood to prove he had not been hurt.

Ghoru brought the assessment to him. "There were nine attackers. The ferines got them all—subdued all but one before they could get to you. You dealt him an impressive blow. But how did they know who you are?"

Bhalkavar spat. "It is my fault. When I laughed I said your name. They must have been hidden nearby. These men are the weapon Ruryo tried against Khoroas. I should have anticipated it. Your ferines are wiser and more alert."

"You see, Generals, Ruryo's weapons don't work. His time is over and this battle has been decided—a formality."

He closed his mouth before his next words came out.

The real conflict will be resolved in Prayadevale.

Ruryo paced across the now nearly empty durbar. Even the throne was missing. Pharmos transported it to Hanarabode. He sneered at the markings left on the floor underneath.

Pharmos makes it clear why he hated the mercenaries so much. They looted before he could.

He heard approaching footsteps outside a side door of the durbar and rushed to open it. A breathless messenger stood in the rays of the morning sun.

"You weren't with the group I sent."

The messenger shook his head, not knowing what the Assessor meant. "No, I came to tell you a Sulatin has arrived to see you. He forced me."

"A Sulatin?" He was mystified but then contemptuous. "Why did you use this door? It is restricted to messengers with my special assignments only. I am waiting for one, and you have disturbed me. Get out. Tell the Sulatin to get out."

"But this is the way he came in. He forced me. He is right here."

The anger on Ruryo's face sent the man flying back into the corridor. But before he could slam the door Luzarain stepped into the room.

Ruryo backed up clumsily. "The Alchemist. What do you want?" He quickly recovered from the surprise and stormed a moment with impatience. Then he attacked. "Do you mean to tell me you are a Sulatin?"

Luzarain smiled. "I came to tell you that your attack on Saina failed."

"What?"

Luzarain paced the durbar in a round as he spoke to Ruryo.

"You are too clever a man. You are right about so much. The Seed Bearers have forsaken the mantle of leadership. The Sulatins have abandoned their charge to protect all knowledge. And no one realizes the truth. Your thinking was brilliant. Make the emptiness tangible. Fill the loss by bringing prosperity to the people. Make them feel self-reliant—no need for flawed leadership and corrupted knowledge. Rule by reason and judgment. But here is your failure. You overreach—and for nothing. You could have had everything you want. I would have helped you at every step."

Ruryo was not listening. He seethed as Murosaya had done before him. "Saina lives still? I sent nine assassins! They are impeccable. They cannot be seen. This is impossible!"

Luzarain laughed cruelly. "They were captured by ferines. No one thinks of everything." He stopped to enjoy Ruryo outrage. "You see? You believe you are patient and faultlessly discerning, but when you are tested equanimity escapes you. It is because you built this edifice in your mind on the anger and jealousy of a Seed Bearer's queen and the resentful submission of his son—not forgetting the help of a few thousand primitives that you carelessly cast aside. Such a foundation cannot support your intentions. Your mind is sucked into the mud by your allies."

"Stop! I do not care or ask for your judgments. Did you bring me more canisters?"

Luzarain raised his palms in disbelief. "No, Assessor. And let me say that I would gladly have forced the flood in the dungeons had my counterpart not thought of it first. I was willing to back you as long as your self-importance remained in check. In the end you proved to have the same failings of the Seed Bearers. You think you are necessary. But all your success and all your failure was just a play in Goddessoma."

"What gibberish!"

"I give you once last chance. I brought you advice on how to earn your power back on your own merits."

Ruryo swore under his breath and sat down on a misplaced wooden chest that was too plain to interest Pharmos.

"Your power lies in your discriminating mind—when it functions so. And in your ally."

"What ally?"

"Seed Bearer Saina."

"Sulatins are fools," Ruryo growled.

"That happens to be true. But I am not here as a fool or to fool you. Saina wants to end the rule of Seed Bearers as surely as you do. He wants to dismantle the Sulatin Order. His weakness lies in his openness and his modesty. He does not appreciate your villainy, nor his own authority. You want to eliminate your enemies. He aspires to redeem his. You are bound by the material just as he is bound by the aethereal"

"You left out that he is a Sulatin toy. He was trained by you. What do I care for anything you have said?"

"You will hear me because for the first time it has dawned on you that your initiative is completely blocked. Nothing is working—you for whom everything was working. Your opportunity, Ruryo, has passed. Saina's has just begun. Do you really want what you have envisioned, or do you just want to be the one who is credited with achieving it. At this moment Saina—even after your blundering attack on him—is willing to negotiate with you.

Ruryo snorted. "What could he possibly offer me?"

"Now who is the fool? He can save you from defeat. You can merge your power and achieve the transformation you both seek."

"You tell a very unpersuasive story, Sulatin. You convince me that this young man deserves whatever I decide to mete out to him."

"If you fight him this day you lose everything. Panjael cannot command his Protectors against their own Seed Bearer. You have none of those canisters I thanklessly filled with the devils of Goddessoma—all of which is far beyond your comprehension. You have had your way cheaply until now. Treachery, traitors, profane allies and supernatural weapons. Now it is time to earn your way. This is your first true test. You have my advice on how to pass it. When the armies line up, you stop the battle. You call Saina out and you offer to join him for the future of the Ten Abodes."

Ruryo gave a quick laugh at the notion. "From your description he will believe it."

"Of course. He is willing to think you worthy. Your test is that *you* must believe it."

Ruryo gave a long stare at nothing. Then he took a slow breath and exhaled. "How do I know this is not a trick to preserve your Order? Why should I believe a Seed Bearer—one trained as a Sulatin—would ever turn against his own?

"Use your discrimination once for something other than killing those who get in your way. You know this is the truth. This time *you* have to change—not trick someone else into it. If you do not change you fail."

"Yes, you make it all very clear. You have had your speech. I will consider your words. Now leave me."

Luzarain strode across the durbar without a word or gesture and opened the great door for his departure. No one challenged him.

The combined armies of Seed Bearer Saina came out of the hills and took positions on the eastern side of the city, forcing Ruryo and Panjael to fight with the sun in their faces and their backs to the river should they come out on the plain. If not, then Saina would surround the city for siege.

Panjael did not lead his troops out until the midmorning sun no longer interfered with sighting. They came through all the gates and bridges on the eastern wall. He segmented his line so that the Satamabode Protectors scrupulously avoided facing each other.

Saina sat upon Grizzle in front of his ferine army. He knew they had no advantage in this kind of fight beyond recent reputation. Not counting the ferines, the forces were equal. The battle would be determined by the will of soldiers with conflicted loyalty.

Finally, Ruryo emerged in the Seed Bearer's ratha with huge wheels and canopy, drawn by four muscled horses. He stopped where he just crossed the bridge to keep escape close behind him.

The walls were crowded with citizens. Having little news of the outcome of events at Alambarat, they could not be fully certain who was fighting for them and against them. They knew that the last time armies formed outside the walls the result was deadly, but their curiosity was stronger than their memory.

There was no wind yet. Everyone on Saina's side of the battle noted it. Ruryo's weapon would be just as effective as it was within the walls.

Saina could sense the gods and demons of Goddessoma as invisible soldiers who would fight a battle parallel to the human one. But he did not sense the demons were stronger. There was no victory to be won— only inevitability. This day was Her incoming breath, taking back into Herself Her entire creation, only to breathe out with what was to come.

That meant there was no restoring Satamabode to its former stature. There would be no need for a Seed Bearer in what followed—no matter who claimed victory. Everything must be cleaned away. Sugorai. Prayadevale. The cognitions of the Founding Seers. Everything. Doing-doing-doing—already done.

Suddenly Saina heard Ghoru galloping to him. "Do not go, Saina! Do not! I urge you!

Saina awoke. "What are you saying?"

"Did you not see the signal? Ruryo calls to you. He wants to confer. It is a trap. He has no honor for truce."

Saina shook his head. "Nor do I. I must go."

"He tried to kill you last night!"

"Yes. And today expect the same. But he failed. So he knows that was his last resort on his terms. Now his risk and mine are the same. He doesn't fight that way. He must ask for terms."

"I'm going with you."

Saina nodded, but he saw Ghoru about to bring up an entire line of riders. "No. Pick nine. That is what they thought it took to kill me. Make four of them ferines—Shib will call them. And send someone to tell Bhalkavar I put him in charge in case of treachery."

"Don't bother. He will hit them like lightning."

Saina took pleasure in that thought as they rode very slowly across the plain between the martial lines, letting everyone see the new Seed

Bearer of Satamabode. Grizzle pranced and turned. He knew what was needed.

They stopped a short distance from the opposing frontline and across from Panjael—too far to talk, but close enough for an arrow. Panjael acknowledged him with a wry smile and a nod. He turned and spread out his soldiers to create an alley to reach Ruryo. Panjael cantered ahead and dismounted next to the Assessor, who remained in the ratha.

Ghoru beseeched Saina not to ride on. "Saina you cannot take this bait. I do not trust your brother either."

Saina heard a voice within. His voice. The voice he must trust. It contradicted Ghoru's advice. He shook his head slowly. "I am certain this is the right course. He is no longer my brother, but neither is he my enemy."

Ruryo hissed to Panjael, "I have archers aiming at your heart. Either Saina dies in the next moments or you do."

Panjael looked into Ruryo's eyes and smiled. *Here I am again. One more chance to kill an Assessor—or a Seed Bearer.*

"Why not aim for Saina. It might be more efficient."

"You don't think far enough ahead, son of Murosaya. You kill him and your men will follow you. They have no one left on the other side."

As his sentence ended a clatter came from the Satamabode Protectors on Ruryo's side. As Saina rode through them, they all were dropping swords and lances and loosening their armor.

"Mmm," observed Panjael, "their loyalty is no longer at issue. If I kill Saina we will both die anyway."

Ruryo swore in a demanding tone. "Just do it."

Saina reached the ratha and dismounted. Ghoru did the same, leaving his hand on his blade as he walked.

Ruryo spoke first from his high seat.

"Seed Bearer of Satamabode. I discern you to be someone willing to talk. Let us share our goals and aspirations for the Ten Abodes. Not fight today—but decide today—a just and justifiable future. I welcome you back to your city."

Ruryo gestured grandly at the walls and stepped down to the ground.

At that very moment a loud sound came from the base of the city wall across the bridge—first rocks breaking and scattering and then a vibrant voice singing. A ragged man emerged running from a hidden escape tunnel leading out of the city dungeon. The citizens at the top of the wall called out in surprise leaning dangerously to view the escapee below. Ruryo turned to look along with everyone else.

The man leaped onto the bridge and raced across. He was a skeletal, filthy, bearded man waving a bow in one hand and a demonic arrow in the other. A sword bounced clumsily at his leg. Now everyone realized he was about to release the weapon they all feared.

Ruryo felt his heart leap. Nacros had found one more canister and a bow. Right now any hero was welcome.

Panjael, Ghoru and Saina all watched in disbelief as he stopped and planted his feet, drawing back the bow. He released it and every eye on the battlefield and on the walls saw it sail in an arc to strike the end of the bridge.

They all took in a rapid breath and from wherever they stood ducked as the arrow split apart, awaiting the vapor they knew was coming. The figure now ran erratically toward them with his sword drawn. But no vapor came, no supernatural presence—only a spray of mud.

Panjael and Saina spoke nearly the same words. "It is Nacros!" "Is it Nacros?"

Ruryo cried out. "Here! He is here! Do it! Do what I commanded! Kill Saina!"

Ghoru's sword was out at once but Saina put his arm across it. "He is mad."

"Mad men kill!"

"But wait!"

Nacros ran at full force with sword extended. He was laughing in ecstasy.

Panjael had an instant to decide who dies—Saina, Ruryo, himself, Nacros. He stepped in front of Saina and blocked the blow. Nacros went down but managed a slash at Panjael's leg. Panjael fell on top of him pushing his blade into Nacros' chest—at the same time letting Nacros' blade slide inside his ribs.

Neither one spoke. Nacros coughed blood and drifted into death. Panjael's hand stretched toward Ruryo without weapon or strength to perform the last act he wished for.

Saina and Ghoru knelt beside them and with wild eyes Ruryo broke into a run across the bridge. Ghoru leaped after him.

Saina felt these two souls of his half-brother and his once half-brother looking at him as clearly as the boys on the monastery roof. He closed his eyes and shook his head.

Nacros, our mother bound us in birth. Panjael, your father bound us in honor. Destiny binds us forever. Welcome to Goddessoma.

Then he rose and immediately followed Ghoru as Shib and his ferines raced ahead of him.

Ruryo looked over his shoulder in panic. There was only one possible escape. He ran to the wall, stumbling over the rocks, and plunged into the darkness of the hole Nacros had opened.

When the ferines reached the hole, they leaped back. They felt the demonic presence. They turned and blocked Saina and Ghoru from entering.

"Saina, tell them we have to get him!"

Shib pushed his companions away and went in. Ghoru tried to follow but he was suddenly filled with panic. Saina felt the panic but more than fear was awe. The weapon that lost the city was a no more than a drop of this power. The city itself rested on top of a cavern of agony and annihilation.

Saina sensed the hole in the base of the wall as an opening to Goddessoma. He went in cautiously to face the presence. In all his aetheric adventures, he had never felt this awful strength. Nothing could compare to it. Nothing could stop it. His feet froze in dank dirt.

Shib's face was just visible ahead but Saina knew if he went further the blackness would swallow him completely. He called Shib back out.

"Not this time, Shib. These devils belong the Goddess. The Being Surrounded by Light will have to deal with this. Even your valor has a limit.

On the battlefield Bhalkavar had surrounded the Hanarabode Protectors. The Satamabode Protectors crossed the field to join in comradeship in the middle.

Bhalkavar galloped to Saina. "Is Ruryo dead?"

Saina shook his head. "He escaped into something worse. You can report to the Regent that his hold on the Ten Abodes is broken."

Saina saw the elation in the general. He felt none himself.

"Remember, without Ruryo, I would not be here as Seed Bearer of Satamabode. I owe him everything.

Bhalkavar gave a stern look. "See it your way. But don't tell her that. She deserves to be herself again."

Saina nodded.

"Your Sulatin companion has arrived—out of nowhere in the middle of the battlefield. Here he comes. I have a lot to do yet. People are pouring out of the city." He called for Ghoru and gave orders to everyone around him. Then he turned to Saina and jerked a thumb toward Daiyenso. "He called you Saina the Destroyer."

"But everything appears to have survived."

"Yes. That was fortunate." There was a look on Bhalkavar's face that he might add something, but he wheeled his horse and took off.

Saina was alone with the ferines at a guarding distance until Daiyenso reached him. "Another victory done."

"But we accept it was never the real fight for us," countered Saina. "Ruryo was just a tool of the Goddess." He paused. "And so am I."

"And so am I. But Ruryo is a broken tool. You are freed to do the work ahead."

"Prayadevale."

Daiyenso did not need to confirm it.

Shib came up behind and draped an arm over Saina's shoulder. Saina turned and looked into his eyes.

"Shib. We need to meet the Being Surrounded by Light."

Shib pointed to the distant mountain where Prayadevale stood. *Eees therr.*

"You take your people there now. We will meet you soon."

Shib let out a melodious call that was answered by thousands.

———∘∘◦❁◦∘∘———

In Virnipal, Bhalkavar's report first caused elation. When the story of how the battle unfolded and concluded was read, the mood settled in bewilderment. Then, when his report introduced a letter from Saina to the Regent explaining the next step—his intention to bring an end to the Sulatins in Prayadevale—a storm blasted through the palace. Though she had come to accept this outcome as a possibility, when faced with actuality—and Saina as its instigator—a sense of betrayal overwhelmed her. Pavim was a streak of lightning crackling with outrage. And for defending Saina, her daughter stood alone, exposed on high ground.

"For a time, Sevrese. For a time, I granted you wisdom—in hindsight. I even faulted myself. I accepted his strange crusade in the Garland Forest as reason to offer my army to him." She paced in the same room Sevrese attacked her and the general for sending Saina with the cadets to the sea. "He had everything. He restored control of Satamabode. He resolved the question of the Seed Bearers. He brought it all back into balance." She breathed deeply several times and began again in a low voice. "Now he wants to destroy the Sulatins. And he intimates that the role of Seed Bearer will perish as well. He is a usurper—no different from Ruryo. He reviles tradition and flaunts expedience. You cannot defend him!"

Sevrese felt anger rising of exact equal measure. "Not as long as you rant and refuse to listen, I cannot." She turned away from her mother.

Pavim waved her hand as if she was perfectly willing to listen—to good sense.

Sevrese stood and walked to the nearest window. "These are not questions that concern me. I have pledged myself to him. I trust him. I don't see Bhalkavar racing to Prayadevale with our Protectors to defend the Sulatins. This is all exaggerated in your imagination. Saina sees behind this world and into Goddessoma. He means to enact his battles on the aetheric field."

"Don't be fooled. When Athayam confronted him in this palace, he was speaking of the end of the Sulatins in *this* world. It was an accusation. Saina did not back away from it."

"And the Intercessor said Saina was right."

"Figuratively."

"You want it both ways. When it suits you, you accept speculation and figurative words. When it does not, all meanings are literal and you lash out. You toy with the idea of the Preceptor's return. But the change that follows, you must deny. If it were not for the Preceptor castigating the Seed Bearers five hundred years ago, you would have no Sulatin Order to revere. Saina brings change, and you cling to the old."

"If this letter was from the Preceptor, you might be right to condemn me. But it is not. No one knows if this person is the Preceptor. All we know is that Saina has replaced Ruryo, but Ruryo's plan lives on."

"Yes, and carried on by one of your own. Seed Bearer of Satamabode. That must gall you. Well, it is all quite beyond your influence now. You did what you could with the Seed Bearers and your censure of them was as bad as Ruryo's and worse than Saina's. You would harness Saina but you cannot and thus your anger. Now you want to harness me. But I won't have it. Thus your anger."

"Then it is nothing to you that he insults me with this incredible communication."

"No. I am sorry for that. I am certain it can be explained, were you to give him a chance." Sevrese paused and closed her eyes, pressing her lips together. What she would say next could not be defended. "Mother, in his letter to me, he asked me to join him in Alambarat. I will do so."

Pavim's pacing stopped abruptly.

"I am leaving today. It is clear you cannot consent, but I am not asking you to. If you intend to imprison me, you have only a few moments to arrange it, for I am off by horseback—alone—as soon as I can saddle."

Pavim turned deep red. "Do not end this discussion this way."

"It is not a discussion! It is tyranny. Is that all you want? Your old ways back? Maybe you should ask what we want—the next Seed Bearers, the next Daughters of the Seed, the next shopkeepers and farmers and warriors."

"Well what do you want? Can you tell me that? You cannot—you want the excitation of change? So whoever offers it is who you will all follow."

"That does you no credit. What are you afraid of?"

Pavim turned away to avoid that question. "I will not have you back here with him." She let the force of her words hit then let go another blow. "I will not have you back at all once your character is sullied by his."

Sevrese did not let the energy behind the words penetrate her. She stood stiff and aloof and livid.

"And, understand Sevrese, I take this sacrilege he plans on Prayadevale to be a greater transgression by a large measure than any exchange of passion between you. If you follow him there, you do so as no Daughter of Ryadabode."

Sevrese's heart pumped wildly. She stared her mother down now, though she was certain her face had gone pale. She knew her mother's will was equal to hers. There would be no victory here. She timed her exit to prevent another attack, and rushed to her room where she grabbed the pack she had put together. She threw off her clothes, changed for riding, and then ran to the stables.

She rode Tamarind. She needed a friend who would be hers forever. As she left she could feel her mother watching from the palace heights, but no one made an attempt to stop her.

Above, away from the window, but still able to see, Pavim witnessed her daughter's departure and then broke down, weeping alone until exhaustion stopped the flow. The first waves of emotion rose from the harshness of their disunion, but a deeper distress, a lifetime's heartache took over—not the loss of her child but the loss of hope. She felt as though everything had fled from her—everything she would defend was now beyond all her power to do so.

When her spasm subsided and she could sink with release, she pondered the very foundation of all her attachments. Her concern was not for Sevrese, for whatever hazard a mother might envision. She knew the girl's destiny was to triumph—at least in love, where she had always held out for the highest.

What forced her eyes to tightly close, her brows to furrow, her temples to pound, was the futility of her devotion to these principles she fervently defended. Were they as important as her own family? She no longer even knew if they were real or fancy.

What did Saina want of her? How could he expect her to act when he strips her of the tenets she depended on to guide all her actions? Surely, there was still a need for leaders to guarantee and uphold all the rights of all the people within their domains with probity and compassion.

But she could not defend even that simple idea. It was not that she faulted the Seed Bearers any more than herself, for who was blameless? She had seen enough of her husband's errors years ago and even as a child seen her father's. And she could not place her own regency upon the judgment scales without hesitation. Could she truly claim to be the guardian of all rights and not just the possessor of all privilege? Or had she just lived out the forms that tradition had established.

She was left without solid footing, without a brace, in a wind so strong her slender form must founder. And Saina had done this to her. He showed her she was blind. But did he have to then push her onto a path she had never walked before?

She felt suddenly a need to beseech a deity—any would do—on behalf of her daughter. Not for protection, but for the courage to fight and for the discernment to know what was worth fighting for.

"Sevrese," she whispered, "compromise nothing of yourself."

EPISODE 9

When word came that a solitary female rider with an escort trailing at a distance was approaching Alambarat from Ryadabode, Saina galloped through the gates on Grizzle. The horse finally voiced exception to the incline and brought their pace down to a walk.

Saina apologized aloud to him.

Grizzle gave him a vivid picture of his discomfort. *Your seat is bristling and tight. You break the flow. What is your problem? Take hold of yourself.*

Saina had no defense. He could feel it in himself. The longing to see her depleted any reserve of patience, leaving him raw and fiery and full of restive thoughts. They all came back to the same fear—what will she see when they meet? Would she accept him as what he had become?

But while that was how he phrased it today, the sensation had been pushing him since he left Sugorai. It began when he took leave of Bhalkavar, handing him the letters to Pavim and Sevrese. The general's hand had hesitated just a moment, but enough that Saina doubted what he had written.

The general had agreed to stay in Sugorai to keep the peace and to remove what he could of Hanarabode's presence. But Saina sensed that the task might have been the general's way to avoid the Regent when she heard of the plan for Prayadevale.

There was no way to soften what would become of the Sulatin Order. Surely she did not envision cruel ferines torturing helpless monks on Saina's orders. And he was convinced she understood the imperative. She heard it from Athayam, and to his reckoning, she accepted it as fact. But the image of Bhalkavar's reluctant hand bothered him, and Sevrese's feeling for him was the only proof he would accept.

They saw each other from the top and bottom of a switchback. They met where the two slopes joined. They did not speak until they touched hands. He breathed a long excited sigh as he looked into her eyes.

Their hands slid along each other's arm and they would have embraced, but the horses were fractious with each other, and they were bumped apart. They turned and made their way back down to Alambarat side-by-side.

"I see you have your escort now, Saina." She nodded toward the riders on a switchback below and the ferines on the slopes.

"Yes." He shrugged. "It is ironic that everyone has the highest expectations of me, but they appear to think I can do nothing alone. You have the same problem. Do you know you are followed?"

"Yes. It was Tamarind who caught the scent. My mother's work, no doubt. Don't be surprised if they drift off once I am seen in the company of your guard."

"Is she well?" It was so flat a question, it could not deserve a truthful answer. Sevrese simply nodded without meaning. He did not know how to inquire beyond that.

He took a long breath to settle himself, but it did nothing. He wondered if there was tension in her as well.

She looked down, not at him, to speak. "All these days since you returned from the training. So much is new."

"Unbelievable. I found a grandmother. I lost two brothers. I gained a half-sister of whom I know too little."

"Not forgetting your stature rose markedly."

"Yes, that. I hope I have your approval. Without yours, well—"

She frowned darkly. "My approval. Is there something I would not approve of?"

"I didn't say it well. It's just that discovering my identity and all the changes that came with it—the fight at Sugorai, the fight that lies ahead. Bhalkavar's wariness—must be hard for your mother to accept. But I cannot feel myself without your acceptance."

"Saina, everyone is thrilled about your true identity. Everyone rejoices at the success in Sugorai. Yet you seem to regret what has happened."

"Then all this has not changed your feelings?"

She stiffened. "No. What are you thinking? I told you my feelings do not depend on circumstance."

He swallowed hard and could not meet her eyes. *What am I thinking? What am I afraid of?* "I'm sorry. Nothing I have said makes sense suddenly. I have been very mindful of your mother's reaction to my plan. I hoped it would not affect your regard."

"Mindful?" She stopped Tamarind. "Saina, the letter you sent"— she stopped for want of the words and just shook her head.

The anxiety boiled in his stomach. "It was not meant to upset her. I had no choice. Since we won Alambarat, I feel like I have just been keeping afloat in a current. There are things that must happen. I only meant to make her aware of them."

"That is not true. I read the letter. I heard you just now. You want approval, but you gave instructions that much would be expected of her after you finish in Prayadevale."

"Those weren't my words."

"As good as. That is how she heard them."

"I only meant, because of her high principles, she had more to give than could be expected from others. Others who would not see the importance of this act. Sevrese, it was an invitation to her to take part in the greatest event for the Ten Abodes in five hundred years."

"I see." She stroked Tamarind's neck before looking at Saina's eyes. "The greatest event in five hundred years is your party. And you sent her an invitation with instructions on how to clean up afterwards."

He suddenly felt angry. This was a willful misunderstanding. "I didn't think she would want to participate. But I could not withhold the truth of what is destined. She is important to that destiny." Then immediately he cut off the emotion, wondering how he could ever be angry at her.

Sevrese saw it flash in his eyes and did not care that he suppressed it. She stared at him in silence.

"What is wrong?" he asked plaintively. Grizzle took several twisting steps.

She looked puzzled, painfully. "How can you ask for my approval and tell me what you do is controlled by destiny?" She shook her head in disbelief and looked away. Then she turned quickly back to him. "You wanted me to come. You wrote for me to come. I expected to enjoy your achievements and those ahead. Now you tell me you are just drifting on a current, as if my coming is not something you choose."

"I want you with me. I want your strength and your guidance and your affection. I am sorry if I have not expressed this very well."

She lowered her brows in troubled thought. "Saina, if there is a cloud of uncertainty around you, I will try to be the sun. But the cloud appears to be inside you and of your making. There is something from our past that is no longer here in your words."

"I don't understand. What is it?"

"Let me explain my coming. I have left my mother for the last time. Your letter insulted her. Devastated her. She forbid me to come and disowned me for my refusal of her. I came with the same intention that brought you to me from the sea camp that night. But you feel I have come to judge you. Lovers don't judge. To ask for approval is to admit you don't approve of yourself. Of course I have thought about all you have gone through from student to sovran. But I believed it would bring something glorious between us. You appear to believe I would be disappointed that you are not the same person I met in the forest. You give me little credit."

Her words made wounds he knew he had no power to close. He felt panic, as if death were coming.

"It has not been easy to live up to the Dowager's revelations. But I accept this destiny and the acts I must undertake to follow it. I regret causing your mother pain, yet I cannot change what is happening. That future is inevitable. But I know you do have a choice. I'm not asking for approval. I am asking if you want to make the choice to be with me."

"You are confused. You don't appear to know me as I thought you did. You certainly do not know yourself as I thought you did."

Tamarind began walking again, and she did nothing to stop her. Grizzle was glad to head back. They fell into the stiff and rhythmless pace of the horses going downhill. The horses balked and bumped each other and once made an attempt to bite. Saina's frustration made him pull Grizzle's head too strongly.

Sevrese shot a disapproving look. "Not with my horse."

He gave a look of apology. He knew he was losing control of himself. He was becoming exactly what she described. He wanted to deny everything. To ride back up the trail and begin again. But he could only ride beside her in silence. When they reached the flat ground near Alambarat, he tried one more apology.

"Sevrese, I don't know how my words went so wrong. I have known every day since we last were together that I love you. And long before that I loved you without knowing the words for the feeling. My feelings have not changed, and I have missed you too much to express."

She replied quietly, "Meeting like this after so much has happened to both of us is unfair. I would like most to take some rest by myself, and let this pressure melt away."

She gave the slightest nudge to Tamarind with her knee, and the horse cantered on. Grizzle did not wait for Saina to recover his balance and took off behind her.

When they reached the city, he took her to rooms that had been prepared near the Dowager's. She closed the door on him without a parting word. He stood immobilized and baffled, in despair. His arm straightened as if he would let the beads fall to his hand, but they were gone now. He looked futilely at the door. He would have knocked. He would have called her. But he was certain she would not answer him.

The rest of the day passed while he alternated between agony and sorrow. He roused himself to find the servants who had been assigned to her. They reported to him that she had refused food. She had in time bathed and had dressed in simple clothes she had brought in her one bag strapped to her saddle. More bags had arrived with her escort but she had left these unopened outside her door. She asked that she no longer be disturbed.

After much pacing in the hall he ventured a knock. He heard her voice, but it requested only that he return another time.

At sundown he pleaded for her to admit him. She did so. Her eyes were swollen. Her face miserable. Her demeanor distant.

"Sevrese, I want only to apologize"—

She cut him off. "Before I hear your apology, Saina, I want you to fully understand what that apology might be for. I fear it is I who must make that clear between us."

He stood still, not knowing how else to take what was coming.

Now her head tossed as she gathered in her emotions. "Please sit," she added and then began to pace the room in rhythm with her words.

He sat upon a cushioned stool to be used by a servant.

"You are right. Bhalkavar disapproves. In the letter he sent my mother, he used the phrase, Saina the Destroyer—apparently your Sulatin ally named it, but you did not refuse it. I was taken aback. My mother's impression was stronger."

Saina wanted to tell her it was only meant to describe the aspect of the Goddess, but she waved off his words.

"I understand you used it as a Sulatin would, but you knew no one else would greet it happily. Bhalkavar dismissed the title as trenchant and included in the letter as a caution to Pavim—his admission that you carry out the Athayam's instructions in spite of her wishes. In short, you relied on her support without respecting her reasons for giving it." She stopped to forestall any rebuttal." I know the conflict was resolved without a loss to her Protectors, but that has no relevance to this."

She stopped and breathed deeply with eyes closed. "Whatever your destiny turns out to be, it has separated you from your allies. It has caused them pain. Your allies happen to be the people closest to me. I have turned my back on them. It is too late for you to ask for approval. If your destiny is driving you, then have the grace not to flaunt it to others or to use it as your excuse to seek their approbation. It dishonors you." She shook when she spoke *dishonor*. "Of course, I defended your words and your actions to my mother, but now I discover I cannot defend your manner and the pride that has settled on your character—a false pride that you are giving in to a current that carries you. That you are not a cause, only a result. And therefore others have to cede to you their expectations and bury their reaction because your destiny precedes theirs. I know, having said this, you will apologize with all your heart, but the hurt cannot be removed from their hearts so easily. Do you think I do not understand what it means to not have control over your actions? That is the burden of a Seed Bearer family. It is not destiny. It is not a curse. It is simply a matter of honor. Ruryo may have exposed the fact that weaker Seed Bearers take the privileges and give nothing. But in my experience others accept the burdens along with the privileges with equanimity. Your Abode, if you want to know, was not among them."

She paused and he dreaded the next words.

"Do you understand and accept the honor that destiny has bestowed upon you? What follows is grace, not approval. If you want me to join you, ask me as Saina—not Saina the Seed Bearer, Saina the Destroyer, or Saina of Destiny. Grace does not inhabit titles, only persons. For a man who knows who he is and who I am and honors the love we have together, I will cast aside everything. You claimed to have measured me by that standard on the ride to the Ryadabode border. You have indeed changed if you think less of me now."

She fell silent with anger, but this time he had no impulse to leap in. She gathered herself and went on.

"It is time you learned what sacrifice means, Saina. It is time you stop yourself before condescension takes over any further. We once joked that I would be your teacher for the skills of riding. You learned that well enough without me. You expressed upon the pillow of my bed that I was your teacher in love. But as a lover you were in no need of a teacher." Her face contorted and her eyes streamed with tears. As she sensed he might rise to her, she took a step backward and stiffened, regaining herself.

"But I will teach you this. I will teach you the mistake of taking yourself so seriously. The mistake of giving no one else credit for their own wisdom, for their talents, for their own destinies—all given to them by the same divinity that speaks to you. Once as an abandoned student you were too fragile to believe yourself worthy. Now you are so swollen by the Seed to apologize for it. Go on this adventure to the Sulatins. Play your game of destruction. Be compelled as an instrument of the gods. Do you think I was not listening that night on the balcony when you returned from the ferines? This change that is coming—it will take place in an eyeblink. The devils will defeat the gods. The Goddess will create anew. An eyeblink. It does not wait for you—for your destiny. And the moment after your victory in Prayadevale, we will all be the same people. There is no reason to bruise my mother or Bhalkavar or me in this process. As you leave tomorrow for Prayadevale, I leave in another direction entirely. I give you no apology, and I do not seek your approval."

She fought off more tears by tightening every muscle.

He rose, but her hand went up as a shield. She turned from him and asked him to go. This time as the door closed he did not delude himself by lingering.

Daiyenso found Saina at dusk sitting on a bench in a dark corner of the common where he had once addressed the city. There were no ferines in a nearby tree. No one took notice. Daiyenso stared for a long time until Saina finally replied to the question he was expecting.

"What's wrong is I forgot to follow your instruction."

Daiyenso gave a small twist of his head to invite more.

"When I asked you about the Seed on our last night here. You said to ask the Goddess."

"I remember.

"I expected the Seed would change me. So I tried to be a Seed Bearer, but I got it wrong. I should have checked with Her, as you recommended."

"What changed is the power of cognition. The gift that Seed Bearers have ignored. You cannot ignore it."

"I experienced Goddessoma as a student. What is the difference?" Before Daiyenso could answer, Saina gave a huff. "I know the answer. I have even explained the difference to others. But it was only words I was taught to say. Are you going to give me words you were taught to say?" Saina stood awkwardly. "Put off our venture to Prayadevale."

Daiyenso waited. Then he said simply, "As you wish."

"The Preceptor wants me to act out something so simple as the destruction and creation of our world, so he has decided I don't need more judgment or clearer instructions. What am I saying? I offend the Preceptor, I offended Bhalkavar. I offended Pavim. Now I have offended Sevrese. The thing is, Daiyenso, Sevrese is greater to me than my destiny. Can you explain that?"

Daiyenso gave him another long look, as if from a great distance. And in that distance he seemed to hear a voice. He listened and replied softly, "I believe I can. You are unsure who the Goddess is. Let me take you to a place here you have not seen. There you may learn."

"And who Sevrese is?"

He nodded.

"And who I am?"

Daiyenso nodded. "Oh yes."

Saina followed listlessly as they walked through the oldest streets of Alambarat, the section of the city that butted up against the first stone walls more than a thousand years old. Daiyenso led him into a house, where he informed the inhabitants that they must leave for the night so that their sovran might have their home. Saina remained dazed by the enterprise, but he did not question it. Once the family had gone off, elated and confused, Daiyenso lit a lantern and led Saina out the back door into a small courtyard that ended in a pile of rocks.

"Before Alambarat was a city, it was a shrine—serving the city of the old ruins further down the valley where the Founding Seer was born. If we move some of these rocks you will find an entrance to the deep sanctuary beneath the shrine."

Soon the entrance appeared, but it was small, requiring them to bend down and crawl. The passage dropped down a long distance until it opened into a natural cavern where they could stand. In the lantern light they could see a solid rock altar, bare of any sign of worship.

Saina stared in each direction. "How do you know of this place?"

"I found it—I was led to it—during the invasion by Hanarabode. I would guess I am the only one who knows."

Daiyenso motioned toward the passageway on the other side of the altar that appeared to lead even deeper into the earth. "This is only the beginning."

"What is the end?"

"Your Goddess. She will hear your problem. She will answer you— and perhaps judge you."

"I'm not ready for that."

"If you were ready, there would be no need."

Saina stared into the total darkness. The hole was as tight as his body.

"Here you are given no room for choice. You must reenter the Infinite Mother. When you emerge you and I will meet as planned tomorrow in Prayadevale."

Saina nodded. He bowed his back and slid into the opening. The sides of the passage were cut with handholds and offered just enough space to push with his arms. He crawled on his stomach. Water was seeping in along the walls, soaking his clothing and his hair, allowing him to slide along the primitive rock. The droplets ran down the curves of his face and mixed with his own sweat as he strained to push along, finding its way into his mouth where it tasted acrid and musky, warmed by some fire deep in the earth.

The tunnel went on for so long that that fear began to creep into his chest. It was so dark and so close and so slick, it was easy to imagine one would never climb back out.

Finally he emerged into another cavern, known only because of the echoing drips and availability of air. He stood to feel the top, but it was far above him. The floor was level, fashioned by human work. And in the blackness his hand traced round the walls until he found an object that could not have been carved by water alone.

In relief upon the rough rock wall, was a smooth figure, larger than human form. He felt legs that might have been dancing, one foot raised in delicate balance. He felt the narrow waist above the rounded hips, then high breasts as arms were raised to a soundless rhythm.

He stretched to reach the head and found long stone earrings and flowing stone hair. The brow was smooth, the eyes open, the nose straight and perfect. But the mouth was agape and the teeth were sharp as knives and the tongue protruded. His touch brought a sense of awe and no less dread. It felt older than the rock.

He sat before it.

This was the Mother of all. The hints he had received—the burst of energy that came in the presence of the women he had known, the glimpses of the energy and spirits of Goddessoma—were insignificant by comparison to the real thing—even in stone.

He was sitting in the womb of all Her power. Not principle. Not abstraction. Here was the true energy—palpable, earthly, native. He could perceive everything in Her creation—even as he was wholly blind in the darkness. He could feel all Her power coiled beneath his legs and moving along his spine. She was pressing upon him in the air. His body was merely the pattern into which and through which She flowed. The transcendent forms of Goddessoma began here, swirling round Her to be flung away and back again with Her breath.

He could only wait. There was nothing to do—only to be.

In time, he was aware of the echoing of the droplets in the cavern building into a rhythm, the pulse through which moved Her energy in successive emanations until he could not interpret the difference between the vibrations of touch and sound.

And then he saw with an eye that pierced darkness. He could not say it was seeing as one saw in the world above. But it was more convincing. And with it he saw that, in all the world, this energy is all there is. One form—yet one manifestation after another it animates. And through it all the energy itself remains unchanged. For all the distinctions, each object it inhabits—a Seed Bearer, a Sulatin, a Ruryo, a Panjael, a Pavim, a Saina, a Sevrese—is one with the rest.

Each manifestation pushes into Her dance with its own limitless desires—selfish and benevolent, belligerent and tender—in a never-ending current of need. All one vibration of waves rising and falling, separated by the illusion of sequence and time and opposites—birth, death, love, hate, victory, defeat.

With this perfect knowledge of all desires in his grasp, a voice reached into his being without passing his ears.

"What do you want?"

It was not a question. It was an invitation. There was energy in this place to make anything. And nothing could be petitioned that would diminish it.

Eyes closed, his attention deep inside him where his own desires were born, he answered aloud, "I want ... to know You." The sound echoed and beat upon the walls and returned in chaos. "I want ... to know myself ... and I want to know her."

Loud was Her reply, as if every fiber in his body had an ear in which Her words vibrated. Then a thousand ears became a thousand mouths that spoke Her answer within him.

"I am one. Without attributes. Unknowable. I breathe out and in a moment my body forms a world of twos. I am God the Father, Goddess the Mother, I am gods and devils who serve me, I am light and dark, truth and untruth, love and hate, seed and tree. I breathe in and all of the mortal world comes back to one.

He sank mentally and physically to a depth where he lost all bearing. For moments or for years—there was no measure. He was so lost he could not question if the stone statue was truly dancing—swirling on top of him, sweeping him along.

"You and she are the first two of creation. One soul divides into two. Yours is the man's soul through whom I speak in the mortal world. Through you my creation advances with congruity—here to there, in gain and loss, a sequence guided by your mastery and wisdom. All you require I have place in your seed.

"Hers is the woman's soul through whom I nourish the mortal world. Through her my creation abides with love—binding, cherishing, celebrating, bestowing, blessing. All she requires I have placed in her womb.

Together you become Me. I inhabit you.

He roused himself to open his eyes to see Her—the statue, the Goddess. She was lit by a white glow. But now the face was not the face he had felt with his hand. Gone were the piercing teeth and the mouth that would devour and destroy. In its place were lips in a smile sensuous and tempting, eyes filled with laughter, arms raised in joy. But as his sight drew closer, the face changed again. The lips, the eyes—they winced, twisted in pain. The face was now Sevrese's face. Her pain flowed into him.

He realized that until that moment he could feel nothing. He had no emotion that could match the depth of hers. Now he had hers. Now he knew her heart. Sevrese's heart, which was the Goddess' heart.

The pain was a deep desire betrayed. She could not breathe out only in. Creation was dissolving. Love was must end.

The voice declared, "Earn your gift. Let your offering come forth. Sacrifice on the altar your acts, so you will experience *who* acts. All *your* action is Mine. What moves, moves with My will. What rests, rests in Me. Sacrifice your singularity. You are a wave, she is a wave, I am the ocean. Sacrifice the love between you. Her loving you is loving Me. Your loving her is loving Me. When you clutch these things to yourself, you have not enough arms to hold them. The loss of any of them brings you pain and madness. How simple it is to accept them thankfully and let them pass to Me on the altar."

Then came the sound of laughter as light as the strings of a harp, fading into the last words of the Goddess.

He stood. Golden sprays of light were raining on the statue and turning into a river in which he was happy to drown. He edged back up the passage, pulled upward by the need to accept the world above. Daiyenso had left the lamp burning on the altar of the first chamber.

Exhausted Saina bent over the altar and gripped the edge tightly. He felt nothing here like the overwhelming presence of the Goddess below. There sacrifice was without intention. Here was nothing but inexorable hardness of the altar and fragile human flesh. Here sacrifice must be an act of will. He brought Sevrese's form to his mind. His thoughts spun in circles as he struggled to capture the meaning of sacrifice.

What came was so simple. *Everything I am and everything I can be I dedicate to you as I dedicate it to Her. I surrender my destiny, my title, my victories, my honor to the Goddess.*

He did not know if it was enough. He did not know where it fell short. He only knew it was true.

—∘∘❦∘∘—

Saina once more knocked on her door, but without apprehension or hope—only patience.

She admitted him but sat a distance against the window, where the gold sky was fading as the sun cleared the mountains. She was dressed, ready to leave.

"Sevrese." He began quietly, but the words that followed came as forcefully as the beating of his emotions in his chest. "You have suffered because whatever wisdom I gained in our time apart did not make up for the ignorance I invited. I have felt the pain in you, and I feel as if I have stolen offerings from a shrine of the Goddess. As deeply as I want to apologize to you, I understand no words will remove it. But, if you allow me, I will never hurt you or those you love in such a manner again."

She took a deep breath through flaring nostrils, letting her eyes rest on him as she slowly exhaled.

"Is that what you have to tell me?"

It was not a question. It was an invitation. He bowed his head slightly and then raised it to meet her eyes and hold them.

"I want much more than to remove your pain. I want the responsibility to bring you all happiness. I want to love you every moment and receive your love every moment. I want that before I want anything else, before I do anything else. That is where everything for me begins. Don't leave, Sevrese. Stay with me."

She bit at her lips. They tightened. Tears came again but did not flow, only moistening her eyes. When at last she replied, her voice began weak, but turned bold.

307

"I spent last night considering what had made me want you. I recounted everything—as if I had preserved every look, every gesture, every word—everything that could stand for who you are to me. Everything I had been shown in our moments together and contemplated in our time apart. In all of it I have seen you many ways—a struggling monk, a struggling warrior, a victorious sovran—but none of these have any consequence in my heart. It was not these that compelled me to you. They are neither good nor bad, advantage nor fault. Do you understand?"

He gave the faintest nod.

"I do not want anything from you that your position can bring me—whether it be low or high. Or your knowledge—Sulatin or Seed Bearer. What I want—what I must have before my love will flow to you—is something that I am certain must flow through every man who is a man." The words came out now in a series of beats, slowly marching, resounding within his head. "It is self-reliance. It is resolution. It is compassion. It is forbearance. It is gratitude and graciousness for the gifts that come. It is everything that animates manliness and makes it great—high or low."

A small smile crossed her lips but turned bitter before it disappeared. "The general has nearly all of that. I suppose I have defined it from a lifetime of watching him." She breathed deeply. "That is what I saw within you—even in the Garland Forest, where outwardly you showed anything but that. And from behind my veil of secrecy when my mother first interviewed you, I saw it more clearly. And each time since, the clarity grew. The night of the boatride. Your return from the ferines. Your steadiness in the face of Athayam's challenge. And certainly in your visit to my bed. That is who you have been in my mind, and when you were revealed as Seed Bearer, I thought it the perfect fulfillment." She paused. "Until yesterday—when I had to wonder, was it all a fancy? For it is one or the other. Truth or void. Of that I am certain."

Her eyes searched his countenance. She gave him one last chance to show his conformation.

He felt strength and quiet at the same time. "If you saw these qualities, you saw the bud not the fruit. Can you allow that they might be covered up without being destroyed?"

Her head nodded slowly. "Yes." No change came to her eyes.

"And if the covering were removed, they could be mastered in time?"

"That is a possibility."

He nodded repeatedly for a few moments, deciding how much to say and not say. "I was taught last night that loving you is loving the Goddess. When I love Her I love you as She does. When I love you, I love Her. All the qualities you spoke just now also come from Her as well. I believe it must follow that loving you can be the way to their mastery."

Her eyes widened, then stared at nothing, as if remembering. "Why do you talk of Her?"

He did not answer. He did not know where to begin.

Instead, she cut in, "I had a dream of Her last night." Sevrese's hand went to her brow and pressed as if that would recall it. "Such a strong impression, but I would have forgotten if you had not said that. As if— as if She truly spoke and comforted me. As if something was released." She took a deep breath in and softly let it go. "My anger. She took it. So many images I have made of Her. Never in my life a dream. Never a word from Her. Only now."

He felt a pulsing excitement in his chest. He felt gratitude as immense as the sky. "Last night She took something from me as well— let's say, my excesses."

She managed a quick smile. "If She visits each of us on the same night, that would seem to be telling."

"I would say, conclusive."

She reached for him, smiling and sad at once, tears welling and a laugh catching in her throat. He pulled her to him and her hands slid up his shoulders and neck to cup his head.

She said, "I am so tired of being apart."

He put his fingers on her cheek. It was polished smooth like the stone of the Goddess but wet with human tears. They held each other a long time.

Off the road to Prayadevale in a dark part of the forest the Preceptor listened to Daiyenso's account of Saina's Sugorai victory. He gave small signs of satisfaction and even delight. Daiyenso had an impression that the effulgence for which he was named by the ferines glowed more intensely.

"Very nearly flawless. So many harsher possibilities were always there."

"Can we expect the same tomorrow?"

"Tomorrow will be my day to come out of the forest. A propitious day. A great day for you. I thank you for all your effort."

Daiyenso did not respond directly. "A great day for Saina."

"No." A laugh started under his beard and broke through his smile. "A hard day for him. The beginning of many hard days ahead. He will have so much work, he will learn what the sacrifice of the Seed Bearer truly is. Has he recovered his strength?"

"From the defiance of two females? It must be so."

The Preceptor gave a second and softer laugh. "Women are very important for his success now. He will be inspired by the strength and steadiness of these two. And his grandmother will show him that life is much longer and fuller than he can imagine now. In turn, he will be able to open his sister's mind to Goddessoma, where she will thrive." He paused and changed his tone. "The loss of his mother was a terrible blow to endure. It is good he could have some time as a monk—to show him the Goddess first. Else, there was the risk that he would not value these women rightly when he needed to."

"He made some mistakes. I may have been the cause."

"Ahh. You have contributed to his sense of destiny. That is alright. Destiny is a puzzle that in the end comes to nothing. Gifts from the Goddess are always earned—more often before receiving, sometimes after. But his gifts are overpowering. He did not see how many futures are always available. Fixedness and resolve appear to give strength. But like any medicine that heals, too much is poison. Better to be ready for all possibilities than only one. It was always in his power to succeed or fail—and remains so."

"It was my lesson as well. I never doubted he would succeed at Sugorai, and the same here in Prayadevale. But I gauge his potential so much larger now."

"All these gods and devils in Goddessoma—they must be employed somehow. We should always keep the widest view and desire without limitation. It is good for life."

A slow chant, barely perceptible, began to rise in the mountains and unfurl through the air, joining the soft rush of the waving trees. The ferines approached.

The two men listened for some time. At last the Preceptor opened his eyes and spoke.

"They announce the dawn with a special song, knowing this day is different. We will join them."

Daiyenso nodded, but there was the faintest hesitation to get up. The Preceptor caught it.

"What is the question? You are always free to ask whatever you wish. You have earned the right over and over again. Why do you hesitate? You are troubled. Release your conceit."

Daiyenso straightened to sit upon his heels. A slow whisper emerged. "Long ago you told me I had my own tests to pass, lessons to learn. Just now you praised me for that, and I am appreciative. Humbled, for I am not indifferent to praise from you. But you have not told me the whole truth."

"No? That would be a very large telling."

Daiyenso gave a melancholy smile. "You know my mind. You know therefore that I myself have chosen one more test. What am I to do about the enemy I have created?"

"*You* have created? What enemy is this?"

"Luzarain."

"Why do you claim to have created him?"

"Yes. That is wrong. We always were rivals."

The Preceptor shook his head. "Where is humility these days?"

"I did nothing to discourage his resentment when I could have. In small ways I am even guilty of taunting him. It was not necessary. When I realized he was guiding Ruryo, I went beyond my reach to affect my own result. It was pride—but the most conceited reaction was resentment, when I realized that he is my cohort—dear to you."

"Yes, you have identified one test left to pass. But it is not the test you think it to be." There was silence for some time. "Here is your question. Not the one you asked. What causes the Divine Mother to forsake Her Oneness for creation? Why does the unmanifest Goddess take a Body and then multiply it infinitely? Do you know?"

"I know the words that are used. They are no more than a child's story. In Her Oneness She felt alone and desired another. But how can any words, let alone these, describe the truth that is indescribable?"

The Preceptor shook his head. "That does not answer. Take the story for only a symbol of truth, if you like. A shadow of the form. It will suffice. Loneliness is something *you* should appreciate. In Her aloneness there is nothing. Truly nothing. There is silence. As soon as you raise the concept of nothing, you create its opposite. Nothing creates something. When you apprehend silence—you create sound. Darkness defines light. Good, evil. Pleasure, pain. Spontaneously. Instantly. Unavoidably. In Her oneness and solitude everything remains commingled, undifferentiated. To create and organize all that we see around us requires only one thought, one whisper, the faintest impression—such as *alone*. That is why we understand creation and destruction as Her eternal and simultaneous work."

"Therefore I *must* have an enemy?" Daiyenso reflected.

"An opposite, yes. But with your tasks, the opposite is naturally an enemy. There is no other way. You have served me. He has served me. You require each other. You oppose each other. Ruryo requires and opposes Saina. To stand up, what must you do? Push down on your feet. Nothing exists without the presence of its opposite. No one gains the power to realize the highest teaching until there is appreciation of the basest ignorance and suffering."

Daiyenso looked inward. "So you called on Luzarain just as you called me. But you never allow him to have your presence. And that is what propelled him to gain more powers and assist Ruryo. It is *right* that we should be opposed—to accelerate destruction and therefore creation."

The Preceptor held fingertips together and let them bend and butt each other softly many times. "You two are warriors of the spirit, chosen to fight the war of the Goddess' creation and dissolution here in the mortal world. A warrior is nothing without his worthy enemy. The nature of your powers inspired Saina. The nature of Luzarain's were the inspiration of Saina's enemy. Yours prevailed and both your natures belong to the Her now. Her compensation is always perfect once the last test is passed."

"Resolve the conflict."

The Preceptor simply raised a brow.

"But—you have just now said that our enmity is necessary."

"Here. Not in Goddessoma. That is where you must take your rivalry. There is a place for you among Her immortals. Take it."

A wave of anticipation gripped his chest. A breath escaped him involuntarily—as if the Preceptor had reached out and struck him. "Your world?"

"Mine? There are too many brothers and sisters to count. They are everywhere. They are guides—for people, for worlds, for passages. They manifest upon the wishes of the Goddess to aid her eternal creation and destruction. They abide within her when not called."

Daiyenso's heart was pounding even harder—yet, in the midst of perfect calm. "And the means to this destination—is sacrifice?"

"Always sacrifice. But in Goddessoma sacrifice involves no loss." His laughed was drowned by rustle of arriving ferines across the trees.

In the afternoon Saina heard the song of the ferines ahead and turned his force off the road to Prayadevale into the meadow where he felt sure they would meet the Preceptor. Currents of purple, yellow, white, blue, and red flowers swayed in the spring breeze. Dismounting and leaving the horses with their long necks bent to the ground and noses snorting into the greens, Saina and Sevrese walked out into the sunlight.

Daiyenso came out of the thick trees on the other side of the meadow. Saina saw different look on his face—a different emotion that he could not recognize. A distant sadness matched by great satisfaction. Then it dawned on him.

"This is the end of your duties for him—at least on my behalf."

Daiyenso nodded. "I have some work of my own to complete."

Without a thought Saina started to go to his knees in gratitude, but Daiyenso held him up. "Not for me, Saina." He pointed to the figure waiting for him under a lone spreading tree on the other side of the meadow.

From their place in the spring sunlight he was hard to see. The Preceptor's dark skin blended perfectly with the bark of the dense trees behind. They walked toward him into the shade and found a man of indiscernible age standing naked with glistening black hair hanging nearly to the ground and beard to his waist. He gave a welcoming wave toward the three of them and meanwhile invited the ferines to come down from the trees. A cry of excitement broke loose, and ferines swarmed him. He touched the heads here and there and accommodated every one that he could. Shib was at his back through it all. The Preceptor spoke to the ferines wordlessly for a short time and then they dispersed. Saina and Sevrese stepped forward.

Sevrese whispered, "Saina, I see the light around him. He is glorious."

Beneath his beard was a faint smile. His eyes were stern yet still inviting. First he took Sevrese's hands in his and slowly gathered them within his own. She immediately bent her head and thanked him, feeling serenity in his touch. She started to lower further but his hands held her up.

"No need for knees. I know you understand humility, but it is for me to appreciate having you here. You have come a long distance and with much difficulty—am I right?"

Tears welled in her eyes, but her composure remained. "A long distance for my heart, yes. But no more than the others."

"Mmm. Your boldness has been your merit. Half of it is your own, the other half is an inheritance. I shall rely on it many times on the rest of our journey together. But just now I rely on your sense of propriety, which is also exalted. I wonder if you would help me."

"Of course, please," she said with anything but boldness.

"I leave the forest now and join the people. My life here has produced an appearance that might startle some. Daiyenso has a robe for me. Will you cut this hair? And the beard? Make it look as dignified as you would expect if you were to present me to your own mother."

She smiled. "My mother requires no decorum. She would recognize you in a moment, clothed in any manner."

"But decorum would be a gift with which to honor her. You appreciate that—especially."

Sevrese closed her eyes and nodded. She wiped the wetness from her cheek. "Thank you—I see."

Then he came to Saina with a piercing look. "Are you prepared yet?" He took Saina's hands in his own and the sensation was overwhelming.

Saina blinked. "I don't know yet what I am to do. I hope I am."

The eyes bore into Saina's. "Hope will not help you or anyone else. Prepare for anything and you master everything. You have faced many challenges in a short time. There are many tests ahead. Today you must finally pass the only one you have failed so far."

It hit him like an arrow. "What have I failed?"

"Are you prepared to give up your belief in your fallibility?"

My fallibility? His mind went back to the Goddess cave. He could possess nothing that did not belong to Her. Was he willing to say his failings belonged to Her as well, or did his pride require that he claim for himself? *Place it on Her altar*, he heard himself urge.

"I am ready to give it up." He felt a rush in his spine—a layer of confidence he did not know he possessed.

"Mmm. That is a start. It is good that we stay together for a while."

He let go of Saina's hands and put his thumb to Saina's forehead and his fingers to the top of his head. From his touch Saina felt a flaming bolt descend his spine. He felt invincible. When he opened his eyes he saw the Preceptor staring, measuring.

"In Prayadevale today you must order the Sulatins to cross a bridge with you. When you do I want you to feel what you just felt. *Not* what you hope to feel."

Saina took a rough breath. The Preceptor anticipated his thought, as his mind filled with the memory of his two friends as they died from a rooftop.

"Once I gave just such an order to two Sulatin students. They had faith in me—the bridge did not hold."

The Preceptor gripped his arm. "Yes. I know of this. Keep in mind, that you did not speak the truth to those two. They still wait for that even to this day. You have never understood why they cling to you. If you want someone to follow your command, you must speak the truth. You learned that from the general, yes?"

"Yes. I made an enemy recently by speaking more than the truth."

"Yes. There is nothing more than the truth. The truth defies embellishment. But maybe what you wrote was the truth that needed to be expressed. Go by your intuition, not by how others may react. You do not know with certainty what they need. So you should apply to your intuition the test of simplicity. Today especially. With that you can trust you will not make enemies."

Daiyenso stepped forward and led Sevrese and The Preceptor away. Saina went back to his men and his general. He addressed them all.

"I do not know yet what will happen when we reach the monastery, but I trust the man who called us here and ask that you trust him as well."

He then spoke to Ghoru so that everyone could hear. "General, I have never expressed my gratitude to you in front of your men. Those of you who were chosen for this mission should hear it and can pass it along to others when we return to Sugorai. General Ghoru came to Prayadevale after the attack by Hanarabode that you all endured. His mission was to bring me back to our Abode, though neither of us knew why. I was utterly ignorant about anything outside of this mountain, but he gave me exactly what I needed at that moment and took me to safety. Again in Alambarat after we won back the city, I was utterly unpolished in the art of leadership, and found out I must master that very fast. Ghoru trained me. Others have made noble efforts to turn around the defeat of Satamabode, but you can trace our success back to Ghoru. So whatever he instructs you to do today, do not question it for a moment. He is right. And his timing is always impeccable."

There was cheering—nervous but heartfelt.

At Prayadevale the Preceptor sent the ferines through the monastery—no less than Saina's order to sweep Alambarat into the square—to corral everyone in the assembly hall.

He ordered Ghoru's Protectors to form a siege semi-circle from where the buildings butted the mountain rock on each side. Then Saina, Sevrese, Daiyenso, and Shib walked through the doors of the monastery in the presence of the Preceptor. An alarming stream of smoke was pouring out of the cone of the mountain above the monastery, rolling into the firmament as if it would break into a rain of fire. The Preceptor gave it a long look, squinting into the sun beyond.

They then slowly proceeded to the assembly hall. Walking the long center aisle between the rows of straw floor cushions, Saina passed many students nudging each other and whispering. He acknowledged them with an unassuming look. Athayam came forward from the front row and led the Preceptor up the dais steps to his seat. He turned to the side of the room and signaled musicians to start.

Daiyenso and Shib returned to the door and stood as if guards.

A single voice took up a song of praise and on the chorus the entire assembly murmured along until the end. Then everyone took seats. It was the first time Saina had ever been so close to the dais. He saw the seat the Preceptor sat down on—until now the Intercessor's—had a base of pure gold, cast from a mold carved in delicate geometric patterns.

Silence descended and the Preceptor spoke.

"I feel honored," the voice drifted softly from the dais to the ends of the room, "to visit this final act of destruction upon you."

Then a gentle peal of laughter rose in him and everyone in the audience broke loose as well. When it faded, he continued, cheerful and calm.

"The work of your Order is finished. The door of this ancient facility is closed at this moment. Let us take time to accept its passing in silence." He closed his eyes and sank within.

A long time went by. Sevrese left her eyes closed, and Saina, wondering at her reactions to his former world, opened his eyes to see her face was lit with satisfaction. He felt another impulse and was drawn to the face of Luzarain, next to the dais with Athayam, staring intently at Daiyenso. Suddenly Luzarain turned and drew his gaze upon Saina. Saina felt it like a striking blow.

Before he knew what to do the Preceptor stirred, and slowly the room began to come out of silence with the shuffling of bodies, a muffled cough or two, a whisper that lasted too long.

The Preceptor looked at Saina and gave a nod. Saina hesitated, rattled by Luzarain. A second nod was more inviting and he gestured with his hand to stand.

Saina gave himself a command. *This is your task. This is your room. Don't hold back. Give up your fallibility. Step off the roof.*

He stood. The room grew still. He looked across the faces, from children to august elders. In spite of his resolution, he could not avoid the thought with this particular group, *Who am I to lead them?* But he immediately realized there was not an audience in the Ten Abodes who grant him trust on sight. His charge was clear—follow his intuition with simplicity.

His eyes were drawn above the crowd to a corner ledge above. There sat the spirits of two boys whose lives he had spent so carelessly. He understood they had waited all these years for him to lead them to their next existence. He owed it to them to step off the roof and complete the play.

"I was one of you for over half my short life," he began. His voice did not carry in the hall, and he could see those in the back question each other suddenly. He cleared his throat and went on. "I was called out into another life by circumstance. I gave up my place here. Forever. Not many have ever done so. Who would want to?

"I return now as Seed Bearer of Satamabode. And I return as a symbol. A symbol that the time of the Ten Abodes has come to an end as the time of the Sulatins has come to an end."

He hesitated. He turned to the Preceptor and tried to feel his thoughts. There was no barrier. He knew what the Sulatins must do. And how to tell them.

"Like me, you must go out into that same world. We have lived in silence, like the silence of all knowledge as it resides in Goddessoma. But the knowledge in the Body of the Goddess must disperse into Her creation. You must become teachers. Share your knowledge so it becomes action. Lift up the lives of the people of the Ten Abodes, who have accorded you the honor of preserving their knowledge for five centuries."

He felt in his spine the same rush of fire the Preceptor had given him. He had passed one test.

"This action requires sacrifice. I remember a lesson learned here in my first years. It is said, the world is born, grows, and dies over what appears to be an enormous span of time—yet in every instant the Goddess destroys and creates the world anew. From our perspective, nothing changes. The hawk soars across the sky, and in that instant all creation ends. When creation arises again, in that same instant, the hawk continues its flight without interruption. The Goddess lets out her breath to animate creation and takes in her breath to dissolve it. And between those two, the Goddess is one in eternal equanimity. You have the knowledge to see and comprehend Her. Your sacrifice is to let Prayadevale crumble and die and move the knowledge into the houses and palaces below. Protecting the cognitions of the Founding Seers is finished. From today you are their exponents."

He gave them a long look in silence. When Saina sat down, Sevrese took his hand and felt the quivering throughout his body. She pressed close to him to calm it down. Without a look, he melted into her acceptance and relaxed.

The Preceptor began again even more delicately than before. "I am indebted to Saina of Satamabode for his courage over these many days and for his eloquence today. He has captured all truth in this address.

As he says, I have come to transform the preservers of knowledge into the exponents of knowledge that will now be distributed like corn from an abundant harvest. To the farmer's field. To the mill. To the market. To sellers and buyers. To kings and shopkeepers. To the animals of the fields and forests and plains and sky. From today, a Sulatin is a guide for all our people and for all peoples beyond the borders of the Ten Abodes and to all beings everywhere.

"The Ten Abodes themselves will be reconstructed, their geographic boundaries replaced by unbounded knowledge. One monarch will rise as the reflection of the people's aspirations and desires. It is he who has just spoken to you. He is both of your world and of the world of the Ten Abodes. His duty will be to complete this conversion. You will follow his progress, work with his blessing, bring enlightenment everywhere.

"I will provide you with your teaching. I will complete all that you have preserved these five hundred years and replace anything that was lost. You will take your knowledge of the body and you will rejuvenate the bodies of the people. You will take your knowledge of the mind and you will deepen their understanding of all things. You will take your knowledge of the spirit and you will welcome them to Goddessoma. For those who become my guides, a life of infinite happiness awaits. For the people who receive your teaching a life of infinite happiness awaits.

"I come as your symbol. From deep within the silence of the caves of the forest. Now is my time to break that silence and speak. The Goddess commands it for new expressions of Her truth. New cognitions. You will prepare for the Seers who next will *see*."

The Preceptor rose. Everyone in the hall stood to honor him. Then they bowed—all of them. The Intercessor himself. The surrender was accomplished.

And then immediately it was broken. Luzarain pushed his way to the front, creating a human wave as everyone separated to let him pass, a wave more of emotion than motion.

As the wave hit Saina he felt within it a surge of aggression aimed at the Preceptor. Instinctively he came forward to intercept it.

Luzarain looked at Saina as if he were a fly.

"A sham," he murmured. Yet, in the silence, everyone heard the word. It came from the Conductor, and they had to give it credit. "These monks are swayed by words of portent and mystery. Might we want to ask for some proof? Proof that you are the Preceptor. Proof that this young man carries the Seed—beyond a few lines scribbled in an Abode scroll by an Assessor Martial who can hardly be trusted. Proof that this glorious vision you have shared with us is any different from what we endured with Ruryo. Fewer dead bodies do not alter the fundamental argument between the rule of ten Seed Bearers and the rule of one grand monarch. And can you truly back up your claim of a new world created with such a simple device as moving a few hundred monks into new quarters? This is an outrageous fraud, and all my brothers have fallen for it."

Luzarain slowly spun to look into the faces of the monks and as he spun they backed up like a spreading fan. Only Daiyenso held his ground approaching the Preceptor, Saina, Sevrese, and Athayam standing behind Luzarain.

"Ahh. Here is Daiyenso. My counterpart. Perpetrator of this fraud. You have been the champion of this young man Saina as well as the Preceptor. Would you like to be the champion of their proof?"

Daiyenso stared into Luzarain's eyes, who met him with equal intensity.

"What proof would satisfy you?"

"The test must be the power behind the words. Does this Preceptor have such power that he can promise the formation of a new order that will bring enlightenment to everyone? I can accept true power. Well, here is his favorite—does this boy Saina have the power?" He laughed. "I do not see it? He can talk to creatures and heal a cut and he is lucky in war. But before I will follow him, I demand proof of something greater. A challenge to prove that our Order is so unworthy as you all conspire to claim. Come. Come first, Saina—you who want kings to bow to you."

Saina knew the man's power, but he did not fear it. Not until he felt Luzarain's intentions encircle him as though they were ropes of twisted metal. Serpent-like, they slipped round his neck and cut his breath annihilated any force within that could defeat Luzarain.

Then Daiyenso stepped in front of him and took Luzarain's attack. Saina was free.

"These are petty objections, Luzarain," he said coldly. "You are too exalted for this challenge. It does not honor you. You have all the proof you need. This is the mortal world. One side had to lose. It is all resolved."

Luzarain looked gratified. "You and I, however, are not resolved. Where should we challenge each other?"

"We both know the right place."

The two Sulatin adepts stared at each other silently, breathlessly. Words were passing between them unspoken. Then Daiyenso turned his head to the Preceptor, as if to seek his blessing.

The Preceptor looked to both of them. He barely nodded—little more than the slow lowering of his eyelids to Daiyenso.

Daiyenso glanced at Saina with half-closed eyes and fell limp into Saina's arms. It was as if every measure of energy passed out of his body. Saina lowered it to the ground and knelt beside what was Daiyenso. On the floor opposite Daiyenso the body of Luzarain had fallen in in exactly the same state.

What happened next, no one would later describe with confidence. An instant of darkness fell over the room, black as a moonless night. And a flash of light cut through it, brighter than a lightning storm.

The Preceptor rose. "Now we can go. All doubt is removed."

He motioned to Saina and Sevrese and they followed him out. Shib joined them at the door. Saina looked back at the two bodies on the floor. The rest of the Sulatin Order was filing out tentatively, wordlessly.

The Preceptor put his hand to Saina's head. A balsam seemed to flow through his spine.

"It is all right. They have given up this flesh for Her Body. They are immortal now."

Saina felt a thousand questions fighting to get to his lips, but everyone exited the monastery to a greater mystery. A violent wind had come up, hot and crackling, filled with smoke particles from the fire within the mountain.

The Sulatins stood with their long hair and their robes whipping against their bodies. Saina urged them to follow the wind down the road to Alambarat. He gave Ghoru orders to send men to gather up the farmer families beyond the road then keep the monks in order.

Saina was pulled up by an older Sulatin, the last emerging from the building, wildly distraught. It was one of the lineage researchers he had worked with. "The library, Saina! The Abode scrolls! The workshops! We must save something or all will be destroyed."

Saina put his arm around the monk's shoulders. "Just bring what you know." He put his hand on the monk's forehead. Everything else, the Preceptor knows. Everything in the library is also here in each blade of grass we stand on."

The man was not yet convinced. He looked at the grass doubtfully. "But we don't know how to read it. We can't find it as we can in the library."

"Even when we had that, we didn't know how to find it or to read it."

A Protector guided the man away, who still looked miserable. The farmers of this valley and the Sulatins and a host of animals converged ahead on the road that would lead them out of this life forever, and they all looked miserable.

Saina took Sevrese's arm. "I don't think I inspired them very much. They don't want to leave."

Sevrese answered. "The mountain will see to that."

They reached the bridge when the initial explosion came. They stopped, but all that could be seen was the huge ash cloud rising over the trees and a shot of fire through the smoke.

Saina was the last of them to cross that same first bridge that took him away from Prayadevale in the summer. He saw his two childhood friends standing on the other side, motioning him to step on the bridge. He did, and as he crossed they vanished into Goddessoma.

Ghoru greeted him on the other side. "Well, we have been here before," he said quietly. "I heard a rumor that you are going to rule all the Ten Abodes. I'll wager that isn't what you thought would come of my visit."

"No," replied Saina. "And if I had, I would probably never have come with you."

"Yes you would. Destiny all over you. I saw it first."

Saina shook his head. "I'm finished with destiny. It's all doing—just that."

Ghoru nodded. "Doing is good. But it never ends as you expect."

In Virnipal, Pavim stood at the balcony window in her new apartment in the palace, the same one she gave Saina when he first came. She had turned her own quarters over to Khoroas and Deserena in expectation of his ascension—if there was anything to ascend to.

And like Saina, she brought nothing of her own to make it hers. She wanted the simplicity. She wanted to face the mountains of Prayadevale—everyone in all the Ten Abodes was looking that direction many times a day now. She walked to the balcony threshold to watch more haze spread across the firmament above her valley on its way to the sea, trying to imagine the Sulatin monastery in rubble or even burned and buried irrevocably.

Out on the balcony stood General Bhalkavar. He was surrounded by a golden orange glow as the walls of the palace received the brilliance of the setting sun, darkened by the ash for a red sunset everyone was getting used to.

"I saw them together only briefly," he continued. "They returned from his battle with the Sulatins with the conviction of bulls. And now the battle moves on to the people of the nine remaining Abodes, whom they will enlighten, whether or not we all understand what that means. They are consumed with a thousand tasks on behalf of this Preceptor. The palace has been given over to a host of Sulatin monks."

"They have no home yet?" she asked.

"Well, he is more a Sulatin than a Seed Bearer when it comes to comfort. They stay in a small room in the city. To be blunt, when they don't work all hours, they only need a bed."

Her brows rose. "Sounds like Khoroas and Deserena."

"Another structure will be constructed to replace the palace, but it does not resemble a Seed Bearer's residence in the least. More of a center for teaching, healing, and service to the people. While I was there Saina and the Preceptor took all the Sulatins into the caverns below the palace for a long ceremonial cleansing. Something good must have come of it—the city had a spontaneous celebration that night and I have never seen anything so happy—even here.

"And I can tell you, the people have come to their aid with much enthusiasm—especially for her. Before the two of them arrived, you should have seen how everyone worked to sweep aside any sign of the invasion—including the signs of Qurmadi's time before that.

"No sign of Ruryo under the palace?" Pavim ask with a faint smile.

He shook his head. They shared a look.

"What is it?" asked Pavim, tentatively.

"There is a change you will have to get used to, but I don't know if I can explain it. In a larger group that I was included in, the Preceptor spoke of Satamabode being no more."

She looked startled but said nothing, waiting for dangerous words.

"He made an elaborate drawing of triangles interlocking. Nine of them. Then he explained something I did not understand and probably never will about these triangles holding all the energy for the Goddess' creation. The nine represent what were the Nine Abodes, and each of the nine will represent some principle of life—instead of property and boundaries. What mystifies me is that I never know if they are talking about the real world or some supernatural plane.

"Apparently what has been Satamabode now becomes *unmanifest*. His word, and I do not pretend to grasp it. That will be the ground upon which the other nine rest. That is the one from which Sevrese and Saina will govern. Apparently this is all from the Satamabode scroll— ironically the only one left after the eruption because of Saina. Despite whatever I have muddled up here, his speech certainly seemed to please Sevrese and Saina and the Sulatins. I had the feeling the monks were eager to accept what their Order is now supposed to be. Athayam, too. No one else seems very troubled by this dissolution either. Sevrese is the benefactor of this mood. It has been a long time since a royal lady graced the city, and she lights it with her intensity."

"What becomes of the other Seed Bearers then?" She had caution in her voice.

"It seems they are to live up to their lineage. The Preceptor is going to turn them into Seers like the Abode Founders."

A laugh bubbled up to her lips. "One has to admire the exuberance. Are they speaking of the Seed Bearers I know?"

"He said the transformation begins with Seed Bearers living the highest ideals of the Founding Seers. That should be near to your heart."

Pavim's chest rose with a trembling breath. "Yes, it is. I would love to see Khoroas fulfill that role."

She also felt pride on her daughter's behalf, but emptiness on her own. She wanted something to steady her and gazed at the mountains again—but they too had changed forever.

"So Prayadevale has simply disappeared? Forgotten."

He let his own eyes drift toward the sky like hers and folded his arms in front of him, weighing more heavily against the wooden rail. "Yes, no sooner had the Preceptor ordered them out and gathered up the villagers, but the mountain boiled over." He paused. "It was all symbolic up to that moment—although two perished. One was the Conductor Luzarain. The other was Daiyenso."

"I'm sorry for them. The Conductor was a dark man. Not at all like Athayam. Daiyenso saved Sevrese and guided Saina. I wonder what it means to die symbolically." She forced her eyes away from the mountains and faced him. "Tell me, Bhalkavar. What will they do about a ceremony? Is their marriage to be sanctified properly?"

"Ahh. I am not sure if the ceremony to sanctify marriage of a couple of their status has been created yet."

Pavim's brows rose. "But, surely, they will keep to the traditions of—well, why should I say, surely. There are no Sulatins and no Abode scrolls and no Seed Bearers left."

He regarded her carefully. He wanted her to accept some the energy he had described, and not fret about formalities. "Sevrese said the

Sulatins have treatments that can make you and I live another fifty years, perhaps a hundred."

Pavim laughed fleetingly. "And that is a good idea, you think?"

"I can tell you she looks as if she will live a hundred more. Radiant—not just excitement or love or independence. She has something inside her now that was not there before she met this Preceptor. And he did it to her. He is very solicitous about her welfare—and, at a distance, the same for yours."

Now Pavim looked away from him, as if to shield some part of herself from The Preceptor's power. "I would not recognize her." Pavim gave a sigh, recovering her composure, and then smiled. "Yes, I would. She is bold. Everything you say about her fits her character. She has not changed."

"Well, you would not recognize him. Imagine, he and Athayam will go to all the Abodes as the emissaries of this conversion, to convince them all to embrace this vision of the future, to bring all the royals to Sugorai for counsel and instruction. Could the boy you last saw here carry out the task?"

She slowly paced the balcony, taking in the fading warmth. Then she came to a stop near him.

"I know you wonder if I will ever lose this melancholy, but in fact I believe it is all true. I believe the Preceptor's power." Her arm swept out from her body gracefully as if the power was everywhere. "The people may never be aware of the change as we have been. They have had their routines, their occupations, their daily desires, their families—they need not contemplate any transformation beyond their efforts becoming lighter with a new age. I believe Saina and Sevrese—with the Preceptor at their arms—have the power to lift them to a new level of living.

"But for us, for me, there remains extraordinary pain. I have lost something—everything. I spent a lifetime preserving my narrow view of righteousness. I saw it challenged. Shaken to its core. I thought I would—all the sovrans would—uphold it in the end. I despaired and yet I believed in victory. But it turned out not to be remotely like the victory I foresaw. Mine has been swept away. The entire struggle—my world, my struggle—consigned to insignificance before what is yet to come. Saina wrote such a story to me, but my pride took offense. Yet he was entirely right."

"He regrets every word. Has he not told you?"

"Yes—very warmly and honorably in a letter when they first came down the mountain. His regret was unnecessary. It was my pride. I will not let him waste any feeling over that."

Tears came out now. Slowly they trailed down her cheek. "Forgive me. Your words are precious for me. Thank you. You know how I love that girl. And the boy, too."

He nodded.

"Let me have the letters now. I will read them." Her hand went out.

He gave them to her, one from each of them, still rolled as carefully as they had presented them to him. She broke the seal and read, winding around the balcony slowly. When she finished she laid them both on a small table and returned to him, closer than before.

Her words came slowly, but now there was a stirring inside of them. "Send word to Saina in my name. Ask him if he will receive me at his earliest convenience. Tell him I want to be his first pupil—if he will have me. And if he will have me, I will join him in his attempt to convert the rest. Tell him."

He nodded.

"And tell Sevrese that I thank her for the honor of her request. She asks to have their marriage sanctified here, so that I might offer blessings of my own, but I prefer to go to them." Her lips tightened. Her neck, her shoulders, her spine followed. "What am I saying? I do not mean to make you a messenger. I will write all this. I apologize. I—I am a bit overcome."

He took a step closer to her, leaving nothing between. Their look could not be broken, though her eyes were flooded.

"And what will you do with fifty more years, Bhalkavar?" she struggled to ask.

A slow smile spread behind his beard. He picked up her hand. "I am glad you ask. You Seed Bearers think only about yourselves. Nobody worries that this new world has no need of generals. So I am planning to finally spend these years with you, and I would ask for at least a hundred."

Her chest trembled with her next breath. Her eyes closed. She nodded and stretched to kiss his lips—too quickly, he thought. But then her forehead dropped to his chest and the last tears spread into his tunic.

He could feel them through the cloth, through the skin, until they flowed through his veins to his heart.

Beyond the border of the Ten Abodes, out in flat, dry, empty wilderness where the tribal peoples wandered with their flocks and herds, a lone man strayed into a nomad camp as night was falling.

The elders of the band welcomed him because he was clearly from the land of the Ten Abodes they had heard so much about in the past year. And, as the man spoke their language to a degree, they expected him to recount the whole adventure. And to explain why their kinsmen did not return.

The man was hungry—dirty as well, but they did not fault that, for a herder's life was not a clean one either. Right away they brought him close to their fire and placed a plate of food in his lap.

The man ate and talked distractedly, but any stories from strangers seemed entertaining to people in these circumstances. Except, when they prodded with questions about their tribesmen, he answered vaguely or claimed he did not know. It irritated them that he did not understand the rules of hospitality—information paid for food and bed. On the other hand, he had nothing worth their killing him for, so it did not matter.

They had a surprise for him that might make him come to life. They watched him fall silent and pass his fingers over the surface of the plate his food was served on. He noticed. They eyed each other with pride.

One of their kinsman had come back homesick after only a few days of fighting. The plate was in his bag of loot. It was silver and from the land of the Ten Abodes. He could at least tell them what was written on it.

The stranger remained silent a few moments longer and then curiously let out a slow, bitter laugh. Even the cold night winds of these plains could not compare to the biting sound from deep inside him.

He said in their language that this plate once belonged in a great palace in the largest of the Ten Abodes, Satamabode. He added that he had once held it in his hands.

This brought murmurs of awe. The coincidence was impossible to credit. They were happy with that.

But then he spoke in his own tongue with a rueful smile. "Not this stupid piece of silver, you sorrowful thieves. No, in this hand I held the Abode itself. I would have held them all."

He carelessly dropped the plate into the dust with a dull clang. He saw the offended faces in the firelight, but he cared nothing for their feelings.

"I made an error. That is all. I should have dealt with the Sulatins. No. Two errors. I should have dealt with the boy Saina. Or three. I don't know"—

He felt tightness in his throat. His breath came roughly. His words gave up on him. *I can't think the way I used to. My mind was lost in that place ... where was that place? In the dark. I don't even remember how I got out. Well, they thought they trapped me but I always win. I'm here, am I not?*

One of the men dismissed him with the wave of his hand and went off to relieve himself. The others shrugged and crossed around to the other side of the fire, where they could watch him if they needed to but otherwise could ignore him and go about their own ways.

He remained oblivious to them, staring into the fire, into nothing. His vacant thoughts were disturbed only later when a woman approached and sat beside him. She handed him a bone pipe with a thin trail of sweet smoke ascending.

He heard the men across the fire laughing uncontrollably, but when he looked he saw that they were engaged in some game of their own. One had fallen off his seat backwards. They were not laughing at Assessor Ruryo.

"That's right," he said aloud. "Only I can laugh at Assessor Ruryo's mistakes.

The woman motioned that he should smoke, and he did. Within a short time he began to feel the warmth of the pipe transforming the very blood in his veins. He felt a softness overtake his body and mind. The fire rose in wild patterns before his eyes.

The woman shared the pipe with him. He had paid her no attention but now saw beauty in her firelit eyes and in the way her dark hair fell carelessly across her face. Her blouse was loose and the curve of her breast glowed as it rose with her breathing. She had nothing of the ugly hardened skin that afflicted this race—no doubt she was a captive stolen on their travels.

But neither the drug in the pipe nor her attractions could entirely dislodge his sour thoughts, or their endless repetitions. He felt her hand on his shoulder. He heard words come from his mouth in a mixture of her language and his, as if he had to explain this one fact to her before he could let go and relax. The words fell clumsily.

"That sanctimonious, fortune-favored, upstart, bastard, Seed Bearer Saina. He rules the world. When his very fingers move, the world moves to respond." He would have gone on but the words became slurred as he watched his own fingers slowly dancing before his eyes. "Bastard," he repeated.

The woman smiled. "My man was in your war. He did not come back."

Ruryo fought the drug's confusion to understand this. He knew that blood feud was like daily food to these people. Was she about to kill him?

Her breasts were exposed to him now. He could not remember when he had last wanted a woman. It had never been his need. It was nothing compared to the sensation of power and control. But perhaps he had been wrong.

"I regret your loss," he whispered hoarsely. "I am sure he died courageously. I am sure he served like a great warrior."

She laughed. "He was a brute. A pig—skin like a pig like all these brutes. I hope some woman cut his throat just before he would have raped her."

Ruryo sank back on his elbows. He found a laugh of his own escaping him. "Do you, indeed?" The laugh came again, gaining momentum. His words slipped out in between. "I did sense a certain lack of delicacy among them. Yes. Pigs. But are lions any better?"

She giggled and stretched on top of him. They shared a long kiss, filled with narcotic lust and lack of control. His hands grasped the softness of her flesh fervently, as if at least he could take hold of this one reward of all his labors. There was nothing else left for him to enjoy.

Then he felt the special character of the drug. Suddenly, he did remember that place in the dark below the palace. It all came back to him. He yelled with horror and pushed the woman off of him. He got up and staggered into the night.

The men considered following and killing him, but the drug made them lazy. The man was a good as dead on his own.

In a region beyond earthbound senses, a small corner of infinite Goddessoma, with only a distant memory of his own identity, Daiyenso came to rest, contented.

That both time and dimension should seem so confused here did not trouble him. At some point, he was aware of a radiance, golden-white, that surrounded him—not only a color, but as well an emotion beyond pleasure, untainted by the fear or sadness or loss.

As if, could he taste it, he would immediately think of honey from a celestial hive. If he could hear it, then he would think of the hush of the wind above a forest or the rhythmic rumble of waves upon sand. If he could understand it, then he would possess all truth. But to him there was no need to go beyond the simple fact of its presence.

The brilliance went everywhere, in a space where boundaries meant nothing. He could look at it as though he had eyes, but the power of sight went forward, backward, up and down, in and out of time.

Within that all-sight he sensed souls merging and disjoining. His own many lives—sorry affairs and glorious deeds—freed from judgment. But other lives as well. He became aware of a rival, recently subdued—but still potent, querulous, and intense—now to be his companion, and having been both rival and companion many times in many bodies. He recalled a young man, modestly bearing the weight of the desires of thousands—friends, adversaries, kings, monks, elders, children. And a master, giving all to rescue them, but never diminished by the effort. None of the names would come, only impressions. He gave up wondering, not concerned whether these events had been good or bad. The recollections were so remote, he could only marvel that they had truly taken place.

He became aware of his own body, seeming to stretch out into the vastness of space, containing all space yet turning continually in upon itself.

But it struck him that this was not his body. This was the Body of the Goddess, lying in the bed of Her creation, and he was simply resting beside it, like her child held in a comfort unimaginable.

This realization gave rise to a soaring flow of devotion. To be inside Her! To feel such majesty. To be home. All separation forgotten. She was the source of the light and expansion and joy. She was removing the memories from his mind, so that he could enjoy only Her in Her domain. She was perfection.

She was breathing now.

A chant began—his voice and Hers. Sound unbound from meaning. A hum spreading infinitely, carrying him across creation on its waves. The world—all worlds—were dissolving within it. At the same time they were ascending, expanding. A new creation was coming.

He witnessed it, utterly detached.

Then, surprised, he felt himself drawn into it. But gently, as if his mother had put him upon the ground to play. And now she was standing back, watching him find treasure after treasure in his delight. She was laughing with his pleasure.

Suddenly, like a child who cannot see his mother, he knew he was apart from Her. The light, the expansion, the joy were threatened. He felt fear and longing. The memory of Her filled him with desire to stay.

But one desire rose on top of another in an endless line, crowding into his consciousness, clouding every sense and aching to be fulfilled. And he understood at last that a new life had come to him—full of need and limitations and doing after doing after doing. This time, more glorious and more burdensome than all those past. In this birth he would not merely serve an immortal but join among them.

Still, was this enough to save his soul from severance with Her?

Oh, Mother, he cried. *This time let me find You and stay there forever!*

But no answer came. The only sound was the eternal hum—flowing out, flowing in—of Her breath. Was it enough of a promise for him?